SOMETHING IN
COMMON

PATRICIA A. PHILLIPS

Published By
Milligan Books

Cover Designed By
Chris Ebuehi-Graphic Options

Formatting By
AbarCo Business Services

Published and Distributed by:
Milligan Books
an imprint of Professional Business Consultants
1425 W. Manchester Blvd., Suite B,
Los Angeles, California 90047

First Printing, November, 1998
10 9 8 7 6 5 4 3 2 1

ISBN 1-881524-46-9

This book is a work of fiction. Names, characters, places and incidents are either the product of the author's imagination or are used fictiously and any resemblance to actual persons, living or dead or locales is entirely coincidental.

Printed in the United States of America.

Dedication

In loving memory of Ophelia Washington, Edna London and Ernest and Florene London.

Acknowledgment

I would like to thank Black Writer's on Tour for their advice and encouragement, and special thanks to Victoria Christopher Murray.

I acknowledge my mother, Myrtle London, my granddaughter, Arabya Hope Royal, my grandson, Aaren Brett Haggins, my daughter, Cassandra Royal, my son-in-law, Chris Royal, my son, Darren Haggins. I also wish to acknowledge Jackie and Michael Baker, Stacey and Kevin Golden, Janice, Diane, Charles and Stanley.

ABOUT THE AUTHOR

Patricia A. Phillips currently resides in Culver City, California. She has 16 years of professional experience in the banking industry. She is now actively pursuing her professional writing career.

As an enthusiastic fan of the romance genre, Patricia A. Phillips was inspired to begin writing a romance novel of her own. It took her three years to complete this novel, but once she started, it all became so natural that she was surprised. She found out that she was as voracious a writer as she was a reader. The experience of creating fictional characters was wonderful and incredibly exciting as she built a world around them.

Patricia A. Phillips plans to continue writing novels. She is certain that with each book she writes, she will reveal more interesting tales than the previous one.

Chapter 1

Helen Graham unlocked the door to her three-bedroom townhouse. She stepped inside her living room, letting her two suitcases drop to the floor and kicked off her shoes. Her tired feet enjoyed the feel of the thick white carpet. She dropped her latest novel on the coffee table and sighed. Helen walked into her office and picked up off the floor piles of paper that had fallen from her fax machine. They would be read later. She flipped on her answering machine. The tenth message was from Darlene. She laughed as she listened to the message from her close friend.

Walking back into the living room, she opened the drapes and stopped in front of her daughter's picture that hung over the fireplace. Lynn had been ten years old when the picture was taken, wearing a white dress and holding an Easter bunny with long ears that flopped over her arms. She had the same wide smile as her father. Helen smiled as she traced the gold frame with her index finger.

She turned from the picture and looked around her living room. She had decorated her house in white – the plush carpet, drapes and furniture. In the middle of the room was the Queen Anne styled couch with an oak coffee table in front of it and two tall chairs on either side.

At the bottom of the stairs she picked up the bag from the Saks on Rodeo Road and walked up the stairs to her bedroom. She pulled out two blouses and hung them in her closet. She stood with her hands on her hips in front of the wall to wall closet and sighed. Some of her clothes still had price tags on them, yet she continued to buy.

Helen grabbed her blue satin robe and trembled as she felt a chill in the air. This one wouldn't keep her warm enough and she decided on her green terry cloth bathrobe. She threw it

1

over her shoulder and walked into the bathroom. As she stood in front of the mirror, she pushed her hair from her face and noticed her tired eyes. She washed her face, brushed her teeth, then pulled her brown, shoulder-length hair back into a ponytail. Her robe stopped above her knees, showing her long, shapely legs. Helen was tall and slender with smooth, ebony colored skin. Her almond-shaped eyes were dark with thick lashes; she had a perfectly shaped nose and high cheekbones.

She walked through her home from room to room as if something had changed, but nothing had. This was just her habit, something she settled into every time she returned home. Helen was a writer and her success gave her a comfortable life. Her daughter was able to go to the college of her choice, unlike Helen who hadn't gone to college at all. Lynn was her only child, the only child she ever wanted. They were close, unlike her relationship with her own mother when she was a child.

Lying back on her bed, Helen thought about her life. Time had passed so quickly. Lynn's father had walked out on them for another woman when Lynn was just eight years old and they hadn't seen him often. So, Helen had struggled hard to make a decent living for herself and her daughter and that was when her desire to write came forth.

She began writing in the evenings – every night when she came home from work. Sometimes she stayed up until the early hours of the morning, determined to complete that first novel. Writing exhilarated her. She felt more alive as she breathed life into her characters. She remembered how wonderful it felt to be in love and she wrote about sadness and despair, the hurt felt deep inside the soul. Lord, she'd had her share. That was what she liked most about writing. She had total control. And now, she also had money in the bank, security and independence.

Helen walked back downstairs and looked at the two suitcases still sitting by the door and decided she'd unpack them tomorrow. It was already past five and she decided to make herself a cup of tea. While she waited for the water to boil, she prepared a ham sandwich, placing it on a silver tray, next to the cup and saucer she'd sat out. The whistling from the tea kettle made her smile and she picked up the tray, carried it into the living room and sat it on the table next to the reclining chair. She sipped her tea, then laid back and closed her eyes, trying to relax. But, she kept hearing her mother's voice.

She had called from the hotel in Los Angeles and told her mother she wouldn't have time to visit her on this trip. After all, why should I? she had asked herself. She never expressed any affection for me. Mama stopped loving me a long time ago. Helen looked at her sandwich, but made no attempt to pick it up.

Even now, she could hear her mother's laughter when she had phoned her years ago to tell her about her first book. Helen had been so excited to accomplish something and make her mother proud.

"Helen, I could understand if it were Harriet, but you? What on earth made you think you could write a book? Girl, stay on your job and make a living for you and your child. Try to make some sense out of your life since your husband walked out on you."

Helen had cringed at the constant reminder of her failed marriage.

"Get that foolishness out of your head," her mother had continued. "Be realistic for once. You always thought that you were more than anyone else. You are black and poor, girl, so act like it."

"And how is that, Mama?" Helen had asked feeling deflated. She had only wanted her mother to feel as proud and excited as she felt.

"You should just work hard, make a living like somebody with some sense in their head. Just look at life as it really is and stop dreaming about writing books."

Helen had hung up the phone with a heavy heart and didn't write for a week. How could a mother say such cruel words to her child?

"I could see if it were Harriet," her mother's words still rang in her ears. She shook her head as if to clear it. Well, to hell with her mother. She had made something out of her life. Her novels had been released one after another and though she knew her mother and Harriet would never read her books, that had not stopped her success.

3

Helen had waited for her mother to mention anything, just one word about her books so that she could throw her words back into her face, but her mother never mentioned anything about Helen's writing.

Now, it had been five years since she'd seen her mother or her older sister Harriet and she hadn't missed them for a minute. But she still got angry when she thought of how hard she worked just to have her mother purposely ignore her accomplishments. By now she should be used to it, but it still hurt. So much that she hadn't wanted to see them in all these years.

Helen rinsed the coffee cup and plate, then walked back into the living room and picked up her shoes that she had set on the bottom of the stairs. She went upstairs to call Steve, her lover. As she dialed his number, she smiled as she thought of the word 'lover'. He wasn't anything more or anything less and she was content with things just as they were. Helen and Steve were the same age and both enjoyed their comfortable, physical relationship. Who said you had to be in love to make love?

She wanted to take a long hot bath before Steve arrived. As her bath water was running, she looked in her closet for something sexy. Their relationship had started a year ago, in a shopping mall when he saw her in a store and asked her advice about a sweater he was buying for his Mom on Mother's Day. She helped him pick one, then they had walked to a Mexican restaurant and had lunch, each paying for their own. They exchanged numbers and a month later, their relationship bloomed. It was all so strange to Helen in the beginning. To have sex and enjoy it with a man she wasn't in love with.

She stepped gingerly into the hot water and slowly let her body sink into the tub. She had an hour before her lover arrived and she planned to relax and enjoy every minute of it.

Helen opened her eyes late the next morning with the sun shining through her windows. Steve had left so that he could start work at seven. She rolled over on her back and closed her eyes, still feeling the sweet sensation of their lovemaking. The ringing phone brought her wide awake.

"Mom, did I wake you?"

"No, love, I'm still in bed, but I'm not asleep. I need to

get up with all the things I have to do today. I guess I'm still a little fatigued."

"You should be," Lynn said. "You went nonstop the entire four days you were here."

"I know, but I enjoyed spending time with you more than anything else during my trip." Helen always enjoyed her daughter, especially since she didn't see her enough.

"I read half of your new book last night and I think it is going to be a best seller. You'll see, Mom."

"So, does that mean you like it?" Helen asked not able to hold back her smile.

"Of course, though I sometimes forget my mother's the author, especially when I get to the sexy parts. I'm proud of you, Mom," she said softly.

"Thanks, honey, I'm very proud of you, too."

"Well, I've got to get to my class now. Lisa is waiting for me." Lisa was her roommate from San Francisco.

"Take care of yourself, Lynn."

"I will, Mom. I'll call you in a day or two. I should be finished with the book by then."

Helen hung up the phone and showered. Wearing her long, satin robe, she took her coffee to the door to get the newspaper. She sat at the kitchen table with two slices of wheat toast, which was what she ate every morning. Finishing, she went through the day, doing all of her chores – from unpacking, to laundry, to replenishing the food in her refrigerator.

The day passed quickly and still tired from her trip, Helen was asleep by nine. The telephone rang at precisely midnight. She jumped and instantly thought of Lynn. No one ever called this late, unless it was bad news. Her hands trembled as she reached for the phone. She turned on the lamp on the nightstand, her heart beating fast and hard against her chest. She put the phone to her ear, but before she could get a word out, she heard Elaine's voice on the other end.

"Helen, it's me."

Helen sat up straight in bed. She felt panic rising in her throat. "Elaine, what is it?" she asked in a shaky voice.

"Mama's dead, Helen. She is dead!"

Helen couldn't make herself speak. Her palms were

sweaty, her eyes were wide and fixed straight ahead on the light from the lamp.

"Helen, Helen are you there?"

"Yes, Elaine. I'm here." Helen felt a chill run down her back and cleared her throat. "Are you all right, Elaine?"

"Yes, I just can't believe it. Mama was just fine when I left this morning," she said, crying.

"Dear God, what happened, Elaine?"

"It was a heart attack," Elaine whispered. "It happened so fast, only a couple of hours ago. One minute she was talking and the next minute she was holding her hands to her chest."

"Elaine, I'll call the airlines and make reservations on the first flight out. I'm sorry you had to be alone through this."

"Harriet's here with me now."

Helen didn't exactly feel any satisfaction with that news. If anything, Harriet would make the situation worse.

"After you've made your reservation, call me back. I'll pick you up at the airport."

"I'll call you in the morning. Just hang in there, honey. I'll be there before you know it."

Helen hung up and sat on the edge of her bed, holding her hands against her chest as if she were going to faint. "Mama's dead." She couldn't believe it. Even as she said the words, she couldn't believe it. Her hands trembled as she closed them into fists.

Her mother was dead and the hurt she felt was over-whelming. Just as overwhelming as when she lost her father and Helen hadn't expected her mother's death to hurt her so. But then, she never thought of her mother dying. Somehow, she just took it for granted that she would always be at the living room window in her old rocking chair.

What hurt the most now was that she and her mother never became friends, never got to know each other, at least not the way a mother and daughter should know each other. But now, it was too late to fix it and in her heart she felt cheated of the mother that she never had. Life is so uncertain, she thought as she laid her head against the headboard and closed her eyes as the tears started to flow.

Chapter 2

Helen arrived at LAX at exactly 8:00, the morning after her mother's death. She was wearing the new gray slacks and gray silk blouse she had bought the day before. That morning, they were the first pieces of clothing she saw hanging in her closet. The only makeup she wore was a soft, red lipstick and her hair was tied back in a ponytail.

She took the escalator to the ground floor to luggage pick-up. It seemed odd; she'd only done this two days before. She walked outside. Elaine was parked in front waiting for her.

Elaine got out of the car and opened the trunk. The two sisters embraced and stood apart to get a good look at each other.

"You look well, Helen," she said smiling. "There's no justice in this world. I workout, but I still have a hard time keeping the weight off."

"But, you do keep it off and you look great," Helen smiled back.

They got inside the car and Elaine drove off, adjusting her rear view mirror.

"So, how do you do it?" Elaine asked.

"By writing all hours of the night and getting very little sleep. I also try to walk three miles every day." Helen glanced at her younger sister. Elaine was tall and thin. Without makeup, she looked as if she hadn't slept well the night before. Her jet-black hair was the same color as their mother's. Her eyes were round and usually alert, but today they looked tired against her ebony brown skin. Helen decided that her sister had a look between wholesome and lovely.

Helen sighed deeply. "I should have gone by the house when I was here two days ago, but Mama always made me feel worse than I did before I saw her. I just never knew what to expect, Elaine," she said with a sad expression. "But, I would have seen her alive for the last time."

Elaine looked at her for a long moment. "Why? It would have been the same. She hadn't changed, Helen. Neither has Harriet. The only reason I could tolerate living there was because I learned to ignore them to where I wouldn't feel so insignificant. But I always felt out of place with Mama and Harriet, you know what I mean?"

"Of course I do. I felt the same way."

"I didn't know that. I thought you'd grown out of it," Elaine said.

"Well, it may have seemed that way, but it wasn't. I just didn't want them to know that they got to me."

"You know, Helen, when we were children, Mama didn't pay much attention to me, but I learned to live with it. You never could. You always let Mama's words hurt you. She did get a little better, but it was only because she was getting older and needed me. She didn't want me to move out." Elaine shook her head and sighed. "She'd dampened the spirits in everyone around her...except Harriet. Look, Helen, don't allow Harriet to get next to you because you know she'll try."

They looked at each other with warm smiles.

"I'll try not to. I want this trip to be as peaceful as possible. It's no time for fighting."

"Harriet isn't going to let it be too peaceful," Elaine replied. "You're going to stay at the house, aren't you?"

"Of course."

Elaine beamed. "Great. Now, tell me about my niece. I haven't seen her in almost two years."

"She's doing really well in school. I'm so proud of her." Helen's eyes lit up.

"Does she still look like you?"

"I think so. At least that's what everyone says. Girl, she has so much energy."

"So did you when you were her age. As I remember, you never got tired and you always had a mind of your own. Not that there was anything wrong with it. I mean, look at you now. You're doing very well, Helen." Helen looked out the window at buildings she hadn't seen before.

"I had to. Thomas left me and I had to do well."

8

Elaine nodded her head in a way that showed she understood. "You must have felt very alone during that time."

"I did, but I lived and made the best of it. I think that no matter what happens, if you try, you can find some good in it."

"That's true," Elaine replied. "Will Lynn come over tonight? I can't wait to see her."

"I'm going to call her when we get home. I called her this morning, so she's expecting me."

"We're almost home," Elaine said, turning the corner to make a left on Slauson.

Home, thought Helen. She hadn't thought of Los Angeles as home since she left twenty years ago. Home was where you had family that loved you or a place that you always remembered with warmth in your heart. It was not a place that you wanted to forget.

"What are you going to do now, Elaine? I mean, now that Mama is...gone."

"Sell the house, put a small down payment on a place of my own."

"Why don't you come to Atlanta to spend some time with me when school is out? You're not teaching summer school, are you?"

"Would you believe that I was thinking of that this morning? I'll see how things go here first." She turned right on Slauson to Crenshaw.

It had been a long time, but everything looked the same to Helen. Some of the old buildings were gone with newer ones in their place.

Elaine parked the car and sighed. "We're here."

Helen stood in front of the house, remembering the past.

She looked at the white fence surrounding the front yard. How many times had her mother told her to stop jumping the fence like those wild-behind boys in the neighborhood? Her eyes took in the entire white house with green trimmings. It had been painted more than once since the last time she was home, but always the same color. Her mother didn't like changes.

Helen looked at the woman standing across the street, but she didn't recognize her. Must be a new neighbor. She won-

9

dered how many of the old neighbors still lived in the neighborhood.

Elaine walked up beside her. "That's Harriet's car in the driveway."

Helen sighed. She had figured as much. "So, she's here? Wonderful."

Elaine touched Helen's shoulder. "Remember, don't let her get to you."

"Yeah, sure." Helen could see Harriet watching them from the window, standing in the middle of the open drapes, watching every move they made. Helen grabbed one suitcase and Elaine took the other. They walked inside and were starting up the stairs when they heard Harriet's footsteps coming towards them. They both stopped and looked at each other as if they were expecting something unpleasant.

"Long time, no see, Helen."

Helen turned to face her sister. "Five years, three months, to be exact."

"Are you always so precise?"

"That depends. How have you been, Harriet?"

"Things could be better, after all, Mama's gone," Harriet said in a dry tone.

"I'm sorry. I know how close you two were."

Harriet looked from Helen to Elaine and for the first time noticed how much they looked alike, though Helen looked like their father and Elaine more like their mother.

"Will your daughter be coming to her grandmother's funeral?"

"Her name is Lynn and she will be here, even though she never got to know Mama." Helen thought of all the birthdays and Christmases and other holidays that her mother had missed. Lynn had only seen her grandmother five times and it was never anything to remember.

"Well, it's good to know she has the respect," Harriet snapped.

Helen's eyes glinted dangerously. She stepped down a stair and stopped when she felt Elaine's hand on her shoulder. Welcome home, Helen, she thought as she turned and continued up the long stairs.

Dinner that night was quiet. Helen and Elaine had fun cooking together in the spacious kitchen. It reminded Helen of the way they used to cook when they were younger. She had forgotten what it was like to laugh in her mother's house. It was nice, just the two of them in the kitchen, while Harriet remained alone in the living room.

"Girl, compared to my kitchen, Mama's is so large. I used to want one like this, but now I'm fine with my small one. With Lynn gone, sometimes I don't cook for days." She looked at the shiny floors. She'd forgotten what it felt like to mop and wax so much floor. When she was younger, it had seemed even larger.

They had roast beef, collard greens, candy yams and cornbread. Helen sat directly across from Harriet and felt as if she was sitting across from a stranger. It was hard to believe that sisters could feel so far apart from each other. Helen sighed and tried to force herself to eat.

Helen noticed that Harriet had aged tremendously. Her almond-shaped eyes were small and suspicious. The constant frown on her face had caused lines around her eyes and mouth that remained even when she wasn't smiling. She had stopped coloring her hair; it was now more gray than black. She was unhappy. It showed in her eyes...and in her drinking as she mixed one drink after another. Helen was glad when dinner was over.

While Helen and Elaine were clearing the table, they heard the doorbell ring.

"Did your sister make it in yet?" Helen and Elaine heard a man's voice.

"She's in the dining room with Elaine, of course," they heard Harriet reply.

Elaine looked at Helen and smiled mischievously. "That's Robert."

"I recognized his voice. It's a little deeper, but I would recognize it anyplace."

"He's really nice, Helen, but you know that already, don't you?" Elaine whispered. "I've never understood their marriage. It is so strange, kind of distant, you know?"

Helen was listening to Elaine, but the anticipation of

seeing Robert was making her palms sweat. She wondered how he looked, how would he react seeing her and why in hell was she so nervous?

Elaine was waiting for her to answer. "Are you still with me?" Elaine asked.

"Oh, I didn't know they were having problems. Mama told me Harriet had the perfect marriage."

The sisters stopped whispering when Robert walked into the dining room. He stood for a few seconds staring at Helen, then he smiled. He walked up to her and extended his hand tentatively, as if he didn't know if he should or didn't know if he was supposed to.

Elaine watched him and smiled. She had never seen him at a loss. He was always so cool and calm. Always knew the right words or right moves.

"It's so nice to see you again, Helen. It's been too long."

Helen smiled and was glad that Harriet had stayed in the living room. His wide smile made chills go down her back and his hand felt warm. "Yes, it has been a long time. I was here five years ago, but I missed you."

"I remember and I was disappointed. I was working on a big case then."

She pulled her hand from his and he looked embarrassed as if he'd forgotten he was still holding her hand. He seemed taller than she'd remembered and was impeccably dressed in a brown suit, white shirt and brown tie. He had the blackest hair she'd ever seen and his eyes were just as black. His skin was the color of dark brown sugar and he had a full mouth and stubborn chin. He was still a very handsome man.

Elaine offered Robert dinner, but he refused. Helen could see Harriet moving around in the living room and noticed Robert watching Harriet with a look of disapproval as he looked at the glass in her hand.

"Coffee anyone?" Elaine asked. Robert and Helen said yes at the same time, but when she asked Harriet, she refused. The three of them sat at the dining room table while Harriet remained alone in the living room.

"Robert, Elaine tells me you've been in the District Attorney's office for six years now," Helen said as she sipped her coffee.

12

Robert smiled. "Yes, I left the firm after the old man died." There was something sad in his eyes. "Things just weren't the same there anymore. I guess when the one who hires you leaves, he takes something special with him. But, I love my work. Sometimes it is very rewarding, other times it can be rough. You tend to help one, but hurt the other at the same time."

"I can imagine with families involved," Helen said, then dropped her eyes as she noticed his hard stare.

Harriet walked into the room and sat next to Robert.

"How is your daughter?" Robert asked with interest.

"She's doing well. She's at USC and she's a good kid."

Robert could see Helen's pride by the gleam in her eyes as she spoke of Lynn.

Harriet's head jerked upright. Not realizing it, she murmured aloud. "I had a daughter once."

Everyone was quiet as though time had stopped. Harriet looked up and saw the pity in their eyes. Quickly, she rose from her chair and walked into the kitchen. She had to get away from the staring eyes, to be alone for a few minutes to compose herself. She needed the air to breathe again, with no one feeling sorry for her.

Robert sat back in his chair with his hands folded in his lap looking after her. "I apologize for Harriet," he said and sighed deeply.

"There's no need to be sorry," Helen said softly. "I had almost forgotten about the daughter you and Harriet lost. Will she be all right?"

"Yes. She just needs some time alone." He paused as he looked into the kitchen. "Anyway, what do you ladies have planned for tomorrow?" he asked, trying to change the subject.

"Elaine and I are going shopping for Mama's dress. We can do it early and get it over with," she said to Elaine.

"And remember we have some cooking and baking to do too," Elaine added. She could feel the tension in the air. God, what is going on here, Elaine wondered, as she looked from Robert to Helen?

Robert stood up and taking Helen's hand pulled her from

her chair. He looked into her eyes as if he knew what she was thinking. "I wish we could have gotten together again under different circumstances."

Helen knew there were no other circumstances that would have brought her family together. She used to meet Elaine every year, but as their mother got older and needed Elaine more, even that had changed.

Helen looked into Robert's face, feeling odd that they were so close. This wasn't supposed to happen this way. After all, they hadn't seen each other in twenty years. She wasn't supposed to feel anything and she wasn't supposed to find him even more handsome than she remembered. Maybe these feelings were natural. She did love him once and she was sure he loved her.

She blinked her eyes rapidly. What the hell am I thinking? Her palms were damp and she abruptly withdrew her hand, feeling as though she was a clumsy child. He was still smiling and she wanted to slap that damn smirk from his face.

Harriet walked back in and looked from Robert to Helen and then to Elaine. "I take it you two can get along without me."

"Of course," Helen said a bit too quickly and Elaine nodded in agreement. "Take as much time as you need Harriet. We realize how hard this must be for you."

"It should be for all of us," Harriet snapped loudly. "She was *our* mother."

Elaine and Helen exchanged glances. "Some things never change," Helen murmured under her breath.

Robert cleared his throat. "Come on, Harriet, so that I can see you to your car." He helped her into her coat and they walked out.

"They're quite a couple, aren't they?" Elaine said as she closed the door behind them. "They seem to be so opposite. I wonder what went wrong in their marriage."

It didn't surprise Helen that their marriage hadn't worked. She knew they wouldn't stay happy long, from the first time she saw them together, standing in the door kissing. She could still envision it clearly.

"Lord, please make these two days move quickly," Helen thought.

14

"I never understood the attraction between them," Elaine continued, as she took the coffee cups into the kitchen. "It always seemed to me that there was never any love there at all."

Helen couldn't bear to think about Robert and Harriet together. She needed to change the subject. "Elaine, do you remember when Daddy moved us into this house?" Helen looked around the room as if she were trying to remember when they first moved in. She stood opposite Elaine. "Oh no, you wouldn't, because you were only four. I was six and Harriet was nine."

"But, I do remember, Helen."

They sat at the table again.

"You do? God, it was so long ago. Life was better for us in those days. We got along, we laughed and played and most of all, we loved each other."

"You and I still do, Helen."

Helen nodded in agreement. "You know, Elaine, I used to wonder if we had stayed in South Carolina if life would have been better. It was exciting moving to a different place. But a few years here and everything started to change. I never understood why. Our family just grew apart."

Elaine shook her head sadly as if she didn't understand any of it either. "I don't think it would have made any difference where we lived. Home is anyplace as long as there's love."

"You're right. Maybe there aren't any answers. I know that I stopped looking for them a long time ago. It's just that seeing Harriet again made me start to wonder. For instance, that garbage about Harriet's marriage, why would Mama lie to me? What was the point? And to think I believed her. You tend to believe your own mother, you know."

Elaine moaned. "You know the answer to that. You had Robert first and it didn't work out between the two of you, so Mama wanted you to think it was going well between Harriet and Robert. That would have made Harriet better for him than you were."

"But, I don't understand. I was her daughter too."

"I know, but that's just the way things were with Mama. Anything to build Harriet and make us feel smaller."

There was silence for a moment. "Elaine, I'm so hurt by

15

Mama's death." She paused. "What about you?"

Elaine took a deep breath. "I am too." She motioned for Helen to follow her into the living room and the two sat together on the couch. "When you left, I had no one for a long time," Elaine said taking Helen's hand. "God, I was lonely. I missed you terribly. Sometimes, I even wished I was you – able to move away and start a new life. I used to be angry that I was the one left with Mama. Then, I started teaching and things got a bit better." Elaine paused and Helen could see the pain in her sister's eyes. "I almost got married once."

"I never knew that. What happened?" Helen asked.

"He called it off," she said sadly. "Another woman was having his baby. I never knew there was another woman. Then, I met another man I loved, but he didn't love me. And, I met another and another. And guess what?"

"They loved me," Elaine continued. "But, I wasn't in love with them. It all happened too fast after Donald called off our engagement." Elaine shook her head. "Good thing I never told Mama or Harriet because I wouldn't have heard the last of it." Elaine held Helen's hand tighter. "You were struggling and making a decent life for Lynn and yourself so I didn't want to lay my problems on your shoulders. And another thing, I was never as pretty as you, Helen. So, it was harder for me."

Helen made Elaine turn to face her. "Look at me, Elaine. That's not true and I never want to hear you say it again. It's just not your time yet."

"Maybe...anyway, I had no one in my life and Mama needed me."

"I'm sorry it's been so hard on you, honey. I wish that I could have been more help. It wasn't fair to you," Helen said apologetically.

"You had your own life and I understood."

"Well, that is one thing that Harriet and I have in common – bad marriages. Tell me something. Does Harriet always drink like that? I saw her refilling her glass one right after another."

"Yes and she is drinking more now. It's not always as bad as today. I think it's beginning to hit her that she is going to be alone for the first time in her life, since Mama's gone.

16

She spent most of her time here with Mama, you know."

"Oh," said Helen. "I guess she's afraid."

Elaine turned to face Helen. "I'm going to make some changes in my life and I think Harriet should too. Like I said before, I'm going to sell the house as soon as possible. I don't want to be here alone.

"That's great. You should get out and spread your wings."

Elaine smiled feeling a new boost of energy. "I'll divide the money among the three of us and I'll buy a place of my own."

"That's exactly what you need. Something for you for a change." Helen kissed her on the cheek. "One thing though, keep my share and put it towards your new home. You deserve it. You stayed with Mama until the end. When you called to tell me she was dead, I felt so guilty. Were you alone with her when it happened?" Helen asked grimacing.

Elaine nodded, the tears forming in her eyes. Helen took her in her arms and laid her head on her shoulder, just the way she did when they were children.

"You deserve so much more, honey," Helen said softly. "I realize how unfair I've been. The years went by so damn fast. Me working five and six days a week and writing taking up so much of my time. But, that's no excuse for not coming around to be with you."

"Don't talk like that, Helen. The truth is, it wouldn't have made any difference to Mama. You would have come and then left with your head hanging down. Anyway, let's start planning what we have to do tomorrow," Elaine said.

"Yes, just one more day and it will be over," said Helen. "I have a book to start writing when I get home."

The two sisters walked into the kitchen to decide what they would cook for the people who would be stopping by the house.

"I've already had five phone calls from people wanting to know what food to bring." Elaine sighed heavily.

They finished in the kitchen and walked up the stairs, stopping at the top.

"When is my niece coming over?"

"The morning of the funeral. I don't want Lynn here

tomorrow night. She wanted to stay over, but with Harriet coming in and out, it would have been too tense."

Elaine nodded and the two sisters hugged, holding each other for a few seconds before they went to their rooms, each thinking of the two days ahead of them.

Chapter 3

March 28, 1994, Odessa Frances Gilmore was put to rest in a brown and gold coffin. It was cold and overcast; the gray clouds threatened to open at any moment. Helen held her head down without really seeing the fifty or so neighbors, family and friends attending her mother's funeral. Many of the people, Helen had never seen before.

She was dressed in all black, Lynn standing on one side and Elaine on the other, each holding her hand. She looked over at Harriet and watched as her body trembled. Robert linked their arms providing Harriet with the support that she needed. It was still odd for Helen to see them together. She hadn't seen them all the years they were married.

Helen was surprised to see her cousin, Mary, standing on the other side of the grave. She hadn't seen Mary in almost twenty years. Mary was wearing a short, tawdry red dress and a blond wig piled high on top her head. Her face was heavily made up with light red lipstick that emphasized the size and shape of her full mouth. Helen looked closely at Mary's face. Life told stories in her eyes and face, eyes that were tired. Mary looked older than her thirty-eight years.

Mary stood alone, glancing at every one who passed as if she was trying to recognize all the people there. Finally she looked at Helen and nodded her head in recognition.

Helen's eyes widened as Harriet moaned. For a moment, she thought Harriet would collapse, but Robert held onto her.

"Ashes to ashes, dust to dust." How many more times would the Pastor say those words?

Three women from the church choir stepped closer to the coffin and began singing a soft melody. Helen couldn't remember the name of the song, but her mother used to hum it when Helen was a child. Her mother would sit in her rocking chair, looking out the window, just humming a song.

Finally, the Pastor finished and everyone started to turn away. But suddenly, Helen couldn't move. She couldn't walk away and leave her mother's body lying in the cold, damp ground. Her legs began to weaken and she felt Lynn's arm around her shoulder. Helen knew she couldn't fall apart – she had to be strong for Lynn and Elaine.

Elaine pulled Lynn from Helen and motioned for her to let her mother have a few minutes alone. Elaine and Lynn walked away.

Tears ran down Helen's cheeks as she stood at the side of the coffin with her hands hanging to her sides. She took a deep breath and sighed. "Well, looks like this is it, Mama. You'll be in good hands and you don't have to worry about anything anymore. You are finally at peace, Mama." Her voice cracked as she spoke. She wondered if her mother had ever had any peace in her life. "I'm sorry I couldn't be the daughter that you wanted, Mama, but I did love you. I've always loved you. The problem is that I've never told you and now it's too late." She wiped a tear from her cheek. "It's too late for a lot of things, but I hope you hear me, Mama. Rest in peace."

As Helen walked across the damp grass, she saw Elaine walking in her direction. Elaine took her by the hand and they walked together.

"Are you all right, Helen?"

"Yes. I just had a couple of things to say to Mama." Helen saw Lynn watching from the limousine. "Is Lynn all right?"

"Yes, she knew that you needed to stay a little longer."

"And, what about Harriet?"

"She's waiting in the car, but she's not talking to anyone."

Helen and Elaine got into the car. Dusk was a dismal bank of clouds, threatening again, but they made it back to the house before the rain began to fall.

At the house, Helen sat at the dining room table with Mary and Lynn. People were still coming.

"Is this your girl, Helen? She was just a little thing the last time I saw her," Mary said as she smiled at Lynn.

Lynn smiled and said hello.

"Do you have any children, Mary?" Helen asked.

"Hell, no, girl! I don't have no time for kids. I've never really liked them anyway." Mary looked at Lynn and laughed. "Just kidding, honey. I just never really had the time and what would I do with a kid on my back?" she asked still laughing.

Mary looked in Lynn's face. "She looks like you, Helen, when you were her age. Pretty like you too. Hey, are you still married?" Mary asked.

"No, I've been divorced for ten years."

"Is that so? I always wondered how you were getting along and I didn't see much of the family anymore, so there was no one to ask. Girl, I've been so removed, I just found out yesterday about Aunt Odessa. You know, it's a damn shame when families drift apart. It makes me sad," she said, straightening her wig on her head. "I just happened to run into Melvia at the cleaners and she told me about your mother. Melvia hadn't called me in months. Not that I really wanted her to."

Helen and Lynn laughed.

"Did your ever remarry, Mary?" Helen asked.

"No, my marriage was hell, girl. Anyway, why are we talking about marriage? The way I see it, you don't have to marry when you can get the same things out of a man if you're single and he treats you better. Shit." She crossed her legs and laughed.

Lynn almost choked, her face turning red trying to keep from laughing out loud.

"You know how stupid men are, girl," Mary continued joking. "You know, Helen, you look like your father. Harriet and Elaine look like Aunt Odessa with all that black hair."

Helen only nodded. Once Mary got started, she would never stop talking.

"You know, Helen, being here makes me think about my mother," Mary went on. "When we were children, Mama used to bring us over here all the time."

"I remember and we had lots of fun," Helen replied warmly.

Elaine came to the table to see if Lynn wanted to meet some of the young people. "I have a nice looking teacher who wants to meet my niece. So, I'm taking her away from you two."

Lynn stood. "I'll be outside for a while, Mom." Lynn smiled at Mary as she turned away.

"Helen, you see that tall, handsome dude in the gray suit over there?"

Helen followed Mary's stare.

"He's one fine dude, ain't he?" she asked. Mary stood and grabbed a chicken leg from the platter, holding it in her hand as she talked.

Helen looked again at the man that Mary admired. His suit could have been nice, if the sleeves hadn't been too short for his arms. He had a gold chain around his neck and his wrists were covered with gold jewelry. His hair was a little too long for Helen's taste.

"I can't wait any longer," Mary said, still holding the chicken leg in her hand. "I'm gonna hit on him, with his fine behind." She winked at Helen. "Watch me, you just might learn something."

As Mary walked away, Lynn returned to the table and sat beside Helen. They watched Mary as she sauntered towards the man, her dress too tight across her narrow hips. Mary stood in front of the man and pushed her blond hair from her face and then, the two walked outside together. A match made in heaven, Helen thought.

Helen and Lynn fixed their plates and returned to the dining room table. Helen saw Robert standing in the living room talking to a few men and she turned her head away before he saw her.

"Mom, tell me about Mary," Lynn said.

Helen noticed that Lynn's hair was getting longer and pushed it behind her ear. "Well, there's not much to tell. She used to be a nice looking woman, but she had a hard life. She got married at sixteen. She and her husband were heavy drinkers and got hooked on liquor and drugs by the time she was eighteen. A year later, her husband was found dead on the East Side in some alley and that made Mary stop drinking – for a while. But then, she started up again, drinking more than before. And, she slept with every man that promised her a drink." Helen paused for a moment. "It breaks my heart to see her like this. We were close as children. But, no matter what happens to Mary, she gets up stronger than before."

People continued to come into the house and after awhile, Lynn went outside. Helen watched as her daughter stood on the lawn with the young teacher. He was handsome and Helen watched Lynn smile shyly. He was average height, with a nice build and his brown skinned looked good in his navy suit. Lynn seemed to be taken with him and the young man seemed just as taken with her.

Helen wandered off alone in the back yard enjoying the peace and quiet. She was tired of the introductions and smiling every time someone wanted to start a conversation. And, she was tired of avoiding Harriet. She was glad she was returning to Atlanta in the morning.

The fresh air felt good against Helen's face. She had changed into a pair of black slacks and a white, silk blouse. Something she could be comfortable in. She was standing against the tall lemon tree, watching two birds in the neighbors' yard when she heard a slight sound and turned around.

It was Robert. He stood tall, his jacket and tie removed. The gray at his temples only made his black hair more prominent. She wondered how long he'd been standing there. She felt an unfamiliar thrill that was frustrating and disconcerting and it frightened her, but only for a moment.

She wondered if he was thinking of their past, the way he had kissed her, had held her so tight that she remembered she had been unable to breathe. She shook her head trying to clear away those thoughts. I've got to stop this silliness, she thought as she took a deep breath.

She stared at him before she spoke. "Why do you stay married to my sister when you're not in love?" she asked, not pulling her eyes from his.

He looked at her as if he was taken aback by her forwardness. He cleared his throat and pushed both hands into his pockets. He took a few steps in no particular direction. "You do get to the point, don't you? But, you always have. I knew that hadn't changed by the books you write. You're very good, you know."

"I try," she said, trying to appear nonchalant as she

23

leaned against the tree. "It's hard to imagine you reading my books. I can only imagine you with the Wall Street Journal."

He chuckled. "Did you really think I wouldn't read your books? Even Harriet picks them up and looks at your picture on the cover."

"That's surprising. Anyway, you haven't answered my question, Robert."

He sighed and looked up to the sky as if he needed help. "I was hoping you'd forget about that," he said as he took another step closer to her. "It's a long story. I've asked for a divorce more than once." He paused. "The first time, she almost agreed. But then, our baby died and I couldn't go through with it. I couldn't leave her in such a state and I wasn't doing too well myself. Losing our daughter in a car accident like that...it was too hard." He sounded shaken and Helen was sorry she had asked the question, but she remained silent.

"So, the years passed and I stayed," he continued. "But we live separate lives. We sleep in separate rooms. We've had nothing in common for years. About five years ago, I asked Harriet for a divorce again, and this time, she flat out refused."

"Why?"

"I don't know. I think she's just used to me being there. But, I've made up my mind. I'm getting a divorce. She can have the house and anything she wants."

Helen was almost frightened for Harriet. She wasn't sure if her sister were strong enough to handle a divorce, especially with their mother's death.

"I'm getting a divorce," Robert repeated, enunciating each word. "I decided two days ago." He looked into her eyes.

"Why did you decide just two days ago?" she asked her voice very soft.

"Do you have to ask?" He smiled, showing his perfect white teeth. "Two days ago you waltzed back into my life. Just as fast as you waltzed out twenty years ago."

An uneasy silence hung between them.

"Robert," Elaine called from a distance. "You have a telephone call."

"Excuse me," he said softly and walked past Elaine, then stopped to look back at Helen.

24

"Everyone's leaving," Elaine yelled now to Helen. "And Harriet says the three of us have to talk."

Taking a deep breath, Helen walked past Elaine and into the house.

"What did I miss?" Elaine asked herself aloud and followed Helen inside.

Harriet was waiting in the living room when Helen and Elaine entered. Lynn walked inside with her coat folded over her arm and her car keys in her hand.

"Let me walk my daughter to the car," Helen said to Harriet. "I'll be right back."

Lynn said good bye to everyone and then walked outside with Helen and Elaine.

"So, you're leaving in the morning, Mom?"

"Yes, at eleven thirty."

"And, young lady, I'm moving into a new house and I want us to get to know each other. You're the only niece I have, Lynn," Elaine said warmly. "We'll go to lunch sometime."

"I would love that," Lynn exclaimed and kissed her aunt on the cheek

"I'll call you when I get home, Lynn," Helen said, hugging her tight.

"All right, Mom. Have a safe trip."

Helen ran her fingers through her daughter's hair and opened the car door. Lynn was still waving as she drove down the street. By the time the two sisters walked back inside the house, Harriet was waiting impatiently.

Robert walked into the living room with his jacket folded over his arm. "Well, ladies. I'm going to call it a day. When are you leaving, Helen?"

"Tomorrow morning."

"So soon?" Everyone could hear the surprise in his voice.

"Yes, I just finished a book and I'm ready to start a new one."

"Well," he sighed. "It was nice to see you." He looked disappointed and Helen knew it was definitely time to return home.

"It was nice seeing you too," Helen said forcing a smile. Not wanting to meet his eyes, she looked away. She knew exactly what he was thinking and her heart was beating faster than ever.

Robert kissed her on the cheek and then he kissed Elaine. He turned to Harriet. "I'll see you at home."

As soon as Robert walked out, Helen spoke, "So, what did you want us to talk about Harriet?" Helen and Elaine waited patiently until she swallowed the last drop of gin in her glass. She set the empty glass on the edge of the coffee table gingerly as if she had had too much to drink.

"Mama's gone. We have to decide what we're going to do with everything. And especially this house," Harriet said.

Elaine spoke first. "I'm going to sell the house. We'll split the money between just us, Harriet, because Helen wants me to have her share."

"Oh, how generous!" Harriet snapped. "Now, what about the rest of Mama's things?" Harriet asked looking from one sister to the other.

"I don't want anything," Helen said. "Except maybe a photo of Mama, Daddy and the three of us." Helen looked at the family album on the small table in the corner.

"And, why is that, Helen?" Harriet asked with venom in her voice. "Isn't anything good enough for you anymore?"

Helen was furious. Avoiding her sister all day had not been enough. She got up fast and this time Elaine couldn't stop her. "You are still intolerable, Harriet. You've been nasty all your miserable life. And, at a time like this, you would think you could be a bit kinder." Helen was still standing. "No. I don't want anything in this house. Damn you, Harriet!"

"Well done, Helen," Harriet smirked. "I had forgotten what a nasty mouth you have. I would've thought you would have changed that by now." Harriet picked up her purse. "Well, maybe after tomorrow, we won't have to see each other again, Helen."

"If I'm lucky, Harriet. Now can we just get on with this so you can leave and I can spend my last night with Elaine in peace?"

Harriet's eyes narrowed in anger. "I'll come back tomorrow so we can settle things between the two of us," Harriet said to Elaine.

Elaine nodded and closed her eyes, trying to hold back the tears. They only had each other now. No mother, no father, just each other and it hurt to see what they'd become. Not even Mama's death could bring them together. Though Harriet got on her nerves, Elaine loved both of her older sisters and she didn't want to have to make a choice.

Harriet grabbed her long, cashmere coat and stood in front of Helen for a few seconds without saying anything. She fidgeted with her coat before she finally said good-bye.

Surprisingly, sadness engulfed Helen. She knew this would be the last time she would see her sister and her eyes watered. She wanted to touch her sister, hold her, but she knew it was too late. "Good-bye, Harriet," she said.

That night, Helen and Elaine sat in the kitchen and talked until midnight. Helen looked around the room and stopped at the old-fashioned white and black stove. She'd never seen another one like it. The white curtains still hung in the window over the sink. The four small pictures of white ducks swimming in a pond were still there too, though the ducks had turned yellow. She looked down at the oatmeal-colored floor, shining from being waxed every Saturday morning. Helen walked through the house, stopping to look at all the pictures and furniture that she would never see again. She felt the loss inside.

Helen and Elaine said good night and walked up the stairs to their rooms. Helen regretted the words that were spoken earlier, but knew they could never be taken back.

After trying to fall asleep for more than an hour, Helen finally got out of bed and went downstairs to the kitchen. She was standing in front of the opened refrigerator when she heard a noise and jumped, then saw Elaine at the door.

"So, you couldn't sleep either?" Helen asked, holding a Coke in her hand.

"No, it's been a long day, but I'm still restless."

"It's been a *helluva* long day, girl!" Helen exclaimed, as she grabbed the bottle of wine from the top shelf of the refrigerator. "I'll bet this puts me to sleep in no time."

"I think I'll have a glass, too," Elaine said.

"Okay, I'll get the glasses. Why don't we go into the living room and sit on the floor like we used to do?"

Elaine giggled. "Good idea."

"Turn the stereo on so that we can have some music."

"Music coming right up."

Helen carried the wine and glasses into the living room and sat on the floor next to Elaine.

"How old is this thing anyway?" Elaine asked as she adjusted the buttons on the stereo.

"Daddy brought it when we were very young."

"I thought it came with house," Elaine laughed. "It's been here as long as I can remember. The needle fell out years ago." Elaine sipped her wine.

Helen looked at the neatly stacked records under the stereo. There were 45's, 33's and 78's. "Mama and Dad used to listen to the 78's," Helen said. "Damn shame we can't play any of them."

They both laughed until they had to hold their stomachs.

"How many times did we sit here just like this with our dates, listening to the music?" Helen wondered.

Elaine looked as if she were trying to remember and laughed out loud again. "I used to see your dates stealing kisses from you. I used to watch from the stairway."

"You sneak," Helen yelled with a mischievous glint in her eyes.

Suddenly, Elaine became serious. "Helen, do you date much? Elaine asked.

"Hell, no. I don't have the time. But, I do have a lover." She smiled as she thought of him.

"A lover?" Elaine questioned.

"Uh huh. Someone that I can count on when I need male company. He's a very nice man. I met him a year ago."

"And you don't feel any attachment to him at all?" Elaine asked with surprise.

"Elaine, right now I am just to busy to have any attachments in my life. I don't need anyone expecting any-thing from me." Helen had to smile at the confusion on her sister's face.

"I can't imagine that. Haven't you met anyone you want to marry?'

Helen didn't say anything for a few seconds. "I used to

want to get married again, but you know Elaine, I decided I needed something in my life besides being a wife and mother. I knew just being married, working nine to five, would never be enough for me. I mean, what if the marriage doesn't work. Well, what do you have left? Your children grow up and leave home to live their own lives. So, I needed something to hold on to when I'm alone and older, the money is a plus. I'm not saying that I would never remarry. I just haven't been in love for a long time," she said as she looked at the empty glass in her hand. "I just hope if there is a second chance of a marriage for me, it will be the right one. It would have to be a man that won't take away my independence." She sighed. "Now, what about you, Elaine? Would you like to get married and have a family."

"Girl, I'm too old now."

"Too old? Girl, you're younger than I am and I know a woman who was 42 and had a baby. You are definitely not too old. Age is just a number. If you don't feel old, then you're not. Get married and go for it."

Elaine sipped her wine. "I think I'm beginning to see double," she giggled.

Helen looked at the glass in her hand. "Oh, hell. I was just thinking that this was our third glass of wine, but I think it's our fourth."

They fell on the floor laughing again feeling like they used to when they were teenagers.

"Harriet should be here with us. Maybe after a few drinks she may get loose and smile for once."

"Oh, no, Helen. A few drinks would only make Harriet meaner. You saw her. She drinks and says nothing to no one. When Robert was working and going to school, I used to try to get her to come and spend time with me. But no. She would come to see Mama, eat dinner and leave."

"Mama," Helen said it and felt tears burning her eyes. "She's gone, Elaine."

Elaine laid her head on Helen's shoulders. "We don't have any parents, anymore, Helen." Her words were sad.

"I know, honey." They were silent for a moment. "I think it's time for us to go up to bed," Helen said finally.

The next morning, Helen awakened with a throbbing headache. She phoned Lynn to see if she needed anything before she left. By ten-thirty, Helen and Elaine were at the airport and Elaine waited until it was time for Helen to board the plane.

Helen looked into her sister's eyes and felt concern. She looked lonely, maybe even afraid. Her life was about to change.

"Honey, I really wish I had more time to spend with you," Helen said.

Elaine took Helen's hand. "I understand and there will be other trips."

Helen kissed her sister on the cheek and for a moment acted as if she didn't want to leave. But finally, Helen boarded the plane and Elaine stood at the large window watching the plane until it was a small speck in the sky. It was only eleven-thirty and Elaine missed her sister already.

Chapter 4

Just as Elaine was about to turn into the In-And-Out Burger lot for her favorite hamburger and fries, a Century 21 Real Estate office caught her eye. Before she could change her mind, she passed the burger place and turned into the parking lot of the real estate office.

She felt giddy with excitement. For the first time, she was on her own – free to make her own decisions. This must be what Helen feels like everyday, she thought as she turned off the ignition. It was a shame that all of this came from her mother's death. She laid her head against the car seat and closed her eyes. Poor Mama, she was never happy, Elaine thought. She was never satisfied; there was no one on earth who could please her.

Finally, she took a deep breath and got out of the car. She moved quickly towards the office. This wasn't what she planned on doing today, but she was glad that she was here. Selling the house would be her new beginning. Her first step forward that she would be taking alone.

A man was already standing at the counter when she entered the office. He looked to be in his fifties, with gray hair and a friendly smile. He was light-skinned, pale actually; there was not enough color in his face.

"My name is Mr. Parker and you look in need of a good realtor," his said, as his smile seemed to widen.

Elaine couldn't help but return his warm smile and relaxed instantly.

"I have a three-bedroom, two-story house to sell and I am also interested in purchasing something for myself. Not too big. I'll be living by myself. A townhouse would be nice."

"Please, come right in, Mrs…"

"Oh, I'm sorry. Here I've been babbling on. My name is Gilmore. *Miss* Gilmore."

"Nice to meet you Miss Gilmore. Why don't you have a seat here at my desk," he said moving into a small cubicle and motioning to a chair. After he sat down, he continued speaking, "I think today is your lucky day. I have a lovely place that just went on the market." He pulled a file from one of the desk drawers and opened it to show her the listing. He pulled out the appraisal and gave her the pictures that were attached.

"While you're looking over this, why don't I get us a cup of coffee, Miss Gilmore?"

"Oh, that would be nice." She still had a headache from the wine she had shared with Helen and hoped that the coffee would help. When he came back, she sipped on the hot cup as he told her about the townhouse.

"An older couple owns it and wants to move to Arizona because of the husband's health. They're willing to accept ten thousand less than the appraised value. They owe so little on the note that they can afford to accept less."

Elaine looked down at the pictures once again. The building was white with a security gate and white carpeting throughout the townhouse. Her eyes widened with excitement. She couldn't wait to see it. "Mr. Parker, I need to sell my house to have the money for the down payment."

"Oh, you won't have to worry about that. I'm sure I'll be able to sell your house for you. I can stop by tomorrow, take a look at it and put it on the market right away," he said trying to reassure her. "Now, I'll stop by your home tomorrow to pick up an extra set of keys so that I can start showing your house right away. Of course, I will always call before I bring anyone over – it's our company policy."

Elaine frowned. "Are you going to give me the keys back every evening?" she asked looking as though she didn't have a clear understanding.

He looked at her strangely, wondering what he had said to alarm her. "Oh no, Miss Gilmore. I may have to show you're house any time of the day. But, if it will make you feel more comfortable, you can always be there." He was beginning to wonder if she was sure about selling the house.

"I've been a realtor for over twenty-five years," he continued. "Trust me. I will sell your house before you know it. And, tomorrow, I will take you to see the townhouse if that is convenient for you."

Her face lit up again. "Yes, I do want to see it."

"Then, it's settled. We'll put your house on the market tomorrow. I'll call you in the morning."

She smiled. "Thank you, Mr. Parker. I'll look forward to hearing from you." She started to get up and stopped. Maybe I should ask Helen if it's okay to give him the keys, she thought to herself.

"Is there anything wrong, Miss Gilmore?" he asked, frowning. What in the hell is wrong this time, he thought.

"Oh, nothing," she responded, shaking her head. "It's fine. I'll have an extra set of keys for you tomorrow."

He walked her to the door. "How long have you lived in your house, Miss Gilmore?""

She turned to face him. "Since I was four years old."

That explains it, he thought. "Well, I'll do my best to help you in any way possible. Sometimes when people live in their homes for so long, they start to have doubts about selling.

"Oh, no, Mr. Parker. I don't have any doubts. I'm ready to make the change."

Elaine stood outside the real estate office and looked up at the sky. The sun was warm against her face. Looks like it's going to be a beautiful day, she thought as she ran through the rest of the errands she had in her mind. She had the extra set of keys made, then stopped at the back, withdrawing $3500 from her savings account. Then, she headed for the beauty salon. She was tired of wearing her hair in the same old style and she wanted a change. Maybe she would wear it hanging to her shoulders, just like Helen. Yes, that is what she would do. Only she would leave it black.

The stylist was a tall, skinny woman with thick hair that was piled too high on her head. Elaine looked in the mirror when the beauty operator finished.

"You look adorable, honey. You should come back and get your hair in that style again," she said teasing the back.

"Oh, I will." She was pleased with it and decided to get a manicure while she was there. "I want the works!" she told the operator.

Afterwards, Elaine went shopping for new clothes. She bought a suit she'd seen in a magazine two weeks before. It was navy with a long jacket and a large pocket on each side. She couldn't stop looking at herself in the mirror. She walked through the store to see if she saw anything else she wanted. Shoes, I need shoes to match my suits, she thought with delight. She gave the saleslady her suits to hold while she went to the shoe department. She tried on a pair to match each suit. Elaine stood at the long mirror as she tried on each pair.

The saleslady walked up to her and smiled. "Which pair did you decided on?"

Elaine swirled in front of the mirror, then looked down at her feet. "All four, please."

Elaine felt the chill of the evening air as she walked to her car. She looked at her watch and was surprised that she had been out all day. She headed for home.

Inside the house, she stood in the living room holding her bags and sighed. This room had seemed so much larger when she was a child. Soon, I'll be walking into a different house, a different life, she thought. But, she would never forget this house. This was where her family was happy and she and her sisters used to laugh and play. She didn't want to forget this place.

Her mother and father loved their home and they kept it up well after their father's death. But now, it was time to heal and go forward. She knew her mother would want that for her.

Elaine walked upstairs and into her bedroom to hang her new suits and put her shoes away. Every time she passed the long wall mirror, she stopped and admired her new hairdo. She looked like a new person and certainly felt like one. She decided to call Harriet to let her know that tomorrow at this time, the house would be up for sale.

For once, Harriet agreed with Elaine. "Sell the house and get it over with. The sooner you move into a different house, the better you will feel. That house is a constant reminder of Mama's death. It is about time that you get on with your life and start acting like an adult. You've depended on Mama far too long, Elaine. You're thirty-six and it's time for you to move on."

Elaine's spirit was deflated. "Okay, okay, Harriet. I didn't call for you to go over my life's story. I'll let you know as soon as I get a buyer."

"Yes and don't let anyone talk you down on the price we agreed upon," she said.

All of a sudden, Elaine felt like yelling through the phone, but she wouldn't permit Harriet to screw up a beautiful day. "I know how to handle business without your advice, Harriet. And, I didn't hear you offer to help with anything," she snapped at her sister.

Elaine heard Harriet take a deep breath.

"I was only trying to keep you informed, since one-third of the money belongs to you. Remember, Helen is giving me her share. Isn't that nice of her? She has such a generous heart."

Harriet's sigh through the phone was the epitome of irritation, which made Elaine smile. Harriet hung up the telephone without saying another word. That'll teach her, Elaine thought. She walked back to the mirror and admired her hair.

After dinner, she got into her bed and watched television. She was exhausted, but prayed all her days would be as exciting as today. Before she fell asleep, she phoned Helen to ask about the key. As always, Helen was patient and understanding. She told Elaine that she had done the right thing. "He needs it to show the house, Elaine, so it's normal for him to ask for the keys. Think about it. He has the key to the townhouse that he's going to show you. Everything will be just fine, honey." Elaine was relieved and fell asleep with a smile on her face.

Harriet set the table for dinner. She wasn't sure if she should be happy that Robert would be home early enough for dinner or if she should be suspicious. Robert was so unreadable. She closed her eyes and tried to remember the last time they sat at the table together for dinner. Or the last time they'd had a real talk. Or the last time they'd had sex. She couldn't remember any of it.

But, he had called and said he'd be home. What did this mean, she wondered? Obviously, he had something on his mind. She remembered the expression on his face this morning before he walked out the door. Did he have something to say? Was it a look of desire? No, who was she kidding? He hadn't touched her in years. Desire died in the early years of their marriage. After they'd lost their child, Harriet lost all interest in sex. She liked sleeping in separate beds and Robert had his work and his interests. She wasn't sure if he'd had any affairs, but if he had, she had appreciated his discreetness. She didn't have to deal with wrong number, hang-ups or anything like that when she answered the phone.

Harriet took the meatloaf from the oven. She'd taken special care with the meal, preparing it just like Robert liked it. Now that her mother was gone, the only person she had was Robert and she didn't want him to leave her too.

She stood in the mirror, looking at the lines that had developed in her face and she shook her head in dismay. Where did all the years go, she thought. She felt shaken just looking into the mirror and she turned her face from side to side. It was as if she had just seen the lines. She looked almost ten years older than Robert. She pushed her hair from her face with the back of her hand, then changed her mind. Too much gray. She pulled her hair forward again.

She walked back into the kitchen to make sure everything was ready. The food was prepared, the wine was chilled. She caught a glance of her reflection in the mirror and looked down at her dress. This was not the time for a dull navy dress. Looking at her watch, she noticed that she still had time to change.

She looked through her closet, pulling out three dresses and decided on the light green jumpsuit that Robert had bought her for her birthday the year before. Standing in front of the mirror, she saw that she was still slender, the jumpsuit fit her just right. She walked back downstairs and was taking the wine out of the refrigerator when she heard the key inside the lock. Her heart jumped.

"Harriet, I'm home," Robert yelled. She felt like a nervous child and before she could answer he was on his way upstairs, climbing them two at a time. Her heart started to beat faster with the anticipation of what the evening would bring.

Half an hour later, they were eating in the dining room.

Robert had changed into a pair of jeans and blue sweatshirt, his black hair shining under the light.

"You're still a good cook," he said, smiling at her. She wondered if he noticed the jumpsuit she was wearing. Looking up from her plate, she smiled warmly, but she could see the strain in his face. Maybe he was as nervous as she was. She sensed that he was just making conversation and she knew this dinner wasn't turning out as pleasurable as she'd planned, but rather was the calm before the storm.

After a while, Robert folded his napkin and laid it beside his plate. "Harriet, we have to talk," he said trying to sound calm.

Here it comes, she thought. Why did he have to do this now? Why couldn't he just wait until they finished? She had all of these questions, but did not voice any of them. She didn't want to make it any worse than it had to be. Harriet waited, feeling numb, her stomach tightening in anticipation and dread.

He cleared his throat. Where to start? He thought. After twenty-one years of marriage, there was just no easy way to do it. "Harriet, we are still young enough to have a happy life. I asked you for a divorce several times and for various reasons, I always backed down when you refused." He leaned in closer, taking her hand. "You deserve better, Harriet. We both deserve to be happy."

She moved from her chair, feeling as if she was getting sick. Was she hearing him right? Did he come home early just to tell her this? "What are you saying, Robert?" she asked, though she knew the answer in her heart.

"You know what I'm saying. Please don't act as if you don't." His voice was even.

"And what if I refuse again!" she snapped feeling as if she were suffocating. Her hands were trembling and she sat down again, folding her hands in her lap.

"I'll file for divorce anyway." He looked straight at her. "And, if I have to do it, the grounds will be infidelity," he said enunciating each word as he wanted no misunderstanding. "But if you agree to the divorce, we can get this over with, no hard feelings."

She pushed her hair from her face, trying to believe what

he was saying. Her eyes opened wide. "What on earth do you mean by infidelity."

"Harriet, did you think that I didn't know about you and old man Penn? I knew when it started and ended. And, so did his wife."

Her mouth fell open. "You never said a word about it."

He sat back in his chair and sipped his wine. "You're right. I never said anything before, but I'm telling you now. And, I'll use it in the divorce if I have to. But, I don't want to fight you that way, Harriet."

She was enraged. "You son-of-a-bitch!"

"Maybe I am. I just want out of this marriage." He saw the hurt on her face and knew he couldn't sit there any longer. Robert pushed his chair from the table. "I'm leaving tonight, Harriet. I'll have my lawyer get in touch with you in a couple of weeks. I want you to know that I want to be fair. I want you to find happiness in your life." He started to walk away.

"Fair, Robert?" She was yelling. "What is fair?" She was shaking her head as if she still couldn't believe what was happening.

He looked sad. He truly wanted her to be happy, but he needed his happiness too. He had to end this marriage. "I realize this may not seem fair to you, especially at this time of your life. But, this is for the best." He turned and walked up the stairs.

Harriet couldn't move. It had happened so fast and it seemed so final. She laid her head back against the chair and closed her eyes. It had been a long time since they'd been happy. But twenty-one years was a long time and now all she felt was numb. She sat still listening to him moving around upstairs. Finally, she heard him come down the stairs and close the door behind him. She heard his car drive out of the driveway. And, then she heard nothing. Robert was gone.

For the next three months, Robert threw himself into his work, focusing on one case in particular. Protecting a child from a sexually abusive father, was the diversion he needed and after several months, Robert won the case, returning the child to its mother. To celebrate, Robert had asked a tall, beautiful redhead to go to dinner with him. This was the first time he was going out since he had left Harriet.

The date was a bore. The only things he found intriguing about the woman were her full breasts and nicely shaped ass. She had talked through dinner – telling him of all the different men that had fallen in love with her, the money they spent on her, and the vacations they took her on. By the time desert was served, she was making plans for her life with Robert. How exciting it was going to be to be with a lawyer, she had told him. Robert had rolled his eyes. Is this what dating was like in the nineties?

He made love to her for hours and she was as good as she looked. But there were no sparks, no rockets taking off for Robert. She was beautiful, but empty. Even after he went out with her two other times, his opinion didn't change. So, he threw himself back into work, occasionally dating, but still wanting the happiness that he believed he'd been missing for over twenty years.

Harriet worked for the Board of Education on San Pedro Street and found her days filled only with work. By nine every night, Harriet was asleep and her weekends were even worse. She'd read, drink and sleep. She thought of her mother often and cried.

She awakened one Sunday morning cold and frightened. She held her hands in front of her. They were trembling. Her stomach was doing somersaults and her head was pounding. She thought she was dying and shuddered at the thought of crawling out of bed, but did slowly. She tiptoed into the dining room, and grabbed a bottle of gin. But when the smell of the drink reached her, she started to cry and threw the glass against the wall, ran into her bedroom and opened her closet door. She stood for a moment looking at her clothes hanging there in front of her. She grabbed a gray suit off the hanger and took a long shower. All the while, crying, with tears rolling down her cheeks. Her hands were cold and still trembling. Then, she dressed quickly and drank two cups of black coffee before she left the house.

She drove to the large Baptist church on 51st and Broadway and sat in her car for a few moments. This was what she had to do. Put her life in the hands of the Lord. There was no one else to love her, no one else to depend on, but the Lord

Almighty. Her steps felt lighter as she walked inside the church. The usher seated her besides a lady whose smile was so warm that it brought tears to Harriet's eyes.

The Pastor asked if there was anyone who needed special prayer. He beckoned them to the front. Harriet was the first to get up. There were other people at the altar, but she knew that no one needed this as much as she did. She walked out two hours later, a member of the church. From now on, she was going to serve the Lord. This was her new home, her new family. And, this was her last chance at life. She felt warm inside. She was saved.

Chapter 5

"Lord, have mercy, Helen. These collard greens are delicious, girl. How did you learn to cook so good?" Darlene asked between bites.

"Mama taught all three of us to cook and clean."

"Well, I'm glad you invited me over for dinner. You know how much I love to eat," Darlene laughed.

"And I enjoy cooking as long as there's someone to enjoy eating it."

"Girl, you know I do," Darlene said, as she buttered her cornbread, then took a drink of her lemonade.

Helen laughed. Darlene Jives was forty-one years old with a wide smile and light brown eyes. She was short and wide, over one hundred and ninety pounds. Her shiny black hair was tied in a ponytail that hung pasted to her shoulders. She was pretty with smooth skin.

"Girl, you're going to have a cholesterol problem," Helen said looking at the butter Darlene had soaked her cornbread and candy yams with.

"Who, me? Why you ask?" She looked at Helen and then at her plate as if she hadn't realized how much butter that she had eaten.

"Have you had it checked lately?" Helen tried to ask the question casually.

"Hell, no. Everyone has to die from something, Helen. Eating is my weakness. It's better than using drugs or drinking."

"You're a stone nut case. Do you want some more lemonade?"

"Yes and add lots of ice and a teaspoon of sugar, please."

Helen got the pitcher from the refrigerator and gave the sugar to Darlene.

"So, you've been so busy with your new book, we never get the chance to talk. How is that bitchy sister of yours?"

Helen let out a sigh and frowned. "Harriet's the same. Bitchy and unhappy as ever. Elaine told me that Harriet has joined a church now. Hopefully, this will help her. Let's go out to the patio, it's cooler out there."

Darlene followed Helen from the kitchen. Helen was wearing cut off blue jeans and a short, white T-shirt. She was barefoot, her hair pinned up in the back.

"So, tell me about Elaine. How's she getting along in that new townhouse?"

"As far as I know, she's doing okay. She's still decorating. She tells me she's got a new hairdo and all new clothes. I hope she doesn't go through her money without thinking."

Darlene heard the concern in Helen's voice. "So, what you're saying is that the girl has a new attitude, huh?"

"I guess you can say that," Helen said.

"Well, good for her. I always thought she was a sweet girl. She needs this time to spread her wings," Darlene said. "Do you know that I haven't set foot in LA since I left. And, after twenty-two years, I don't plan to." Darlene sighed and leaned back in her chair. "I have such a wonderful life here. I have my bakery and my house. Atlanta is where I belong," Darlene said, taking another drink of her lemonade.

"I love it too, but we were so young when we came to Atlanta. We probably would have done just as well in LA."

Darlene shook her head. "I'm not so sure about that. Hell, nothing good ever happened to my family there."

"Well, I'm sure my mother thought I was going to run back home after Thomas left me, but I had no intentions of going back. Now, I go out there just to see Lynn and Elaine and then bring my ass back here where I belong." She looked serious. "But, I am glad I ran into you all those years ago."

"So am I," Darlene laughed. The sun was still warm against their faces, but every once in a while they could feel a breeze. The sky was clear and the two friends sat on the patio continuing their talk as they did at least once a month.

"Anyway, how is Walter?" Helen asked.

Darlene stopped laughing. "Girl, I'm tired of his little

42

skinny, good-for-nothing ass. He never has enough money to take me out. He comes over, eats my food, watches television and then screws my brains out," she said, folding her arms in front of her. "Just thinking of him makes me angry."

"How often does he come over?"

"Two, maybe three times a week."

Helen looked at her friend. "Do you love him, Darlene?"

She was silent for several moments. "I like him a lot, but I don't think I'm in love with him."

Helen wasn't convinced and she was sure that Walter was only using her friend. He didn't love her. Helen was certain of that. Darlene has a big heart and he knows it, thought Helen. Not to mention that Darlene's banana nut bread was now in the stores and bakeries. She is doing pretty good financially, and the bastard knows it, Helen thought feeling disgust.

"How's your new book coming along?" Darlene asked.

"It's selling. I like it better than the last one, but I always say that, don't I?"

Darlene nodded in agreement.

"I'm almost half through the next one, but for some reason, I keep losing my train of thought. Guess it's writer's block, but I'm sure it won't last too long."

Darlene could tell that something was bothering her friend. "Okay, I've waited long enough. So, let's have it. What's bothering you, Helen?" she asked warmly. Darlene tilted her head. "You haven't found yourself a man that you haven't told me about?"

Helen laughed. "You've got to be kidding. I am not looking for anyone. And who would put up with me anyway? When I'm writing, I don't know if it's day or night."

"But something is bothering you," Darlene continued to probe.

Helen sighed. "I can't put my finger on it, Darlene. My mother's death made me realize that I don't have parents anymore. Mama and I were never close, but I never imagined her not being here. And now, I'm worried about Elaine. I never get to speak to her. She's always busy, either coming or going when I call."

"Helen, the woman is grown for Pete's sake. You

said she is free for the first time in her life. She is probably not used to living alone yet and stays out late sometimes because she has no reason to rush home anymore. You said yourself that she needs to spread her wings and get used to living a life of her own."

Helen still seemed unconvinced. "I just don't know, Darlene. It just worries me."

"Think about it, honey. She can now come and go as she pleases. Once she is used to it, she will calm down and realize there isn't anything new out there in those streets. Just trust me on this one, Helen."

"But, there is something more that is bugging me, Darlene."

"Like what, honey?"

"For instance, like selling the house. I keep thinking that I should have gone back until it was sold," she said still not sure what the problem could be.

"But, Helen, she sold it and brought her own place, didn't she? Besides, Harriet is there if she needs any help. All you need to do is relax a little. Elaine sold the house and brought a new one. She did it, so stop worrying over nothing. How can you keep your mind on writing a book? If you are so worried, then phone Harriet and have her drop in on Elaine."

"I guess you're right. Maybe I'm making too much out of this. Like you said, it's still new to her. She will settle down sooner or later," Helen said, nodding her head.

The bright lights were glittering on Peachtree Street and the night was beautiful. The sky was filled with bright stars shining enough to brighten the city. The night club was busy. Most of the women wore sleeveless dresses in the August humidity.

Helen wore her hair up, a short black dress with thin spaghetti straps, black hose and pumps. Darlene wore a long, black sleeveless dress and a pair of black flat shoes and her bright brown eyes gleamed with excitement.

"This is the best birthday present you've given me, Helen. You know how much I love James Brown and I know he's going to sing all his old songs. Those were the best, you know," she said smiling.

"Yeah, they were. I don't like what he sings now." Helen remembered the good old days when she and Robert used to dance to "Try Me" and "Bewildered". She shook her head as if she were trying to clear it. It was all so long ago.

Darlene was saying, "As old as he is, he can still sing as good as he used to."

They were standing in front of the night club, which looked like an old movie theater. Helen was furiously digging in her purse for the tickets.

"Oh, no, girl! You didn't forget the tickets, did you Helen?" Darlene asked.

Helen cursed under her breath, then breathed a sigh of relief. "No, here they are." She pulled the tickets out and waved them in front of Darlene's face, but Darlene was distracted. "Hello," Helen said, then followed Darlene's gaze. "Who are you looking at? Do you know him?"

Girl, look at that man standing on the corner. I have never seen a White man so fine."

The man looked in Helen's direction and their eyes met. They smiled, then he turned away. A tall Black woman on his arm kissed his cheek as they entered the club.

"My, my, my. I wouldn't mind walking in her shoes tonight," said Helen.

"I know, the way you were flirting with the man, Helen," Darlene said and laughed.

"Come on. Let's go inside. Maybe I'll run into him and take him home with me," she said playfully.

"Dream on, honey." They laughed their way inside.

They were only six rows from the front. The place was packed and the music was loud. When the unknown group came on the stage, Helen went to buy a cold drink. Darlene stayed behind.

The lobby was crowded and Helen walked into the ladies room to check her makeup. As she walked across the lobby, she felt a hand on her shoulder and froze when she turned around.

Robert was even more handsome than she remembered. It looked like the divorce was doing him good.

"Hello, Helen," he extended his hand and she took it. His

hand was warm, large and strong. "How have you been?" he asked, looking as if he could see straight through her.

"I've been okay, thank you." She managed another smile and looked around to see if anyone was standing off to the side waiting for him.

As if he could read her mind, he spoke, "I flew in with a couple of guys earlier today. We're flying out tonight."

"So soon? You couldn't have seen much of the city in that short time."

"No, I didn't. We had business here and thought a little pleasure would be nice too." He looked at her as though he was memorizing every inch of her, the same look she saw in his eyes when she was in LA. "You look beautiful, Helen."

She smiled, her palms sweating. He made her feel like she was nineteen. No other man made her feel so erratic. She took a deep breath and held her purse in front of her, forcing her fingers to stop quivering. "I'm sorry about you and Harriet."

"We weren't happy. The divorce was the best for both of us."

I guess so," she said. "Well, we'd better be getting back to our seats. It was nice seeing you, Robert." She started to walk away, when he called her name.

"If I can get away for a few days next month, I would like to see Atlanta. Maybe you could show me around. I know you're busy and I don't want to put you out, but maybe you could spare a day."

She wondered what it would be like spending a day alone with him. "Yes," she heard herself say. "I would love to show you the city. Just call and let me know."

"Of course."

They both stood there as though they were at a loss for words.

"Well, my friend is going to wonder what happened to me. I'd better get back. Have a safe trip home, Robert," she said, with a strain in her voice.

"I will and I'm looking forward to us getting together."

She turned and walked away, feeling his eyes on her.

"What took you so long? I started to go out to see if you were all right," Darlene said looking strangely at Helen.

"I ran into Robert, my sister's ex-husband."

Darlene looked at her in surprise. "What's he doing here?"

"He said he's here on a business trip..." Before Helen could continue, James Brown started to sing, "Please, Please" and Darlene turned her attention toward the stage. Helen turned in her seat and saw Robert sitting only a few rows behind her. She could feel his eyes on her.

The rest of the concert was a daze to Helen and she was glad when they were outside, walking to her car. She looked around for Robert, but he was no place in sight. She was relieved and disappointed. This is silly, she thought. By tomorrow, this feeling will be gone and forgotten. She and Darlene got into the car and headed home.

The next day, Helen was at home standing at her patio door waiting for Harriet to answer the telephone. Dammit, where is she? She was about to hang up when she heard Harriet's voice.

"Hello, Harriet, it's Helen." There was only silence.

"Are you there, Harriet?"

"Yes. What's wrong, Helen?" Hearing from Helen only meant bad news.

"I need you to do me a favor, Harriet. I haven't heard from Elaine in three weeks. I called today and her phone is disconnected with no forwarding number."

There was a long silence on Harriet's end.

"But, you said that Elaine could have your share of the money from the sale."

"What the hell does that have to do with anything, Harriet? Why do you always have to be so difficult? I'm not calling about the money. I need to know if my sister is all right and why her damn phone is disconnected!"

"There's no reason for such foul language, Helen. I understand you quite well."

"Then act like it," Helen snapped.

"Well, Helen, Elaine just told me that she is going to call you tomorrow and give you her new number."

"Why did she get her number changed in the first place?"

"She said that someone kept calling with the wrong number at all times of the night."

"Well, I thought something terrible had happened to her."

"No, Helen, the Lord is watching over her just as He does with all of us. But some of us go to church to thank Him for it."

Helen ignored her remark. "Does Elaine like her new place?"

"She says she loves it."

"Harriet, I saw Robert last night at a concert. I was surprised. He said he was here on a business trip."

Harriet sighed deeply. "I don't want to ever hear that man's name again, do you hear me? He is a sinner, not a child of God."

Helen was shocked to hear the bitterness in her sister's words. "I'm sorry, Harriet. Well, since I know that Elaine is fine, I won't keep you any longer."

"Good, I have to go to Bible study and I don't like being late."

"Take care, Harriet," Helen said feeling like she had just completed a conversation with a stranger.

The next morning, Helen received a phone call from Elaine.

"I'm sorry to call you so early, but I'm so excited. I have a million things to do today. Did I tell you I'm buying all new furniture?"

"Did you get rid of all of Mama's things?" Helen blinked her eyes wide. She was really wide awake now. It was hard to believe that Elaine had gotten rid of everything that belonged to Mama, she thought with disbelief.

"Of course. Why would I furnish my new house with old furniture?"

Helen didn't say anything. The distance made it harder for her to realize that her mother was dead, but with all of her possessions now gone, it left her with an empty feeling inside. Mama is really dead, she thought.

"Helen, I brought a new white couch like yours. Remember how much I loved it?"

"Yes," was all Helen could say.

"How's Lynn, Helen?"

"She's fine. She asked me about you last week."

"I'll give her a call next week," Elaine said.

"I've been worried about you Elaine. Whenever I call you're either too busy or not at home."

"Why do I have to be home every time you call?" Elaine asked with an irritated edge in her voice.

"You don't, honey. I just want to make sure you're taking care of yourself. But you sound happy and that makes me happy."

"I am excited about my new life, Helen. I even have a new boyfriend."

"Really? Tell me about him."

"Oh, Helen, he's absolutely wonderful. He's tall and good looking, has a good sense of humor. He keeps me laughing. That's important, don't you think?"

"Yes."

"He's twenty-four, but looks younger. He takes good care of himself."

Helen coughed and dropped the phone. She picked it up and put it back to her ear. "Did you say, twenty-four?"

"Yes, but we're in love, Helen. He makes me happy."

Helen sat on the edge of her bed. Elaine gave her the new number.

"I'll give you a call next week. Bye, Helen."

Elaine walked back into the bedroom where William was already dressed. He went to her and put a joint between her lips and kissed her on the cheek. She puffed twice and set it in the ash tray. She had never had a joint until she met William. It made her laugh and relax and forget things she didn't want to remember.

"Baby, I need five hundred dollars to pay my rent. It's due today," he said as he kissed her again and again.

"But William, I keep telling you to move in with me. It'll be cheaper that way. It doesn't make sense that we're paying rent in two different places."

He kissed her hard on the mouth and pushed her against the wall. "What don't make sense is for a man to move in on his woman while he's out of a job." He took another hit on the joint and passed it to her.

She nibbled at his neck. "Move in with me today, William."

"No, not until I get a job. Can't you understand that, baby?"

"No, I need you here with me, William. Every night."

He pulled away so that he could see her face. "I feel the same way, but not until I find a job."

She unzipped his pants, pulled off her jeans, not taking her eyes from his. He led her to the bed and kissed her.

"After I make love to you, give me the money, so that I can get back early. We can spend the day together and I'll cook dinner."

She lay on top of him. "Whatever I have is yours, William. You know that," she whispered.

"Yeah, baby, I know that."

Helen sat in the kitchen with her breakfast in front of her. Tonight, she would have to call Harriet again. She was sure she'd heard a man's voice while she was talking to Elaine. Helen put her coffee cup down. Twenty-four years old. She couldn't believe it. What was happening to her sister? Whatever it was, it was happening too fast. Harriet would just have to find out about this William.

Helen tried to remember her conversation with Elaine. Maybe it wasn't as serious as she was envisioning it to be. At least that's what she hoped. She shuddered at the thought of this man having access to Elaine's money.

The next day, Harriet returned Helen's call. "I've met the man, Helen. I don't like him, but we can't decide who Elaine should be with. It's not our business."

"Well, does he live with her?"

"No, he left before I did. I happened to peek inside her closets and saw no men's clothing, no sign of a man living there. I'm going to talk to her about joining church. That's what she really needs. She doesn't need a man to guide her around. She needs the Lord. You do too, Helen. Try the Lord instead of writing trashy books."

Helen sighed. "I don't feel like arguing with you today, Harriet. Look, thanks for returning my call. It takes a load off my mind."

When she hung up the phone, Helen changed her clothes so that she could get out of the house for a while. As she dressed, she thought about Elaine. Maybe she was just being overprotective. Elaine had a right to live her own life. But twenty-four? Helen couldn't get that out of her mind.

She walked out the front door into the warm weather. And as she stepped into the street, a white convertible flew by. The young woman that was driving lived across the street and lived with a man about fifteen years her senior. Helen had never met the woman, had only seen her driving out of the garage, always at top speed. She prayed that they'd never be driving at the same time. Lord, help the person she runs into. For sure, it would be their last day on earth because she would never stop in time.

Chapter 6

Helen parked her car in the parking lot of the Westin Peachtree Plaza Hotel. She was meeting Robert for breakfast before she showed him the city. He was going to be in Atlanta for the entire weekend and she hoped she'd be able to fill their time until Sunday evening.

She was surprised at the excitement and anticipation she felt and her heart thumped even harder when she saw him standing tall in white slacks and a blue short-sleeved shirt. He was standing with his hands stuffed in his pockets and she had to smile. Even when they were kids, he stood straight that way. She would have recognized him a block away.

He smiled as she walked towards him. He took in her black slacks and gray silk blouse and noticed how her hair looked almost red in the sunlight. She looked radiant.

She reached out her hand to him, but he leaned over and kissed her cheek. He hadn't realized until this moment how much he'd wanted to see her.

"What time did you arrive?" she asked.

"A couple of hours ago. I've unpacked and even had time to freshen up a bit."

"You're not tired?"

"No, I'm ready to go, girl. I've been looking forward to this trip."

Helen couldn't stop smiling. "Well then, you'd better be in shape because you have a lot of walking to do, Mister," she kidded with him.

He led her to the hotel restaurant and they were seated at a corner table.

"You look pretty, Helen," Robert said, admiring her.

"Thanks," she replied and looked outside onto the busy

street. "Are you ready for our hot weather? Atlanta is very different from LA, you know."

"So I've been told. I don't mind. A little hot weather never hurt anyone," he laughed.

"Well, we can always stop for a cold drink if it gets too hot for you."

"Fair enough. I really appreciate you spending these three days with me."

Was he kidding? Her excitement had not stopped building. "I've been looking forward to this. I've been suffering from writer's block and getting away from my writing for a few days will help."

They ordered ham, eggs, and wheat toast, orange juice and black coffee. The restaurant was beginning to get busy with tourists pausing to take pictures.

"So, how is everything on the home front, Robert?"

He sighed. "I've been working long hours, seven days a week."

"No time to play at all?" she smiled.

"Not much. Just lots of work. That's why I'm glad for this trip. It gives me a chance to get away and relax a bit. Take my mind away from everything."

"I understand," Helen said. "I've felt the same way lots of times. Have you seen Elaine lately?"

"As a matter of fact, I saw her in the post office last week. She looks well and seems to be excited about all the new things in her life."

"That's what she said the last time I spoke to her," Helen said.

He nodded and looked around the restaurant. "This is a nice hotel."

"That's why I recommended it. I knew you would like it. This is where my agent stays when she comes to town."

He smiled, unable to take his eyes off of her. She barely looked thirty years old.

"Have you seen Harriet?" she asked.

"No, not since I moved out. I couldn't take it any longer, Helen. My life was just passing me by and I needed to get away." He shook his head. "I just couldn't live out the rest of my life that way." He looked sad and she nodded in agreement, letting him know that she understood.

"It must have been lonely for you both," Helen said. "Were you two ever in love?" she asked then held up her hands. "I'm sorry if I'm being too personal."

"No, not at all. Maybe we were happy once. But..." his voice trailed off. "Are you happy here, Helen?"

The question surprised her. "I guess I am. I'm looking for the same things that everyone else is looking for. Companionship, someone to be a friend first, before a lover. That's important, don't you think?"

"Yes," he nodded.

"I guess I could be happier," she said in a low voice. "But then I wonder is there anyone who is completely happy?"

"Maybe not completely, but I think one can be very happy if they have the right person." They were silent for several moments. "Helen, do you realize that I've only seen you twice since you left LA all those years ago? I used to wonder about you all the time."

She smiled. "Well, I think we've talked long enough. Let's get going."

He placed money in the middle of the table and they walked out. The day was warm and sunny. Robert inhaled deeply, enjoying the warm air.

"Why don't we walk in that direction?" Helen pointed. "There's a lot to see just by walking up and down Peachtree."

They walked slowly, feeling as if no time had passed between them. Almost no time.

"You know, you asked me about Harriet back in the restaurant. And, I think I need to explain. I thought I loved her once. After you had left me." When she said nothing, he continued. "After Harriet and I were married for a few years, I admitted to myself that I was trying to replace a love that I lost."

She looked up at him, hoping that the conversation wouldn't get too deep again. She knew he was talking about her.

"And, maybe I was trying to replace the love I never had as a kid. I wanted a family to love me and for me to love. I wanted children so that I could give them everything that I missed out on. After my father left, my mother's way of

54

showing love was to put food in my stomach and a roof over my head. She never showed me any affection."

Helen nodded, understanding what he was feeling. "What happened to our parents, Robert? What could have happened to make them so remote toward their children?"

"I just don't know," he said. "Life was hard, they had to work so much that they didn't have time to say, 'I love you.'"

"But not all parents were like ours."

"That's true." He held her arm and led her across the busy street. "I should have brought my camera," he said purposely changing the subject.

"We can buy one inside the mall."

Leaving the heavy conversation behind, they spent the day sightseeing around Atlanta – the Historie Building and Structures, AG Rhones Memorial Hall and the Victoria Romanesque Revival Building. They stopped for lunch at the Fish Market and talked about their lives. As they talked, the twenty years seemed to disappear. They had become friends, and without knowing it, they were falling into a comfortable relationship.

Chapter 7

The day had gone by faster than they realized. They had shared so much of their lives, things they never got to know about each other and things they had forgotten. Neither of them wanted the day to end, so they went to Helen's house for dinner.

After eating a fruit salad, they sat at the patio table and talked for a few more hours. The patio was small with plants in every corner, a round table and three white chairs. Helen could feel the cool, gentle breeze blowing across her face and she inhaled, feeling peacefulness surround her. They sat opposite each other, sipping on wine and it was a while before Helen realized they had been holding hands. She didn't know how long they'd been in this position, but she didn't pull her hand away. It felt good, it felt safe and comfortable.

He gently pushed her hair from her face. He didn't quite know why he did, except to touch her. He had wanted to touch her all day and now her hair felt like silk against his hands, as it fell through his fingers. Looking at her beautiful face, he wanted to trace her lips with his finger tips. There had been other women since his divorce, but Helen was different. He could sit and hold her all night and just listen to her talk. He wanted to hold her in his arms, to protect her and make her smile. He knew then that he still loved her.

He had noticed that she'd only had one phone call – from Darlene. And he was glad that so far, there were no male companions calling her. It would be harder knowing that she had a lover, especially since he had to return to Los Angeles.

"Helen, I want to remember you just the way you are now," he whispered, so close to her. She smiled, but still didn't pull her hand away. They talked until after ten and finally, she took Robert back to the hotel. He gave her a kiss on her forehead and smoothed her hair from her face. This could easily become a habit, he thought, as he looked into her face and then watched her walk away.

Helen walked into Darlene's bakery at ten the next morning. Darlene was wrapping her fresh bread and pies for her delivery man to pick up for his daily route. Her two employees were in the kitchen baking.

Helen peeked into one of the boxes. "When did you decide to bake pies?"

"Last week. I told you."

"No, you said you were thinking about it," she said, holding a sweet potato pie in her hand.

"Well, I thought about it and now I'm selling pies."

Helen picked up another. They were all so perfect. "I want to buy one," she said.

"Have one. There's a couple in the kitchen."

Helen poured herself a cup of coffee and sliced a piece of banana nut bread that was on the counter for customers to sample. While Darlene worked, she noticed that Helen was barely eating and hadn't said a word.

"I can tell you need to talk. What's up?" Darlene asked her friend.

"How can you tell that I need to talk?" Helen asked.

"Girl," Darlene started with one hand on her hip. She was wearing her hair net and long white apron. She pulled a stool to the counter and sat next to Helen. "How many years have we known each other? I can always tell by that faraway look in those big browns of yours. Besides, when you just look at my banana bread and don't eat it, honey, I know something is heavy on your mind." Darlene folded her arms in front of her.

Helen was looking at the red polish on her toes. "Well, you know I was with Robert yesterday. We went back to my place last night and ate, listened to a little music, talked..." she said, waiting for Darlene's reply.

Darlene was looking at her as if she was expecting more. "So, how did it go?"

"Pretty good..."

"Well, what do you two have planned for today?"

"I don't know yet. We're just planning as we go along. It's more fun that way. And, planning doesn't turn out the way you plan anyway."

Darlene got up. "I need some cold water. It's getting hot in here. Do you want a glass?"

"No, thanks." Helen sighed and hesitated. "You know while we were talking last night, we ended up holding hands. I told him things about my marriage and my family that I have only told you. I even told him about my love affairs. We talked about everything and it felt good. It is not often that a woman can tell a man about her past affairs, wouldn't you say?"

"No, it is not very often, and when they tell us about theirs, it's a lie, never completely the truth," Darlene said laughing.

"I know this sounds crazy and I'm scared to death, but I think I'm falling in love with him. Even if he was married to my sister."

Darlene wiped her hands on her apron and sat back on the stool with a glass of water. "It's not like you and Harriet are close sister and you didn't see Robert and Harriet enough to recognize them as man and wife."

"I know, but she is still my sister."

"And she was your sister when she took him away from you twenty years ago."

"That's true, but we were only children," Helen said and frowned as Darlene wiped sweat from her forehead with the back of her hand. Funny, thought Helen. She didn't seem to feel as warm as Darlene obviously felt. "You're too young for hot flashes, aren't you?"

"Go to hell, Helen!" They both laughed. "I've been baking since three this morning and I'm just tired!"

Helen got up and started to pace the floor. "Why am I feeling this way about him? And, so soon. This is crazy and frightening, Darlene, damn frightening."

"Girl, just relax and enjoy it. Life is too short to worry about every little thing or feeling you get about someone," Darlene explained with wisdom.

"I know I should, but we live so far apart. We'll hardly see each other."

"Well, that may be good. It'll give you time to think about what you're doing."

Helen sat back on her stool. "I knew this was going to

happen when I was back in LA. I didn't want him to come out here, but I thought this was just a feeling that would go away. I thought that I was just being foolish. I was thunderstruck when I ran into him at the James Brown concert. Who would have thought that he would be there?"

"Well, maybe this happened for a reason, Helen. I sure as hell wish it would happen to me," Darlene said jokingly. "The last time I saw Robert, he was a lot of man. I could crawl up and down..."

"Oh, shut the hell up," Helen laughed. She looked at her watch. "I promised him that I would be at his hotel by eleven. Girl, I feel like a young girl on my first date," she said gathering her belongings in a rush.

"You still look young, Helen."

"Yeah, but I don't feel so young sometimes," she said.

"When you always had to struggle the way we did to make it, you have a right to feel older than your years," laughed Darlene.

"Yes," Helen laughed. "Don't I know that."
Darlene walked with her to the car and looked up at the sun. "Now, don't talk to me about hot flashes. Hell, it's hot out here," she said feeling all heat and no air.

"Well, I have only one more day with Robert, so I probably won't see you for the rest of the weekend," Helen said giving Darlene a wicked smile.

"Enjoy yourself, Helen. For a change, stop worrying about things."

Helen arrived at the hotel at exactly eleven and Robert was waiting in the lobby. She was dressed in white sandals, while slacks and a white cotton blouse with ruffles on the sleeves, that hung off her shoulders. He gave her a kiss on her cheek and she held her breath to keep control. They held hands as they walked to the small coffee shop.

"I'm going to miss you," Robert said. "Will you come to LA a little more often?"

"Yes, I think so," she said as she nodded and smiled up at him. She showed him the rest of Peachtree Street and he took pictures, mostly of her. After dinner, they ended up back at his hotel room. She spent the night with him and the next morning, they had breakfast in bed, watching the rain as it drenched the city. For the rest of the day, they held each other, making love through the day into that night. Finally dressing for dinner, they went to the Pierremont Plaza, then to Atlanta Nights, a nightclub that a friend of Robert's had recommended. It was the most romantic weekend that she could remember ever having. If she spent the rest of her life with Robert, she would always remember their special weekend of falling in love again, and getting to know each other, mind, body and soul.

The next morning, he checked out of the hotel and stayed with Helen until Monday morning. The morning of his departure was sad for both of them and they held each other as if it were their last time together. Helen knew people just didn't get second chances like this.

After she returned from the airport, she stayed inside, listening to the rain hitting her windows and thinking of Robert. She'd never know such love before, the binding love that one felt growing stronger every minute they were together. When she dressed, he helped her button her blouse. When the wind blew her hair, he pushed it from her face. His attentiveness and thoughtfulness was more than any woman could wish for or dream of. In an unconscious gesture, she pushed her fingers through her hair. Finally, unable to take the quiet anymore, she went to Darlene's bakery.

"Girl, your eyes are sparkling." But Darlene saw sadness in them too. "Was he that good?" she asked playfully.

Helen laughed out loud. "Yes! Now, take this coffee before it gets cold." Helen looked around the room. "Where is everyone? I don't hear anyone in the kitchen."

"They're already gone. We've been here since three this morning, you know. Let's go into my office. It's cooler in there." Darlene pulled off her hair net and apron and sat on the leather couch opposite Helen. "Wait a minute before you start. I just want to put these papers away and get a couple of slices of banana nut bread. Honey, I don't want to miss any of your hot weekend." She turned to face Helen. "And, it's about time, too, Helen, that you let your guard down and enjoy it."

"Now, my doors are locked; I'm closed for the day and I'm ready! Tell me about Robert."

"This feels like the first time I've been in love. I'm not used to this."

"Well, you're older now. This could be real."

Helen nodded. "You're right about that. I feel safe with him, Darlene. I've been afraid to trust or believe, but Robert is a gentleman and he needs love in his life as much as I do. He talks about his life, his desires with me. And, what I love about him the most is that he gives as much as he takes. That's important to me," she said.

Darlene nodded and remained silent.

"He made me realize how much I needed someone. And, I had him, if only for the weekend."

"Only for the weekend? Helen, it could be better this time around. You're older and you both know what you want and need."

"I want and need him."

"Then, go after him. Let him know how you feel. Tell him how you feel."

"I did that all weekend. And so did he." Helen's face glowed.

"So, what's going to happen now?"

Helen didn't say anything for a few seconds. She had already asked herself that question. "Well, I'm just going to go on with my life as it was before. I'm not sure if I'll see him again and I still have a life of my own." She sighed audibly and took her seat again, feeling all the hope that she had felt just seconds before depleting from her.

"And, what about Steve?" Darlene asked her.

"We haven't seen each other for a while. I guess we just grew apart. We were never in love. We may not see each other as lovers, but we will always be friends."

This is very confusing, Darlene thought, and she knew it was for Helen as well. First, she's in love with the man and within seconds, she may never see him again. She tried to understand what Helen was feeling, but it was hard for someone as spontaneous as Darlene.

"I'm really unaccustomed to feeling this way. I usually run the other way."

"I don't think you should turn your back on this, honey."

"I just want to keep my head on straight."

"That's wise. But don't turn your back on Robert if he makes you happy. Since your divorce, no man has been able to get this close to you. Maybe it's time that you break that barrier that you've built around you. You did let it down for the weekend."

"That was only for the weekend. But the big problem is that Robert lives so far away. He could play around on me and I wouldn't know and there would be nothing I could do about it," she said sounding as if she was getting angry.

"He doesn't have to be far away to cheat on you. Remember Thomas?"

"Of course. He slept with women right under my nose. There's no way I can forget it. He had a woman two blocks from our apartment, one on his job, and left Lynn and I for another one. And you're right, Robert doesn't have to be a hundred miles away to play on me."

Robert sat behind his desk trying to concentrate. He walked to the coffee maker and poured himself a cup of black coffee. He stopped at the large window and took in the view of downtown Los Angeles. So much smog, he murmured. He sighed and went back to his desk. He tried going back to work, when his phone rang. It was his informer, but it wasn't what he needed to close his case. Damn, he wanted to finish this case. He needed one more piece of information to complete the puzzle. It was frustrating, and it was the obstacle that prevented him from putting all the pieces together.

Hours had passed and he looked at his watch again. It was seven by then and he wasn't any closer to solving the case than he was earlier. He was weary. He looked at this watch forty minutes later. The phone rang and bingo...the missing piece he needed. If the shooting took place at seven-thirty, and he was sure it had, the man had time to drive all the way home and was there by eight, since he lived so close. The witness lied. He let out a sigh of relief. He had his answer and he would win this case. Damn, he wanted to finish this case.

He closed his eyes and saw her face. Her hair in disarray from their love making. Her sweet mouth, the way she kissed him, held him. He took a deep breath, closed his eyes and whispered, "sweet Helen." He phoned her every night, but that wasn't enough. He needed to be with her. He needed her next to him when he woke up in the mornings.

Three weeks later, Robert put a down payment on a two-story, three-bedroom white house with black trim. There were two rooms that could be used as offices – one for him and one for Helen. He would see her a few more times before he asked her to marry him. He wanted her now, but wasn't sure if she'd be willing to moved back to LA. At least with Lynn and Elaine living here, it increased his chances of her saying yes.

Robert went back to Atlanta to spend another weekend with Helen and when he returned home, he was totally convinced of his decision. He would make Helen Graham his wife.

After working day and night for the next few weeks on his big case, his break finally came. The witness had lied. He had his answer and would win his case. A week later, when the verdict came in giving him the victory, the first person he wanted to speak with was Helen.

Robert hadn't heard from her in four days. The last time they'd talked, she'd gotten a call in the middle of their conversation and had never called him back. He hated the call waiting service on the telephone. As far as he was concerned, that was the worse invention the telephone company could have created. If the line was busy, all one had to do was hand up and call again. He couldn't wait to speak to her.

Mr. Holly was a short, middle aged man who had lived next door to Helen for five years. He had asked her to arrange his silk flowers because he'd admired the arrangement in her apartment.

"You should be an interior designer as well as a writer," he had complimented her.

She had gone over to Mr. Holly's apartment, leaving her door slightly ajar and when she heard her phone ring, she asked Mr. Holly to answer it for her.

The man's voice took Robert by surprise. He was flabbergasted and slammed the phone down. So, that's why she's been so busy, he thought angrily. He got up and walked to the window and stood with his hands in his pockets. Just when I thought I'd gotten to know her, she springs this on me! Just like she did twenty years ago.

He grabbed his coat and walked out of his office. He was finished here today. Screw it, he was finished with Helen too. He left without giving her the benefit of the doubt.

Chapter 8

She added all the checks and calculated the figures twice. Five thousand dollars and she hadn't heard from William in three weeks. With the last three thousand that she had given him, he'd said that he was coming back to take her out to dinner, but hadn't returned. "Lord, how could I have been so gullible?" she moaned as tears rolled down her cheeks. "He must have been waiting for a fool like me." She sat at the table shaking her head, just like she'd done for the last three weeks.

She thought of Harriet and the sermon she'd given her last time they'd gotten together. "You don't need a man in your life, Elaine. All you need is God. Look at me," she said filled with pride. "My divorce is final and I feel good. I feel peace in my life. No, Elaine. You don't need a man to satisfy your every need. All you need is the Lord."

She couldn't sit and think about Harriet now. She had to find William. But as her hands quivered, she knew she'd never find him. She'd already tried. The apartment that he rented belonged to a friend; the man said William had never lived there.

"You look like a nice lady, so just forget William. He only uses my place for his women to hide them from his wife. He'll never leave his wife and baby."

She'd been shocked when the man told her that. This was all her fault – especially smoking those joints with him. He'd probably given them to her so that she wouldn't realize how much money she was giving him. She had to do something, to try to get some of her money back. She tried the man at the apartment again, hoping he would tell her where William lived.

"Sorry, but I can't do that. Besides, what good will it do you, lady? Forget him."

65

She sat in her car parked in front of the apartment for two nights, hoping to catch William, but there was no sign of him. Her money was gone. She cried and hung her head in shame.

The next morning, Elaine awoke to the ringing phone. It was Helen saying that she would be in LA next week. When she hung up, she cried again. Another frustration, she thought. "Why does she want to come to LA now?" Company was the last thing she wanted and she decided she would spend one day with her sister. She got out of bed and looked out the window. The sky was filled with gray, dark clouds. Just like she felt.

That night, she couldn't stay at home any longer, thinking of William and coming up with no answers. Nick's Place was packed with people talking and drinking. Elaine stood at the door for a few minutes, trying to adjust her eyes to the darkness, before finding a table in the bar. As she drank and listened to the loud music, her thoughts kept returning to William. She had to forget him, if only for one night. After-ward, she'd go home, get some sleep and start a new day tomorrow. William was out of her life and so was her five thousand dollars. So few men had noticed her, but William had made her feel beautiful. Now, she felt like a loser. But how was she to know these things. William was such a smooth talker.

"Miss." She jumped. "I'm sorry, I didn't mean to frigh-ten you."

Elaine looked up at the man like she'd forgotten where she was. "What did you say?"

"I asked if you were waiting for someone and if not, may I buy you a drink?" His voice was deep and sexy like Barry White's. He was dark skinned, impeccably dressed in a dark gray suit as if he'd just gotten off from work. He smiled. "So, may I buy you that drink?"

"No, thanks. I won't be here too long."

He looked disappointed, his arms fell by his sides. "May I sit for a while?" he asked, as he stood in font of her. "You look as though you could use some company. A pretty woman shouldn't be alone."

She looked up at him again. "Why not?" she said. Maybe she needed someone to talk to – to take her mind off of William and this man seemed to be a gentleman.

He sat across from her and introduced himself as Jake. He motioned for a waitress and ordered rum and coke for the both of them.

They chatted casually; he told her that he was an engineer for a large company. She asked if he were married; he said no. He looked at her skeptically, wondering why she'd asked. He told her about his childhood, his sisters and brothers. He asked if she lived alone, if she had family that lived near her and what kind of car she drove. She thought his questions were strange, but she answered them anyway. With what she'd been through, nothing was normal anymore.

"Do you come here often, Jake?" she asked.

"No. There's a place near my job that some of us go to after work, but I'm glad I passed by here today. I wouldn't have met you if I had gone with my friends." He smiled at her again, giving her the sweetest smile she'd ever seen – so sweet and innocent. "Would you like something to eat, Elaine? They serve good food here."

Elaine declined, but they continued chatting. She felt comfortable with him. "I've never come to a bar by myself before. But this place seems safe and it's not far," she said.

He counted her fourth drink. "Are you driving, Elaine?"

"Yes, but I'm fine. Don't worry about me."

"But what if you're stopped by the cops? They aren't easy on drunk drivers. I know someone who lost their license. Why don't you let me drive you home?"

She finished her drink and sat her glass down. "No, I shouldn't. We just met..."

"I know, but I'll feel better knowing you are safe. And tomorrow, you'll thank me," he said with that warm smile that she was beginning to love. "I'll wake you up tomorrow morning and bring you back to your car."

Elaine knew that he was just concerned for her safety. "I can walk home or call a cab."

"Well, why don't you come home with me, sleep on the couch and I'll bring you to your car in the morning? On my word of honor, "he said and touched her hand softly. "It really wouldn't be good if you were stopped."

When Elaine looked at him, she saw double and wondered what would happen if the cops stopped her. She hesitated, but when she looked down at her keys and saw two sets, she was worried. "Maybe it would be a good idea to go home with you. But you do promise to bring me back to my car first thing in the morning?"

"The moment you open your eyes," he said.

She looked at him again, then, picked up her glass and gulped down the last drop of her drink. She didn't realize how much she'd had to drink until she stood up. He led her to his 1986 brown Seville and she slid into the front seat next to her. Jake turned on the radio and Elaine leaned her head back listening to "My Girl" by the Temptations.

For a moment, she felt frightened and as if he read her mind, he told her that he would take her home now, if she wanted him to.

"No, it wouldn't be fair to you. You're so close to your house now." And, she did trust this man.

"Well, good. Because I could use the company, if you feel like talking," he said, with a teasing smile.

The drive to Jake's house was only about twenty minutes and she was thankful for that. Her head felt heavy and she just wanted to get inside so she could sleep. At that moment, her mother's face flashed in front of her and unsettled her. Was she watching over her, she wondered? Or was the drinking taking over her mind?

The apartment was small and stuffy and a chill ran down her back as she stood in the middle of the living room. The apartment was decorated in brown and black, but didn't feel like anyone had been living here, it was just a place to sleep. There were no rugs or plants, nothing to make this place a home.

She felt uneasy. "Maybe, you should just drive me back to my car. I'll be fine."

"No. We've come all the way here so you can stay here tonight. You'll get some sleep and I promise I'll take you back in the morning. Now, have a seat and relax."

She was apprehensive, but finally agreed. After all, what could happen?

"That's a good girl, relax," he said with that warm smile as he took her jacket.

"I won't put you out of your bed. I can sleep on the couch."

"You just undress and make yourself comfortable," he said, walking from the room. He came back with a pillow under his arm. "I'll make the couch into a bed."

She stood and looked around with frightened eyes. "Oh, no, Jake. You don't have to go through so much trouble. I can sleep on the couch just as it is. All I need is a blanket to keep me warm."

Ignoring her, he pulled the couch out and Elaine noticed there was already a sheet and brown wool blanket on it.

"There's no bedroom here, is there?" she asked, afraid to hear his answer.

"No, my apartment is a single, so we'll be sleeping together tonight."

She felt a pain in the pit of her stomach. She had to swallow hard to keep from throwing up. She decided to leave, walk back to her car or catch a bus. Anything would be better than staying and the fresh air would sober her up.

She glanced at Jake and now he seemed strange to her. What happened to his warm smile? His soft voice had become hard and raspy. She watched as he pulled his belt from his trousers, looking as if he was moving in slow motion. Her heart began beating faster.

As she watched him, he raised his hand high in the air and the thick, black belt came down hard across her shoulders and back, and again, and again, stripping away her silk blouse. She tried to gasp for air, but shock kept her from breathing. His voice quivered as he called her name and laughed. She held her hands against her face, desperately trying to prevent the belt from hitting her face. She grew more frantic with each lick and she wondered how long this would continue. She screamed and begged, but he only hit her harder.

Finally, the beating stopped and he held her head with one hand as he unzipped his trousers with the other. He pulled his penis from his pants and forced her mouth open, pushing every inch of himself inside her mouth. He was hard, rough, pulling her hair, bobbing her head backward and forward so fast that she felt dizzy. She couldn't cry out, she could barely breathe. She was trying to keep from choking and she felt as if she would suffocate as he plunged deeper and deeper, his penis now larger and harder, hitting the back of her throat again, and again, faster and faster. Finally, he exploded and pushed her down. She felt the cold, hard floor hitting against her back and she moaned, feeling the pain of the welts.

She was trying to focus when she heard his deep, cold, harsh voice.

"Get up, you bitch, and undress."

There was pleasure in his voice and she had to hold onto the couch for support. As she gagged, still crying, he laughed, enjoying every minute of her horror. Slowly, she peeled off what was left of her blouse and begged him to let her go. But, he slapped her hard and she fell to the floor, hitting her back against the small table in the center of the room.

"Do you think I drove your drunk ass out here just to turn around and drive you back?" he yelled.

"I can walk, I was willing to walk. I promise, I won't say a word about this. Please just let me go," she pleaded and cried.

He laughed an ugly laugh. "Who would believe a tramp and whore anyway? You're all alike." She cried as his words hit her. Is that what she'd become?

"You go to a bar looking for it and when you get it, you all cry and beg like damn babies. You knew what you were doing when you came home with me," he laughed again. He grabbed a handful of her hair, pulling her up until his face was close to hers. "Sure, bitch. I'll let you go when I'm good and finished with you."

She wanted to die. She was sure that he would kill her and she wanted to just get it over with. How stupid she was to trust him, a complete stranger. She closed her eyes and saw her mother again. She reached out to touch her, but felt nothing but pain traveling through her trembling body. But, she was sure that her mother was trying to tell her something. Maybe that they would be together soon.

He peeled off his clothes, not taking his eyes from her. Elaine curled her body under the blanket like a wounded mouse.

"Now, Daddy's gonna give you what you wanted."

She whimpered and begged him to let her go, pleading with him until she was hysterical and he pulled her up on her knees.

He turned her onto her stomach and entered her. The pain was so excruciating that she felt like her body would break into pieces. The room spun, then total darkness, then pain again...the darkness, darkness, then nothing.

She awoke with pain in her lower body and she couldn't move. Dampness and chills ran up and down her spine and now she felt the pain in every part of her. She heard voices and slowly opened her eyes. A White face was close to hers. He was talking to her, but she couldn't understand a word he was saying. The darkness and pain returned and she fell asleep, drifting slowly, floating far, far away as though she had no control of her mind or body.

Chapter 9

"Are you related to Elaine Gilmore?" They both jumped at the sound of the doctor's deep voice.

"Yes, we're her sisters," Helen said, as she grabbed her purse from the couch and rushed in front of Harriet.

"I'm Doctor Welsh." Helen shook his hand and introduced herself and Harriet. The doctor was tall and slender with blond hair that was almost white. He had deep blue eyes and a healthy tanned face.

"How is my sister?" Helen asked cautiously, afraid of what she might hear.

"She'll be all right, but she'll need a lot of rest and extensive counseling. This was traumatic for her."

Harriet and Helen looked at each other and though Helen wanted to cry, she held back her tears. She had to be strong for Elaine's sake.

"She was a little beaten up, but she'll be able to go home in a few days," the doctor continued.

Helen sighed, relieved. "Can we see her now?" she asked.

As the doctor led them into Elaine's room, Helen felt her legs weakening with every step as she got closer to the bed. Helen kissed Elaine on her forehead, keeping her face from showing her shock at the way her sister looked.

Elaine's face was bruised and one eye was swollen. Harriet stood back, away from Helen and Elaine and Helen wondered why her older sister was so quiet.

"How do you feel, honey?" Helen asked.

"Sore from head to toe," Elaine whispered in a hoarse voice that Helen barely recognized. Tears ran down Elaine's face and she wiped them with the back of her hand. "I was sure that he would kill me, Helen. I was leaving the bar and he grabbed me from behind, dragged me to his car and forced me in." There, she'd said it. It was a lie, but there was no other way. She couldn't face them if they knew the truth.

She thought of her mother and closed her eyes. It bothered her to think that her mother was watching while she was being beaten. And if her mother had been watching, then she now knew that Elaine was lying and she cringed thinking that her mother might know the failure she'd become.

Harriet walked to the other side of the bed. "You went to a bar?" she asked with an edge of anger in her voice. "I asked you to go to a prayer meeting with me and you went to a bar?" Harriet repeated contemptibly. "If you would have gone with me, none of this would have happened to you. Bars are for tramps, Elaine. You should have been at church."

Helen didn't like where the conversation was going or the tone of voice that Harriet was now using.

"If you would have gone with me, then none of this would have happened to you." She stood straight. "Bars are for tramps, Elaine. You should try joining the church," she snapped. Harriet moved closer to the bed. "What happened to you was your own doing. You brought this terrible thing on yourself."

Helen gave Harriet a long threatening stare. "How dare you waltz in here so holy after all the years you've been..."

"Stop it, just stop it, both of you!" Elaine cried. "I can't stand this."

Helen took her hand. "I'm sorry, honey."

"I've got to go," snapped Harriet.

"Go ahead, I'll stay with her," Helen said without facing Harriet giving Elaine her complete attention. "I'm sorry," Helen apologized again after Harriet left the room without saying another word.

"That's okay. We both know how Harriet is." Elaine paused, then continued. "How...how did you find out?"

"I told you I was coming out and when I got to Lynn's place and called you, there was no answer. I kept calling and then finally called Harriet's office. When her secretary told me that Harriet had gone to the hospital to see her sister, I jumped in the car and drove here in a panic. I couldn't imagine what had happened." She took her sister's hand in hers.

Elaine closed her eyes and Helen could see tears escaping from the corner of her eyes, falling onto her pillow. Helen felt angry and hurt as she looked at her sister and saw her pain. Helen knew she had to say something to make her sister feel better.

"Honey, you were just in the wrong place at the wrong time. There's nothing wrong with going to a bar. Darlene and I do it sometimes."

Elaine opened her eyes. "But, I'm sure you and Darlene handle yourselves much better than I did, Helen."

Helen looked at her as if she didn't understand what she meant. She looked so small, so fragile. Helen wondered if it was the medication that prevented her from thinking clearly. "Don't be so hard on yourself. What happened to you could have happened to any of us, Elaine."

When Elaine shook her head, Helen continued trying to calm her sister. "Look, the man grabbed you. There was nothing you could have done to prevent it."

Elaine started to speak, but couldn't. And, what would she say anyway? She had gone into a bar to forget about William – another mistake. She had followed a man home. A stranger. There were no excuses. Harriet was right, she had become a tramp. She closed her eyes and wished for sleep.

"Have you heard anything I've said, Elaine?"

"Yes," Elaine whispered. "But you don't know how I feel. No one does."

"Then tell me. How do you feel?"

She sat up to relieve the pressure from her back and laid her hands across her stomach, never taking her eyes off them. "I feel like sleeping my life away, but I wish that I had no feeling at all."

Hearing her sister, Helen knew that Elaine needed counseling. But she couldn't talk about that now – later, when the time was right.

"I'm really tired, Helen. Why don't you go spend some time with Lynn?"

"Are you sure you want to be alone right now?"

Elaine slid down, pulling the blanket to her chest. "Yes, I'm tired and need some sleep." Elaine closed her eyes. "I need peace and quiet."

74

Helen stood up. "Okay, I'll call you later, honey." She patted her sister's hand, then turned and left the room.

Helen arrived at the hotel an hour after she left Elaine. She changed into her short, blue satin bathrobe and picked up the phone to call Robert. She hadn't heard from him in awhile and wondered what was wrong, but before she dialed the last number, she hung up the phone. If he doesn't want me, I don't want to have anything to do with him. As Helen lay back on the bed, her thoughts were filled with Elaine and Robert and both of them made her want to cry. She just hoped that there would be better days ahead, for all of them.

Helen and Lynn took Elaine home from the hospital at noon as planned. Elaine unlocked the door to her townhouse. Lynn ran through admiring her aunt's place.

"It's beautiful, Aunt Elaine," Lynn said, beaming. "I love it."

"Yes, Elaine. Lynn is right. You did a wonderful job with the décor."

"Thanks," Elaine said dryly. She walked slowly to the couch. She was drowsy from the sleeping pill that the nurse had given her the night before. Lynn walked into the kitchen and Elaine turned to Helen. "I didn't want Lynn to see me like this, Helen. Did you have to bring her here today? I hope you didn't tell her what happened!" Elaine sounded angry.

Helen was sitting next to her on the couch. "She's not a child anymore, Elaine and she understands that these things happen to people. There's a cruel world out there and she needs to know about it."

Elaine laid her head back on the couch. "I wish someone had told me about it," she said as her eyes watered.

"I know, honey." The phone rang and Helen answered. It was Harriet. "Are you coming over today?" Helen asked.

"No, I have a prayer meeting and another meeting tonight. How is Elaine?"

"Not very well," Helen said with disappointment.

"Well, tell her that I will pray for her. I don't have time today, but I will try to see her tomorrow."

"You'll try?" Helen said sarcastically.

"I'm busy, Helen. And like I said, Elaine inflicted this on herself. She had no business hanging around in a bar." Her voice was hard and uncaring. "I bet she'll never take her behind into another bar again."

Helen tried to control herself knowing that Elaine was listening. "I'll tell her that you'll see her tomorrow," Helen said stiffly. "And Harriet, don't ever let me hear you say anything like that again."

"I speak the truth and sometimes that hurts. You should both live for the Lord, Helen. Then you'll understand what I'm talking about."

"Harriet, if you were standing in front of me this moment, it would take the Lord to get my hands from around your neck," she snapped.

"See what I mean? Just listen to yourself, Helen..."

Helen cut her off before she could finish. "Good-bye, Harriet."

Lynn walked back into the living room. "I could stay the night if you'd like, Aunt Elaine."

"Oh, no, honey. I won't be very good company. I'll probably fall asleep before night and you'd be alone."

"But, I wouldn't mind. I could read or watch TV."

Elaine took one of Lynn's hands in hers. "Not tonight, Lynn. But when I'm feeling better, I want us to spend some time together. I would love to have you come around more."

"Do you need anything, Elaine? Maybe something to eat?" Helen asked.

"No, I ate before you got to the hospital."

"But, you left most of your food on the tray, honey."

Elaine put one hand up to stop Helen before she continued. "I'm okay, Helen. I have food if I get hungry. Why don't you take Lynn shopping or to lunch? I'm not dead, you know. Just a little tired," she said looking in no particular direction. "Next time you come out, we can do something together, the three of us."

"Yeah, sure we will," Helen said and got up. "I'll call and check on you before I leave tomorrow," Helen said as Elaine walked them to the door. She touched Elaine's arm.

"Are you sure you don't need anything from the store, Aunt Elaine?"

"I'm sure. Now, you two run along and have a good

time. I'll be just fine. I'm going straight to bed." Elaine grabbed Helen's hand. "Helen, thanks for everything."

Helen smiled, kissed her on the cheek and walked out.

Elaine stood at the window and watched Helen and Lynn climb into the car. They looked like sisters, both wearing jeans. They were the same height, same hair color and Helen was as slim as her daughter. As they drove away, Elaine sighed with relief, went into her bedroom and got into bed.

Helen and Lynn had lunch and shopped in Beverly Hills.

"Mom, I had a good time today. I'm glad you came out."

"So am I, love."

Lynn could see that her mother was still worried about Elaine. "I think I should go and visit Aunt Elaine more. You know, kind of check on her to see if she needs anything. She looked so sad; it was hard to leave her today. I'm concerned about her, Mom."

"I'm worried about her too and it would be great if you could check on her since you're here in person. If I phone her, she'll just say that she's fine, even if she's not."

Helen parked her car in front of Lynn's dorm. She put her arms around her daughter's shoulders. "I'm so lucky to have you, Lynn. You've always been a blessing to me."

Lynn's eyes began to water and she hugged her mother. "Thanks, Mom," she said, a bit embarrassed by her mother's sincerity. She wanted to change the subject. "What're you doing tomorrow, Mom?"

"I'm going home. Elaine doesn't want any company and you'll be working."

"Well, why don't you come inside for a while?"

"Sure, I can watch you try on your new clothes and shoes," she said and smiled. She got out of the car and opened the trunk to get Lynn's boxes. "Here," she said playfully. "Now, tell me that you don't try on your new clothes as soon as you bring 'em home?"

Lynn laughed as she swung the bags in her hands. "Yeah, I still do that. I try them on in the store and again when I get home." She unlocked her door and Helen followed her inside.

"Wow, it's nice and clean in here, Lynn," Helen said surprised. "Who cleaned up, your roommate?"

"No, Mom. I did. I had a feeling you might drop by."

Helen walked around. "I'm proud of you, Lynn. Now, try on your clothes while I sit and rest my feet."

Lynn tried on the yellow dress that Helen picked out for her. She stood in the middle of the floor and twirled in a circle.

"Beautiful! I told you that dress would look good on you," Helen said admiringly.

Lynn tried on the white sandals with the dress. "How do you like these two together?" Lynn asked, standing in front of the mirror.

"It looks good with the dress," Helen said and lay across Lynn's bed. Lynn finished and hung up her clothes.

"Thanks for all of the clothes, Mom, but you don't have to keep buying for me. I'm working now and have my own money." She sat on the bed next to her mother.

"I want you to use that money for things you might need. Besides, I love buying your clothes. It reminds me of when you were a little girl."

They sat in the room and talked for two hours. The next morning, Helen phoned Elaine and Harriet was with her. But Elaine said that she still didn't want any company. Then, she called Lynn who was on her way to work.

I'm not needed here, Helen thought. It's time to go home. By ten, she was on the 747, in a window seat looking out at the clear Los Angeles weather. "Good-bye, Robert," she whispered. That was the first time she'd actually said the words. It was time to move forward. It was clearly over between them.

As Helen was in the sky on her way back to Atlanta, Robert was boarding his plane in Atlanta. What a fool he'd been for traveling across the country to see her, he thought angrily. She hadn't been home for days and didn't return any of his calls. Fuck it, he thought, madder than he was before he'd left Los Angeles to see her. It is over.

Chapter 10

"You did what, girl?" Helen asked.

"You heard me, and yes I did, because I'm tired of men messing over women," Darlene said.

"Tell me everything!" Helen said, still trying to believe what Darlene had done.

"Wait, let me close the door so my employees won't hear. Want another slice of banana bread, coffee?"

Helen held up both hands. "No, I just want you to sit your silly ass down at this counter and tell me what you did." Helen patted the stool next to her. "Come on, sit right here next to me."

"Well, I was walking outside of Glovers Market when Walter, his wife and daughter walked out. I had my neighbor's kids with me; I had the baby in my arms. When Walter saw me, girl, I thought he would collapse. He tried to turn around, but I yelled, 'Hey, baby, where've you been?' His skinny hussy of a wife was looking at me with her mouth wide opened. I said, 'Baby, I've missed you. And look, your baby misses his daddy.' I pushed the baby I was holding right in his face. Then, I said, 'Walter, where have you been? I'm sorry, baby, if I made you mad at me."

Helen's eyes were wide and eager. She laughed, holding the counter so she wouldn't fall off the stool.

"Girl, I thought Walter was going to pee in his pants," Darlene continued. "The coward couldn't do anything but open his mouth and close it again. I mean, not a sound came out of him, Helen." Darlene laughed. "You should have seen his sorry face. Helen, you would have died laughing."

"Girl, I can't stop laughing now. I can't imagine how hard I would have laughed if I had been there. I can picture that little weasel. He got what he deserved." Helen was glad it happened. Walter was a fool and a user.

"The only thing he could say was, 'Darlene.' That skinny wife of his started beating him over his head with her purse. I watched her beat him all the way to their car. Girl, she was mad as hell."

"What was he doing while she was hitting him?" Helen asked, unable to stop laughing.

"The only thing he did was throw his hands up trying to stop her from hitting him on that empty head of his. I've never seen a woman beat a man's ass like that before."

"What in heaven's name made you do that?"

"Like I said, I'm just tired of lying men. I didn't deserve the lies he told me, Helen," Darlene said sadly.

"No, you didn't, honey. You deserve better and one day you'll have it."

"He even had the nerve to call me the next day, but I hung up on his ass. Where are all the good men?" Darlene sighed.

Helen sucked her teeth in disgust. "I don't know. Before I got back with Robert, I had decided I would never get married again. But now, I think about it sometimes though most of the time I think I am better off single."

Darlene could tell that her friend was still hurt by not hearing from Robert. "Well, so much for the men in our lives. How was your trip?"

Helen shook her head. "It was nothing like what I had planned with Robert when he was here."

"What happened?"

"To make a long story short, Elaine was raped."

Darlene stood up, her mouth opened. "Oh, no, girl," she exclaimed.

"Yeah. She went to a bar and as she was getting into her car, some man grabbed her from behind. He beat and raped her all night."

Darlene put her hands over her mouth and eased back on the stool. "How is she now, Helen?"

"She's home, but not good. I talked to her before I left this morning. She's really depressed. I am so worried about her. I tried to get her to come here for a few weeks, but she refused. She wouldn't even let me see her today." Helen paused, fighting back her tears.

Darlene held Helen in her arms.

"I get this way every time I think of her, Darlene. You should have seen her – the bruises on her body, her swollen eye…" Helen sat back on the stool. "I'll be all right, but Elaine is really out of it. I just have to make sure she gets some help."

"But, what can you do if she doesn't let you?" Darlene asked.

"I don't know, and I feel even more helpless since I'm so far away."

"Well, at least Harriet is there with her."

Helen shook her head. "Not really. Harriet is so into her church that nothing else seems to matter. She says that Elaine brought this on herself. Can you imagine? Every damn thing is a sin now that she has joined the church." Helen threw her hands in the air. "So, Elaine is really out there alone. But there's something else that is bothering me. I don't think Elaine is telling me everything."

Darlene frowned. "What do you mean?"

"I just have a feeling, that's all. She doesn't want to talk about it."

"Of course she doesn't. It's not pleasant; it has to be hard on her. Imagine what she went through," Darlene said, as she trembled feeling chills down her back.

"I understand that. I really wish she would consider coming here."

"Well, you asked her and she said no. So, that's all you can do. Maybe she just wants to work things out for herself."

They both sat quietly for a few minutes.

"Well, how is our girl?" Darlene asked.

"Lynn is doing well. But she loves LA, a little too much for me."

"Do you think she'll stay there when she finishes school?"

"I don't know yet, but I wouldn't be surprised. It seems like LA takes everything and everyone I love," Helen said sadly, thinking of Elaine and Robert.

Darlene nodded in agreement, but said nothing.

Two weeks passed and Elaine had only left the house when it was necessary. She cooked dinner for Lynn one evening and was thankful for the company. She hadn't seen

Harriet since that one time she'd come to visit. Harriet had called once after that, but Elaine didn't expect anything more from her sister. She hadn't seen anyone else and her days and nights were beginning to run into each other. Elaine felt safe as long as she was home.

She opened the blinds and the sun was already shining brightly, warming the inside of her house. Her roses were blooming. She walked outside to her patio to water her plants when she realized it had been weeks since she'd noticed the weather. She put a plastic flower pot on the table and looked up at the sun. She jumped, as she heard a noise, and ran back into her apartment. She looked back onto the patio and discovered that it was only the empty flower pot that had fallen to the ground.

She walked inside her living room, sat on the couch and laid her head back. As she closed her eyes, tears spilled down her cheeks. She couldn't continue living this way, she thought. She had become so frightened, jumping at every sound. Every day, she checked the doors and windows over and over again. At night, she slept with a chair against the door.

She got up again and looked out the window. It was just too nice to stay inside. But, where could she go? Where could she feel safe? She needed to go to the supermarket, but what if she ran into Jake? Chills ran through her body.

She went to the bathroom, showered and got into bed. She closed her eyes, thinking of all the things that had changed in her life in such a short time and finally drifted into a restless sleep.

The ringing phone made her jump. She was relieved to hear Helen's voice.

"Are you all right, Elaine? You sound out of breath."

"I'm fine. I just have a headache, that's all. And when the phone rang, I jumped too fast."

"Maybe you should go to the doctor."

"It's only a headache, Helen." Elaine could hear Helen sigh through the phone and she was sorry she snapped at her sister. "I'm sorry, Helen. It's just that all I have is a headache. You don't have to worry about me."

"You'll call Lynn if you need anything, won't you Elaine?"

"Yes, and Lynn has been very good about calling me. She was here for dinner the night before last. And, I am feeling better. How's your new book coming?"

"I've been writing like crazy. I've also been thinking about promoting this one more than the last two, you know, traveling, the whole thing."

"That's a good idea. We shouldn't talk too long, Helen. The bill is going up."

"I don't mind. I love talking to you, but I know you're not feeling well, so I won't keep you. Call me if you need anything, Elaine."

"I will and thank you."

"I'll talk to you soon."

After Elaine hung up, she got out of bed and walked into the kitchen to put on the tea kettle. Sipping her tea, she watched a bird eat something on the patio, then fly away. The bird was freer than she was. Was this the way she was going to live her life? Like a hermit?

Living alone wasn't so great after all. When she lived with her mother, she felt safe – unhappy, but safe. But, who said you had to be happy? After all, she didn't know anyone who was completely happy. Or maybe, happiness was only for some and not for everyone. Or maybe it was just her.

When night approached, she did as she had done for weeks. She read a novel, took two sleeping pills and slept. She had gone into a world of her own. This continued for weeks, until one morning she stood in front of the mirror and noticed how thin she'd become. And the dark circles under her eyes scared her.

She ran to the store and brought iron pills to increase her appetite. She sat the bottle next to her other medications lined across the counter. Pills for her headaches, pills to wake her up in the morning and pills to help her sleep at night, pills for her nerves and now pills to increase her appetite. She was depressed just looking at all of the bottles.

She lined them up in the order she would take them and realized this was what her life had become – pills, listening for noises, and checking all of her doors. And, when she finished doing all of that, she would read until she couldn't keep her eyes open and sleep.

Chapter 11

Lynn took the long way around to get to the dorm. When a friend of hers called her name, she waved, but kept walking. "Damn, I know I saw Maria go this way. Where did she disappear to so fast?" she thought. Finally, she spotted Maria sitting alone on the steps of the Science Building. Silently, Lynn stood in front of her.

"Hi, Lynn. Where are you on your way to?"

"To see you," Lynn said in a cold voice, her brown eyes condemning her.

"Oh," was all Maria said as she frowned. She knew something was wrong. Lynn wasn't smiling and she always smiled.

As Lynn stared at Maria, she could see that Maria's face was strained, her eyes sad and alone and she was sniffing as if she'd been crying. Lynn sat down beside her. "I saw you take the money from the cash register today," she said.

Maria sighed and pushed her hair from her face. She was embarrassed; it was bad enough she was a thief, but now her integrity was bruised. She wanted to hide. "Oh, no, Lynn, you're mistaken," she said, as her voice trembled. "I didn't take any money. How can you accuse me of that? I know that you think I'm just a poor Mexican, but…"

Lynn shook her head. "Don't give me that. I saw you take the money." Lynn stopped talking when two girls walked by. Then, she continued. "I think you should put the money back. You're going to get caught and you'll end up getting fired, or arrested or both. And then, it will be harder on the rest of us. Don't you see that?"

Maria stood up facing Lynn. "So what? You don't need the money. You're one of those uppity Blacks who have a lot of money," Maria snapped.

"I'm just not getting through to you, am I? First of all, my family didn't always have money, and there were times when I wanted things, but I didn't steal. And even though my mother has money now, I like doing for myself." Lynn let out a deep sigh. "Come on, Maria, I'm only trying to be your friend."

Maria's expression didn't change. "The hell you are. You're just looking out for your own hide because you don't want anyone to think it was you."

Lynn's eyes narrowed. "I'm wasting my time here. If this is the way you want it, fine." She started to walk away.

"Wait, what are you going to do?" Maria asked in a state of panic.

Lynn answered without looking back. "You'll find out soon enough. I'm not going to take the blame for something you've done and I won't let anyone else be blamed either." She stopped and turned, facing Maria. "I tried to be your friend, but I'm not wasting anymore of my time."

"Wait a minute. Do you really want to be my friend?"

"That's what I've been trying to tell you," Lynn yelled back at her.

"I don't have any friends."

"Why?" Lynn asked as she walked back toward Maria.

"I go to school and work late. I haven't had time for friends and anyway, everyone thinks they're better because I'm here on a scholarship. But, no one knows me. I'm going to school so that I can be somebody. But, it doesn't seem to matter. I feel out of place here." Lynn frowned, while Maria continued. "My roommate is White and she's nice and friendly when it's just the two of us. But when her friends come around, she doesn't have much to say to me."

"That happens to me too, Maria."

"No, it's not the same. Your mother has money. You wear the same clothes they do. You drive the same car. I have nothing," Maria said, wiping tears from her eyes.

Lynn touched her arm. "Come on, let's go to my room so that we can talk."

"Where's Lisa?" Maria asked referring to Lynn's roommate.

"She went home for the summer."

85

When they entered the room, Lynn took two Cokes from the small refrigerator and gave one to Maria.

Maria sat down and looked around the room, noticing the two telephones, hot plate and thirteen-inch television.

"You guys have so much here – everything you'd need."

"Don't you have the same things in your room?" Lynn asked, as she kicked off her shoes and sat in the middle of the bed, folding her legs Indian style.

Maria smiled. "See, you take for granted that my room has everything that you have because you get things so easily. Well, that isn't the way it is at all. I have a bed and clothes, of course. But the rest belongs to my roommate. I don't even have a telephone." Tears rolled down her face. "Do you think anyone else saw me take the money?"

"If they had, you would already be fired or at the police station."

"I like working at Robinson's May, and I really need the job. It's the only way I get money."

Lynn wished there was something she could do. Even before her mother became a writer, she never really went without anything she needed or wanted. Listening to Maria made her realize how lucky she was.

Maria finished her Coke and got up to leave, when Lynn took her by the arm and asked her to stay. She went to the bathroom and brought back a box of tissues. Maria thanked her and blew her nose that was as red as her eyes from crying.

"What should I do about the money?" she asked, looking at Lynn with a frightened expression. "What if they arrest me tomorrow?"

"I don't think you have anything to worry about." Lynn paused. "Have you taken money from the store before?"

"No! I swear! I don't know what came over me. I have no money, no one to turn to. My parent's can't help me because there are too many to feed at home."

Lynn nodded, trying to understand what Maria was feeling. "You're not on drugs, are you?"

Maria's eyes widened. "What? No!" She was appalled by the question.

"Then, why did you need the money?"

Maria just stared at her. Hadn't she just told her? Why couldn't she understand? She looked down at the colors in the rug. "I have to send my entire paycheck to help my family. I'm the oldest of eight children and my parents need my help. I didn't have enough money to buy lunch and we don't get paid for two weeks. What was I to do?" She moistened her lips with her tongue, pushed her long brown hair from her face with eyes as round as dark brown marbles.

"Do you send money home each pay day?"

"Yes."

Lynn looked at her oddly. "But, what about you, Maria? Maybe it's time that you start thinking about yourself. I don't mean to sound selfish, but don't you realize that you didn't make your parent's life the way it is?"

Maria shook her head in agreement. She'd thought the same thing herself, but knew how much her family needed her help.

"I know what you're saying, but I have younger sisters and brothers to think about. My parents are not the only ones there."

Lynn nodded, understanding. She got up and looked inside her purse, pulled out a twenty-dollar bill and stuffed it in Maria's hand.

Maria shook her head. "I can't take this," she said, trying to return the money. "But I do appreciate the offer. I don't want you feeling sorry for me because I don't feel sorry for myself."

"I don't feel sorry for you, and I'm not giving this to you either. This is a loan and you can pay me back in two weeks."

Maria hesitated for a few seconds. She had no money, except the ten dollars she'd stolen. "Thank you and I will pay you back."

"Well, now that we have money, why don't we go to the 33rd Street Market and get a big ice cream soda. It's hot in here," Lynn said, and took her keys from the table, locking the door behind them.

When she returned to her room, she wrote her mother a letter. After hearing about Maria's situation, Lynn knew how lucky she was. She thanked Helen for making her life comfortable and for being a terrific mother.

Lynn and Maria became friends. When school started and Lynn's roommate, Lisa, returned, all three became friends and Maria no longer felt like an outsider. Lynn taught Maria how to budget and Maria was able to purchase some new clothes while she still sent money home.

Things changed when Maria's brother Juan showed up and stayed with a Hispanic family on the East Side. From the way Juan behaved – always borrowing money and hanging out with a group of low riders – Lynn and Lisa suspected that he was on drugs.

One night, a phone call came on Lynn's phone for Maria. Juan had been arrested for robbery and auto theft. And since he was already on probation, his was sentenced to two years in prison. In support of her brother, Maria blamed Juan's situation on their father, or the neighborhood he was living in, or the friends he was hanging around with.

Lynn tried to explain to Maria that Juan had choices, just as she had and he only had himself to blame.

"Well, we stick together, no matter what. You just don't understand, Lynn. You said you were my friend, but you don't understand me at all," Maria said angrily.

Two months passed before Lynn saw Maria again. One night as she was reading, she heard a light knock on the door. Lynn hesitated, when she saw it was Maria. She wasn't sure if she should close the door or just stand and leave it open. After all she'd done for Maria, Lynn was hurt that Maria had turned her back on her.

Maria looked like she had been crying. "Aren't you going to ask me in, Lynn?"

Lynn sighed impatiently. "Yeah, sure, come in," she said, standing with her arms folded in front of her. "What can I do for you, Maria?"

Maria took a step forward. "Look, Lynn, I know that I haven't been fair, but I was so upset about Juan..."

Lynn cut her off. "So, why are you here, now?"

"I want our friendship back," she said softly. "I've missed you, Lynn, and just didn't know how to come and say it."

"And, it took you two months to say it? No, I don't think so, Maria. You see, there are some things that one can't get back, like trusting our friendship again."

Maria looked shocked and hurt. "Lynn, you don't really mean that?" She felt shattered by Lynn's words. She put up both hands as in a sign of defeat. "I won't take any more of your time. If you decide one day that you can forgive me, just let me know. I really do miss you and Lisa. Like I said, I never had friends before and didn't realize how important friends could be until I lost you guys."

"No, Maria, until you turned your back on us."

Maria nodded her head in agreement and started to walk out of the room, then stopped. "By the way, where is Lisa? I haven't seen her lately."

"She dropped out of school to get married. You remember, Donald, don't you?"

"Yes, he seemed very nice."

"Donald is a nice guy."

"So, who's your new roommate?"

"I don't have one yet."

There were fresh tears in Maria's eyes. "Remember, we used to say if there was a room for three, I would move in with you guys?"

"Yes, but things changed. You changed, Maria."

Maria knew Lynn was right. "Too bad I didn't see Lisa before she left. I wish I could've said good-bye."

"Lisa said the same thing about you."

Maria walked out. Lynn started to call her back, but changed her mind and closed the door. Then, she called her mother.

"What's up? Are you all right, Lynn?" Helen was sitting in the livingroom drinking a tall glass of lemonade and watching "Some Like It Hot" on television. Detecting something not quite right in Lynn's voice, she sat up straight on the couch.

Lynn sighed. Her mother could always sense when something was wrong. "Maria just left my room and remember when I told you that Lisa had dropped out of school?"

"Yes...so, is Maria moving in with you?"

"I think she wants to, but I was very cold to her," Lynn said sadly.

"And, now you wish that you weren't?"

"You know me so well."

"Of course I do. I knew you before you were born."

Lynn smiled for the first time that day.

"Hang up and go make things right between you and Maria. Besides, I'll feel better knowing that someone will be in that room with you."

"But, she really hurt me, Mom."

"I know, but you two were friends. She's hurting as much as you are."

"I'll sleep on it and maybe I'll talk to her about it tomorrow."

"Call me and tell me what happens, love," Helen said.

"I will and thanks, Mom."

The next day, Lynn and Maria went to the administrative office and got permission for Maria to move in. Three months later, they received the news that Juan had been stabbed to death. Maria was hurt, but realized there was nothing she could have done. Juan had chosen his own path. Maria finally had a friend, and she wouldn't do anything to lose their friendship again.

Helen felt good this morning. She was up at three making coffee. By seven, she had finished her book. This one was going to be her favorite, she could feel it in her heart the whole time she was writing. She glanced at the clock, when she heard the phone ring. Must be Lynn or Darlene, she thought out loud.

She heard Darlene's hardy voice. "You're up already, girl?"

"Sure am. I was just about to shower and come to the bakery to have a cup of coffee with you. After that, I may do a little shopping. I want to buy something for Elaine's new home."

"You're just getting around to that now?"

"Yes, I just found out what colors she's using," Helen said as she pulled her robe tighter around her waist.

"Go to that Black art store. Girl, they have everything in there. Anyway, I take it you finished your book?"

Helen took a deep breath. "Yes. Sometimes I feel as if I can't get on with my life when I'm in the middle of writing a book. But now that I'm finished, I want to do something special today. I might even go out to dinner."

Darlene smiled. "Well, congratulations, Helen." For a few seconds Darlene was silent.

"Are you still there?" Helen asked.

"Yeah, I'm just not having a good day. I think I'm tired and I have this nagging headache."

"Well, no wonder your head hurts. You're up before dawn every morning and you put in all of those hours at the bakery. You know what you need? A vacation. We should go on vacation together. We could both use the rest."

"That's something I should think about. It's been a year and a half since I went to visit my sister Valerie. Since then, I haven't had time."

"That's too long. We'll plan it when I get there. I'll be out at there in about forty-five minutes. I'll stop and pick up some decaffeinated coffee."

"Hey, why decaffeinated?"

"It's better for your health and face it, we're not in our twenties any longer. I've been drinking too much of that other stuff. If you're feeling better after we have coffee, why don't you go out shopping with me?"

"I think I'm going home to take a nap after you leave."

"On your way home, stop and get some iron pills. Women need plenty of iron."

"I'll remember that, Doctor Helen," she said smiling.

Less than an hour later, Helen walked into the bakery's office where she thought Darlene would be doing some paperwork. The office was empty and Helen went into the kitchen. "Darlene," she called. There was no answer.

Helen frowned. She began to feel leery and all the doors were unlocked; Darlene had to be around somewhere. She went back to the office and stopped, frozen in her tracks. "Oh, God, no!"

She dropped her purse to the floor and ran to the desk. Darlene was stretched out flat on the floor. She felt Darlene's wrist and waited, finally feeling her pulse. She grabbed the phone and dialed 911, not taking her eyes from Darlene. She remained on her knees, holding her friend's hand, letting her know she wasn't alone. She looked up at the ceiling. "Lord, why didn't I get here sooner?" A tear rolled down her face. Her heart was beating so fast that she was afraid that the paramedics would find them both unconscious.

In the hospital, Helen waited for Darlene's sister Valerie to arrive. She lived in San Diego and Helen had called her right after they'd arrived at the hospital.

"I should have phoned her, Helen. I was just thinking about her this morning. We talk, but haven't seen each other in almost two years. I just hope that this doesn't mean that I won't see my sister alive when I get there..." Valerie could hardly get the words out and Helen knew she was crying.

"Don't say that, Valerie. Just think positive." Helen proceeded to fill Valerie in on what she knew. "The doctor said she had a mild heart attack, but she is out of danger. Her blood pressure is too high and they'll give her medication for that. And, she's overweight; she'll have to watch what she eats. But she is resting and she will be all right."

In the cafeteria, Helen decided to have a cup of tea and sandwich. She took the food back to the waiting area and the quiet was broken when an older woman cried out. From what the nurses were saying, the woman's husband had just died of a massive heart attack and they had to drag her from the room.

Helen thought of her own mother's death. Everyone had been so careful not to mention it. No one spoke of her anymore, no one said they missed her. Was it purposely, she wondered?

She sat her tea cup on the small table and laid her head back, closing her eyes. The couch was soft and comfortable and she would sleep on it if she had to. She had to stay close to Darlene. She didn't know what she'd do without her best friend. She remembered the day they'd run into each other after so many years.

Helen had been walking out of the Five and Ten Cent store, holding nine-year-old Lynn, with one hand and her shopping bag and purse in the other. She was looking down at Lynn when she bumped into Darlene, knocking a large shopping bag out of her arms.

"I'm sorry," Helen said, quite embarrassed. She was stressed from the job interview she'd gone on earlier. She knew without a doubt that she would not get the job and she needed the higher pay.

Helen and Darlene dropped to the ground at the same

time to pick up the pans that had fallen from Darlene's bags. When they stood up again, both women were laughing, hugging and crying.

"The poor child looks frightened to death with all this ricketiness going on around her." Darlene bent over and patted the top of Lynn's head. "And, a pretty little child."

"I'm sorry, I had so much on my mind," Helen apologized. "I looked down for only a second and bumped into you." She sighed. "It's good to see you again, Darlene."

"Now calm down, Helen. It's all right." She laughed out loud again.

That was the beginning of a life-long friendship. When Helen's husband walked out, she could always depend on Darlene for support. She watched Lynn when Helen worked two jobs and when Darlene started to bake in her home, Helen helped her get her business off the ground. Those were what they called their struggling days, but they had each other.

"Helen?"

She opened her eyes when she heard Valerie. Valerie looked tired and strained. The two women held each other.

"Here, sit on the couch next to me," Helen said wiping tears from her eyes.

"How is she?" Valerie asked.

"She's still sleeping. Like I told you, it was a mild heart attack."

"Oh, Helen. A heart attack sounds so serious," Valerie said in a panic. "And, she's been asleep for such a long time."

"They gave her a shot to make her sleep. The doctor said that she really will be fine."

Valerie kept repeating the words 'heart attack' as if she was still trying to believe it. "And, I know my sister's weight didn't help any of this. She's too heavy, you know." Valerie stood up. "I knew this would happen. I've told that girl over and over again to leave those pork chops alone. Pork isn't good for you. And, she eats too much fatty foods. She's always been too hard-headed, you know, Helen?"

A nurse came into the waiting room. "She's awake now, ladies."

Helen and Valerie jumped from the couch and the nurse led them to the room.

Darlene held her head up when she heard Helen's and Valerie's foot steps and she tried to remember what had happened.

Helen kissed her on her cheek. "You gave me quite a scare, girl. How do you feel?" Helen held back her tears.

"Pretty weak, my chest still hurts." Darlene's voice was soft.

Valerie stood close by, taking her hand. "I told Helen that I was just thinking about you this morning."

Darlene tried to smile, but was cut off by a cough. Helen picked up a glass of water on the table next to the bed and held it to her mouth.

"Easy, don't drink too fast."

Darlene laid her head on the pillow. "What about my bakery?" she asked, still struggling to get her voice back.

"Now, you don't have to worry about that," Helen said. "The bakery will be up and running as always. I'll go in and I know Mrs. Beasley will help me. I know that I can handle it."

Darlene looked up at Helen. "I know that you can handle it too."

"And what about me, you two?" Valerie piped in. "I'll go in with Helen and give her a hand. We'll take care of everything."

"Helen, you have keys to the house, don't you?" Darlene asked.

"Yes, and I'll give them to Valerie. Don't worry about anything. Just get better so that we can go on our vacation together. Now you'll have a chance to think of someplace that you want to go."

Darlene nodded, but moments later, she was asleep.

Darlene stayed in the hospital for four days and Helen and Valerie ran the bakery as planned. While Helen was efficient and worked well with Darlene's employees, everyone had problems with Valerie. She complained constantly.

Three days after Darlene got home, she begged Helen to pick her up on her way to the bakery. Helen agreed, but made Darlene promise not to do any work.

"I want you to stay in one place. Do you hear me, Darlene?"

"Yes, Helen."

"You can give a few orders and tell us how to take short

cuts, but I won't have you doing anything strenuous. I mean it!"

"Okay, okay. I know when I'm whipped."

"That'll be the day," Valerie said, walking back into the room.

Ten more days passed and Darlene and Valerie were snapping at each other. When Helen and Darlene were alone, Darlene complained about her sister. "I love her, Helen, and I do appreciate her, but, she's gotta go. She's been here too long. Anything over five days is too long and she's driving me crazy."

"Has her husband called her to come home yet?"

"Hell, no. He's probably hoping that she'll stay another five weeks so that he can have some peace. She tells me how to run my home and my business, she tells me what I should eat and what time I should go to bed. Can you imagine that?"

Helen laughed.

"It's not funny. I can't take much more of this."

"Oh, don't start getting frustrated. It won't be long before you're up and working again. And then, you can go visit Valerie for a few weeks to rest some more," Helen said as she laughed at the expression on Darlene's face.

"I know you're kidding."

"Now, Darlene. You know it wouldn't be Valerie if she didn't tell you how to run your life. She even gave me a piece of advice on my writing."

"And, this is a woman who won't even pick up a magazine. What did you say to her?"

"I didn't say anything. I kept doing my work. Besides, I was so stunned, I think I opened my mouth, but nothing came out."

Hearing Valerie's footsteps, they stopped talking. Helen picked up her newspaper and Valerie sat opposite Darlene.

"Darlene, don't you think your delivery boy should dress more professional? He's wearing the same clothes he wore yesterday. And, honey, this is a business."

Darlene didn't answer, but knew then that her sister would really have to go.

That night, they had dinner at Helen's house. Helen prepared baked chicken, brown rice and a Caesar salad.

"The dinner was delicious, Helen," Valerie said.

"It was, but what's for desert?" Darlene asked.

"Darlene, you know that I don't keep sweets in my house. I would eat it all myself if I did. What about some peaches or grapes?"

"I'll have a peach."

"Good!" Valerie exclaimed. "That's what you need to be eating. Fresh fruit. It's good for you. And, you'll lose weight too."

Helen held her breath, waiting for the explosion, but instead Valerie announced that her husband wanted her to come home.

"I'm afraid I'll have to leave the day after tomorrow. But, I can come back next week."

Darlene's eyes lit up. "Oh, no! Your husband need you and I'm feeling so much better." Darlene looked at Helen for help. "Besides, Helen's here when I need her and I will just feel too guilty keeping you away from your husband any longer. Why don't you leave tomorrow?"

Valerie sighed. "I just hate to leave you so abruptly."

"Valerie, I will keep you informed with what's going on with your sister. You don't have to feel bad about leaving. You have your own business."

"You've been a big help to me. I don't know what I would've done without you."

Helen wanted to laugh at the performance Darlene was putting on for her sister.

"Well, you do look better, and I think you're losing weight too. I can see it in your face," Valerie said.

"Why don't you leave tomorrow?" Helen asked, smiling at Darlene.

"Well, as long as I know that you'll follow the doctor's orders."

Darlene held up both hands as if she were trying to defend herself. "I know when I'm beat, and I know I have to take better care of myself." Darlene touched her sister's arm. "And you don't have to come back here next week either. You are needed at home with your husband and your business."

Valerie was convinced. "Okay, I'll leave on the first flight out tomorrow morning. May I use your phone, Helen?"

Helen smiled. "Sure. You can go into the living room so that you can have more privacy."

When she walked out of the kitchen, Helen and Darlene put their hands over their mouths and hooted with laughter. They laughed so hard, tears rolled down their cheeks.

"You did a damn good job, Darlene. And you were so sincere. Such a liar!"

"Me?"

"Yes, you. I wish you could have heard yourself." They laughed again. "She means well, Darlene. Hell, if it were me who was sick, Harriet wouldn't make the effort to see me at all. You're lucky to have a sister who cares."

"I know. It's just that she's such an old hen. We're only two years apart and she acts like she's my mother."

"That's the way she feels about you."

The next morning, they took Valerie to the airport and waited until she boarded the plane.

"Please take care of yourself, Darlene," Valerie pleaded.

"I will. Just don't worry so much about me." Darlene hugged her sister. "You did a good job at the bakery and I do thank you for that," Darlene said sincerely.

Helen hugged Valerie too. "We'll talk soon. Call me any-time, Valerie."

"I'll do that," Valerie said and smiled as she picked up her small piece of luggage and walked to the gate. Darlene and Helen stayed until the plane took off. Then, they walked back to the car and headed home.

Chapter 12

"Helen, do you think the good Lord is a man?" Darlene asked as they turned the corner and saw the restaurant. "There it is," Darlene said. "I knew it had to be in this block."

"I wish you had remembered before I parked my car three blocks away, and these shoes are killing me. And shit, it must be one hundred degrees out here."

"Oh, stop complaining, Helen. You'll enjoy the food."

"Yeah, if I can forget the pain in my feet." Then, Helen remembered the question Darlene had asked and she hadn't answered. She wondered what was on Darlene's mind. "Why did you ask me if I thought God was a man?"

"I don't know, just wondered. Haven't you wondered the same thing?" Darlene asked.

"I guess I have – everyone probably has at one time or another."

"Well, do you think God is a man or not?"

Helen paused as if she was thinking of an answer. "I used to think God was a man. Every picture that you see has him that way. And then, look at life. Men don't get any bullshit. They don't go around believing everyone who says, 'I love you', they don't get PMS and they don't have labor pains. They run the world, fuck it up, then blame us for it."

Darlene was surprised to hear the anger in Helen's voice. "You're taking this conversation too personally, Helen. You're thinking of your own experiences with men." Darlene knew Helen was thinking of Robert.

"Yeah, maybe I am. I just get so tired."

"I know." Darlene looked up at the hot sun beating on their heads, but it was a nice Saturday evening. And, she was glad to be going out to dinner and glad to be getting Helen out of the house. She looked in Helen's face again and smiled.

"Helen, don't you think there was more to the relationship with you and Robert?"

Helen whipped her head around. "What on earth are you talking about, Darlene? It's over between me and Robert, so how can there be more? Now, you see why I think God's a man. Who ends up with the broken heart?"

"Yeah, I know," Darlene answered and sighed heavily. "Here we are."

They walked inside.

"It feels cool in here," Helen said, looking around the busy restaurant. They were led to a table and once seated, Helen turned in her seat to see where the laughter was coming from. The people at the next table were enjoying themselves and Helen smiled. It felt good to be around happy people. She realized that she had been feeling sorry for herself because of Robert. But, no more. She wasn't the first woman to be lied to or hurt by a man. She just didn't understand why Robert had done it to her.

"The catfish is very good," Darlene said. "Stop daydreaming and look at your menu."

Helen opened her menu and decided on catfish as well. She took a deep breath. "Coming here was a good idea. All of a sudden, I'm hungry and what else would we be doing on a Saturday evening?"

"I knew you would like it once you cooled off and rested your feet," Darlene said.

Helen laughed for the first time that day.

"And you need to start getting out again," Darlene continued. "You're still hurting over Robert. Maybe you should pick up the phone and call him."

"The hell I will. You know, the crazy thing is we weren't even together that long, but we spent the best weekends of my life together," she said with a slight smile as she remembered. "You know, Darlene. Robert made me realize that it's not the length of time you spend with a person, but the way the time is spent that counts. The time we spent together was magical, then boom, it's over. He pulled the rug from under my feet, just as fast as he put it there," she paused, fighting back tears. "It's over and that's that," she said releasing her breath heavily.

"By the way, you look good, Darlene. Have you lost more weight?"

Darlene nodded. "Ten more pounds and I feel good too. It's not so easy since I don't run everyday like you do."

"I haven't run in a couple of weeks. I'm trying to get back into my normal routine." She looked around. "We got a good table with a view."

"And a good view of the men coming in too," said Darlene.

"That one in the corner has been watching you since we walked in."

"Where?" Darlene asked.

"If you look now, you'll look right into his face. He's watching you now. He's good looking too. I'll let you know when you can look," Helen said.

The jukebox began playing "Love On My Mind," by Natalie Cole. Helen looked around as if someone had touched her. The song filled the room and she sat back in her chair. "Just what I needed to hear," she whispered under her breath, as she recalled the night she and Robert danced to this song the last time they were together.

The walk back to the car didn't seem as far as it had when they arrived.

"I might be leaving for New York and Detroit next week. I'm still trying to decide which city to go to first."

"Is this for your new book?" Darlene asked.

"Yes, and I think it would do me some good to get away for a while."

"Good girl. If I wasn't just getting back to work, I'd go with you."

They climbed into the car and Helen drove off. It was still early so Darlene and Helen stopped in the shopping center downtown.

"This store has all kinds of gift items," said Helen, looking at the jewelry. "I thought I might see something to buy for Lynn."

"What about the bracelets over there. I'll bet she'll like one." Darlene motioned for Helen to follow her to the glass display in the middle of the floor. As they were browsing through the display, they ran into Steve. He was with another woman about ten years younger.

How original, Helen thought. But, she really didn't care. Steve had been a great lover, but he was in her past. He walked up to Helen and kissed her on the cheek.

"You look good, Helen. You know, I've always loved you in white." He smiled, revealing even teeth as he held Helen's hand.

"Thanks, Steve, you look good too."

"It's been a while," he said, looking back at the woman and Helen followed his gaze. "I've been seeing her now for a couple of months," he explained.

Helen smiled. "She's very pretty. I wish you luck, Steve. You deserve it."

Steve kissed her again, acting as if he was at a loss for words. "Call me sometimes, Helen. It would be good to hear from you from time to time."

She nodded. "I will," she said. He squeezed her hand gently and walked away.

Helen watched him and the woman walk from the store holding hands. She walked over to where Darlene was standing. "I hope he's happy. He's a nice man."

Darlene looked in his direction. "Too bad you two couldn't make it."

"We were too different, or maybe too much alike. Whichever, the two don't go well together if you're trying to move beyond friendship. I'll always like him, but I could never fall in love with him. I don't know, I may never fall in love again," Helen said sadly.

"Girl, yes you will. You're just feeling angry and hurt and disappointed right now."

"I guess you're right. But I won't go through any more disappointments. It's bad on the ego," Helen laughed, and picked up a pair of earrings, but decided she really didn't like them. "You know what I need?"

"What?" Darlene asked.

"An affair with a good looking man. One that can make me forget everything," she laughed.

"So do I." Darlene laughed with her friend.

"Would you like to get married, Darlene?"

"I think so sometimes, but every married couple is not as happy as they seem. We may not be missing too much by being single." They were silent for a few moments. "So Helen, go and have your affair," Darlene laughed.

"Hey, this is perfect for Lynn, don't you think?" Helen asked.

Darlene held the gold bracelet in her hand. "It's beautiful, Helen. She'll love it."

"I think I'll buy one and send it to Elaine along with a gift for her house."

"You know, I'm going to buy one and send it to Valerie," Darlene said, smiling.

"She'll love it, Darlene, and she'll be so thrilled that you thought of her."

As they drove home, Helen said, "I wonder what Harriet's up to? I was thinking of her this morning. Not even Elaine has spoken to her lately. Sometimes I worry about her, Darlene."

"Now, you know Harriet, Helen. Elaine's not talking to her is nothing unusual, is it?"

"No, not really, but I've been thinking of her. Especially since Valerie came here to take care of you. If I got sick, I could never count on Harriet, but if the situation were reversed, I would be there for her in two heartbeats," Helen said, parking the car in front of Darlene's house.

At that very moment, Harriet was home looking at a picture of her sisters when they were children. She almost smiled. They were now adults and so much had changed. Where had the time gone? It seemed like yesterday when she would go see her mother and watch her sitting in that old rocking chair, looking out the living room window.

She replaced the picture and phoned Brother Watson to invite him over. She needed someone to talk to and she knew that Brother Watson enjoyed her company. After so many years of marriage, who would have thought that she would have to call a man for company? She sighed. I guess that's what years of an unhappy marriage do to you, she thought filled with regrets.

Brother Watson had called her twice, but she was always

too busy. Tonight, she needed to know that she was still a woman, and Brother Watson lived by the Word of God. He was a good man, a kind man, but deep in her heart, she knew that Robert was kind to her, too. It was just that the marriage had been over for a long time and there was no love left between them. And, Robert was lonely, whereas, she was complacent with their marriage the way it was.

She sat on the couch, wondering what she had missed in her life and why there was such a void inside of her. She sighed. I have to stop thinking of this unhappiness and with the Lord's help, go forward. Pastor Jones says the Lord wants all His children to be happy and I'm a child of God, she thought out loud.

Harriet changed into a lime green dress that she hadn't worn in over a year. She wanted to look different from the way Brother Watson was used to seeing her at church. She picked out a pair of flat shoes, then combed her hair. As she looked at herself in the mirror, she was still as slim as when Robert left, but she did have more gray hair.

She put on a pot of fresh coffee and took the sweet potato pie from the refrigerator. She ran to the door, when the bell rang and opened it as he stepped inside with his hat in his hand.

"Hello, Harriet. I'm glad you called me."

"I'm glad you could come for a visit, Brother Watson. Come on and have a seat. Make yourself at home." She was a bit nervous having a man around for the first time. He followed her to the couch. "Let me turn on the television."

He was a pleasant man with a wide smile. He was tall and thickly built with black hair receding in the front. His nose was large. He had dark, round eyes, a square chin and a round-shaped face.

Harriet stood in front of him and smiled. "I have a surprise for you, Brother Watson. Wait here."

He watched her walk out of the room and return with a tray of coffee and two slices of sweet potato pie. His smile widened. "This is a surprise, Harriet. And, you bake the best sweet potato pie of anyone I know. Everyone in church knows that. Having a homemade pie is such a treat for me."

"Well, I'm glad I baked this for you."

After they finished, they talked, though Charles Watson did most of the talking. He told her he'd been divorced for over three years.

"Don't you ever get lonesome here by yourself, Harriet?"

"Sometimes. But I talk to the Lord."

"That's all fine, but the Lord don't want nobody being lonely or unhappy, Harriet. You know, I talk to the Lord myself, but I need the company of a nice woman," he said trying to read the blank expression on her face.

She nodded in the affirmative. "Yes, I agree, Charles. I needed company tonight," she said not believing that she was admitting it.

"I need a good woman and I've been looking and looking. But maybe I never realized that the woman was already here right in front of me. I'm talking about you, Harriet."

She felt nervous, not sure if she had made a mistake by having him over. She had only wanted a man to talk to – she wasn't ready to jump into a relationship. "Well, Charles, I never knew that you felt that way." She sat up straight and smoothed her dress.

"Well, like my Daddy used to say, 'Charles, you can't see for looking,' and I've been looking all the time. And, all this time, you were there in the church with me," he explained. He licked his bottom lip and sighed. "If you just give me the chance, I'm gonna make you a good man." He put one hand on his knee and took a deep breath. "Now, I've put my cards on the table. You just think about what I've said. If you decide you don't want me to court you, then we can just be friends."

Harriet said nothing. She knew Charles had been watching her with those sad eyes of his, but she never knew what he felt and now she was sorry she'd invited him over. "I had no idea that you would have so much to say, Charles." She looked up to face him. "Why don't we start as friends, Charles, and then see what happens? We have lots of time and don't want to rush into anything we may be sorry for later."

"What could we be sorry for?" he asked with disappointment. "We're not strangers."

"I just think that we should wait and become friends before we start anything else."

"Don't wait too long, Harriet," he said in a low, even voice.

She was taken aback by his bluntness and all of a sudden, she felt tired and drained. Everything had gone wrong today – from her leaky sink to driving around Westwood for an hour trying to find The Bible Store to running into Robert who was with a beautiful woman. And now this with Charles.

After he left, she washed the dishes and went to bed with a headache. She looked at the clock on the nightstand, realizing it had been sixteen hours since she had climbed out of bed this morning, and her body and mind felt every hour of it.

She closed her eyes, thinking of Robert and their failed marriage. But, she wasn't the one who had failed. He was the one who walked out. Finally exhausted, she fell asleep.

Elaine looked in the mirror and cringed at the dark circles under her eyes. At ten in the morning, she was already tired and disgusted at what her day would be like. She took her morning pills, and wondered when all of this would end. She held her hands in front of her and saw they were trembling. Maybe if she rested for another hour she would feel better. She climbed back into bed and closed her eyes, but it was impossible to sleep. She had just taken her wake up pills.

Three weeks later, Elaine stood in front of her bedroom mirror and noticed she had lost more weight. She dressed and went to the drug store to buy more pills for her appetite when she saw the pharmacist staring at her. Her hands started to tremble and her palms began to sweat. Her vision became blurry and her legs weakened; her mouth felt so dry that she couldn't swallow. She remembered feeling the heat in her face, the perspiration in her forehead. When she looked at the pharmacist, he was out of focus, seeming to be far away and she knew she was in trouble.

She awakened in the back of Smith's Drug Store, lying on a brown leather couch with smelling salts under her nose. She jumped, not recognizing where she was and struggled to get up.

"Shush, be quiet and drink the water," a man said softly.

She didn't think that the water would stay down, but it did, thank God. Before she could say anything, a cup was at her mouth and she took a long swallow. He laid her head back and placed a wet towel to her forehead. She tried to get up again, but she couldn't will her body to move.

"Miss, you better wait a minute before you faint again." She lay back slowly. "There, just relax for a while. Close your eyes and take a deep breath." She was slowly breathing in and out. He was on his knees besides her. He seemed to be a tall man, but gentle with a quiet way that made her feel at ease.

"Mr. Smith," she heard a woman's voice from the doorway. "Do we have a box of thermometers in the back?"

"No, but we will on Friday. I ordered them two days ago." His voice was warm and friendly.

He turned his attention back to Elaine. "Okay, now sit up slowly so you won't get dizzy." She did as she was told. She looked into his eyes, wondering what he thought of this woman who had fainted in his store, but his eyes only showed concern. He leaned forward and helped her up with both hands.

As she sat up, she felt a stab of pain in her head. He held her arm again.

"Maybe you'd better sit for a few more moments, Miss," he said as he helped her back on the couch.

"My name is Elaine."

"Okay, Elaine. And, I'm Dan Smith."

Elaine noticed the way he pronounced every word slowly. She took a deep breath. "Mr. Smith, I really don't want to be any trouble and I know that I'm keeping you from your work."

He was still on one knee in front of her. "Don't worry, Elaine. This is my store and Miss Wright can run things fine without me for a while."

She was surprised at how safe she was feeling with him. Maybe it was because they weren't alone, or maybe it was because of the gentleness in his eyes. But, it had been a long time since she had been anywhere near a man.

"I feel better now, Mr. Smith, and I want to thank you for all you've done. I just feel so lucky that this happened here and not while I was in my car."

"From the look in your eyes, if you don't leave the drugs or whatever it is you're taking alone, next time you may not be so lucky."

She flinched. "I'm not doing drugs." He just didn't understand what she'd gone through.

"Something is harming your body and whatever it is, you need to stop today."

She got up fast and felt light headed, but he didn't notice.

He knew that he had insulted her, but somebody had to tell her, and she was in his store, so he told her.

She was insulted. She walked to the door and turned to face him with tears in her eyes. "Thank you again, Mr. Smith," she said and walked out the door without looking back at him.

She cried all the way home. When she arrived home, she ran inside, straight to her bedroom and pulled out the business card that the doctor had given her when she was released from the hospital. It was time that she faced it – she needed counseling; she couldn't do this alone. All of the hurt and shame she felt about what she'd been through. Today was a close call, tomorrow could be worse. The only way to close the chapter was to seek help. She looked at the card and sat on the edge of her bed as she dialed the number, still crying when someone answered.

That week, she went to her first group session on the third floor of the Kaiser Permanente building. There were twelve women of all ages. They cried and laughed together, all sitting in a circle, all in support of each other. Elaine listened as each told their story, though she was afraid to stand up and tell hers. She wondered if they would think it was her fault, if they would think she was crazy. Her heart beat faster and faster as she listened to each one talk.

By the third meeting, she didn't blame herself for what had happened. She'd made a stupid mistake by drinking too much and jumping into a car with a stranger. But, she didn't deserve what he'd done to her.

At her fourth meeting, she almost got up to leave, when a pretty blonde woman, gently held her arm to keep her there.

"Running won't help, darling," the woman said. "If you leave now, you'll never be back for help."

Elaine returned to her seat and looked around, preparing herself to speak. Finally, she stood up and once she started, she couldn't stop. The words came out of her much easier than she expected. She cried and to her surprise, some of the women cried along with her. She felt like she belonged there. She had something in common with these women and she felt strong and whole again.

After her fifth meeting, she returned to Smith's Drug Store. She knew it was because of Dan Smith that she'd made the decision to get help and she felt she owed him an explanation. She could face him and this time, with dignity.

She was going to drive, then changed her mind. The store wasn't far, she would walk. She felt good, dressed in green slacks and a matching silk blouse. She was only taking sleeping pills once or twice a week and all of the other pills had been trashed after her second meeting. She was back to exercising and eating regularly.

Elaine walked into the drug store and noticed Dan Smith right away. My, he's a big man and so tall, she thought. He wasn't very handsome, put his spirit made him beautiful. His eyes lit up when he saw her standing quietly, waiting for him to look up from the prescription he was preparing.

She saw the surprised expression on his face and she cleared her throat. "Mr. Smith, I don't feel that I thanked you properly when I got sick here two months ago. I was very embarrassed at my condition and appearance."

"I'm sorry if I insulted you that day, Elaine," he said. "But, I felt you needed to be told."

She was impressed that he remembered her name. "Oh, no. You were very kind. If you hadn't said what you said...who knows. I went home and took a good look at myself," she said, waiting for his response.

He smiled, looking at her and noticing how attractive she was.

"Have you had lunch yet, Mr. Smith?"

"No, and call me Dan."

"Okay, Dan. May I take you to lunch? I could use a hamburger from Tommy's down the street. I haven't had a good hamburger in a long time."

"Hold on for just one second." He walked over to the woman who worked in the store and told her he would be back shortly.

They walked to Tommy's Burger about a block away. It

was warm and she saw flowers blooming all around them. How could one miss so much, she wondered? She stopped and picked a red rose from a bush. She smiled as she inhaled the scent from the rose.

"So, you love roses?" Dan asked.

"Yes," she replied.

"I'll remember that," he said looking down at her.

She looked up at him, wondering what he meant.

Their lunch was hamburgers, fries and Cokes, but she felt as though it was the best lunch she'd had in a year. They sat outside on the small patio and she felt the warm air against her arms and face.

"I'm so glad that I'm not taking the pills any longer. School starts in a few weeks and I love teaching. I owe it to my students to do my best." She looked away and he patted her hand.

"You'll do very good, Elaine. And, the next lunch will be on me; hopefully that will be soon if it's all right with you."

She didn't know what to say and she could feel the heat in her face. "I'd love to, Dan," she said, feeling her heart skip a beat.

Elaine and Dan started dating a month after that lunch. They saw each other evenings after work. She never imagined that she could feel so loved and happy after the rape. But she was making it through, though it was difficult.

The first time he touched her, she froze. And, as they sat in her living room listening to soft music, she told him about the rape, but didn't mention how it took place. She had learned from going to her meetings that the 'how's and why's' weren't important, only the rape.

After she told him, he was patient and she felt safe with him. They had a comfortable, easy relationship and they took their time getting to know one another.

"Harriet, woman, I've been taking you to dinner for three weeks. Taking you to the best restaurants, too. And to the movies and all the church functions. I'll give you anything you want and need, Harriet. But, I don't want to be your fool. I ain't complaining none about the money, even though it don't grow on trees, you know. And, I have more where it came from. But, am I gonna be your man or not? I have to know,

Harriet. So, what you gonna do?" he asked, looking straight into her eyes.

Harriet's eyes widened in disbelief at the pragmatic way he put his words. It was so unromantic.

"I know that I ain't as smart as that ex-husband of yours, but I'm doing all right for myself."

Lord, please don't let him be proposing marriage, she thought with a silent prayer. She wasn't that fond of Charles, but she did like him. It felt good to be with a man who desired her and he was proud to be seen with her. And, he was a man who served the Lord.

Yes, it was true that he wasn't as educated or as smart as Robert. But he had his own home and didn't wear cheap shoes. That was important to Harriet. So what if women didn't look twice when he passed. She wasn't getting any younger either. And, he always told her that she was pretty and smart and desirable. Hell, she didn't have to be in love as long as she enjoyed his company.

She sighed, and looked at Charles while he waited for his answer. She knew he wouldn't let her off easy like he had so many times before. Suddenly it hit her. Was this about sex? She hadn't had sex in years and wasn't sure if she was ready for it. She knew Charles was more than ready for it.

She looked up to the ceiling. Lord, what to do?

"Well, Harriet?"

It's time, she thought. She put her hand on his arm and kissed him on the cheek. "Why don't we just try to be closer and see what happens, Charles?" she said in a low voice. "I already like you very much." She smiled shyly when he looked at her.

Charles eyes were wide and he laughed out loud. "I was hoping you would say something like that, Harriet. I've been waiting so long for you, honey." He put his arm around her shoulder and looked deep into her eyes. "Can I kiss you now?"

"Yes, Charles," she whispered.

He kissed her long and hard and it felt nice.

Chapter 13

"I've lost fifteen pounds, Helen," Darlene said, as she stood in the kitchen and spun around in a circle to model her new figure. "I'll be able to wear a size fourteen in no time at all." She stood in front of Helen and laughed. "What do you think?"

"I think it's wonderful and I knew you could do it. When you get down to a size fourteen, why don't we go shopping in New York for some sexy new clothes? We never did take that vacation and you've been so good with your diet, Honey," Helen said taking a seat at the table. "You deserve it."

"I have been good, haven't I?" she asked, posing with her hands on her hips.

"Damn right," Helen said. "Too bad Valerie can't see you now."

"When I get down to a fourteen, I'll go visit her."

"Tell you what. We can go together. I haven't been to San Diego in a while and we can rent a car and go to LA the next day."

Darlene's smile faded as she poured hot water in their tea cups. Helen was watching her.

"Is there something wrong, Darlene?" Helen was sitting with her hands folded on the table in front of her.

"Yes, Jimmy's cousin called me last night and said that he's very sick."

For a few moments, Helen looked as if she couldn't remember Jimmy. "You mean the Jimmy you were dating about seven years ago?"

"Yes," she said sadly. "He has cancer. Sharon says he's been sick for over a year."

The phone rang and Darlene walked out of the kitchen to answer it. Helen waited in the kitchen, sipping her tea.

111

Darlene's kitchen was white and as immaculate as the kitchen in her bakery. A green plant hung from the window in a white flower pot. Helen walked over to the small window and looked into the back yard. Red roses were growing near the window. She walked back to the table and waited for Darlene.

When Darlene returned to the kitchen, Helen said, "Your rose bush is growing pretty tall."

"Thanks, I do well with roses, but I can't seem to grow any other flowers."

"Now, tell me how you feel about Jimmy."

"I don't know, Helen. It's been so long since the last time I saw him. I'm sorry he's sick."

"Of course. Are you going to see him?"

"I guess that I should. I wonder if he will want to see me. We broke up on bad terms, you know. What do you think?"

"You didn't do anything to him. I don't know why he wouldn't want to see you. Hell, he probably wanted to see you even before he got sick. Besides, people don't want to die thinking someone is angry with them. At least, I know I wouldn't. Just think about it for a couple of days."

"You're right. I hate it when your past pops up like this. I got over Jimmy years ago," she said throwing her hands up in the air.

"Just give it a rest now. My mother used to say tomorrow is another day." Helen sounded sad when she mentioned her mother. She paused for a moment. "Tomorrow you'll feel better."

"Have you heard anything from Harriet lately?" Darlene asked.

"You've got to be kidding. If Elaine didn't tell me about her, I wouldn't know anything at all." Helen sighed. "I wish that one day Harriet and I could sit down and talk out our differences. We're not kids anymore, after all. I wish I could make her listen to me, talk to me."

"She won't listen, Helen. She loves being miserable and making you miserable along with her." Darlene took a bowl of strawberries from the refrigerator and put them in the middle of the table before she grabbed one for herself.

"Girl, just forget about Harriet. Now, tell me about

Elaine." Darlene said and popped another strawberry in her mouth. "I'm hooked on these things since I haven't been eating as many sweets."

Helen looked happy again. "Elaine and I talked yesterday and she sounds wonderful. She seems to be happy for the first time in years. She's back at work." Helen sighed. "I was really worried about her. I asked her to come and live out here, but as always, she refused."

"You see, Helen. It just took time for her to get herself together after what happened. Did you tell her about you and Robert?"

"No, I didn't want to do that on the phone." Helen got up and put her cup in the sink.

They walked into the living room and the phone rang again. Helen looked at the shining hardwood floors, and the white and black rug in the middle. The large painting of Darlene and Valerie hanging over the fireplace had been painted five years ago during a Fourth of July weekend. Darlene's house was cozy and warm.

"That was my delivery boy," Darlene said as she hung up the phone. "He's sick so I had to call Mrs. Beasley's husband. He said he'll deliver my breads tomorrow," she said with a sigh of relief.

"Well, I guess I'd better go so I can stop by the store on my way home," Helen said. "I hate it when it rains for two or three days in a row, don't you?"

"Yes, girl. And, you better get started before the rain starts up again," Darlene said, looking through the window. "The weatherman says today should be the worst."

"I'd better get out of here." Helen was already standing in the door.

"I feel better since you dropped by."

"You mean about Jimmy? He'll want to see you, I'm sure, but you should do what you feel is best," Helen said as she rushed out into the cold rain.

As she was putting her key in the front door, she could hear her phone ringing. She rushed in to pick it up before the answering machine. "Hello," she said in a hurried voice.

"Hi, Mom. You sound out of breath."

"I just got home. It's beginning to pour rain out here. How's the weather there?"

"Beautiful and warm."

"And, how's Maria?"

"She's doing real good. She's even able to save a little money now. One day, I'll bring her home so you can meet her."

"I'd like that." Helen took off her coat and let out a tired sigh. "Now, I can sit down and talk to you. But you seem a little quiet. Is something wrong, honey?" Helen asked with concern in her voice.

"It's nothing, Mom. Just boyfriend trouble."

"With Don? What happened?"

"He's seeing someone else named Melinda."

"What's she like?"

"Nothing special – tall, blond and fake," Lynn said. She sounded sad.

"There's a lot of that going around. Leave him alone, Lynn. It's his loss. You remember that when he comes running back," Helen said with a chilling edge of anger in her voice."

"I hear you, Mom."

"Do you love him, honey?"

"No. It's just that I had to find this out through someone else."

"He didn't even have the balls to tell you himself? You are too good for him and don't you ever forget that."

"Mom, don't get so upset. I just want to forget him. We were only together for three months anyway."

At least she sounded determined, Helen thought.

"But, you know what I've been thinking, Mom?"

"What?" Helen sat sideways with both legs hanging over the arm of the couch.

Lynn hesitated for a moment. "After I graduate, I may stay out here. I love Los Angeles. I love the weather and it's not like I don't have family here."

Helen sat up straight. She didn't like what she was hearing and instantly felt a lump in her throat. "You're only feeling this way now, Lynn. You'll feel differently when you finish school. There are as many opportunities for you here as there are in LA."

"That depends on the job you want."

Helen sighed through the phone. "I don't want to discuss this tonight, Lynn. You still have time to think about it."

Lynn just wanted to prepare her mother. She was certain that she would stay in LA. "It's not as if we won't see each other, Mom. You can come out her anytime you want. I'll have my own apartment and you can stay with me. Aunt Elaine was just saying yesterday that the next time you come out, you can stay with her."

"You sound as if you've already made up your mind."

"No, I was only thinking about it. Like you said, we can discuss it at another time. Mom, please don't be upset," she said softly. "What have you been doing since you finished your book?"

"Nothing much. I help Darlene out some days. Hey, she's lost twenty pounds."

"Great. Tell her to lose fifteen more by the time I get home for Easter break."

Helen laughed for the first time during their conversation. "I'll tell her. She'll love it."

Lynn was glad to hear her mother laugh. "I'll call you in a day or two, Mom."

"Okay, honey. I have five chapters to proofread, so I better do it before I get too sleepy. Take care of yourself, love, and forget about what's his name."

"I will."

As soon as Helen hung up the phone it rang again. The last thing she needed was to be on the phone all night when she had work to do. She needed to get away. After this phone call, she decided she would make reservations at the Ritz Carlton in New York City.

Chapter 14

Lola Doverwood was waiting for Helen at John F. Kennedy Airport in New York. Helen was dressed in all burgundy – her suit, shoes and long cashmere coat. Her hair was up in a French roll with bangs. She was ready to promote this book. Usually, she did a few book signings, but this time she wanted to do more. She knew that would mean she'd have to travel more, but hell, why not? What else did she have to do? This would help replace the loneliness that she felt.

Lola watched her step off the plane, walking confidently, her head held high. Helen saw a nice looking man smile at her and she lightly returned his smile. Lola would take her to the hotel, just as she had done years ago when she wrote her first book. But this time, they would make plans for promoting her book.

Lola smiled and took Helen's hand. "Dear, how splendid you look. I was very happy you decided to come out. It's been a while and this will be a good experience for you. From here, you're planning to go on to Detroit?"

Helen was smiling. "I'm thinking about it. We'll see. I'll let you know in time so you can make the schedule for me with the bookstores. But I have to admit, Lola, I'm getting excited."

They were walking through the airport. "Darling, is there someone special in Detroit?" she asked with a teasing smile.

"Oh, no. A few months ago when I was in LA, I met someone from Detroit. I might look him up."

"Sounds like fun, Helen. You should go and enjoy yourself. Now come on, let's get your luggage and we'll be on our way. I know you must be tired from the flight. I get tired when I fly to Atlanta."

Helen smiled because Lola never stopped talking. But, she was a warm, sweet lady.

"What book is that you're carrying, dear?"

"The Promise, by Danielle Steele. I love all of her books. I've read them all," Helen said.

"So have I. I love her work."

"Now, tell me what kind of schedule do I have?" Helen asked as they stood waiting for her luggage.

"One that will keep you busy. But, you'll still have lots of free time on your own to go to plays or go shopping."

After Helen's luggage came, they walked to Lola's red Mercedes Benz.

"Is this new?" Helen trilled.

"Yes, darling. Isn't it fun?"

Helen stood in front of it, then she walked around it twice and stood back again. "I love it!" Helen exclaimed, as she buckled herself into the seat, admiring the cream interior and plush seats.

They sped out of the parking lot laughing and talking all the way to the hotel. As Helen walked into her hotel suite, she noticed the vase of roses and a card from Lola and she smiled, grateful for her relationship with her publisher.

On this trip, she had decided to stay in the best hotel. It was time for a change. She walked through the grand suite with a wide grin on her face, then kicked off her shoes and spun around like a whirling dervish. She was enjoying this and it was only the beginning. It was time to start the second half of her life and put the first half behind her.

She undressed and hung her suit in the large walk-in closet and started looking over her schedule. She'd be in New York for three days and then maybe she'd move on to Detroit. She would decide when it was time to leave New York.

Suddenly, she felt hungry and called for room service. Less than a half an hour later, she was served with an incredibly scrumptious luncheon. She had smoked ham and Brie on a croissant, tossed salad and herbal tea. It was already four o'clock; she'd have to get used to the time change.

While she ate, she looked through a Conde-Nast, then decided to make phone calls. She phoned Lynn to give her the name and number to the hotel. Then, she called Darlene.

"Why don't you hop on a plane and come out?"

"I will as soon as you get off the phone. My taxi is waiting to take me to the airport."

Helen screamed with delight. "You must be kidding."

"No, I'm not. Give me your room number and I'll see you tomorrow morning. It'll be too late when I get in tonight. I booked my own room; I know how you hate my snoring," Darlene joked.

"You don't have to do that. You can stay with me," Helen said.

"I know, but I like having my own suite."

"Okay, but don't say I didn't ask. I'm just so happy that you're coming."

"I thought about what you said, and I said hell with it. Mrs. Beasley can handle things for a few days. Now, girl, I got to go. My cab is waiting."

Helen jumped out of her chair. They would have a great time together. It was only five o'clock, but already dark so she took a shower and watched television, then finally completed her unpacking.

She planned the next day in her mind. She and Darlene would have breakfast in her room, then get a taxi to the bookstore on Verrick Street. Darlene could assist her in signing her books. She was always asking Helen what it was like and now she would see for herself. Later, they would stop and have dinner and maybe see a play or go dancing. Helen even thought of canceling her trip to Detroit altogether so that she and Darlene could spend a few extra days in New York. Helen fell asleep early, smiling with thoughts of the mini vacation she and Darlene would have.

By ten o'clock, Darlene arrived at the hotel, exhausted from the flight. She walked to the balcony connected to her suite and looked out at New York City. She smiled and inhaled the cold air, then walked back inside. She opened her large closet and smiled again. She hadn't stopped smiling since she decided to take this trip. Then, she laughed, seeing the roses that Helen had sent her. Her eyes watered. "Isn't this just like Helen?" She took a shower and went to bed, excited about her time in New York.

The next morning at eight, Darlene was at Helen's door. "Did I wake you?"

"No, come on in," Helen said as she pulled Darlene inside and hugged her. "I'm so glad to see you, girl." Helen showed Darlene around her suite.

"This is beautiful," Darlene said.

"Now, why don't I call room service and we can go over what I have planned for today?" She ordered ham and eggs, toast, coffee and orange juice. They sat at the table and made their plans.

When they finished, Helen leaned back in her chair and smiled. "I am so happy you're here. What made you do this?"

Darlene was silent for a moment. "You know the day I had the heart attack? I thought, what if I had died?"

Helen frowned. "Don't talk like that, Darlene!"

"It could have happened, Helen. So, I decided to enjoy my life. I can afford it."

Helen smiled. "If you couldn't afford it, I would have paid just to have you here with me."

"And you know what else?" Darlene continued. "I think we'll be friends forever."

"I already know that." They laughed and hugged. Helen felt tears stinging her eyes and held her breath to hold them back. "Okay, it's time for us to get ready," Helen said.

Darlene finished her coffee and stood up. "I'll go get dressed. I'll meet you in the lobby, Helen. You know it takes me almost two hours to get dressed."

Several hours later, Helen sighed and whispered to Darlene. "In three hours, I think I've signed two hundred books. I bet all of them haven't even read this one." Helen glanced at her watch. "It's time for us to leave and let's get out of here before anyone else comes."

A few minutes later, they stood outside the bookstore looking at the traffic.

"I'm hungry, Darlene, aren't you?"

"Yes, starved."

Helen looked across the street. "What about that place over there?" She pointed so that Darlene could see it. "It's called the Eat-All-You-Can restaurant. I wonder what they serve in there?"

"I don't know and I don't really care. I'll say it again, I'm starved."

Helen laughed. "Well, let's try it."

The place wasn't fancy, but it was clean and that was all they cared about. The tablecloths were red and white and there were fresh flowers on each table. Helen ordered a BBQ beef sandwich with a small salad and Darlene ordered BBQ chicken with a salad.

"This beef is tender," Helen said.

"So is the chicken."

They ate everything on their plates and then had a cup of coffee as they looked outside and watched people passing by.

"New York is just too busy a city to live in," Darlene said.

"I know. Everyone is always in such a damn hurry. Anyway, let's go over to Park Avenue."

"What's on Park Avenue?"

"I used to think it was all rich people. I got that idea from reading Harold Robbin's novels. All of his rich characters lived on Park Avenue so that first time I came to New York, I took a cab over there. Of course I was disappointed. Nothing is ever the way you read about it. It's the same when people go to Los Angeles. The first place they want to see is Hollywood and Beverly Hills, rich and famous Beverly Hills. The houses are beautiful and too damn expensive. But, it's different in the books. But, I still love riding and walking down Park Avenue."

"So, what did you do when you went there for the first time?"

"I walked up and down the streets. Looked at the tall buildings and then went back to my hotel. I just thought you would like to see it."

Helen crossed to the curbside and signaled for a taxi. They told the driver where they were going and Darlene edged closer to Helen so that he couldn't hear what she was saying.

"He's a strange looking man, Helen. I wouldn't ride with him if I was alone."

"Darlene, this is New York. Like Hollywood, you'll see lots of strange looking people."

The taxi driver drove like a madman from Varrick Street through the city and Helen laughed when she saw the look on

Darlene's face. When they got to Park Avenue, Darlene took pictures of everything she saw and Helen asked the driver to stop so she could take a picture of Darlene standing under a street sign that read Park Avenue. It was cold and was getting dark, so they took the cab back to the hotel.

"Why don't we have dinner in the restaurant here?" Helen suggested. "There's a nice piano bar and dancing."

"That sounds great. I haven't danced in a long time. I want this to be a vacation to remember," Darlene said with excitement in her eyes.

"We can always come back, Darlene. This doesn't have to be your last time."

They went to their rooms to shower and change.

"I'll be at your room at six-thirty," Helen said.

"I'm not very hungry, Helen, are you?"

"No, not really. I think I may have just a light salad."

"Yeah, a salad sounds good. What are you going to wear?"

"My red Donna Karan dress."

"All right then, girl," Darlene laughed as she walked off.

They met in the lobby, had a light dinner, then went into the piano bar. The room was cozy with small oak tables and a grand piano in the corner. A Black man wearing thick glasses was playing. He had a long braid hanging down his back.

"This man can really play," Helen said after they ordered some wine.

When the piano man took a break, slow jazz music filled the room and a tall, good looking man asked Helen to dance. She accepted with a smile. As she danced, she saw someone ask Darlene to dance and Darlene readily accepted.

This was the perfect vacation, Helen thought as she watched Darlene. They continued dancing and talking with their partners until well past midnight when they all said goodnight and went to their rooms.

Before Helen could kick off her shoes, the phone rang. She laughed, knowing it was Darlene.

"Girl, I hope we run into those guys tomorrow night. It was fun."

"It was and John is a smooth dancer," Helen said.

"So was Darrell. I love the way he slow dances," Darlene laughed.

"I noticed you two were practically glued together."

"Well, he kept holding me tight. And, the man felt good. They said to be there the same time tomorrow night and I say, let's be there," Darlene said.

"Sounds good to me. We have to be at the book store by eleven in the morning." Helen groaned as she eased her feet out of her shoes. "I'm dead tired."

"So am I, but I am so glad that I came to New York. When was the last time we went out and danced past midnight?"

Helen laughed. "I'm glad you're having a good time."

The next day, they finished at the bookstore by two, then had lunch and went shopping. Helen took Darlene to the Bronx so that she could see what it was like and they returned to the hotel by seven.

Helen changed into a red, low cut dress that showed her cleavage and Darlene was in a navy dress that revealed her smooth back. Her dress was two sizes smaller since she lost weight.

"You look great, Darlene," Helen said when they met in the hallway.

Darlene whirled around. "Do you really think so?"

"Yes. See what a vacation can do for you?"

"Well, honey, in that red dress, you're going to set someone on fire tonight."

"Come on, let's go," Helen laughed.

When they walked into the piano bar, the two men were waiting and stood up when they saw Helen and Darlene.

"They were looking for us," Darlene whispered. "Did you see Darrell looking at the door?"

"Yes, with that hunger in his eyes. You better watch out, girl," Helen chuckled.

They ordered wine and chatted like old friends. When Helen and John slow danced, he kissed her gently on the cheek.

"I'm sorry, but I had to do that. You feel so good and smell so sweet."

Helen smiled.

"I love your smile," John said. His dark eyes sparkled. The gray around his temples made him look sophisticated. "I wanted to kiss you last night. But when I held you in my arms tonight, I couldn't help it."

That was all right with Helen since one kiss was all he would get. She noticed that he eyed every single woman who walked by him and she didn't play that. Sure, he was single and could do as he pleased, but if he wanted her, then at least he could keep his eyes in his head when he was with her. He was a smooth talker, knew all the right things to say. But, Helen had heard it all before.

Again, after midnight, the men walked Helen and Darlene to their rooms. But this time, John kissed Helen full on her mouth. He's a good kisser, Helen thought. When he let her go, she stepped back, opened her eyes and took a deep breath. I'll be damned, she thought.

"Good night, John. I had a good time." She walked into her room, leaving him standing at the door. And again, before she could kick off her shoes, Darlene was on the phone.

"Girl, Darrell wanted to come inside, but I told him I was too tired. I'm sure they think tomorrow night will be a sure thing," Darlene hooted with laughter.

"But, you and I will be on a plane without even saying good-bye to them," Helen laughed. "They think they are so damn slick and women are stupid. I'll bet one of them is married."

"Probably, but I didn't care enough to ask. They say they're from Los Angeles, but I bet they live right here and the all day meetings they were telling us about is just them working and coming here when they get off. Darrell never invited me to his room."

"Neither did John."

"Anyway, are you still going to Detroit?"

"No. Maybe next month. Lola hadn't made any arrangements and I ended up having more fun here with you anyway."

Helen and Darlene slept until ten the next morning and had breakfast in Helen's suite. After breakfast, they went out to purchase more gifts and were on their plane to Atlanta while John and Darrell were waiting for them in the piano bar, planning a long, hot night and watching every woman that passed by.

123

Chapter 15

Helen walked in the door, kicked off her shoes and sighed. She'd gone through this routine so often, it was automatic. She dropped her suitcases in front of the stairs; she would take them up after she checked her messages. She turned on her answering machine loud enough to hear her messages from the next room. She stood still at first and listened, but she wasn't mistaken. It was Robert's voice. "Why now?" she moaned. She'd planned her life without him.

She heard an edge in his voice. "Please call me back," his voice said.

Fat chance. She clicked off the machine and went upstairs to her bathroom. She looked closely at her face. Her tiredness showed. "Too much dancing," she said aloud and smiled. She pushed her hair back and went into her bedroom. As she sat on the edge of her bed, she thought about Robert's call. Why now? What did he want? She stared at the ceiling as if an answer would appear from nowhere.

She was changing her clothes when the phone rang. His voice came through loud and clear, and for a few seconds she was silent as nervousness crept through her body. "Hello, Robert."

"Helen, I called you three times."

"I'm sorry, I was out of town. Is there something wrong?" she asked casually.

"Yes, and if you give me a chance, I want to fix it."

"What is there to fix?" Her voice was low.

"Our lives. Please give me a chance, Helen. I've called you many times, but you've refused to return my calls. I got mad as hell when I called once and a man answered. That's when I knew why you hadn't called me back."

She sat up straight and frowned. "What man?"

"Don't play with me, Helen," he snapped. "It's not like

you. I hung up, called again and he answered again."

Helen sighed. "Robert, I don't know what you're talking about."

"It was a Friday afternoon. A man answered your phone."

She could hear the anger in his voice that matched her own. "Robert, I seem to remember calling you and..." Out of the blue, she remembered. She laughed. "I remember now. It was my neighbor." She talked fast, explaining that she had been in her neighbor's house arranging flowers when he'd called. Now, she remembered that Robert had stopped calling right after that.

He told her that he had flown to Atlanta to get things right between them, and she told him that she was in Los Angeles that same weekend. She lay back on her bed and looked at the ceiling. She was so happy that she agreed to spend the weekend with him. She realized that all of the anger she'd carried was because she still loved him. They made plans for her to fly to Los Angeles the next day.

"Yesss," she shouted when she hung up the phone. She felt an excitement she hadn't felt since the last time she was with him. After she showered, she unpacked, then packed a new suitcase.

The next day, she was on the plane filled with anticipation and when she exited the plane, the only person she saw was Robert. He held her tight with one arm and gave her a dozen roses. They left the airport holding hands.

It rained the entire first day she was in Los Angeles and they stayed inside.

"Do you realize we haven't been out of bed since I arrived?"

"Yes. And, this is where we belong. We have been apart for too long." She was lying in his arms. "Would you like to go out for dinner?" he asked.

"I don't want to move."

"Neither do I." He kissed her hard. "Baby, I can't get enough of you," he whispered.

She moaned and held him tightly.

Dressed in their bathrobes, they ate leftover pizza that Robert had ordered for himself the night before, then sat in the living room listening to soft music until midnight. They talked about all that had happened since they were last together.

"Two days is just not long enough, Helen."

"I know, love. The time seems to go so damn fast for us."

"We can have next weekend together," he said, pulling her closer.

"I'm planning on it."

She was as happy as a sixteen-year old on her first date. And when she returned to Atlanta, she couldn't concentrate on anything for the entire week. When Friday finally came, she went to the airport early, eagerly waiting for his arrival. They went straight to her townhouse, where they spent the first day in bed. The next day, she took him to dinner and dancing afterwards.

"Why can't life be like this for us always?" she asked.

He kissed her forehead. "It can be and I promise that one day it will be." He nipped at her ear.

They were sitting on the couch, and he had his arms around her. She was wearing a short, black bathrobe and black satin slippers. He took the pins from her hair and it fell to her shoulders.

"Remember when you were standing against that big tree in your mother's backyard the day of her funeral?"

She nodded.

"Helen, I knew then that we would get back together," he said slowly, running his fingers through her hair. "I just knew that I had to have you back. If you only knew how many times I'd thought of you and I together. And, how many times I regretted losing you. It was like losing a part of my life that I couldn't take back." He held her hand to his lips and she trembled.

She looked into his eyes. "I never knew that's how you felt. I thought you were in love with Harriet. That's why I married Thomas. I don't think I was ever in love with him. I was just young and unsure."

"It's a shame that this all comes out twenty-one years later. We've missed all that time of happiness," he said. "But, we can make up for it now." He ran his fingers through her silky hair again. He loved the way it felt in his hands.

She sat on his knee, kissing his neck. Then, she kissed him fully. "I wonder how many children we would have had together if we'd married," Helen pondered.

"Probably four," he laughed.

"Why four?"

"Because I always wanted four children with you."

"When did you decide that?"

"Every time we were together."

She laughed, covering her mouth with both hands. "You know, I remember you telling me that once," Helen said. "We were kissing in my parent's backyard. My parents didn't know that I had gotten home from that party. You kissed me and asked if I would have four children with you – two girls and two boys. You scared the holy hell out of me, Robert."

"You remember that?" he asked as he kissed her. He held her so tight she could hardly breath and she wanted this feeling to last forever.

Their last night, they cooked and had a quiet dinner at her apartment. And, when she took him to the airport the next morning, they held each other and kissed until he had to board the plane. Helen watched until the plane was completely out of sight.

When Helen arrived at the bakery the next morning, Darlene smiled at her.

"Well, Miss. How busy we've been lately," Darlene said mischievously. "You're glowing all over. What did that man do to you?

Helen laughed. "A little of everything."

"Well, come on. Let's go into my office. So, how do you feel about your relationship this time?" Darlene asked.

Helen sighed deeply. "I'm in trouble, Darlene. I love him more than before."

"That's not trouble, Helen. The man loves you. It will probably be smooth sailing from here."

"I don't know. But, I'm going to think positively about it."

Darlene heard the tea kettle. "Oh, I forgot I was warming water. Wait here and I'll get us a cup of tea."

"Bring me a slice of banana bread, too."

Darlene returned and sat the tray on the table, giving Helen her cup. She sat on the leather couch and put her feet up.

"Now, this feels good," Darlene said. "Anyway, where were we?"

"I was saying that I'm going to think positively about Robert and I."

"Just remember, Helen. There will be some rough spots, but tell me what relationship doesn't have them?"

"Not very many," Helen said as she took off her sweater and laid it over the chair.

"So, just relax and enjoy it," Darlene told her friend. She smiled. Helen looked like a woman in love.

"So, what did you do this weekend?" Helen asked.

"Not much. Rested, read and watched a couple of good movies on TV. I was a little tired when I left Friday. Mrs. Beasley was home sick with the flu and I had to do a little more than usual. Oh, and Valerie called me Sunday. She's still checking up on me. I talked her out of coming out next month."

"Are you sure you're all right, Darlene? You know I don't mind coming in to the bakery and helping you."

"Now, don't you get started too, Helen. I feel fine now. All I needed was rest. And, I don't overdo it like I used to. I'm feeling fine."

The two friends continued to chat until Helen left. On her way home, Helen thought about Darlene; she was still worried about her friend's health. She would have to watch her a little closer. It frightened her to think of Darlene having another heart attack.

After stopping at the drug store, Helen went home and went to her computer to write down ideas for a new book that had been playing in her mind.

Chapter 16

Mona Greene passed her exam, scoring higher than anyone on the waiting list. She'd been waiting for three months, jumping every time her phone rang. And now finally, the job was hers.

She stepped off the elevator, dressed to kill in her professional navy suit and pumps. She walked with an air of confidence and several guys passing by gave her an admiring smile. She smiled back, knowing that she was attractive. And there was no doubt she would use her looks without a second thought to get whatever she wanted.

She was told to ask for Anita, the senior secretary, who would take her to her new boss, Robert Wilbertson. I hope he's not too old and grumpy. And, I certainly hope he doesn't think I'm going to bring him coffee every morning. As she stood at the reception desk, she waited for Anita to get off the phone. Anita was a small woman with a lovely face, but she wasn't smiling as she talked and Mona was glad she wasn't the person on the other end of the telephone.

Anita led Mona to the corner desk. "This is where you'll be sitting. Mr. Wilbertson gets in around nine, if he doesn't have an appointment. Now, let me tell you how things are done around here." Anita spoke, straightforwardly without cracking a smile. "You'll be doing most of Mr. Wilbertson's typing, or doing something for one of the other D.A's. This is a very busy office. Now, let me show you where you can get coffee or tea."

Anita showed Mona the small café and brought herself a cup of tea and coffee for Mona. As they walked back to their department, two men stopped them, asking Anita if Robert was in yet. Anita was annoyed. She knew they only asked so that they could get a better look at Robert's new secretary. As they continued down the hall, Anita continued her

orientation. "You'll get an hour lunch and two fifteen-minute breaks. Always let someone know when you're leaving."
They were at Mona's desk when Anita looked behind them.

"Here comes Mr. Wilbertson now. He'll probably want you to call him Robert, just like the rest of us do," Anita said and Mona noticed that she still had not smiled.

As Mona looked up at her new boss, she was breathless. He is so fine, she thought. Anita, noticing Mona's glassy-eyed stare, stepped in front of her and spoke to Robert.

"Good morning, Robert. This is your new secretary, Mona Greene."

Robert smiled and extended his hand. "Welcome aboard," he said, then disappeared into his office.

"Is he always so abrupt?" Mona asked surprised that he hadn't reacted the way she was used to men acting toward her. No stares or admiring looks. Totally business.

"Not always. But, he's a busy man and he's had quite a full week. Don't worry. He is a nice man."
Anita showed her where the supplies were kept and told Mona to take what she needed. She showed her the phone directory and explained how to cover phones if any of the other secretaries were away from their desk. Anita kept the conversation on a business level and Mona knew she'd get no further than that.

"I'm going to leave you in Robert's hands. I'll introduce you to the other girls later; call me if you need anything."
Anita walked away, leaving Mona alone at her desk. Welcome aboard, she thought.

When she turned around, Robert was standing in the doorway. "I have coffee in my office. You're more than welcome to a cup if you'd like."

"Thanks, Mr. Wilbertson. I think I'll take you up on your offer." She smiled and followed him into his office. "Is there anything I can do for you this morning, Mr. Wilbertson," she asked as she poured coffee for both of them.

"You can call me Robert, and if it's all right with you, I'll call you Mona. We go by first names here."
She gave him her best smile. "Okay, Robert."

"Have a seat, Mona. Now first, I need two letters typed

130

and they must go in the first mail drop. Someone will show you where the mail room is."

She sipped on her coffee. "I'll get right on it." She returned to her work area. On her desk was a computer, telephone and pad. On the other side stood a filing cabinet. The desk was filled with supplies. She got started on the work Robert had given her.

The day went well and Mona was tired when she got home. But, every time she thought of Robert, a smile crossed her face. He had complimented her and she was fascinated with him. He'd taken her to lunch at a Chinese restaurant and she enjoyed her time with him.

After dinner, she took a bath and prepared for the next day. She chose a green jersey dress that was businesslike, but revealed her figure. Robert was a class act, but he was still a man. And she knew men loved looking at her body.

She found out that Robert was divorced. Loose and free, was what one of the secretaries had told her. It really didn't matter to her if he were married or divorced, if she really wanted him. With six sisters and four brothers, she'd had to fight for everything she wanted. She excelled when there was competition.

Mona went to bed, but unable to sleep from excitement, she decided to call her mother. As soon as she heard her mother's voice. Mona knew she was in pain.

"Hi, Mama. Did I wake you?"

"No, baby, you didn't. I can't find a comfortable position to lay in. My back is hurting me something terrible. Been this way for four days now. Mack came over this morning because he and Sandra had a big falling out. He's going to stay here for a few days. I told that boy to leave her." Mona heard her mother groan and she knew she was changing positions again.

"The child is not his anyway, so why stay?"

Mona sighed. She didn't call her mother to hear about her brother's problems with his wife. Every time she called her mother, there was something new with one of her sisters or brothers. She didn't understand why her mother put up with it. With all of her pain, she wished her siblings would stop putting problems on their mother's shoulders.

"Mama," she said. "When are you going to understand that there isn't anything you can do about Mack's problems? Now, what are you taking for your back pain?"

"The doctor gave me stronger pills, but I can't find them anywhere. I took one the day before yesterday and then Bobbie came over and brought Tashia with her. Well, you know she ain't nothing but a pillhead. She probably took my pills thinking they would make her high."

Mona was depressed. "I've got to go, Mama. I hope you feel better, and make Mack help you around the house while he's there." She hung up, now in a gloomy mood.

The next morning, she was in the office before Robert. She had already made coffee and was working on the computer when he arrived. He was wearing a charcoal-gray suit and gray shoes. Expensive, from head to toe. A man that dressed that way would want his woman to look just as good, she thought with sparks in her eyes. She could picture the beautiful gifts he would buy her.

The days passed by quickly and between Robert and Anita, Mona was always busy. But she loved working with Robert. He was always polite and businesslike. And she was impressed that he worked long hours. One morning, he asked her to come inside his office.

"Where have you been all my life, Mona?" he asked complimenting her. "I told Anita that you are one of the best secretaries in the State of California," he said with a smile that sent her heart in flames.

That night as she lay in bed, she closed her eyes and could smell Robert's cologne. He always smelled so good. She imagined his hands touching her body, fondling her, making her moan with desire. Soon, she would no longer have to fantasize about him. He would be in her bed, inside her and he would keep coming back for more.

The next morning, Mona sat at her desk listening to his voice as he talked on the telephone. What is happening to me, she thought. She knew she had to figure out a way to get him. She worked as closely with him as she could – bringing him lunch when he couldn't get away from his desk and working late even when he said she didn't have to. There were several times when she noticed the way his eyes would slowly glide over her body, focusing on her breasts, and she knew that he was no different than any other man. In time, he would be hers.

Several weeks passed and one morning, Robert buzzed Mona into his office.

"Mona, I've got to finish this case. Please hold my calls until two. Except for Helen Graham, of course. Always put her calls through to me."

She cleared her throat. "Helen Graham?"

Robert simply nodded and turned his back to her returning to his work.

As Mona walked out of the office, she repeated the name in her mind. Why does the name sound familiar, she wondered? She couldn't forget the expression on his face and the soft tone of his voice when he said her name. Who was this woman and what did she mean to Robert? But, somehow, Mona already knew. Well, what did she expect? A man in his position, with his looks had to have someone in his life. Mona chuckled. That wasn't going to stop her.

When the call from Helen came through that afternoon, Mona stood at Robert's closed door and listened. "I love you, too," was the last thing Mona heard Robert say before he hung up. Mona's heart dropped, but then she held her head high. This was just an obstacle and all obstacles could be removed.

Over the next month, Mona heard Helen and Robert talking on the phone on several occasions and suddenly, Mona felt like she wasn't making any progress with Robert at all. But one day, her chance came. She was in his office taking notes, when he made an announcement.

"I purchased a house in Baldwin Hills," he said with pride. Her eyes lit up. "How wonderful, that neighborhood is so beautiful."

"I'm very excited about it."

"So, when can I see it?" Mona asked.

The abrupt question caught him off guard and he didn't understand why he felt so odd. After all, what harm could it do to show her? She was new to the area and probably just wanted to see homes in different neighborhoods. "Let's go this evening after work."

"I'll be looking forward to it," she smiled demurely and left the office.

Anita was waiting for her as she came out. "I just wanted to drop these off for you," Anita said handing Mona some files.

"What are you so happy about?"

The smile had not left Mona's face. "Oh, nothing, except that I'm going to see Robert's new house this evening," Mona almost sang the words.

Anita frowned. She'd been watching her for weeks and knew that Mona was after Robert. It was a common thing for the new girls to come in thinking they could marry one of the D.As. In fact, she'd had the same idea when she first met Robert years ago. But, he was married and she respected that. Over the years, they'd become close friends and even after his divorce, Anita valued their friendship more than a cheap affair that wouldn't last. But, she knew it was different with Mona. Her type wouldn't back off no matter what. Anita decided she had to watch the situation closely. She wasn't about to let Mona take advantage of her friend.

That evening, when Mona and Robert left the office together, Anita made a mental note to maybe bring it up with Robert. She had to do something.

It didn't take them long to drive into Baldwin Hills and when Robert drove his black Mercedes up the long driveway, Mona was excited. The lawn of the two-story house was perfectly manicured and it looked like the type of place that she had always dreamed of living in.

"Now, the house isn't furnished yet," he said as he put the key in the door. "I only have a few things since I moved in three days ago."

Mona smiled. It was time she found out just how much Helen Graham meant to Robert. "Has your friend Helen seen it yet?"

"No, but she will soon," he smiled.

They stepped inside.

"It's absolutely beautiful, Robert. This living room is bigger than my entire apartment."

He showed her through the house, taking her from room to room. He showed her the backyard that he was especially proud of. This was where he planned to marry Helen. As they walked back into the house, Mona wandered through the living room. Yes, this was the kind of life she wanted – the house and the man. She was daydreaming when she heard Robert call her name.

"I'm sorry, I didn't hear you, Robert."

"I said to wait here. I'm going to run upstairs, then take you home. I know you've got to be a bit tired. You've had a long day."

He ran up the stairs and Mona went over a plan in her head. When he returned, he found her still staring out the window.

"It's so beautiful here, Robert. I hate to leave."

"Well, we'll invite you to our first barbecue."

"I would like that very much," But she wanted more, much more and she knew she had to move fast to get it.

He was ready to take her home. Just as they were about to walk out the door, he heard her whisper his name, and turned to her just as her eyes were rolling up into her head.

"Oh, God. What's wrong?" He grabbed her before she hit the floor and looked around. There was no furniture in the living room and he carried her up to his bedroom, laying her on his bed. He ran to the bathroom and returned, laying a wet towel on her forehead. She stirred and slowly opened her eyes.

"How do you feel, Mona?" His voice was filled with concern.

"I feel better, and stupid," she whispered. "I must've fainted." She tried to hold her head up and he helped her.

"Have you fainted before? Maybe I should take you to the hospital."

She tried to lift her head again. "Oh, no. I don't think it's anything more than not having anything to eat. I haven't eaten since seven-thirty this morning."

He stood up. "You didn't have lunch?"

She shook her head. "I went to the post office to mail a gift to my Mom and my time ran out. I couldn't be late while you were working so hard, Robert," she said with a vague look in her eyes.

"I'm sorry, Mona, but don't ever go all day without eating. Next time take the extra time."

She nodded.

"Do you feel like some Chinese Food?"

"Oh, no, Robert. I can't intrude on you like this." She held her face in her hands. "I guess I'm still a little dizzy."

"I owe you dinner and I didn't want to eat alone anyway. Now, just don't move until I get back."

She smiled as she heard his car start up and she curled up in his bed and waited. When he returned, he came up to the bedroom.

"Do you feel up to coming downstairs?" he asked, still concerned.

"Oh, no. I'm fine now. I guess I just needed a little rest." He helped her down the stairs and they sat on stools at the kitchen counter. They ate and talked about their jobs.

"Feel like a glass of wine?" he asked.

"That would be nice."

He filled their glasses and it wasn't long before they finished the entire bottle.

"I think it's time for me to take you home," Robert said finally.

"Okay, just let me go upstairs and get my purse."

He waited in the kitchen and turned when he heard her footsteps. She was completely nude. He looked at her smooth, brown skin and flat stomach. He opened his mouth, but no words emerged. She moved closer to him, her breasts so close that he could actually taste them. Her eyes were full of deviltry and she smiled at the shock on his face.

"No," he said as he closed his eyes and shook his head from side to side.

"No, what, Robert?" No, you don't want me? No, not tonight? What do you mean by no?" She moved closer to him.

"You know you want me, Robert. If not tonight, then tomorrow or the night after." She touched his thigh, her hand slowly circling the budge in his pants.

He was still sitting on the edge of the bar stool and she was standing so close, he could smell the wine on her breath and the sweet scent of her perfectly shaped body. She gently placed one of his hands on her breast and moaned, and Robert felt like her nipple was burning through the palm of his hand. He placed his other hand around her waist and shook his head as if he was coming out of a dream. He removed his hands from her body and removed her hand from his thigh. This had to stop before things got more out of hand.

"No, I can't do this," he whispered. "This isn't right."

She smiled, ignoring his words and placed his hand back on her breast as she leaned against him. She moaned, closed her eyes and kissed him hard on his mouth.

He was out of his head, kissing her, feeling her, and after they both pulled at his clothes, tearing them off, he gently picked her up and carried her upstairs. He sat her down in the middle of his bed and made love to her. His desire was so strong, she knew that it was pure lust. But she knew that the next time, he would really be making love to her. What surprised her was that she responded to him. He made every muscle in her body cry out for mercy and she knew she'd fallen hard for him.

At six the next morning, Robert took her home. He stood at her front door, unmoving until she stepped inside.

When he turned to leave, she asked, "No kiss good-bye?"

He smiled and gave her a quick peck on her forehead. She threw her arms around his neck and kissed him on his lips, noticing that he didn't kiss her back. She watched him drive off and felt an emptiness deep inside. She took a deep breath. He'll be all right. He's just feeling guilty, she thought. A few more times with him and he would be hers. All she needed was time. After all, she was here with him everyday, not Helen.

Back at his home, Robert took a long, hot shower. He leaned against the wall, thinking of Helen. Why have I been so stupid? I'm going to marry Helen. The worst part of it was that he'd have to see Mona everyday. Not that he thought it would ever happen again. It wouldn't. It shouldn't have ever happened. He dressed, drank a cup of black coffee and before he left for the office, stopped to call Helen. Her answering machine picked up and he left a message for her to call. He needed to hear her voice.

Mona arrived at her desk a half-hour earlier than usual. She wanted to have Robert's coffee waiting for him when he arrived. She was sitting at her desk, enjoying the memories of last night, when the phone rang. It was Helen.

"Please tell Robert that I'm sorry I missed his call this morning. I was in the shower. I'll call him later."

Mona was polite, but was fuming when she hung up the phone. She had no intentions of giving Robert any messages. And, to think he had taken the time to call Helen this morning. "Damn him! Well, it's time for me to break up this nonsense. I'm his woman now!" She sat with a wicked smile, until she saw Anita watching her.

"Good morning, Mona. You're early today," Anita said, looking at her watch.

"Yes, I have some important work to do."

"Well, don't come to work too early. You'll have Robert too spoiled for his *next* secretary," Anita said and turned away.

Mona was stunned. What did she mean by *next* secretary? Mona didn't like the way Anita had looked at her.

When Robert arrived, he looked grim and spoke in a dry tone of voice. After pouring himself coffee, he buried himself in work. He gave Mona letters to type and phone calls to make as if nothing happened between them. She followed his lead, behaving as professional as possible. She knew this was just an act. He would want her again – maybe even tonight.

When he asked her to go to lunch with him, she was ecstatic. It was working. Everything was falling into place – the fake fainting spell, the love making, and now, the day after. He took her to a restaurant not far from the office. It was a small place and they arrived a half-hour earlier than the normal lunch crowd.

He ordered spaghetti and garlic bread. She ordered the same, though she was almost too excited to eat. But as the lunch went on, she knew something was wrong. He was quiet and it wasn't until their plates had been taken away, that he cleared his throat to speak.

"Mona, I feel awful about last night. I don't know what came over me. Please believe me. This has never happened to me before and it can never happen again. I don't want this to interfere with our work relationship either. Can you under-stand what I'm saying?"

She heard his words, but they weren't registering. Maybe she wasn't hearing him clearly. Her face remained blank and she remained speechless.

"You're an excellent employee," he continued, feeling uncomfortable at her silence. "You're smart, efficient and so much more..." As he talked, he saw her eyes blaze and he wondered if she was hearing anything. "Do you think we can start all over and forget what happened?"

She wanted to slap him, kick him, anything that would make him feel her pain. She forced herself to answer. "Yes, Robert, of course," she said with a tight smile. "Why don't we start over? I love my job and don't want to leave."

He took a deep breath and released it. "Mona, thank you for your understanding. And, I am truly sorry about this."

"Then, it's settled," she said sipping her iced tea, afraid she was going to explode.

He felt relieved. And, lucky that the air had been cleared between them. It was much easier than he anticipated.

Chapter 17

Mona arrived at work early the next morning, tired from lack of sleep. Her brain was on overload; she'd been thinking of Robert all night. And that meant, she was thinking about Helen. Helen was a problem that she hadn't counted on. But, with a timely plan, she could resolve the problem and she and Robert could get on with their lives.

She had tried to convince herself Robert wasn't worth all this. But then, she'd remembered their love making and that big house. How exciting to be married to a lawyer, live in a gorgeous home, drive a Mercedes and wear expensive clothes. It would be a great change from the deadbeats she'd dated in the past. She had left the last man she lived with without as much as a good-bye. Sometimes, she wondered if he were looking for her. She almost jumped out of her skin one morning thinking she saw him, but it wasn't him. He said that he would kill her if she ever left him and she believed him. She closed her eyes again. Maybe she would have her mother move in with them after the first year of their marriage. Her mother deserved to live in style after all she'd been through. Mona's father had left when she was just fifteen years old, saying that he was tired of supporting a family. Her mother had sat around and cried for years after her husband left. In the beginning, Mona had wanted to cry along with her mother, but as time passed, she learned to block out her mother's tears. Her mother was weak and she wasn't going to be anything like her. I'm going to fight for what I want, Mona thought. Fight for what belongs to me. And, Robert is mine. She smiled a wicked smile. The challenge of Helen made her want him more than before.

With a new gust of energy, she marched into Robert's office and looked under the G's in his Rolodex. She spotted Helen's information and wrote it on a piece of paper then went back to her desk. She leaned back and thought for a moment. She'd have to figure out just how to use this. Just writing a letter or making a phone call wouldn't do. It had to be something that would stick, make Helen never want to see Robert again, no matter what he said. She had to convince Helen that Robert was in love with another woman. She smiled with a sparkle in her eyes. She knew what she had to do. The ringing phone interrupted her daydream. It was Helen.

"I'm sorry, Miss Graham. But, Robert isn't in yet." Mona could feel the muscles tightening in her body. "I gave him your messages yesterday and I'll let him know that you called again."

She hung up the phone and returned to the computer. Robert would get no messages from her, Mona thought as she banged on the keyboard and tried to concentrate on her work.

For the next few days, Mona and Robert worked closely together as if nothing had happened. His work load had increased as he was now in court. Robert was cool and unapproachable, talking only about work.

Anita could see the change. For one thing, Robert was very cool with Mona. Sure, he could be very abrupt and straight to the point. And, he did work hard, but he was warm and easy to work with. Mona didn't seem as happy as before. There was a definite change in their work relationship. And, Anita was trying to pinpoint what it was.

Robert and Helen talked almost every night and he promised her that he would be on the first flight to Atlanta as soon as his court case was over. He hated being apart and knew things would be much better if they were married and living in the same house. They had already wasted so many years and now his work was keeping him away from her. Once this case was over, he would ask Helen to marry him and show her the house he'd brought for the two of them.

Another week passed and as Robert was sitting at his desk, studying papers, Mona walked into his office. She stood in front of his desk and cleared her throat.

He looked up. "Yes, what can I do for you, Mona?"

"Robert, when I was at your house, I mean...when we were together..." His expression changed, but she continued.

"Anyway, I think I lost my ruby ring. My mother gave it to me and I'm really upset about it."

He laid his pen on his desk and ran his fingers through his wavy hair. "When did you realize you lost it at my house? Do you think it could be someplace else?"

With an expressionless face, she tried not to reveal the irritation that was simmering within her. Keeping her voice leveled, she answered, "I haven't seen it since we were together. I didn't want to be reminded of that night, so I didn't say anything about it until I was sure that it was no where else. I'm sure you understand what it means to me to get it back."

And, to get back into my house, thought Robert. "When I get home today I'll look for it," he said, then lowered his head returning to his work.

"Robert, I was wondering if I could come over and look for it myself. I promise not to take too long."

His gaze narrowed on her face as if he couldn't believe what she was asking him. "Excuse me?"

She knew that he had heard her. "Please, Robert. It should only take a minute and I remember every room I was in. I know I can look for it better than you can. And, if I can't find it, I'll know that I did look for it myself..."

He made an exaggerated sigh. "Okay. You can follow me home if you're leaving on time today. I'll be too busy the rest of the week. By the way, has Helen called me and you forgot to give me the messages?"

She turned back, looking him straight in the eye. "Oh, no, Robert. I wouldn't forget that."

He shook his head and picked up his pen.

So, that's what his bad mood is about, Mona thought. She smiled as she walked back to her desk. The entire time they were talking, his smooth, deep voice rang in her ears and her heart ached because she couldn't touch him or feel his strong hands touching her the way they had that night. "Soon," she thought aloud.

That evening she followed him home and he let her go up to the bedroom while he remained down stairs. She looked under the bed and throughout the room and within a few minutes, she ran down the stairs, calling Robert's name.

"Look what I found," she said, holding out her hand so that he could see the ring.

Robert smiled, the first smile she'd seen on his face that day. "Looks like it was a good idea that you came to look for it. I probably would have never found it myself." He walked her to the door. "I'm glad that you found it."

"I don't know what I would have told my mother if I lost it. I wear it every time she sees me."

They walked outside to her car, but before she got in she stood on her toes and kissed him on the cheek and lost her balance. He grabbed her shoulders with both hands. She held on to his arms for support.

"I'm so sorry, Robert." He stepped back. "That was suppose to be a thank you for your time, and patience with me today. I feel so much better. You just don't know how much better."

"I'm glad that you found it." Maybe he had been too hard on her today. He could have been more understanding since it was a ring that her mother bought her, he thought, as he opened the car door so she could get in.

She drove off with a sigh of relief as he stood looking after her. He walked back inside. Well, that didn't take long, but he would have to handle Mona very carefully so she wouldn't get the wrong idea about him again. He walked into the kitchen and looked inside the refrigerator to see what he could eat for dinner. There was nothing except cold pasta left from the night before. He grabbed a beer and picked up the newspaper he left on the counter and walked into the den, flipped the news on the T.V.

As she drove away, she sighed with relief. When she arrived at her apartment, her brother was sitting on the sofa watching the news.

"What took you so long?" he asked.

She held up the small bag. "First, I stopped at the store to pick up a few things. Then, I picked up a couple of hamburgers. I'm starved."

"Me too."

She dropped her shoes in the corner, then sat on the couch with her feet up on the table in front of her. "Did you get a good shot?" she asked as she bit into her hamburger.

He nodded. "The pictures should come out good. I got two shots. One as he opened the door as you two walked out and the other when you kissed him. In that picture, it will look like he's embracing you."

"Sounds good," she laughed mischievously.

"What are you up to, anyway?"

"Something very good, my brother."

He laughed. "Something good to you could mean killing someone."

She threw a pillow and it landed on his head. "I'm not that bad. How soon will the pictures be developed?"

"I'll have them for you tomorrow evening."

"That's great." She stood up and opened the blinds. "This apartment doesn't get enough sun. Have you talked to Mama today, Junior?"

"Yeah, she wasn't feeling too well. Her back is hurting again."

Mona sighed with a look of discontent. "I guess I should call, but she might not feel like talking and I don't feel like hearing her complain."

Junior stood and stretched and Mona looked at her brother. He was handsome with the same coffee-colored complexion as she. "I gotta go now. I promised Mary I would take her to the movies. Besides, today is her payday."

Mona walked him to the door. "I'll see you tomorrow with those pictures. I need to have them right away and will have your money then."

She watched him drive away and chuckled. She knew she could count on her brother. Anything for a price.

Helen walked inside with the mail in her hand. She usually met the mailman at the mailbox, a habit she'd started when she was waiting for an answer on her manuscripts. She pushed aside the electric bill and glanced at the large envelope. She was about to open the envelope, when the telephone rang. It was Robert and she smiled as she heard his voice.

"I got your card yesterday, Robert. It was a great surprise." She was feeling light-hearted and in love. Just hearing his voice made her weak in the knees.

"Just something to remind you how much I miss you,

baby. Things are slowing down and I'm looking forward to seeing you real soon."

"And just how soon is that?"

"In a couple of weeks. Should we do your place or mine?"

"Yours, and I can visit Lynn and Elaine while I'm there."

"I can't wait to see you, Helen. I love you very much."

Helen noticed that he sounded serious. "I love you too, Robert. These next two weeks are going to be the longest weeks."

He sighed deeply. They had to get married and end this foolishness. "Well, I better get going, babe. I can't wait to see you. But, I'll speak to you tomorrow."

Helen sat at the kitchen table and looked at the card Robert had sent her. It was white with a small red rose on the outside and large red print on the inside that said, 'I love you. Have to see you soon.' Her heart had flipped when she first opened it and she had to blink back tears. She missed him terribly. It had been a month since they'd been together. And, she had stopped calling him at the office because he was never there and recently never returned her calls. But she understood, knowing how difficult this case was for him. He always made her feel special, calling her when he could. How lucky they were to get this second chance. Life couldn't be any better.

Turning back to her mail, she opened the electric bill first, then set it aside. She picked up the large envelope and noticed it was missing a return address. She tore at the opening, and the phone rang. It was the wrong number.

She hung up the phone and started to walk into the living room, when she remembered, she still hadn't opened all of her mail. No big deal, she thought. It's probably some advertisement. Tearing open the envelope, her heart started racing and her stomach was in knots. She looked at the picture over and over again. As she slumped into a chair, the pictures slipped from her trembling hands onto the floor.

After a few minutes, she picked the pictures up and stared at them. She couldn't tell if the woman was coming or leaving. But, what difference did it make? It was clear to her now why Robert was so busy with work. The pictures made it very clear. She put the pictures face down on the table.

She looked at the stove, not remembering if she'd turned

on the water for coffee, but she hadn't and there was no need to now. There was no way that she could get coffee or anything else down at this moment. But it didn't matter. Nothing mattered. The tears started to flow and one dripped onto the pictures. This was so unfair. She loved Robert as she loved no other man. God opened her heart to him twice, she believed in him just to be lied to, cheated on.

She got up and threw the pictures and envelope in the trash, but then picked them up again. No, she thought. I might need them to remind me what kind of fool I've been. The tears she was holding inside were choking her and finally she released them, crying out. Her shoulders shook as her entire body trembled. How could he do this to me? She was sure they had something special. That's what he told her a million times. And, she had believed him. "Bastard, shit," she screamed.

Hours later when she opened her eyes, she thought she was awakening from a nightmare until she felt the ache in her heart. It was like an itch she couldn't scratch. She had laid on the couch the entire day and now, it was dark outside. She hadn't eaten all day, but she knew food would make her sick. She lay still on her back, listening to the deafening quiet of her home. The worst part was there was nothing she could do to ease the pain. She prayed for solace.

The telephone rang and she let the machine pick it up. She got up, closed the blinds in the living room, then in the dark, climbed up to her bedroom. She crawled into bed, wishing she could stay there for the rest of her life. It was just seven-thirty and she wondered just how long she had slept. She couldn't remember.

She tossed and turned into the night, questions floating in the air unanswered. By two in the morning, she'd had enough. She went into the bathroom and pulled out a bottle of Tylenol PM, filled a Dixie cup with cold water and returned to the bedroom. She sat in the chair next to the window and stared out into the night. It looked like rain was coming; the sky was such a dark blue. Funny, she thought as a tear rolled down her cheek. She felt as dark and quiet as the sky. The Tylenol was starting to work and she lay in her bed, welcoming the effects of the pills. "Damn you, Robert," was the last thing she remembered thinking before she fell into a deep sleep.

Helen heard the buzzer, once, then twice. Someone was at the front gate. The buzzer sounded again and she jumped up. It wasn't the gate; someone was at her door. She pulled herself out of bed and stumbled to the door without looking in the mirror. She looked through the peephole, sighed and let Darlene in.

Darlene walked inside and frowned. Helen looked tired and sick. Her hair was limp and her eyes were inexpressive. Darlene opened the blinds and walked into the kitchen leaving Helen standing in the middle of the living room. She opened the blinds in the kitchen, then walked throughout the house, letting light in. When she returned to the living room, Helen was still standing in the same spot. Darlene took her by the hand and sat her on the couch. Helen held her hands against her face, trying to block the sun from her eyes.

Darlene sighed. "Honey, why didn't you call me and tell me you were sick? I left three messages."

Helen looked straight ahead. "I'm not sick. I'm just not feeling well."

Darlene was still holding her hand. "Hell, girl, if you don't feel well, then you're sick."

"I'm not sick," Helen whispered. "I said I'm not sick. I'm just fucking fed up."

"Fed up about what?"

Helen stood and paced the floor. "Men, lies, cheating. All the faking and pretending. You name it and I'm sick of it." She ran her long, thin fingers through her hair. From the moment she opened her eyes, she felt the pain and anger again.

Darlene was taken aback. "When was the last time you had something to eat?"

"Yesterday, some time. I'm not hungry."

"I'm cooking breakfast."

Helen started to raise one hand to stop her. "No, really. I can't eat anything."

"Look, I'm not going to fight. I'm going to cook breakfast and I'm not going to eat until you do. And, I'm starving."

"Whatever you say. But, don't blame it on me if it all comes back up."

147

"Don't worry, it won't." Darlene went into the clean kitchen. It was apparent that Helen hadn't been eating.

Helen followed Darlene into the kitchen. "I'm going to take a shower."

"By the time you finish, breakfast will be ready."

Helen stood under the shower with her face up to the water. The water woke her up and relaxed her. She stepped out and looked in the mirror as she dried off. She must've terrified Darlene. She put on her underwear and dressed. Then brushed her hair back.

"The coffee smells good," Helen said as she entered the kitchen.

Darlene was putting the food on the table. Helen stared at the bacon and eggs, wheat toast and coffee and wondered how she would eat. But she knew Darlene would bug her, so she picked at the food. As they ate, Helen told Darlene what happened.

Darlene shook her head in disgust as she looked at the pictures. "You said he called yesterday morning when you got these?"

"Yes. He's probably called today; he calls everyday."

"That doesn't make sense. I think we have to figure this out," Darlene said.

"What's there to figure out, Darlene? It's already figured out. It took me too damn long to see it."

"Then, why does he keep calling? Come on, Helen. Listen to the messages and see what he says."

"I don't want to hear anything he has to say. It's over. There's no more hope."

"All I know is that I've seen this man with you and I know that he is in love."

"I thought so too. Obviously both of us were wrong," Helen said as she put the pictures back into the envelope.

"Why are you keeping those pictures? It will only hurt you to look at them."

"I won't be looking at them. I just want to keep them to remind me not to believe anything Robert ever says." A heavy silence fell over the room and Helen reached across the table, touching her friend's hand.

"I am glad you came over. I was so depressed, but now I'm up and ready to face the world. I'm going back to promoting my book. And, I have an idea in my head for a new one."

"So, no more lying around and moping?" Darlene asked.

"No, I'm ready to go on with my life. You know, I can't believe I'm back to where I was a few months ago. I said then, I was going to go on with my life without Robert and look at where I am now? All I have to do is get to the point where the knot in my stomach disappears when I think of him."

"It will, Helen. It just takes time. You'll see."

"I won't fall in love again, Darlene, I promise," she said, as she wiped her eyes with the corner of her napkin.

"Yeah, sure. I think you've said that before."

"No, really. This is my last time around. It's not meant for everyone. And it's obviously not meant for me."

"You're too young to feel this way. This will pass."

"I am forty years old and too old to be going through these ups and downs."

"That is still too young to give up on love. I'm 43 and I want to fall in love. I miss being in love and I don't want to be alone without love in my life." Darlene looked so wistful and sincere that Helen couldn't argue with her. She did deserve someone loving, a good man that she could fall in love with and would love her back.

Darlene looked at her watch. "I don't like leaving you like this, but I've got to get going..." Darlene stared at her friend. She'd never seen her spirit so damaged before. She looked empty.

"I'll be all right," Helen said as if she read Darlene's mind. "I just need to clear my head. I've done all the grieving I'm going to do. It's time to move on."

Darlene stood and put her cup in the sink. "Was I this bad when Luther and I broke up?"

"Hell yes, girl. I thought you would commit suicide or something. I almost called the paramedics when I found you in that bar, drunk, dog tired and talking lots of bullshit."

Darlene felt a chill run down her back. Just thinking of that time in her life made her angry. "He was the lowest,

149

Helen. He never paid me back my money and when I asked him for it, he knocked me down! Had women calling my house, telling me about what they did with him. That was a love affair from hell. And to think I stayed in it for four years," she said disgust in her voice.

Helen didn't mention that she'd seen Luther a few weeks before with a tall, high yellow woman hanging on his arm. He hadn't even asked her about Darlene, not that she had expected him to. But, he should have asked if Darlene was all right, especially after everything she'd done for him.

After Darlene left, Helen listened to her messages, erasing the ones from Robert and returned Lynn's call. They didn't talk long; Lynn wanted to give her mother a report on Elaine.

"She seems happy, Mom. Much more alive than I've ever seen her. I met the man she's dating and he's very nice. I had dinner with them last night. He owns a drug store and reminds me of a large teddy bear. He's gentle and patient. I think they're in love, Mom. Are you listening to me, Mom?"

"Of course and I'm very happy for Elaine. It's time she had someone good in her life; Lord knows she deserves it."
Lynn mentioned again that she might stay in Los Angeles when she graduated; all Helen would say was that there was still time to think about it. But, Lynn sounded as if her decision was already made.

"Are you sure you're all right, Mom?"

Helen cleared her throat. "I'm fine, just getting over the flu. I'll be totally fine in a few days, honey. Kiss Elaine for me and take care of yourself, love."

After she hung up, Helen sat in the kitchen and sipped another cup of coffee. Lynn was going to stay in Los Angeles, she knew it. She was losing her daughter to Los Angeles, just like she had lost Robert to a woman in Los Angeles. She ran upstairs and threw herself across the bed, her tears flowing freely. Her life was so unfair. She cried until she was empty, then got up and dressed in a pair of shorts and T-shirt. She went into her office and turned on her computer. She read her faxes, then started on her new book. When she stopped for another cup of coffee, it was already 6:00 PM. She closed the blinds and started writing again. When she stopped a second time to make herself a sandwich, it was past midnight. She wrote vigorously into the night, until she could no longer keep her eyes open.

Chapter 18

She stood at the glass doors to the patio watching the rain falling hard on the ground. Her plants were in the corner, a good spot so that the rain could get to them. They were always greener after a good soaking in the rain. It had rained constantly for two days and two nights.

Helen sat in the living room in the white high-back chair and closed her eyes. Robert's face appeared and she blinked him away, though she couldn't get him out of her heart. She had to find a way to forget him, but the memories were still too new to go a day without thinking of him. The wound was still wide open. She walked back into the kitchen and poured herself another cup of coffee. What a morning, she thought, as she went back into the living room. Walking from the kitchen to the living room was all she seemed to do. She hadn't taken the time to shower or dress.

It was raining harder now and the rain depressed her. She rested her cup on the coffee table. Three cups were enough for anyone. She didn't know why she had poured another cup anyway. She laid her head back against the couch and a smile slowly creased the corners of her mouth. It was a rainy, quiet day like this one that made her decide to write novels.

She thought about the days when she sat at the kitchen table with her old typewriter and dictionary. She would get home from work at five-thirty, cook dinner, help Lynn with her homework and then write until well past midnight. She'd get up at six the next morning to take Lynn to school and go to work. That was her life until she finished her first novel, "Disappointments." She received an advance of $2000 and small royalty checks. After that, she wrote two short stories which sold for $125 each. She was about to give up, when she decided to change her writing style – giving her characters a more unpredictable life. Her second novel, "Season's End," was good. It was a passionate love story and she felt every word as it came to life on paper. Helen mailed the first three chapters to her agent, who then asked for the entire manuscript.

Almost two months passed and Helen heard nothing. She had decided to move on to something else once again, when one Saturday morning, she received a call from Lola Doverwood. Lola started the conversation by telling Helen what a good job she'd done. And then she went on to tell Helen that she had an offer from a publisher for a two-book contract. The contract was for $250,000. Helen's mouth fell open, yet no sound emerged. Her heart stopped, her entire world stopped. But yet, everything was just beginning. She'd made her mark. She was a writer and all the sacrifices were paying her back now in full. All the long nights and tiring days, her weekends and holidays filled with work, her sleeping and eating with her characters – all had paid off. Her dreams of making a comfortable life for herself and her daughter had come to life.

Lola hung up and Helen sat at the kitchen table, crying softly, with both hands against her face, feeling like she could cry all night. "I'm a writer," she whispered, "I'm truly a writer. Oh God, I've wanted to say those words for so long." She wiped the tears from her eyes. She had to tell her daughter. Lynn was lying across her twin bed watching TV with a book in front of her when Helen walked in, hugged her and told her the news. They hugged and laughed and cried. Then, they grabbed their sweaters and jumped into the car, driving straight to Darlene's house.

"The lights are on, so she's home. I got so excited, I forgot to call and see."

Lynn giggled, still filled with excitement.

They rang the doorbell and with the third ring, Darlene peeked through the blinds.

"What are you two doing out? I thought you had cramps an hour ago," Darlene said to Helen as she cast a critical eye over her.

"I did, but now I feel better. We thought we would come by to see you on our way home," Helen said smiling at Lynn.

Darlene looked at the two of them and knew something

was up. She motioned for them to follow her into the kitchen. Helen and Lynn watched as Darlene fixed them each a tall glass of lemonade.

"Guess what, Darlene? I'm quitting my job. In about two weeks."

Darlene gave Helen her glass and frowned. First, Helen had cramps too bad to come over, then a half-hour later, she pops up with no cramps at all. Now, she's going to quit her job. Darlene took a seat, facing Helen. "I don't think I heard you correctly. Are we missing something here? Like, how are you going to live when you quit your job?"

Helen and Lynn just looked at Darlene, their eyes beaming, lit up like marbles and Darlene sighed.

The telephone rang and Darlene answered it impatiently. It was Valerie calling from San Diego, telling Darlene about her trip to New Orleans, how her business was going, asking when they would take vacation again. Darlene sighed again and shook her head. She wanted to get off the phone. As she looked from Helen to Lynn and saw their smiles, she wanted to know what was going on. Finally, Valerie hung up and Darlene stood before Helen waiting for the news.

"I sold my book for $250,000," she screamed. "I did it, girl."

Darlene jumped up and held Helen so tightly, Helen thought Darlene would crush her. "I can't believe it, Helen. Oh yes, I can. You are good. Come on, let's go into the living room."

The three sat on the couch, trying to talk at the same time.

"It paid off, Helen. Thank the good Lord!" Darlene said as she patted Helen's hand. "Honey, you did it and I'm so happy for you. We're proud of you," Darlene said as she looked at Lynn.

Helen looked at her daughter. She'd gotten as tall as her mother and at only fifteen, was already making plans for college. They could finally sit back now and relax.

"Now, tell me everything and don't leave anything out," Darlene said.

Helen took a drink of her lemonade. "I got the phone call from my agent and I wasn't excited at first. I didn't want to hear about another $2,000.00 check, even though I knew this book was worth much more. When she said the deal was closed and told me the amount of money, I nearly died."

Darlene and Lynn laughed.

"I don't get all the money at once; it's spread over the two books. But, I'm getting enough to turn in my resignation as soon as I put the money in the bank. And then, I'm going on a shopping spree. With the money I saved up and now this, I can buy a townhouse that I really like. Not just one that I can afford, but one I like…" Helen was babbling.

The three enjoyed the rest of the evening, making plans for all the things Helen could do now. It was eight o'clock before Helen and Lynn walked inside their apartment. Helen was hungry and ordered a pizza.

As they sat enjoying their dinner and the excitement of the day, Lynn asked, "Mom, are we rich now?"

Helen gave her daughter a warm smile. "No, love, just comfortable. I'll invest some of the money so that it can make more money, and of course, I'll keep writing." Helen bit into her pizza and wondered how she would sleep with all these thoughts. And, she wondered how long before she got the money.

Six weeks later, Helen had a new car and new clothes for herself and Lynn. When her ex-husband called after he heard the news, she told him to go straight to hell. Too much time had passed without hearing a word from him. And, he had not been a good father. "Too little, too late," she told him before she hung up on him.

Helen also gave Darlene a $15,000 loan to expand her business. But it wasn't until three more weeks passed that she reached out to her family. She wanted to tell her mother the good news and knew that she'd have her approval this time. Helen remembered that telephone call.

"Hi, Mama."

"Is that you, Helen?"

"Yes, Mama, it's me."

"Well, speak up, girl. I can hardly hear a word you're saying."

"I have some good news, Mama."

"Well, I'm listening."

"Is Elaine there with you?"

"No, she went to the store. She forgot to get me some

canned milk for my coffee tomorrow and there are plenty of other things she's not doing…"

Helen knew it was best to let her mother finish.

"That girl will forget her head if it wasn't connected to her neck. I'm telling you she would. I don't know where her mind is sometimes. What is this phone call about anyway, Helen? It's long distance and with that pitiful job you have, you can't afford to pay for small talk. I told you not to move away from here. You could have gotten the same things right here in Los Angeles…"

Helen felt disappointment creeping in her as she lost control of the conversation. But what she had to say would turn it around. "I wrote a novel, Mama, and I'm getting paid $250,000 for it."

She heard her mother clear her throat. "You said, $250,000?"

"Yes, Mama," Helen said with pride.

"Well, that's wonderful, but it's about time. You've been talking about your writing for the longest time. Elaine will be happy to hear it and I'll tell Harriet, though it took you a bit longer than it would have taken her. You know, Helen, once Harriet makes up her mind, she can do anything."

Helen felt as if she had been struck in the chest with a bullet. What a fool I was for calling. Odessa would never be proud of anyone, except Harriet. "I've got to go, Mama. Like you said, this is a long distance call."

"And, my favorite talk show is coming on. Good-bye."

Helen hung up and sighed. Serves you right, Helen. What in hell made me think she would be proud of anything I would do?

The phone rang and Helen jumped from her daydream. She took a deep breath and looked toward the sliding doors. It was still raining. The phone stopped before she picked it up. So much for a sensible day, she thought. God, how long was I dreaming? She touched her coffee cup; it was cold. She sat back and smiled, thinking of the new book she had to complete. This was the best medicine to take her mind off Robert Wilbertson. So, get your ass in gear, Helen Graham. Get on with your life.

Chapter 19

Charles parked in front of Harriet's house, walked her to the door and kissed her good night. She'd sold the house she had lived in with Robert. After she gave Robert his half of the money, she bought herself a smaller two-bedroom house.

Harriet could see from Charles' expression that he was disappointed, but he left without saying so. The truth was, this was her last night out with him. He was nice and made a decent living working at Hughes Aircraft, but he was just too cheap, too selfish, and too complex to deal with. Harriet understood that much of his complexity came from his upbringing – he'd grown up poor in a family of eight children and there was never enough to go around. So now, Charles held on to his money and prayed to God that he would never go hungry again.

Harriet hated when they went out to dinner and he reviewed the check three times to make sure he wasn't overcharged. But, it was worse when he came to her home for dinner and ate until he couldn't move. And then, there was the sex. It had been a long time, since Harriet had had sex and when she finally allowed Charles to take her to bed, she found that she didn't enjoy sex any longer. There was no way she could take another night with him. His moans sickened her and he was always finished quickly without any consideration for her. He had no sex appeal. Now she understood why his ex-wife had run off with another man. Their two-month dating had to end.

The next day, she came home with a headache from her evening commute. The commute which normally took 45-minutes, took almost two hours because of an oil spill on the 405. As she was hanging her clothes in the closet, the telephone rang.

"Harriet, how about a movie tonight?" Charles' voice boomed through the receiver. "We can go to the drive-in because you know I don't like those high-priced theaters."

She shook her head in disgust. "No thanks, not tonight."

"Well then, I could come over and we can just watch TV."

"I'm not feeling well tonight, Charles. But, I do need to talk to you about something, and then we'll call it a night. I'm really tired."

In less than an hour, Charles was at the house with a large grin on his face and flowers that he had picked from his yard in his hand. She offered him a seat in the living room, while she went into the kitchen to get the coffee.

"Charles, you know that I like you. We've had some good times together." She sighed deeply, wishing she had waited until tomorrow for this. "I've been doing some thinking about our relationship."

He looked puzzled. "You've been thinking about what, Harriet? Have I done something to offend you?"

"No, nothing like that. It's just that I don't think I'm ready to become so involved and I'm uncomfortable."

"But Harriet, this takes time. It don't happen overnight," he said facing her.

"I'm just not ready yet, Charles. I don't know if I'll ever be ready for this kind of a close relationship." She was getting fidgety.

He looked at her, not understanding. Hadn't he treated her nice and respected her, he thought.

"What do you mean you're not ready? Have I been pushing too hard?"

"No. I need to do a lot of soul searching. Find out what it is I want to do."

"Harriet, listen to me," he said taking her hand. He was getting nervous. "Harriet, don't do this. I already know that I want to spend the rest of my life with you."

Harriet realized that she had waited too long to break it off. God, why did it have to be so difficult? "Charles, I had no idea that you felt that way." She closed her eyes.

"Harriet, why would I have spent so much money on you if I didn't love you?" He was still holding her hand. "Just tell me what you want, Harriet and I'll do it. Whatever it takes to make you happy." His voice was so sad it made her heart swell.

She didn't want to hurt him, but she was too tired to continue. Her headache was getting worse and now she felt pain in her stomach. "Charles, I don't want you to do anything. I want us to be friends like I suggested in the beginning. But, I got into something with you that I wasn't ready for. We can only be friends."

When he reached for her hands, she gently pulled away and his eyes widened in surprise. "Why did you jump, Harriet? I only wanted to touch you. You don't have to be afraid of me, I won't hurt you."

"You just caught me off guard."

He looked into her eyes and Harriet could see that he was hurt. He got up and paced back and forth with his hands stuffed in his pockets. He had to think of something to make her change her mind.

Finally, he returned to the couch. "I knew that you weren't in love with me, but I was hoping that after awhile, you would feel differently." He looked into her eyes. Did she feel anything for him? As she sat with a blank stare, he got angry. "You know what I think, Harriet?"

She folded her arms in front of her. "No."

"I don't think you can love anyone. I think you're one of those people that ain't capable of loving." He paused. "You're just an old cold fish and I'm glad I found out before it was too late."

She turned to him with trembling hands. "How dare you, you big jackass. You can't talk to me this way." She got off the couch and opened the door with her chin high. "Good-bye, Charles."

He stood, silently facing her.

"Leave my house now," she said in an angry tone of voice.

He walked out without a second glance and she slammed the door behind him. She couldn't believe he had talked to her that way after all she had tolerated with him. But, what cut her to the quick, was that he'd said the same things that Robert said before he left.

She sat back on the couch, still trembling with tears rolling down her face. This definitely didn't go as she planned, she thought as she finally got up from the couch and returned the coffee cups and tray to the kitchen. She continued to wipe the tears from her eyes and walked out of the kitchen. It was time to go to bed. She walked through her home and turned out all the lights.

Robert was completely baffled. He had even called Darlene's house, but she told him that Helen had been in New York.

He was upset. "Darlene, I've been calling her for five weeks and she hasn't returned my calls. I don't know what happened."

Darlene didn't want to talk to him. She still didn't understand why he kept calling Helen when he was involved with someone else. She was almost tempted to ask him why, but decided to stay out of it, especially since Helen was going on with her life. Leaning against the sink, she said, "Robert, someone's ringing my doorbell. Sorry, I can't help you, but I really have to go."

Robert hung up and stood at the window looking at the cloudy sky. He shook his head. They had gotten so close. They had a past together and Robert was hoping for a future. Maybe she has someone in her life and doesn't want me anymore, he thought as he looked down at the busy streets. No, he didn't believe that. He knew Helen loved him as much as he loved her. He walked back to his desk, but he couldn't concentrate on work.

Standing outside his office, Mona overheard his entire conversation with Darlene and she smiled. Everything was going as she planned. She had envisioned herself over and over again, living with Robert in that big house. She even imagined having his child. She was only 32 and could do that if he wanted. She hoped he did – once she had his child, he would never leave her.

She would be waiting for him when he got tired of waiting for Helen's calls. He was worth it. She knew that he was hurt, but she could help him forget. He would need her to pick up the pieces; he would need her for everything. She would make sure of that. And, it would be very soon.

160

Chapter 20

Elaine was too sick and dizzy to teach school today, but she was also nervous. She had used the home pregnancy test twice and both times the results were the same – she was pregnant. She had stopped thinking about having a baby years ago, never thinking that she would have someone like Dan in her life. But with marriage or no marriage – she was going to have this baby. It seemed impossible that something so wonderful could happen to her. She wanted to tell Helen, but she had to tell Dan first.

She smiled as she thought of him. She was madly in love and he said he loved her too. This was a happiness she thought she'd never experience. God, how lucky I am to have a baby with that man, she thought as she touched her stomach and tried to imagine the baby growing inside of her. But then, her smile disappeared. Dan had never said he wanted to get married and they had never discussed children. She was beginning to feel frightened. Would he ask her to get rid of it? She shook her head. No matter what, this was her baby and no one could take it away from her. She was going to have it no matter how Dan felt.

Helen was up with the sun. She showered and walked back into her bedroom, standing in front of the mirror in her panties and bra. At least she didn't look as thin as she had a month ago when things had first changed with Robert. She was home and it felt good to be home again, but it only gave her more time to think of him. The contented expression on her face changed as she thought of the long, empty day that loomed ahead.

She had been busy in New York with her book, but she's had time to shop for herself, Lynn and Darlene. Now, she looked at the piles of boxes from Saks and Bloomingdale's and sighed before picking them up. I guess for now, I'll just have to buy happiness, she thought with a twinge of sadness in her heart. Her life wasn't very happy right now, but one day it would be. Life is what you make it, she said to herself and wondered who had said that.

She went downstairs to the kitchen and sipped coffee and ate wheat toast while she glanced over the newspaper. But, her mind kept going back to her trip. When she wasn't with her editor, she was shopping, taking in a movie or play. Men tried to talk to her, but she wasn't interested. She wasn't ready for an intimate relationship. Not until she could find herself and get peace in her life. It was just too soon. Trying to get over Robert made her feel lonelier than before. She was still hurting deeply from his lies. But she had made up her mind to forget him and go on.

She knew she wouldn't be able to sit in the house all day and she went to the bakery to spend time with Darlene.

"When did you get back?" Darlene asked.

"Last night around nine. I started to call you but I was exhausted, and I know how early you have to get up."

"I wasn't asleep. I was watching "Back Street" with Susan Hayward. Have you ever seen that old movie?"

"Yes. I cried all the way through it. Elaine and I watched it the last time she was here," Helen said as she inhaled. "What is that luscious smell?"

Darlene followed Helen into the kitchen. "Look," Darlene said as she opened the large commercial oven.

"Pound cake?"

"Yes, I decided to try this and give samples to my customers. I want to see their reactions."

Helen took off her coat. "It feels nice and warm in here. It's cold as hell outside."

"Tell me about it. You should have been up at four this morning."

"Here, this is for you since you wouldn't go to New York with me," Helen said, giving Darlene a bag from Bloomingdale's.

They went into Darlene's office and Helen watched as her friend pulled the blouse from the bag with excited eyes. She stood in the middle of the floor and modeled for Helen.

162

"It does look good on you, Darlene."

"I love it. I saw a pair of slacks this color a couple of weeks ago." She gave Helen a bear-hug. "Did you do a lot of shopping?"

"I did more than I anticipated. But, so what? You only live once."

Darlene sat in the chair opposite her. "I'm sorry I couldn't go with you, but I couldn't leave Mrs. Beasley right now. She's just getting back on her feet after that terrible flu. It really got to her and she is getting older."

"Oh, I understand, Darlene. You have to take care of Mrs. Beasley. She is seventy."

"I know. I worry about her. I don't trust anyone the way I trust Mrs. Beasley."

"You know what you need to do? Hire someone who can run the bakery for you. Someone you'll be able to trust. Remember we always said that once we made some money, we would travel and do all the things we couldn't do before. Now is the time to enjoy yourself."

"Let's go into the kitchen and I'll make us some hot tea."

Helen took a seat at the table while Darlene put the kettle on the stove. "Now, like I was saying, don't you know that when you die you can't take this damn bakery with you? It will be standing in this same spot when you're dead, buried and gone," Helen said.

"Valerie was saying the same thing a few days ago. Have you two been talking about this?"

"No, but if we're saying the same thing, then it must be right."

Darlene took two cups from the cabinet and poured the tea.

"You know, you could help me promote my new book," Helen said and they both laughed.

"You never give up. Okay, I'll think about what you're saying. Maybe it is time to find someone to help Mrs. Beasley."

"That's good. Get someone as her assistant and then the two of them could run things while you're away. I'm going to L.A. soon and you could go with me."

"I'll think about it. Now, tell me about your trip."

Helen's head was resting in her hands with both elbows on the table. "It was okay. I worked, shopped and went to a play. Kimberly, my editor, took me to a couple of places I hadn't been before. It was good to get away, but it's always good to be home. Do you have any lemon?"

Darlene watched Helen squeeze the lemon into her tea.

"Guess what," Helen started casually. "I had two messages from Robert."

"I'm not surprised. He called me to find out where you were."

Helen looked at Darlene with wide eyes. "Get out of here. Why is he calling me, Darlene? What does he want?"

"I don't know. Maybe you should ask him that question. After all, he owes you an explanation, don't you think?"

"No. Not anymore. I don't want to talk to him." Her voice was beginning to crack and Darlene knew her well enough to know how obstinate she could be once her mind was made up.

Darlene changed the subject. "How's our girl?"

"She's doing good," Helen sighed.

"And?"

"Damn you, Darlene. You know my every mood! Anyway, Lynn is still trying to decide if she's going to stay in Los Angeles or come home to Atlanta where she belongs. But I'm sure she has already decided on L.A.," Helen said sadly. "I can feel it in my heart. She always brings up the subject as if she's trying to prepare me. I don't understand why she doesn't come right out and say it."

"Maybe she knows something is bothering you."

Helen looked up from her cup. "What do you mean?"

"Girl, don't you think Lynn knows that there is something unsettling in your life right now? You two are so close, Helen."

Helen closed her eyes. "I hadn't really thought of it. I don't want her to worry about me. She has to keep her grades up."

"That's true, but she is your daughter and knows you well."

"I'll remember that the next time I talk to her," Helen

said. "So, what are you doing for the rest of the day?"

"Well, I'm finished with all of my paperwork and I'm bored to death."

"So am I even though I do have some letters to read and calls to make later. I also have to go over some things with my editor…" Helen stopped and looked at her friend. Darlene looked tired. "Are you getting enough rest?"

"Yeah. I just couldn't sleep last night. I tossed and turned all night."

"I've had nights like that. But except for looking tired, you look good. You're still losing weight, huh?"

"Yeah, I am. I have been feeling better. Staying on the diet is hard, but I am walking in the evenings, just like the doctor ordered."

Helen nodded. "Walking is good for you. I feel guilty if I miss walking too many mornings." Helen stood and put on her coat.

"Where are you going?"

"Home – to do all the things I said I needed to do. When I finish, I think I will curl up in bed and read a book. I'm still a bit tired."

Darlene walked her to the door. "Call me later if you get tired of reading."

"I will, but you should go home and try to catch up on some of that sleep you lost last night."

They hugged and Helen went to her car.

She drove with no destination in mind. It was only two and she was having one of those days where she couldn't sit in one place for too long. Not only that, it was warming up. The sun was shining and she didn't want to be inside. She ended up driving to Peachtree and walked up and down the street enjoying the view. She felt better already. It was only March, but Spring was in the air.

She brought an ice cream cone and walked through the streets window-shopping. She was wearing black slacks, a white blouse and her hair hung loose. The only make-up she wore was a pink lipstick, which gave her a wholesome, lovely appearance. She was walking slowly, enjoying the day when she heard a voice behind her.

"Hello, Helen."

She knew who it was before she turned. He had the same distinct, deep voice. "Hello, Thomas. Long time, no see." She smiled pleasantly because after twelve years the animosity was gone. He hadn't been a good father to Lynn, but it didn't matter since she was able to provide for her and her daughter well. He was still a good-looking man – older, but then she was sure she looked older to him.

"How's Lynn?" he asked, looking around to see if she was there, too.

"She's fine. She's still at school in L.A."

"She's not home for the summer?"

"No, she has a job out there."

He stood, staring down at her and Helen wondered what he was thinking.

"I can't believe it's really you, Helen. I often think of you and Lynn and how you're doing. I think about Lynn a lot."

Helen tilted her head to one side. "Do you really think of your daughter, Thomas? Why haven't you tried to get in touch with her?" She had finished her ice cream and wiped her hands with the napkin before tossing it in the trash can behind her.

He didn't answer her question. "I could use a cold drink. What about you, Helen?"

"Just water for me."

They walked into Ruby's, a small place that they were standing in front of, and took a seat at round table. The place had a seventies décor, with large pictures on the wall of Richard Barry, The Impressions, Etta James and Bobby Darren. "Shop Around" by Smokey Robinson and the Miracles, was playing on the jukebox. The waiters and waitresses were dressed in red and white which matched the tablecloths on the tables. Helen felt as though she was sitting in another time.

Thomas took a deep breath. "You asked me why I haven't tried to get in touch with Lynn," Thomas started. When Helen just looked at him, Thomas continued, "Well, I got married right after our divorce and it was really too soon. My mistake."

"I thought you left us so that you could get married."

He sighed and nodded. "I did, but a month after I left you, I wanted to come back. But, I knew that I had hurt you too much. I knew you wouldn't take me back."

"You're right."

"And, I couldn't have faced you anyway. Anyway, I went ahead and got married and the next year, I was laid off from my job. The year after that I was divorced."

"Are you married now?" Helen asked.

"No. Probably never again."

"Good idea. You're not very good at it," she said looking him directly in the eye.

He looked away knowing that he deserved everything she was saying. "You're right. If I couldn't do it with you, Helen, I know I can't make it with anyone."

She didn't say anything. No use beating a dead horse.

"Anyway, after the years past, I thought too much time had gone by and that Lynn probably hated me by then anyway. I guess you could say that I was too much of a coward to find out."

She opened her purse, taking out her wallet. "Here's a picture she took two years ago."

He held the picture wordlessly, and Helen saw his smile widen and his eyes begin to water. She didn't know what she was feeling for him – he was the one who had walked out on them.

"She's a pretty girl, Helen," he said, still staring at the picture.

"She is. She's nineteen now."

"I remember. I only saw her in my mind as an eight year old, but I knew she was nineteen."

"She's quite a young lady and very smart, too," Helen said proudly.

"She looks exactly like you did at her age. As a matter of fact, you don't look that much older now."

Helen chuckled. "I think you've gone blind."

"No, I haven't. Who would have thought that we would have seen each other today? It must be my lucky day."

"Yes, I guess it was." Helen took out a pen and wrote Lynn's address and phone number on the back. "Try writing her, Thomas. I can't promise anything, but you can write and see what happens."

"This really is my lucky day." He looked at the picture once more and put it in his shirt pocket.

They walked outside and stood in front of the soda shop. Thomas told her that he worked in the IBM building and was on his lunch hour.

"I'm not much of a reader, but I have read two of your books. They were great. You're a good writer and a good person, Helen. It took me too long to get my head together, but I want you to know that I realize it now even though it's too late."

"Some people never get their head together, Thomas."

"I appreciate you giving me the picture and Lynn's address. God knows I don't deserve it." He kissed her on the forehead and started to walk away, then stopped. "Damn, it was good seeing you again."

"Guess it was your lucky day," she said. He laughed and walked off and she watched as he walked faster, obviously late from his lunch break.

For some reason, Helen felt better now. The restlessness she'd felt early was wearing into tiredness. Now, she could go home and relax. It had turned out to be a nice day after all.

Elaine woke up sick again and sat at the edge of the bed. She touched her stomach and closed her eyes. She got up and went into the bathroom, looking in the mirror as she splashed cold water on her face. She took deep breaths until she felt better, then went back into the bedroom and climbed into bed. Good thing there was no school today. It was only seven-thirty and she decided that she could sleep another hour.

By evening, she was feeling better, but nervous because she had to tell Dan the news. As she brushed her hair back, she thought of the baby. This child was going to be loved. That's exactly what I'll say to Dan, she thought, as she walked into the living room looking from one corner to another. If I'd known I was going to have a child, I would have bought a house, instead of this townhouse. She wanted her child to be able to play in a big yard, a place where they could run and play ball, play with toys and feel free. Maybe she would sell the townhouse and get a home for her and the baby.

She looked around again and smiled. She was really her own person now. She had come such a long way since she was raped. Feeling dizzy, she sat back on the couch and closed her eyes until the dizziness passed. Twenty minutes later, she got up again smiling, singing, knowing it was a wonderful day in her life.

Elaine called the store and invited Dan over for dinner. He was concerned when she mentioned that she hadn't been feeling well.

"Are you really okay, Elaine? Is there anything I can do for you?"

"No, Dan. It's nothing serious." She smiled. This was more than serious, but she wasn't going to tell him over the telephone.

For dinner, she baked chicken, brown rice, black-eyed peas and cornbread muffins. She wondered if she should serve dinner first or tell him about the baby first. She decided to wait until after dinner since she had already waited two weeks. She was trying to prepare herself just in case he didn't want the baby. It didn't matter though. She would tell him that she would keep it and raise it herself. She didn't need anyone. This baby was a gift from God.

When the doorbell rang, she jumped and looked in the mirror one last time. She hoped that he couldn't hear her heart rapping hard and fast. She opened the door and he stepped inside with a box of See's candy in his hand. He kissed her cheek and handed her the candy. He was always so thoughtful. He knew she loved chocolate candy and See's especially.

They talked for a while, then sat down to dinner, but it was a disaster. Elaine spilled water on her lace tablecloth and kept dropping her fork in her lap. Her hands trembled so much she was afraid to pick up her glass again. It seemed that Dan watched her more closely than usual, but she didn't blame him since she kept dropping things. To make matters worse, the smell of the chicken was making her nauseous and she pushed her chair from the table, not being able to tolerate the food any longer.

Dan jumped from the table and was at her side in less than two heartbeats. She ran to the bathroom, falling to her knees in front of the toilet. She tried to motion to Dan to stay outside, but he stayed with her. And when she finished at the toilet, she burst into tears. This wasn't the way it was supposed to go.

"I messed everything up," she mused between sobs.

He was on his knees beside her and he gently pulled her close to him. She laid her head on his shoulder and he gave her a cold towel to wash her face. Finally, he helped her up and they went back outside into the hallway. "Now, sweetheart, what can be so bad," he whispered softly in her ear.

She couldn't stop crying. "It's not really bad, I mean, I'm just handling it badly."

He didn't let her go. "Tell me, Elaine."

She buried her face in his shoulder. "I'm going to have a baby." She sighed as the words finally came from her and her legs suddenly became weak. For a few seconds that seemed like hours, Dan was silent and Elaine's heart started to beat so fast she was sure he could feel it against his chest.

He held her at arm's length, so he could see her face. "I wondered when you were going to tell me."

Her eyes questioned him. "What?"

"I already knew. You haven't been feeling well, you eat those chocolates like you can't get enough, some foods make you sick as a dog. And if there were any doubts, tonight confirmed it." He paused. "We are having a baby."

"Yes," she whispered. She still couldn't tell if he was happy.

"I'm going to be a father. I was hoping...that you were pregnant." He grabbed her and held her tight against him. "Oh, Elaine. I love you so much." When he looked in her face, he showed nothing but love. "I've always wanted to be a father, but I thought it was too late for me. I'm the luckiest man in the world and it's all because of you." There were tears in his eyes as he led her to the couch. "There's one thing though."

"What?"

"Will you marry me? I love you and I will be a good husband and father. I will give you and the baby everything. Honey, I want to wake up each morning with you beside me. And our child in the bedroom next to ours. I want to marry you."

She cried, nodding her head.

"Is that a yes?" he asked.

"Yes, yes, I'll marry you, Dan." She saw the devotion in his eyes and she cried ecstatically. She had never felt so happy in her life.

"When, Elaine?"

"I don't know when," she said as she accepted a tissue and wiped her eyes.

"We should do it before the baby is born. Even before you start to gain weight. I don't want people saying things that aren't true."

"What kinds of things?"

"I don't want anyone to say that I only married you because of the baby. You know how people are. I love you and I want us to get married as soon as possible." He sat back on the couch and pulled her into his arms. "I want you to relax."

They sat silently for a few minutes. "Will you move in with me when we get married?" she asked.

"Yes, your place is bigger than mine, but we'll buy a house soon."

"You know, I was wondering...do you think I'm too old to have a baby?"

He laughed. "Are you kidding? You're only thirty-six and women are having babies well into their forties. Anyway, you'll never be too old for me."

She kissed him on the forehead and he picked her up, carrying her to bed. It was like a bed of roses that night for Elaine. He made love to her and she slept in his arms until the next morning.

After he'd left for work, Elaine called Helen. She could tell that her sister was groggy when she picked up the phone.

"Hi, Helen."

"Are you all right, Elaine?"

"Isn't it just like you to think something is wrong when you hear my voice."

"I'm sorry, honey. It's just that you never call me before you go to work unless it's important."

"Well, this is important but I've never been better in my life."

Helen smiled and started to relax again. "Good."

"I'm getting married in a month and I want you to be here."

Helen sat straight up in her bed, her eyes wide. "Married? When in hell did all this happen?"

"He asked me last night. And you haven't heard all of it, Helen."

"What else is there?" Helen smiled because Elaine sounded so happy.

"I'm going to have a baby. Isn't it wonderful?"

Helen laughed. "Oh, I just love it! How many months are you?"

"I'm only six weeks, but I have a doctor's appointment tomorrow."

Helen started to cry. "I am so glad for you."

"I can't wait for you to meet Dan. You'll love him, Helen."

"I'm sure I will. Lynn speaks so nicely of him. She loves him already."

"He's the best."

"Well, when is the wedding? Give me all the details so that I can start making arrangements now."

When Helen hung up the phone she smiled and went downstairs to make herself a cup of coffee. She still felt a bit tired and could feel a sore throat coming on. With her coffee, she crawled back into bed and thought about Elaine. She wondered what their mother would say and suddenly she felt an ache in her heart for the loss of Odessa. It would have been nice if she could have shared in this with Elaine.

All of a sudden, Helen's heart dropped. What if Robert went to Elaine's wedding? She didn't want to be anywhere near him. And, what about Harriet? Without a doubt, she would be there. It didn't matter – she had to attend Elaine's wedding no matter what.

The phone rang and she cleared her throat.

"Mom, are you awake?"

"Yes, love."

"You don't sound too well."

"Would you believe it, now I have a sore throat. I'm tired because I stayed up until three this morning reading. You know I can't stop when I'm into a good book."

"You should take it easy for the rest of the day. You push too hard sometimes and you never catch up on your rest. You need a break, Mom." There was concern in Lynn's voice.

"I know and you're right. Hey, enough about me. I just got off the phone with Elaine."

"She called me too, but I wasn't surprised. I knew they were in love. Anyone could see it, and he's so nice, Mom."

"I'll be there for the wedding of course."

"Great, we can spend some time together. I was busy working and studying when you were here last time."

Helen knew something was bothering Lynn. "What is it, honey?"

"I got a letter from Dad yesterday."

Helen sighed. "I gave him your address and a picture of you."

"Mom, what should I do?"

"This is your call. Do whatever your heart tells you to and everything will take care of itself."

"But, I'm just not sure."

"Then, don't do anything. Take your time. Eventually, you'll know what to do and I'll be behind you whatever you decide."

"That makes sense. I'll be glad when you get here, Mom."

"I'm looking forward to it, sweetheart." She was happy about seeing her daughter and Elaine's wedding. It was the rest of what could happen that was bothering her.

After she hung up from Lynn, Helen decided to stay inside, rest and work on the cold she was getting. She had to make sure she felt fine for her trip to L.A. next month.

That night, Helen finished six chapters of her new book. And as she reread them, she felt sad. This part of her book was very depressing. The character watched her child die in her arms. Maybe I'll change it, Helen thought. She would change it to watching her husband die in her arms. Or maybe he would die alone.

Chapter 21

Robert walked out of the restaurant feeling better than he had for months. It was time for him to move on. Helen had ignored every one of his phone calls. That sweet, loving woman had turned out to be someone he didn't really know at all. He never imagined she would drop him without an explanation – without so much as a five-minute phone call. They had known each other too long to have it end this way. But, it was over.

He still hadn't furnished the house, holding on to the hope that she would one day make things right between them. He still wanted to marry her and wanted her to decorate his house as she pleased. But it looked like that would never happen. And, he just didn't understand it. It had been so long since he loved someone so much. But, just as fast as she had returned to his life, she was gone again and this time it was worse. This time, he truly loved her. It wasn't anything like the young love they'd had before.

He was driving down Wilshire, back to the office after his meeting with two well-known lawyers. In fact, one of them – Brad Lawson – had defeated Robert in his very first case. Brad was smart, quick thinking, and Robert had never forgotten him. He never imagined that Brad and his two partners would ask him to join their firm. The first time they'd met, he'd asked for a couple of days to think it over. The next time they met, he accepted. He had gotten his experience at the City District Attorney's office, but it was time to move on and make a change.

He turned onto Spring Street, still thinking of Helen and what could have been. He tried to imagine her in every way, except for in the arms of another man. He even thought of driving straight to the airport and flying to Atlanta right now. But, what if she was with another lover? Sure, he thought, he could always kill the man with his bare hands, but that wouldn't get her back. He sighed. Why do I keep banging my head against this wall, he mused as he parked his car. It was over!

It had been a long day. Harriet had worked ten hours with no lunch break. She walked inside the house and the first thing she did was take the phone off the hook. Charles had become a nuisance, calling her day and night. She couldn't even hide in church. He was always waiting for her when she arrived and he'd take a seat right next to her. He followed her around, begging her to give him another chance. As far as Harriet was concerned, he was a big man with a small brain and it seemed to get smaller everyday.

After a few weeks, Charles gave up and two months later, he was married. Velma Turner, his new wife, was also a member of the church and had had her eyes on Charles for years. She was quiet, tall and wore a light brown wig and homemade clothing that was poorly sewn.

Harriet was relieved to be rid of Charles and kept herself busy in the church. She continued to teach Sunday School and attended every prayer meeting. She had accepted Elaine's invitation to her wedding, but later remembered it was the same week as the church retreat. And, who would marry simple Elaine anyway, she thought? She wondered if that sinful sister of hers, Helen, would be coming for the wedding. Probably. And, she would bring that no-good daughter of hers too. Harriet was content to live her life without her sisters. She wasn't even sad anymore over her divorce. She was happy now, in the church where she belonged. The church was where she would stay, because she didn't have anything or anyone else.

Robert turned in his resignation just as he finished one case and before he could be assigned to another. He'd made a lunch date with Anita. Though they were friends, they hadn't spent much time together lately, and he needed someone to talk to. They walked to their favorite Chinese restaurant and asked to be seated at a table in the back where they could talk in private.

Anita was glad to have this time with her friend. She knew something was bothering him. "You've been quiet lately,

Robert. It seems you have a lot on your mind."

"I thought I had been doing a good job hiding it, Anita."

"Maybe from everyone else, but not me. We've known each other too long, dear."

He tried to smile. "You're right."

She reached across the table and touched his hand. "Would you like to talk about it?"

He nodded as the waiter brought their iced teas. "I don't know what happened, Anita, but I've lost Helen. I think I'm just accepting it, even though I've been hoping something would change for weeks."

"When was the last time you talked to her?"

"It's been months. If was off, just like that," he mused.

"No explanation?"

"Nothing. I didn't think she was the type to drop out of sight and not say why..." As Robert spoke the words, he wondered about the night he had spent with Mona. But, Helen couldn't know about that, could she? "If I did something to her, you would think she would call me and curse me out."

"Unless it was something so bad that she can't even talk about it," Anita said.

"I think she has someone else in her life."

"Do you really believe that, Robert?"

"I don't know. I have a hard time believing that she doesn't love me anymore. We were so good together."

Anita sighed. "Well, something has happened, Robert." She touched his hand again. "Maybe she doesn't love you anymore and you're having a hard time facing it. Sometimes things hurt us so badly, that we can't admit them to ourselves."

Robert shook his head. "No. I could face it, if that was the truth. But, it's not. Like I said, we had too much together. We had a magic that one finds only once in a life time."

"If you really believe that, then maybe you should go and talk to her, Robert. Get to the bottom of this."

"I've tried that. But it never works."

"What happened?" Anita asked with surprise.

"Nothing. Either she was out of town or not home. She refuses to answer any of my calls."

As they ate shrimp fried rice, noodles, egg rolls and soup,

Anita continued to listen to Robert though she was having a hard time believing his whole story. She knew Robert – if he wanted to get to Helen, he would at all costs. But, there was some reason he was afraid to face her. What could it be, Anita wondered? She wanted to ask if it had something to do with Mona. She hadn't seen Robert and Mona together too much recently, but she had caught Mona snooping through Robert's desk. And, even though Mona had come up with an explanation, Anita knew she was lying.

Robert continued talking and Anita nodded, only half listening. She had to have a plan to help her friend. She would look through Mona's desk today, after everyone had left. Maybe she would be able to find an answer to all of this.

Mona looked at her desk and saw the brown envelope with the second set of pictures. She would hold on to them in case she needed to remind Helen of Robert's unfaithfulness. Not that anything had happened between her and Robert since that night, but it would. Mona only needed time and it would all fall into place for her. She got him into bed once and she could do it again.

She glanced at the small clock on her desk. It was after one and Robert and Anita hadn't returned yet. She was told that they used to go to lunch together often. Well, that would stop. Robert was hers, and she was not going to share him with anyone. He was probably spilling his guts to Anita about his breakup with Helen. Mona smiled. So what? There wasn't anything anyone could do to help him now. She gathered her purse and walked out of the building into the warm air.

It was six o'clock before Robert got himself together to leave. He passed by Mona's empty desk and stuck his head in Anita's office.

"What are you still doing here?" he asked. "Shouldn't you be home waiting for some lucky guy to come over?"

She laughed. "I wish."

He waved good-bye and walked out. When he was gone, she leaned back in her chair. She had fallen in love with Robert on the first day he started and over the years, they'd become good friends. He was a good, decent man and she didn't like seeing him hurting this way.

177

She hurried to Mona's desk and started rummaging through the drawers. She looked at the Rolodex, still not sure what she was looking for. She thumbed through the phone numbers and looked at papers on top of the desk. Nothing. Anita stood up straight, one hand on her hip. Damn, there had to be something here. She pulled open the file cabinet and found a brown envelope sitting in front of the files. She opened it and frowned in shock. One by one, she looked at the pictures in disbelief. How had this happened? Why would Robert do this if he loved Helen?

She eased the pictures back and sighed. Maybe if Helen didn't live so far away, he would have had no reason to play house with Mona, she whispered, as she turned the envelope over. It was then that she saw the name and address – Helen's address. Oh, no, she thought. Did Mona mail these?

She pulled out the pictures again and studied them. Somehow, these weren't the pictures of two people in love. Robert looked strained. She could see it now, but she wasn't sure that Helen would be able to see it that way. She wondered if Robert even knew that these pictures had been taken. And, who took them anyway? This is really getting messy, she thought. That's what Robert had been so afraid of – that Helen knew about this affair. This was why Helen hadn't returned his calls.

Her thoughts were interrupted when she heard footsteps and with trembling hands, she dropped the pictures to the floor. She looked up and saw the maintenance crew walking in her direction and she managed to push the pictures back into the envelope before one of them got close enough to see them. As the maintenance crew walked past her to the other end of the office, she wondered what she should do next.

She grabbed her coat and with the pictures left the office. She wasn't sure what she would do, but she would take the pictures home and then decide. She didn't care that Mona might discover them missing in the morning. What could she do about it, anyway? She couldn't go around the office asking for them. Anita smiled, pleased with the image of Mona when she discovered that the pictures were missing.

Anita got in her car and headed home, but within a few

minutes, changed her mind. As she headed towards Baldwin Hills, she looked at the envelope in the seat beside her. Robert, my friend, you have truly fucked up big time.

Anita rang his doorbell twice before he opened the door. He was surprised, but could tell by the expression on her face that something was terribly wrong. She walked past him, saying nothing, as he closed the door behind her.

"I hope I'm not disturbing you," she said, still looking very serious.

He was worried. "No, what is it?"

"Something very important. Something that couldn't wait."

"Okay, come on into the kitchen," he answered, frowning.

She followed him and when they got to the counter, she said, "I think you need to sit down before I show you why I'm here."

He sat slowly on the stool, wondering what was going to happen. "What is it, Anita?"

She was silent for a moment. "Why didn't you tell me about you and Mona? Not that you owe me an explanation. But, when you told me about your breakup with Helen, you said she broke it off without a word. You only told me half the story."

He ran his fingers through his hair and sighed. "For Pete's sake, Anita, what are you talking about?"

She gave him the envelope. "Turn it over and see who it's addressed to and then ask me what I'm talking about."

When he looked at the name on the brown package, he was more bewildered than before. "What is this?"

"Open it and see for yourself."

When he looked at the pictures, he paused, then looked at Anita as if he was looking for an answer. He turned the envelope over and over, looking at Helen's name and then it hit him. "These pictures were sent to Helen." It was more a statement than a question. "Where did you get these?" he asked, as he threw the pictures on the counter. "Where did this trash come from, Anita?"

"I found them in Mona's desk. This could just be a second set."

"Oh, God, Anita. This isn't what it looks like." He banged his fist on the counter. Pain ricocheted up his arm as he cursed in frustration. "Damn, how could she do this to me – to Helen?"

Anita grabbed his hand. "Well, how did she get these pictures, Robert?"

He got up and paced. "It's a long story," he said angrily. "I could just break her neck, Anita."

"How can you say that," Anita said, as she pointed to the pictures. "You two don't exactly look like sister and brother, you know. How can you break her neck for something that you participated in?" she asked with disgust.

"It's not what you think," he snapped.

"Well, the pictures say that you two have been together."

He told Anita about Mona's first visit to his house and said these pictures had to be taken the second time she returned. "I knew she was up to something when she asked if she could come over here. But I had no idea she would go to such extremes."

"She is treacherous, Robert. There's no doubt about that. What are you going to do about her?"

"I'll take care of it. I'm going to let her know that it doesn't matter what happens between me and Helen, there is no way I want to have anything to do with Mona."

Anita smiled and nodded her head.

"Oh, Anita. I hope it's not too late for me and Helen."

He walked her to the car, kissed her on the cheek and watched as she drove off. He went back into his house and looked at the pictures again. Damn. He tore them into small pieces and tossed them into the trash basket. He wanted to go to Mona tonight, but knew it would be better tomorrow – when he had cooled off a bit. It was a good thing he had accepted that new job. He sat on the bar stool with his hands covering his face. When he looked at the clock, it was already past nine. It had been a long, tiring day and he knew it was going to be an even longer night.

Chapter 22

Darlene watched as Helen closed the suitcases and sat them on the floor by the couch. "Girl, you're throwing those bags around like you're angry or something. What's bothering you?"

Helen took a deep breath. "I just don't want to go. I'm only doing this for Elaine's sake. It's a damn shame that I don't want to go home, though I don't really call Los Angeles home anymore."

"Maybe it won't be so bad," Darlene said. "And, the wedding should be nice."

"Yeah, I spoke to Elaine last night and she sounds so happy. But, damn, supposed Robert is there? And what will Harriet say to me? Shit, Darlene."

Darlene got up from her chair and sat next to Helen on the couch. "Calm down, Helen. I think you're worrying for no reason at all. Elaine has enough sense not to invite Harriet and Robert to come under the same roof."

Helen looked up to face her. "You know, I'll bet you're right. Why would she invite Robert when Harriet doesn't even want his name mentioned in her presence? Why didn't I think of that?"

"Yeah, and even if he did come, this would be your chance to say good-bye to him. You guys still have unfinished business and I think you'll feel better when it's all done. It would take a load off your shoulders."

Helen was nodding like she agreed, but said, "I don't think I can do that. It's too soon for me. I'm still too angry. Anyway, I can't keep sitting around wondering what's going to happen. I just have to face whatever is ahead of me, right?"

"Right! So, come on so that I can get you to the airport and take my tired ass home. I've been awake since two this morning."

Helen sighed. "Tell me about it. I didn't get any sleep either worrying about this weekend."

"Stop worrying! Just go to the wedding, go out with Lynn and enjoy yourself. Now, let me get you to the airport."

They picked up the suitcases and walked out the door.

The weather in Los Angeles was beautiful. The sun shone warm, and the minute Helen stepped outside and felt the sun against her face, she felt better. She would make it her business to have a good time.

Lynn picked her up from the airport and they stayed with Elaine. Elaine ordered pizza and beer for dinner and they sat in Elaine's bedroom laughing and talking.

"Elaine, have you thought of Mama at all today?" Helen asked.

"It's funny you should ask that. I thought of her all day. I wish she could have been here for my wedding," Elaine said, as she looked down at the threads in her king-size bed spread. "Maybe my getting married would have made her respect me more."

"Honey, you deserved respect whether you were married or not. She was our mother and shouldn't have respected us just because of that," Helen said.

Lynn looked from her mother to her aunt and listened to their discussion. She couldn't understand her grandmother's way of thinking. She wished she could have known her better," she thought as she took a drink of her mother's beer and frowned at the bitterly tingle.

"Still, I wish Mama was here," Elaine said.

The next morning, they were up at seven. Helen cooked breakfast: eggs, bacon and grits.

"I can't eat anything, Helen," Elaine said as she walked into the kitchen looking as though she was ill.

"Yes you can. You have to have something in your stomach." Helen pulled a chair from the table. "Now, sit and have a good, country breakfast."

Lynn stuck her head in the door and inhaled. "Smells good, Mom." She sat next to her aunt. "I haven't had breakfast like this since I was home."

"That's what I figured," Helen said, and poured orange juice for Lynn.

"Since you cooked, I'll do the dishes. And then you can help Aunt Elaine get ready." Both Helen and Lynn smiled at the nervous bride-to-be.

Helen and Lynn loved Dan and were convinced that he would make Elaine very happy. Helen could see that he loved her sister and it warmed her heart. She would have no reason to worry about her sister any longer. The second half of Elaine's life would be wonderful.

Every time the door bell rang, Helen jumped. But to Helen's surprise, Harriet never came. She never called or anything to congratulate Elaine on her wedding day. Though Helen was sad that Harriet didn't care about Elaine, she knew it was better this way. If Harriet wanted to stay away, that was her choice.

The wedding took place in a small chapel on Beverly Boulevard. It was a small gathering, only 18 people including Dan's brother, Larry, who was a large man with the same red hair as Dan's. They celebrated at Elaine's apartment after the wedding and shortly after, the newlyweds left for Mexico City. Helen spent the next day with Lynn, enjoying the day shopping, going to the movies and having dinner together.

Lynn had gone back to her dorm and Helen was packing her bags preparing to leave when she heard the door bell ring. Since all of Elaine's friends knew that she was on her honeymoon, Helen decided not to answer the door. But then, she thought it might have been Lynn and she rushed to the door. When she opened it, she felt the heat creep into her cheeks.

"Harriet! We thought you were away."

"I just got back, Helen," she said as she walked inside. "I flew back earlier than I had planned."

"Well, you're too late, sister dear. Elaine and her husband already left."

"I didn't come here to see Elaine. I wanted to talk to you." She looked at the suitcases sitting by the door. "And, it looks like I'm just in time."

Helen followed Harriet into the living room. "Well, what is it that you want, Harriet? I know you're not here to inquire about my health," Helen said angrily, upset that Harriet didn't even ask about her sister's wedding.

Harriet almost smiled at her sister's remark. Helen always did have a smart mouth. "I talked to my Pastor and he told me that I needed to talk to you. He feels that I shouldn't carry this around in my heart. We might not like each other, but at least you should know why."

Helen just looked at Harriet. She couldn't imagine what Harriet had to say and her heart started to race. "What is it, Harriet?

Harriet sighed and took a deep breath. "There's a lot that you don't know and now is the time. It all happened when I was fifteen years old." It was coming back to Harriet as if it had just happened. "You and Elaine were in the backyard playing and Elaine was crying because you kept winning. I laughed as I watched the two of you and then walked into the kitchen. Mama and Daddy were arguing loudly and they didn't know that I had come into the room. I stopped, because I heard Mama say my name and I wanted to know what she was saying about me. I thought I had done something bad." Harriet closed her eyes as if she were seeing the moment in her mind. "Mama was saying that it wasn't my fault. I remember thinking, what wasn't my fault? I hadn't done anything wrong."

Helen moved to the edge of her chair. Her throat felt dry, but she couldn't move.

"I hid so that Mama and Daddy couldn't see me," Harriet continued. "And I kept listening. Mama said that she was tired of hearing the same old thing every time he got mad about something. She said she was tired of him throwing this up in her face. Daddy said that if she would have told him that she was pregnant with another man's bastard, he wouldn't have married her. Daddy said that I was stupid, just like my drunken daddy and that I would never be as bright or as pretty as his children – especially you, Helen."

Helen sat up straight in her chair, her eyes wide with shock. A horrendous migraine had suddenly filled her head. "You mean...you mean, Daddy wasn't your father?" Helen stammered.

Harriet nodded. "Mama was pregnant by another man when she and Daddy got married. She said that she would always protect me, take care of me because he would never love me. Mama said that Daddy only loved you so much because you looked just like him."

"I can't believe this..."

"It's true. Daddy even asked Mama if Elaine was his and she cried saying that she never let another man touch her after they were married. I think he knew she was telling the truth, but he was just mean and bitter. He laughed in her face and called her a whore." Harriet sucked in her breath. "I ran down the back alley and cried for hours. I couldn't believe it, but I had heard it with my own ears. The man I called Daddy wasn't my father and he hated me. And from that day, I hated him. I hated you and I hated Elaine. I felt like an outsider and that's why Mama loved me so much. She knew that I was hurting deeply and that I had no one but her. And, she felt guilty and responsible for me."

Helen felt tears burn her eyes. "But we were her children too, Harriet. We needed her too. She shouldn't have turned her back on me and Elaine because of a mistake that she made. That wasn't right."

"I know, but that was her way of making me feel loved."

"And, Elaine and I felt hated and unwanted," Helen snapped.

"That was just her way. She had to do something because there was no love in their marriage. I never saw them kiss or touch. I guess he found out about me right after they married. It was miserable living in the same house with a man that I knew hated me."

"I can't believe that he hated you, Harriet. You were probably just a reminder of what Mama had done. I don't think he blamed you for it. I just wish I would have known."

"Why? It wouldn't have made a difference," Harriet sighed.

Yes, it would have because I would have let you know how much Elaine and I loved you. But, I always thought you knew." Helen felt a tear roll down her cheek. "Did Mama ever tell you about your father?"

"No, she said it didn't matter."

"But, don't you want to know him?"

"To tell you the truth...no. It's too late," she said as she fumbled with the keys to her car. "My Pastor said that I should tell you all of this so that you would understand. It won't change things, but at least you know."

Helen got up and walked closer to her sister. "Now that it's all out, can't we try to be like we once were? We were so close," Helen said with a glint of hope in her eyes.

Harriet looked at her for a few moments. "No, I'm sorry, Helen. I've felt this way for so long. Things cannot go back to the way they were when we were children. Everything has gone too far and gone on for too long."

The sisters walked to the door together. Helen wanted to hold Harriet in her arms, but like Harriet had said, too much had happened.

When Harriet stepped outside, she turned to face Helen. "How's Lynn?"

Helen smiled. "She's fine, Harriet. Thanks for asking."

"Good. I'm glad she's okay."

They stood facing each other as if trying to hold on to this last moment together. Both knew it their hearts that they would never see one another again.

Harriet turned to leave and Helen closed the door behind her. Leaning against the door, Helen wanted to cry, but knew it wouldn't make things any better. How could all of this have happened? So much had gone wrong in their lives. That night, she boarded the plane with a heavy heart, knowing that her life would never be the same.

Robert had been trying to decide, but he knew it would do no good to get on a plane and go to Atlanta. What would he say to her anyway? The pictures said a lot more than he could. He remembered how Anita had reacted and he knew Helen's response would be the same or maybe even worse.

The visit to Mona's apartment that morning had been ugly. She had denied everything until he pulled the pictures from the envelope and shoved them in her hand. She dropped the envelope and tried to hold on to him, but he pushed her away. He told her that he was leaving to work for another company and that he didn't ever want to see her again.

"Can't you see how much I love you, Robert?" she begged.

"I can't believe you have the unmitigated gall to use the word love. You don't know what it is to love. You are too selfish to know." She reached for him again, but he pushed her so hard it frightened her. "Go to hell, Mona. Just stay out of my way. I'll have Anita change your job duties; I don't want to see your face." He stormed off, not looking behind. He knew if he had stayed any longer...he didn't want to think of just how bad he could have hurt her. How could he have been so blind? He was so angry, he didn't go to work at all that day. He couldn't stand the thought of being near her.

That night, he sat at his desk trying to read, but he couldn't concentrate. He stood at the window, looking out into the large back yard. He had waited over twenty years to see Helen, to hold her, kiss her and love her. But now it was over. He couldn't keep making a fool of himself running back and forth between Los Angeles and Atlanta. His hopes and dreams were ripped to shreds, thanks to Mona and one night of weakness. But, he had to find a way to go on with his life. He sighed. How many times had he said that? But that was before he knew about the pictures.

The next morning, when Robert walked into his office, Mona had not reported for work. Just as well, he thought. He didn't want to be any place near that woman.

Anita walked into his office before he had a chance to sit down. "I see you're secretary isn't here yet, and it's almost ten. She didn't come in yesterday either and she hasn't called or anything. I don't know what happened."

"I saw her yesterday morning," Robert said hanging his jacket on a hook.

Anita sat in front of him and saw the tiredness in his eyes. "So, how did it go with her?"

"She lied, of course, until I showed her the pictures. Then, she said she loved me, but I didn't believe a word of it. I have never been so angry in my life," he said with frustration, and Anita nodded, understanding what he must be feeling.

"You got yourself into a mess, my friend. Be careful the next time you unzip your pants for someone."

He groaned, and she got up and went to her desk to try to find help for Robert. She was sure that sooner or later, Mona would call in sick.

The next morning, Anita rushed into Robert's office.

"Have you heard the news, yet?" Anita's voice trembled.

He laid his pen on the desk. "What?"

"One of the secretaries brought me this." She unfolded the newspaper for Robert. "Here, read it."

He read the first paragraph word for word. A man Mona once lived with had shot her twice in the chest. She was dead on arrival at the hospital. The man had been arrested and would likely be charged with murder since he had already confessed. With trembling hands, he put the paper down, before picking it back up and rereading the short article. "Did you see what he said about why he shot her?" he asked Anita.

"Yes," she said her voice still shaking. "She stole $15,000 from him. She closed the account out, leaving him with nothing. The rest of the article said that she had been accused of doing this before." She frowned as she watched Robert stand and go to the window. "Are you all right?"

"Yes...it's just that this is a bit shocking. God, you never know what is going on in a person's life."

"I feel sorry for her. I hope now, she has some peace."

Robert nodded as Anita left his office and closed the door behind her. Robert picked up the newspaper and read the article over and over again. He couldn't believe it. Finally, he folded the paper and set it aside. He had a lot of work to do. But, he couldn't keep his mind focused. When he thought of Mona, he thought of Helen. And, when he thought of Helen, he thought of Mona. It was such a shame. Mona was so young; she had so much to learn about life. But people had to know that there was a price to pay for using others. And, Mona had paid a high price.

Chapter 23

Helen went to visit Darlene at the same time every morning, but for the first time since the bakery was opened, Darlene wasn't there. Mrs. Beasley told Helen that Darlene was back in the hospital. Helen was shocked. "But why? What happened?" she asked afraid of what she might hear.

"We don't know yet. She wasn't herself yesterday. She had a bad headache," Mrs. Beasley said in her shaky, high-pitched voice. "I told her to go home and rest and not to worry about coming in this morning. I knew she was ill when she took my advice without an argument. But, when she went to see the doctor yesterday, they admitted her to the hospital." Mrs. Beasley was talking so fast, all her words seemed to be running together.

Helen headed for the hospital. She was upset. Maybe it was time for Darlene to sell that damn bakery, she thought. She drove hurriedly, almost hitting another car and the sound of the brakes frightened her. When she felt beads of sweat on her forehead, she pulled the car to the side of the road and took deep breaths until she composed herself.

When she got to the hospital, she was told she had to wait – the doctor was in with Darlene and she would be able to go in as soon as he finished. She anxiously paced the long hall-way until the nurse informed her that she could go in.

Helen walked into the room and pointed her finger at her friend. "I leave for a few days and what in the hell do you do? I can't trust you alone, Darlene."

Darlene coughed, feeling weak as she tried to laugh. As Helen pulled a chair close to the bed, she noticed that Darlene looked as weak as she sounded.

"What did the doctor say, honey?"

"The same thing as before. I have a weak heart and it has

weakened even more. He says my heart is getting weaker everyday."

Helen was glad that she was sitting, because if she had been standing, she knew her legs would have given out. She was frightened out of her mind. "Have you called Valerie?" was all she could think to say.

"I did this morning. I almost didn't, but you never know what may happen..." she squeezed Helen's hand.

"Don't talk like that! Nothing will happen. But I am glad that I am here with you," she said, her voice shaking with fear.

"So am I. I missed you, Helen Graham." Darlene was choking back tears. "Valerie will be here in the morning."

"Good, I'll pick her up at the airport," Helen said. She wondered if Darlene was telling her everything. Darlene looked tired, so Helen stood to leave. "You look tired, honey. I think you should rest."

"I am a bit tired today. The doctor gave me a shot so that I could sleep. I can feel it now."

"Okay, I'll be back later."

Darlene nodded.

"If you wake up before I get back, call me. I'm not working today, so I won't be doing anything."

Darlene was almost asleep as she nodded again. Helen walked out the room with the feeling that her friend was much sicker than she was admitting and Helen was more afraid than ever. She walked to her car with tears running down her cheeks.

The next morning, when Helen arrived at the airport to meet Valerie's plane, she was informed that the plane had landed a half-hour early. When Helen looked around, she realized that Valerie had probably taken a cab to the hospital and by the time she got there, Valerie was just walking in the door. They headed to Darlene's room together.

Helen was shocked. Darlene looked even weaker than she did yesterday and she hoped it was the medication. Darlene had dark circles under her eyes and couldn't sit up very long by herself. The tears in Valerie's eyes began to form as she looked at her sister. They talked for a short time, but then the doctor told them that Darlene needed her rest.

Helen drove Valerie to Darlene's house and helped her

carry her luggage inside. "Seems like we just did this not too long ago," Helen said.

"Nine months, two days to be exact," Valerie respon-ded as she wiped her eyes with a tissue. She sat down on the couch and Helen joined her. "While you were saying good-bye to Darlene, I talked to the doctor and he said her heart is getting weaker. It doesn't look good."

Helen's mouth flew open. She had to hold on to the arm of the couch for support.

"Our mother died of the same thing," Valerie continued. "She was overweight, eating everything that she should have stayed away from. Heart disease runs in our family. That's why I'm so careful of what I eat and that's why I'm so hard on Darlene."

Helen was shaking her head in disbelief and tears were running down her cheeks. She couldn't think about losing her friend; she had lost so much during the past year. "We shouldn't give up so quickly," Helen said. "She's not dead. All she needs is a little rest – just time to recuperate. She needs time away from the bakery. Maybe she even needs to sell it. She doesn't need the money."

Valerie nodded with Helen, but Helen wasn't facing the truth. She knew what was happening to her sister. Their mother had been in and out of the hospital when she and Darlene were children and now Valerie felt like she was reliving it all over again.

"I wished I had stayed longer the last time," Valerie said.

"That wouldn't have done any good."

"I don't know. Maybe. But, at the least I would have been here close to her. She's my sister." And, it would have given me more time with her, Valerie thought to herself, but she didn't dare say that to Helen. She could tell that this was hard on Helen and it would be even harder if Darlene were to die.

Helen was tired of this talk. She knew that the only thing that was wrong was that Darlene needed rest. Valerie was simply overreacting.

Valerie reached for Helen's hand and said, "Why don't you go home and get some rest. We'll all be sick if we don't get some sleep. You know the nurse will call us if anything changes."

Helen managed a smile, but it was hard. Valerie put her arm around her shoulder and walked Helen to the door. "Maybe Darlene will be stronger by the time we go back to see her later," Helen said with such hope that it made Valerie want to cry.

"Yes, maybe."

As soon as Helen left, Valerie went straight to the phone and called her husband, asking him to take the next flight to Atlanta. She was preparing for the inevitable and she knew in her heart what was going to happen. She lay on the couch and cried herself to sleep.

Several hours later, Helen picked Valerie up and they returned to the hospital. Helen held up a gown she had bought for Darlene. "How do you like this?" Helen asked.

Darlene opened her eyes wider. "It's beautiful. I'll wear it tomorrow." Her voice was still weak and shaky and Helen noticed that Darlene drifted in and out of sleep.

Helen sat on the edge of the bed and had a terrible feeling that she was losing Darlene. This can't be happening, she thought as she tried to push the negative thoughts out of her mind. Tomorrow would be a better day. She had to believe that.

They left the hospital at eight that night and Helen drove Valerie home without a word spoken between them. When Helen got home, she couldn't eat or sleep. She felt as if she was losing control of her life. She was up all night and prayed that her friend would be better when she returned to the hospital the next day.

She got up early the next day and showered as the daylight peeked through her blinds. She phoned Valerie, but there was no word from the hospital.

"Well, no news is good news," Helen said.

"Maybe..." That was all she had the heart to say to Helen.

As she stepped from the elevator, they saw two nurses and a doctor running into Darlene's room. Helen felt her knees buckling beneath her. Valerie ran to the door, but the nurse stopped her and said they would have to wait outside.

"Please take a seat in the waiting room. We're doing everything we can for your sister," the nurse said, remembering Valerie from yesterday.

"But, what happened?" Valerie pleaded, as she held onto the nurse's arm.

"I'll get back to you as soon as I can. I promise." The nurse was gone before Valerie could say another word.

Helen took Valerie by the arm and led her to the waiting room. This was like a nightmare and it was happening so fast. They held on to each other and cried, both knowing what was about to happen.

As another nurse ran from the nurse's station, Valerie jumped up and caught the nurse by the arm. "Please tell me what's going on?"

The nurse hesitated. She really didn't have time to stop, but she could see the fear on Valerie's face. "Your sister had a heart attack," the nurse said, then ran down the hall.

They watched her disappear into Darlene's room and then they returned to their seats, both in shock. They sat silently, each lost in their own thoughts, before Valerie started crying silently. Helen needed to get away. She went down to the coffee shop to get coffee for both of them. She returned to the waiting room and paced the floor, hoping that they would know something soon. She stood at the window and watched the cars move in and out of the parking lot. It seemed cold outside though she hadn't noticed earlier. She was sure that if anything happened to Darlene, she would leave Atlanta. She shook her head. She couldn't think of life without Darlene.

Thinking of that made her think of Robert. She hadn't seen him in months, but at this moment, she needed him. She looked at Valerie sitting on the couch, leaning back with her eyes closed. They had been waiting over an hour. What was taking so long, she wondered? At that moment, the doctor came out of Darlene's room and started in their direction. Helen and Valerie looked at each other and when the doctor stopped in front of them, he didn't have to say a word. Darlene was gone, they both knew it.

The doctor started to speak, moving his hands and Helen thought she would scream. She took a deep breath and inhaled from deep inside. "Valerie," she whispered.

Valerie held Helen's hand tight. The doctor was saying that he was sorry. That was just the way the actors in the movies started when they couldn't save a patient, Helen thought.

"Her heart was too weak, too damaged." He apologized again. He went on and on, but Helen couldn't hear his words any longer. She saw the doctor finally walk away and felt her legs disappearing from under her. Her best friend had just died and yet, everyone was still talking and moving around her as if nothing had happened.

Valerie began to speak, but Helen couldn't hear her words. Instead, she fell into the darkness that had begun to take over. Her body and mind were floating away from the pain and grief into a sea of darkness.

When she opened her eyes, Valerie was standing over her. "How do you feel, Helen?"

Helen sat up and looked around the small, white room. "Where am I?"

"You don't remember?"

Helen closed her eyes and opened them again. And, the tears started flowing. "Oh, God, Darlene." She held her face in her hands. "What time is it?"

"Five o'clock."

"What happened?"

"The doctor said that your brain couldn't take anymore and your body blocked some of the pain – at least for a little while. We'd better go home and get some rest. My husband flew in an hour ago. He's at Darlene's place. There was no reason for him to come here," she said, choked up. "I asked him to come yesterday."

"That was smart." Helen picked up her purse from the small table beside the bed and sighed. "Yes, Lord, I'm ready to go home."

They said very little on the drive to Darlene's house. Valerie was still crying.

"I'm taking her body back to San Diego so that she can be next to our mother, brother and grandparents."

"When are you leaving?"

"The day after tomorrow, if.... she's ready by then. I may have to stay an extra day. I just want this over with as soon as possible. I can't take this for very long."

"I'll go with you."

"I could use your help, Helen. After the funeral, I'll come

back and pack her things and close up the bakery," Valerie continued to cry.

"I'll help with that too." Helen turned her head so that Valerie couldn't see her tears.

When Helen stopped to let Valerie out of the car, she asked, "Won't you come in for a cup of tea, Helen?"

Helen sighed. She didn't want to be alone. "I guess I could use one."

They were sitting at the table in the kitchen. Darlene's house was always so neat and organized, just like the bakery. It was impossible for Helen to imagine that Darlene would never be here again, sitting in this kitchen like they did so often. Her laughter would never be heard again. Helen's morning trips to the bakery were over. Their morning conversations would never take place again. But, all of these things would always be in Helen's heart.

"Helen, Helen?"

She almost dropped her cup on the table. "Oh, I'm sorry." Helen looked up and saw Valerie's husband standing in the doorway. He was so quiet, she had forgotten he was in the house with them. "My mind had wandered off." Helen felt tears trickle down her cheeks.

Valerie reached across the table and held her hand. "Honey, why don't you go home, or better yet...sleep here?"

Helen ran her fingers through her hair. "I do need to get some sleep. And, I have to make my reservations. There's so much to do; I don't know where to begin."

"I'll make reservations so that you can go with us," Valerie said, and her husband smiled and nodded in agreement.

"Thanks. Oh, dear. I just realized how much I have to do." Helen grabbed her purse and keys and headed out the door. Holding hands, Valerie and her husband watched Helen drive off.

"Darlene was my sister, but Helen is going to miss her terribly, John. I don't know what she's going to do, but I know she's a strong woman and she'll make it."

Helen parked her car in the garage and sat back, closing her eyes. This was one of those times the car found its way home by itself. She didn't remember stopping for lights or stop signs. It was frightening as she realized it.

She walked into the living room and closed the blinds. She was exhausted. Whatever the doctor gave her at the hospital, she could feel it. She walked slowly up the stairs, pushing herself up one step at a time, and lay across her bed. How did this all happen so fast? Darlene seemed a bit tired before she left for Elaine's wedding, but for it to all end this way was more than she could understand.

Just last week, they were sitting in the bakery drinking coffee, eating banana nut bread, laughing and talking. And today, it was all over. She's gone, Helen thought.

She needed to tell Lynn. She picked up the phone, but then put it down again. She would call her tomorrow. After taking her shower, she crawled into bed, but she couldn't sleep. She went into the kitchen, made a cup of warm milk, then returned to her bedroom. She sat in her large chair, facing the window. The night was clear and quiet. The stars sparkled as though they were lighting up the world.

She closed her eyes. It would be easier to make a move now that her friend was gone. There was nothing keeping her in Atlanta. She knew that Lynn wasn't going to be returning and this was her chance to move closer to Lynn and Elaine. And, Elaine would be able to use her help after the baby was born.

Yes, she would move to Los Angeles. Her only wish was that she wouldn't run into Robert. She never wanted to see him again. She felt a pain in her stomach and the swelling of her heart. And she hurt for all of her losses. She wiped her eyes with a tissue, got back into bed and slept.

She slept until eight the next morning, surprised that she was able to get some sleep. Now, she had to get ready to help Valerie. They had to take care of Darlene. And, after that, it would be time for her to take care of herself. She had to make her plans to return to Los Angeles.

Chapter 24

"Oh, no, Mom! Not Aunt Darlene!"

"Yes, honey. I know it's a shock, but try to calm down." Helen was trying to hold back her tears while she talked to her daughter.

"When? How?"

"Yesterday. She was in the hospital when I got back. I knew she hadn't been feeling too well, but I had no idea she was so ill. I thought she only needed rest."

"Do you want me to come home, Mom?" Lynn asked as she cried.

"No, honey. Valerie is taking Darlene back to San Diego and I'll be going with her. We'll be there the day after tomorrow and Valerie expects the funeral to be in about three days." Helen sipped her coffee and took a small bite of her toast.

"Did Valerie see Darlene before she..." Lynn paused. She couldn't say the words.

"Yes, thank God. They got a chance to talk." At that moment, Helen remembered that Darlene had told her she had called Valerie. She must have known, Helen thought.

"I'll meet you in San Diego, but are you sure you're all right? You don't sound so good."

"I'm fine, considering..." Tears were falling from Helen's eyes, but she was trying not to break down for Lynn's sake. "I'm glad you'll be coming to San Diego, but make sure you don't drive at night. I don't want you on the road alone."

"Okay, I'll be fine..." she paused. "Mom, I can't believe Aunt Darlene is gone."

"I can't believe it myself," Helen said as she poured herself another cup of coffee.

"Call me as soon as you arrive in San Diego. When you get there, I'll come right down."

"Okay, honey. I love you. Good night."

Lynn sat on the edge of her bed holding a book and drinking her Coke. She hated being so far away from her mother at a time like this, when her mother needed her support. Maybe she should move back to Atlanta after all – so that she could be closer. What if it had been her mother instead of Darlene? Would she have gotten back in time? Best not to think about things like this, Lynn sighed. She slipped into her shoes, put on her jacket and walked to the library. But no matter what she did, she couldn't stop thinking about her Aunt Darlene.

Valerie called the next day to tell Helen that they would be leaving the next morning. She pulled out her suitcase. She didn't plan on taking much – just her black suit and a few casual clothes. She couldn't concentrate on anything. All she wanted to do was be free of the loneliness and grief that engulfed her.

She showered, washed her hair, made a ham and cheese sandwich, cup of tea and sat in the chair by her bedroom window. She thought of Darlene and the many memories that would always be with her: Darlene's last birthday, their four days in New York and the many other times they had cried and laughed together. My life won't be the same without you, honey, she thought as she crawled into bed and closed her eyes, falling asleep immediately.

The next day when Helen, Valerie and John arrived in San Diego, it was warm and as beautiful as Helen remembered. John and Valerie wanted her to stay with them, but she declined choosing a nearby hotel that she could stay at with Lynn. After getting settled in her room, Helen took a cab to Valerie's house. Married for over twenty years, their home was beautifully decorated with antiques. Valerie and John owned their own business and without children, they doted on one another.

The next day, the house was filled with family and friends and Helen and Lynn stayed with Valerie through the day. That evening, Lynn and Helen returned to the hotel and Lynn noticed how thin her mother looked. They watched television until midnight and went to sleep. Helen woke the morning of the funeral, surprisingly refreshed. This was not a day she was looking forward to, but she knew she had to be strong – for Valerie and Lynn.

They arrived at Valerie's house early, to help her with whatever she needed before the services. Helen and Lynn waited in the living room while Valerie and John finished getting ready. Lynn was watching her mother closely. She was quiet and still not eating much and Lynn was worried.

"Mom, it may do you some good if you stayed here an extra day." Lynn ran her fingers through her mother's hair.

Helen got up and stood at the window. She'd heard a car and wondered if it was someone coming to the house. But, it was the funeral cars arriving and Helen felt her stomach begin to cramp with nerves. "No, I'm going to leave as soon as this is over," Helen said still looking out the window. She was wearing her black Donna Karan suit, a pair of pearl earrings and a matching string of pearls around her neck.

Lynn got up and stood next to her mother. "I wish you would consider staying."

"I can't. I have to go to New York next week to see my editor."

Lynn put her hand on her mother's shoulder. "Mom, is there something bothering you?"

"Yes! My best friend will be buried today."

They looked at each other and hugged.

"I'm sorry, honey," Helen apologized. "Actually, there is something else on my mind." She took Lynn's hand and led her to the couch.

Lynn searched her mother's face for some sign. She looked so sad and lonely.

"I know that you want to remain in Los Angeles after you graduate…"

Lynn held her breath. Just yesterday, she had decided to move back to Atlanta. She knew her mother needed her.

Helen took Lynn's hand and held it tightly. "Well, I've been thinking of moving to Los Angeles. There's nothing for me in Atlanta anymore and you and Elaine are here in California. I think it's time for me to make a serious move."

Lynn grabbed her mother, her eyes cloudy with tears. "I'm so happy, Mom. It would be so neat for us to live closer together."

"Well, that's another reason why I have to get back to Atlanta. You know once I make up my mind, I waste no time."

Lynn's eyes lit up. "But Mom, you can stay an extra day to look around for a place to live. I can go with you."

"I'll be back in a couple of weeks to look around. First, I have to go to New York and then get back to Atlanta to put my townhouse on the market."

Lynn jumped up and down like a child. "I'm so happy, Mom. We'll be able to do so much together."

Their moment was interrupted when Valerie walked in, wiping her eyes. She looked at Helen as she slipped into her jacket. "It's time for us to go," she said solemnly. "The cars are waiting."

John took Valerie's arm and led her to the car. Helen and Lynn joined them, sitting across from them in the family limousine.

The service at the church was short – just the way Darlene would have wanted it and before Helen realized it, they were standing at the cemetery. Standing in front of the casket, listening to the Pastor seemed so familiar to Helen. It was just a year ago that she heard the same words at her mother's funeral. She looked up, and was surprised to see Elaine and Dan standing across from her. Elaine smiled and Helen smiled back. She didn't know they had returned from their honeymoon. Helen continued to glance around and noticed a tall, handsome man standing next to her. She could feel his eyes on her more than once and she wondered who he was. She hadn't seen him before.

After the services, everyone gathered at Valerie's house and Helen spent some time with Darlene's friends. As they chatted, Helen got up to get a glass of punch when she saw the man who had been standing next to her at the cemetery.

He looked at her and smiled. "Hi, I'm George Atkins. I went to high school with Darlene. Valerie tells me that you and Darlene were very close friends."

"Yes," Helen paused fighting back the tears that continued to come. "By the way, my name is Helen," she said shaking his hand.

"I know," he said. "Valerie told me and I also read your last book."

Helen smiled at him. "You don't look like a man who reads romance novels." Her eyes glanced over his body. He was well over six four, blessed with wide shoulders and a nice face. His eyes were slightly slanted and he had short cut black hair. His smile made her relax.

Helen and George sat down and talked for over an hour. He lived in San Francisco, had moved there right after high school. Helen told him she was moving to Los Angeles and he made her promise to call when she got settled.

"I'll take you around, show you all the things that have changed since you moved. And, it would give us a chance to know each other better, Helen."

Helen didn't want to tell him that she needed time to herself. She wasn't ready for a relationship and she was relieved when George left. She put his business card in her pocket and looked at her watch. It was already four.

By eight, Helen and Lynn were back at the hotel. They had said their good-byes to Valerie and John. Helen would see Valerie in a few days when she returned to Atlanta to finish up all the loose ends for her sister. Everything about Darlene will be gone, Helen mused. Her bakery, her home, her presence. Helen still couldn't imagine her life without her best friend.

"It's been a long day, hasn't it?" Helen said as she undressed and got into bed.

Lynn turned on the television and lay back on the bed. "I'm so tired. But, I figured I'd leave about noon tomorrow."

"I'm going to catch a morning flight. I'll get a taxi to the airport."

"Okay." Then, Lynn giggled. "I saw you talking to that handsome man."

"Yes, he was handsome. And he was nice too."

"I saw him give you his business card. Are you going to call him?"

"Do you think I should?"

"Yeah, why not?" she laughed and winked at her mother.

"Well, maybe I will. After I move to Los Angeles." Helen had never told Lynn about Robert and now she was glad she hadn't. There was nothing to tell.

Lynn talked until she noticed her mother wasn't answering and she saw that Helen was fast asleep. Lynn smiled and laid her head back on her pillow. She watched TV until her eyelids got heavy and she turned it off. "Goodnight, Mom," she whispered. She lay in the dark room and envisioned her mother living no more than thirty minutes away from her. She smiled and fell asleep.

Chapter 25

Lynn walked around her room, looking at all the spaces where Maria had kept her belongings. She stood in the spot where Maria had kept her plants and sadness swept over her. That was one thing she would always remember – Maria loved beautiful, green plants.

Lynn couldn't believe that she had lost her room mate, but family circumstances were pulling Maria from college. Maria's father had deserted his family and now Maria had to return home to help with her sisters and brother. Maria told Lynn that this was temporary – she would return to UCLA with her younger sister and go on with her life as she planned.

"This is just the way it has to be, Lynn," Maria had said before she got on the bus. "I have no choice. My people stick together in a crisis. I am just doing what I have to do. But don't worry. One day you'll see me and my sister at your doorstep."

"I hope so. I want you to come back as soon as you can. You know, I'll miss you."

"I'll miss you, too. But, we can visit each other. You can come to my house any time you want." Maria paused and shook her head. "Maybe you shouldn't come. My house is nothing like what you're used to. But, I promise to keep in touch."

"I want you to write often. Tell me everything that is going on, especially with all of your boyfriends."

Maria sighed. "Boyfriends? I won't have any time for that. I'll be working and going to school and cooking and washing. It won't be easy. But, I'm hoping the time will go by fast."

Now, as Lynn stood in her dorm room, she missed Maria

terribly even though she'd only been gone one day. And, she needed her friend now more than ever. Lynn had finally agreed to see her father and now she wondered if she had made the right decision. So many years had passed and she had such mixed emotions. But, she was curious enough to agree to the meeting. She wondered if she would even like him. She lay across her bed and closed her eyes, trying to visualize him the way he was the last time they were together. She remembered his smile and that he was tall. But, that was all. What does he want now, she thought to herself. But, it didn't make sense for her to sit in her room and ask questions. It was too late to change her mind. She picked up her purse and walked out the door.

As she drove to the hotel, Lynn wondered what her mother would think. Helen had left only two days ago, but Lynn hadn't mentioned this meeting. Though Lynn knew Helen would let her make her own decision about this.

She parked her green Mustang in the Airport Hilton and walked inside the lobby. She was wearing jeans and a white cotton blouse and her hair was tied back into a ponytail. The first person she saw in the lobby was Thomas. It had been years, but she knew it was him. She felt her palms getting sweaty and wondered if she was really getting a headache or just imagining it. As she got closer, she noticed his smile, but he didn't seem as tall as she remembered. He definitely looked older, but he was still handsome and his soft, brown eyes seemed to laugh. She noted his hair was gray around the temples, but he still wore it close cut. Funny, she couldn't imagine him being married to her mother.

She stopped in the middle of the lobby and he walked up to her. They stared at each other as though they couldn't look away.

After what seemed like minutes, he spoke. "I would have known you anywhere. You look like your mother. But your eyes – they're like my mother's eyes. They always were, even when you were a baby."

"I would have known you too...Dad. Or would you prefer if I called you Thomas?"

"I'd prefer Dad, if you don't mind," he said. "Dad sounds good. Have you had lunch yet?"

"No." She hadn't had breakfast either, but she didn't tell him that.

He reached out to her, but she didn't take his hand. "Let's go inside," he said pointing to the lobby restaurant. "The food is pretty good. I had breakfast here this morning."

They were led to a table and as he pulled out the chair for her, he noticed how tall she was. He sat opposite her. "Does your mother know that I'm here?"

"No, but she knows about your letter and that we had talked."

Thomas sat back and folded his hands in front of him. "How did she take it?"

"She left it up to me. She knows I can handle it. She's smart, you know," she said with pride.

He smiled. "I know. So, is she doing well?"

"Yes," Lynn replied and wondered why he was asking so many questions about Helen.

When the waitress came, they ordered the same thing: a hamburger, fries and iced tea. As they chatted, Lynn sensed that her father was as nervous as she was.

"What are you majoring in?"

"Communications."

"That's good. It seems your mother has done a great job with you."

She didn't say anything for a few seconds. "Dad, what brought you to L.A?"

"You, and my job. But the truth is, you. I wanted to see you, Lynn." He paused. "Maybe it's because I'm getting older or I'm finally growing up."

The waitress brought their lunch and as Lynn picked at hers, she asked, "Are you still married to her?"

He had to sit his glass down before he could answer. He had tried to imagine all the questions she would ask and this was one he hadn't expected. He shook his head. "No, it didn't last very long. I just wasn't ready to be married and committed to anyone."

"I used to think you left because of me."

"No, absolutely not!"

"I thought having me was just too much responsibility for you."

He looked at her and she looked like she was about to cry. He reached across the table and took her hand. "No, baby. I left because of me. I was selfish, thinking only of myself and I've paid for that. But, don't ever think it was you. It wasn't you or your mother." He cleared his throat. They ate in silence for a few minutes. "Do you think we can be father and daughter again?" he asked with hope in his voice.

She sighed as though she was undecided. "I don't know. We might not even like each other."

He laughed. "I doubt that. I've always loved you. And, I always will, even if you don't want to see me anymore."

"If you felt that way, why didn't you call me before now?"

Thomas was silent until a passing couple was out of hearing distance. "I wanted to call you. And, a few times I did and spoke with your mother. But I knew if I'd spoken to you, you would have asked me to come home and I couldn't."

But he had been gone for years. Surely, he couldn't believe that she would have still asked him that. She studied her father's face and wondered if she would ever trust him.

"I know I haven't been the father you deserved, but I am your father. And, if you give me a chance, I would like for us to become friends. I can't ever make up for the time we've lost, but this could be a new beginning."

She paused before answering, wanting to make sure she was doing the right thing. The corner of her mouth turned into a smile and the frown on her face disappeared. "Okay, we can try and see what happens."

He smiled widely. "I have to go back to Atlanta tomorrow, but this time, we'll keep in touch. Next time, I will stay longer so that you can show me Los Angeles."

"That'll be great. Mom will be moving out here soon, did you know that?"

"No. What made her decide to move?"

"She says there is nothing in Atlanta for her anymore. And, I'm glad she made the decision. I miss her a lot. And, since her best friend died, I want her here with her family."

He nodded in agreement.

The next morning, Lynn was at the hotel at nine. They had breakfast together and then she took her father to the airport. She stayed with him until he boarded the plane. He

206

was her father and as much as it surprised her, she was glad that he was back in her life.

Robert was walking out of the gym when he saw a young girl walking out of Baskin Robbins with an ice cream cone in her hand. She was pretty, her ponytail bouncing past her shoulders and she reminded him so much of Helen. She had the same walk and was about the same height as Helen...he stopped in his tracks. He could see her face clearly now. She was Helen's daughter. He started to run after her, when he saw a red Camaro speeding in her direction. His heart froze inside his chest. "Oh, God. No!" He couldn't remember her name even though he'd heard it a thousand times. He yelled, waving his arms in the air. The first sound was screeching brakes, then screams. Her ice cream flew into the air, and her purse was still hanging on her shoulder as she fell to the ground. The driver jumped out of his car with a wild, scared expression on his face.

Robert was beside Lynn in two heartbeats and he prayed that she wasn't dead. She was unconscious, but he felt a pulse in her slender hand. He yelled for someone to call 911.

The driver was kneeling beside Robert. "Is she alive, Sir?" he asked, his voice shaking with fright.

"Yes," Robert said. "But, I don't know how bad it is. We've got to get her to a hospital fast."

The young man's blonde hair stood straight on the top of his head. His pale face was now turning pink and beads of perspiration were forming on his forehead. "I didn't see her, honest. She was just there in front of me." He rubbed the top of his head. "My parents are going to kill me."

They heard the sirens and the boy stood and waved both hands motioning to the paramedics. Robert stayed on his knees, holding Lynn's hand and praying the entire time.

Helen had just unpacked her bags and wanted to call Lynn to give her the telephone number of the hotel. She dialed Lynn's dorm room, but there was no answer. She shook her head and sighed. How many times had she told Lynn to make sure her answering machine was on when she went out? Guess I'll just have to try later, she mused. Helen decided to go out to eat. Maybe if she left the room for a while, she would shake off the ominous feeling setting in her chest. She hated when she felt like this – like something wasn't going right.

But what could go wrong, she thought. She hadn't planned this trip to San Francisco. It was just good to get away. She had been running on overload ever since Darlene's death. After a few days, she would return to Atlanta, put her house on the market and help Valerie close up the rest of Darlene's affairs.

She changed into comfortable pants and a sweater. The more she thought of her move to California, the better she felt. It was always exciting to do something different. She would be sad leaving Atlanta and all the things that she loved, but it was time. This would be a big step in her life because she loved Atlanta. She loved Peachtree Street, the Peachtree Road Race every Fourth of July, the jogging around Piedmont Park. She loved everything about the city, but she would make the adjustments. Once could jog or write anyplace in the world if that's what you want to do. She went to the lobby and asked the doorman for a recommendation for a good restaurant. From the lobby phone, she once again tried to call Lynn, but there was still no answer. Oh, well, she shrugged. She'd try again when she got back.

Robert stayed with Lynn as she was taken to UCLA Medical Center. On the ride in the ambulance, he looked in her face. She looked so young, so innocent, so much like her mother. God, how was he going to call Helen and give her such dreadful news? Maybe he should call Elaine and she could contact Helen. Robert moved aside so that the para-medics could check Lynn's pulse again.

"She's lucky, you know."

"Will she be all right?" Robert asked.

"I think so, but we can't tell if there are any broken bones or what is going on inside. We'll just have to wait until we get to the hospital." Robert sat back and closed his eyes. He could only hope.

The phone was ringing as Helen rushed into her hotel room. "Elaine! I'm glad you called. I just walked in. I had lunch and did a little sight seeing around the city. Gee, the weather is cold, but not too bad. I'm wearing slacks and a warm sweater." Helen's voice was light and joyful. Going walking made her feel better and she was glad to hear her sister's voice. So, you remembered that I was going to be in San Francisco."

"Actually, Helen, I wasn't sure what day you said you would be there. But when I phoned your house, that's when I remembered."

Helen heard the edge in her sister's voice. She pulled the chair from the table and sat down. "What's up?" Helen asked. "Are you feeling all right, Elaine? It's not the baby, is it?"

"No, it's not the baby."

"What is it, honey?" Helen could feel a pit in her stomach.

"It's Lynn."

She held her breath. "Oh, God, what is it?" she asked, holding the phone tight in her hand. Her voice was so low that Elaine could barely hear her.

"She was hit by a car, Helen. Robert is here at the hospital with her. He's the one that called me."

Helen couldn't comprehend all of the information. Lynn was hit by a car. She's in the hospital. Robert's with her. "How is she now, Elaine?" Helen almost screamed and had to pause to fight back her tears.

"She's conscious. I talked to her for a few minutes. The doctor is with her now."

Helen was trembling and didn't know what to do first. She stood up. Pull yourself together, she thought as she reached for a tissue. "Elaine, I'll make reservations and be down there as soon as possible."

"Okay, I'll meet you at the airport."

"No, I don't want you to leave Lynn. I'll take a taxi." She hung up without saying good-bye. She was able to make reservations on a flight leaving in less than two hours and she packed her clothes hurriedly. She ran out of her room and to the front desk to check out. A taxi waiting in front of the hotel, took her to the airport.

Less than four hours after she received the call, a taxi let her out in front of the emergency unit of the hospital. Robert and Elaine were in the waiting room and they both looked up as she entered. She held Robert's eyes for a moment before she spoke and even though he could tell that she was frightened, she still looked stunning. She walked up to Robert first, her keen eyes piercing. He could feel the daggers shooting from her eyes as she looked at him.

"Hello, Helen. I wanted to stay with Lynn until you arrived."

"Is the doctor still with her?"

"No, she's just sleeping right now, but I didn't want to leave her alone."

"She wouldn't have been alone. Elaine is here."

"I know, but I still felt that I should stay with her until you arrived."

"Well, your gallantry is commendable, but it's really not necessary that you stay any longer."

Elaine's mouth flew open. It wasn't like Helen to be so rude. After all, Robert had stayed out of concern. Elaine stared at her sister. Why was she being so cold?

Helen dismissed Robert and turned to Elaine. "What room is she in?"

"I'll take you," Elaine said as she looked at Robert, not understanding what had transpired between him and Helen.

Helen rushed into Lynn's room like a gust of hard wind. As she leaned over her bed, she softly called her daughter's name.

Lynn groaned, opening her eyes slowly as if every muscle in her body ached. "Hi, Mom," she whispered. "What a terrible reason to have to come back and visit me, huh?"

Elaine walked behind Helen and whispered in her ears. "The doctor gave her a shot so that she could sleep."

Helen took Lynn's hand. "I'm so glad you're all right, baby," she said with tears burning her eyes. "I thought I was going to die when your Aunt Elaine called me."

"Please thank Robert for me, Mom. He was really great."

"I have already, honey."

Helen ignored Elaine's stare. She wasn't going to answer any questions or give any explanations. How the hell did Robert get involved in this anyway? She kissed her daughter again as Lynn drifted off to sleep. Helen peeked under the blanket and saw the bruises on Lynn's legs and knees. She had a small bandage on her forehead and right arm and Helen wondered just how bad her injuries were.

Helen and Elaine tiptoed out of the room.

"I've got to talk to the doctor," Helen said with concern.

Elaine nodded. "His name is Doctor Clarke." They walked to the nurse's station.

Helen introduced herself to the nurse as the tears that she'd been trying to hold back filled her eyes.

"Are you okay?" The tall nurse asked sympathetically as she handed Helen a tissue.

Fighting to control the shaking in her body, Helen shook her head and blew her nose. "I'm sorry. It's just that I am so worried."

"I understand, Miss Graham." The nurse led Helen to a chair. "You wait here and I'll get the doctor."

"Lynn will be all right, Helen, now that you're here with her." Helen nodded and took Elaine's hand.

The nurse returned with the doctor. He was a short man who at first appeared to be impatient, but took his time talking to Helen.

"Your daughter is going to be fine, but she does have a fracture in both legs. There are no other internal injuries, thank God," he said, looking Helen straight in the eyes. He turned, looking at Elaine and noticed her bulging stomach. "Are you all right?"

"Yes, thank you," Elaine nodded.

He turned back to Helen. "Your daughter will be fine, but she'll be in pain for a while. She'll have to take it easy." Doctor Clarke could see the fear in Helen's eyes. "She's a strong girl and she'll be fine in no time. Just give her a few weeks to recover."

"What about her legs? Are you sure she'll be fine?" Helen choked the words out.

"There's no medical reason to believe that there's any problem. She'll be up and around in a few weeks."

Helen nodded, though tears still stung her eyes.

The doctor touched her hand. "I would tell you if there was any reason for concern. The car involved in the accident almost came to a complete stop before it hit her. She'll be able to go home in a day or two." The doctor stood. "You should get some rest. Your daughter will be fine." The doctor walked off to see his next patient.

"The doctor is right, Helen. You look like you're going to collapse any moment. Let me take you to my place so that you can get some sleep."

Helen shook her head. "No, I can't leave her alone. Just make me a reservation at the Hilton on Wilshire. It's not too far and I can rent a car to get back and forth."

"You don't have to do that. Dan and I would love to have you with us."

"You guys are newlyweds and I don't want to intrude. Besides, I really do want to be close to the hospital." Helen kissed her sister on her cheek. "Thanks for being here for my baby."

Elaine wanted to ask Helen about Robert, but she knew this wasn't the time. In a few days, she'd speak to Helen about him.

"Let me walk you to your car, Elaine. You must be tired and it's getting late."

"Are you sure that you'll be all right here?"

"Absolutely."

The sisters hugged. Elaine drove off, leaving Helen standing in front of the emergency unit. Helen took a deep breath, noticing for the first time how beautiful the night was. She looked up to the skies. So peaceful, she thought, but inside her heart felt as if it was breaking into little pieces.

She went back into the hospital and as she got off the elevator, she bumped into Robert. "Excuse me," she said, surprised to see him and she tried to walk around him.

"Oh, no, lady, not so fast."

She swung around with tension filling her face. "What do you want? I already thanked you for being with Lynn." She took a step back, giving herself some space. "Now, would you please go away? I'm sure you have someone waiting for you at home."

Robert stepped closer. "No, not until you hear me out," he said, determined to have his say.

"This is not the time or the place, Robert. The nurses are about to move Lynn to the third floor and I need to be there with her." And anyway, what could you possibly have to say to me, she thought? "I think you just need to go home to your wife or whatever the hell she is. You don't belong here, Robert."

It was just as he suspected – the damn pictures. He could see the hurt in her eyes.

Helen was afraid that she would crumble. She could feel the heat rising in her face and she started to walk away, but he grabbed her arm.

"We've got to talk," he said. Without a word, he guided her down the hallway to a small couch that was not far from Lynn's room, but provided them with some privacy. Helen couldn't imagine what he had to say to her, but she didn't want to hear it. She was tired of all the lies.

She listened as he told her how he had happened to be with Lynn and she shook her head. "Of all people, why you?"

"I'm glad it was me. Besides, everything happens for a reason. Even us."

"I don't think so!"

"Helen, I won't leave this hospital until you listen to me. I'll stay the entire night if I have to."

She sat back and rested her hands in her lap, but she remained silent.

He breathed deeply and turned to her. "First of all, I'm still very much in love with you."

She looked at him as if he was completely out of his mind. "How can you be in love with me? I thought you were involved with someone," she muttered.

"That's what you were supposed to believe."

She frowned in confusion. "What do you mean?"

He sat back and told her the entire story about Mona, including her death. When he finished, he sat back waiting for her response.

"How many other women were there?" she asked.

The question took him by surprise and he cleared his throat. "I guess I deserve that, but it was only that one night, Helen. And, I regretted it, even before it was over. There has never been anyone else."

She stood. "I believed in you, Robert, and you let me down. And now you think with that simple explanation I should just fall into your arms? Well, that is not going to happen. I don't believe a word you're saying."

"But, it's true."

"Well, it doesn't matter because there will never be anything between us again. In case you haven't heard, I'm moving to Los Angeles, but not with you, and it's important for you to understand this." She heard a noise and looked down the hall. Lynn was being moved. "Now, if you will excuse me, I have a daughter to attend to." She started to walk away. "Good-bye, Robert."

Helen followed the nurses to Lynn's new room. She sat beside the bed and stared at her sleeping daughter. Helen gently pushed the hair from Lynn's face. "God, what would I have done, if I'd lost you, Lynn?" she whispered. She looked up to the ceiling as if she expected an answer from God. But she had her answer. Lynn was alive.

She walked out of the room and sat on a couch outside. It seemed that her life was just falling apart. First she lost Robert, then Darlene and now Lynn's accident. She curled her legs under her and tried to sleep, but thoughts of Robert, Darlene, and Lynn kept drifting through her mind. She thought about the story that Robert had told her. Could it be true? Could someone really be that malicious? She shook her head as though she was trying to clear it. There were so many unanswered questions. But, it didn't matter. He still cheated and lied to her. Would he jump in bed with every manipulating little tramp that came along? Could she ever believe him or trust him again?

She fell asleep and woke up in the middle of the night. She checked on Lynn and noticed that her daughter was still in the same position. Was something wrong with her leg or was it the medication? She would have to check with the doctor in the morning.

The hallway was deserted with only one nurse at the nurse's station. Tomorrow night, she would sleep at the hotel, but for now, she needed to be by her daughter. She found her eyelids getting heavy and drifted to sleep. When she awoke, Robert was sitting next to her with two cups of coffee in his hands. He handed one to her.

She hesitated before accepting her cup. "Thank you."

He smiled. "I thought you could use this. Did Lynn sleep through the night?"

"Yes."

"How much sleep did you get?" he asked.

"Not much."

He sipped on his coffee. "Are you going to stay here all day?"

"Maybe." She looked down at her wrinkled shirt. "I have to shower and change."

"I started to come back last night, but I'm working on a deposition and a few other things. I was up until two-thirty this morning."

"I can't believe you're up and out this early," Helen said as she glanced at her watch.

"I'm always up early, even though sometimes I work until three or four in the morning. All I need is a shower, a cup of coffee and I can begin my day."

"You sound like me. When I get caught up with my writing, I work until all hours of the night." She realized that they were sitting close and she was surprised that she was enjoying his company.

"How are things at the D.As office?"

"Oh, I left there. I'm a partner in a private law firm and I love it. The opportunity is good and it is a well-known firm." He touched her hand. "I'm on my way to the office, but I had to stop by and see you...and Lynn. Do you need anything?"

She looked down at his hand on hers and thought about all the times she and Darlene drank coffee together in the mornings.

"Helen?" Robert called her name.

"I'm sorry," she said looking as if she was a thousand miles away. "I guess I'm tired. What were you saying?"

"I was asking if you needed anything. But, I think you need a few good hours of sleep."

"I'm going to go to the hotel after Lynn wakes up and the doctor checks on her."

He nodded. "You know, Lynn might have quite a recovery period. I'm sure you're going to want to be with her. Will you be staying out here?"

"I think so, though I haven't thought that far ahead yet. It'll depend on a lot of things."

"You know, you wouldn't have to stay in a hotel. I have two extra rooms at my house. Lynn may not be able to go back to her dorm for a while and staying at my house will be much better than staying in a hotel. And, Elaine's place isn't big enough for all of you." He watched as her eyes widened in surprise. He pulled his business card from his pocket. "You can reach me at the office if you need anything. If I'm not there, my secretary will be able to contact me." He stood and she looked at the length of his long body. "Think about it, Helen. You can stay with me as long as you need to."

As he walked away, she stared at his straight back and wide shoulders. His black suit was tailored to his perfectly shaped body. Damn him!

Helen looked up as saw the nurse walking toward her. She stood up, feeling every muscle in her tired body start to stiffen. The nurse gave her a warm smile. Helen released her breath, and sighed with relief.

"How are you this morning, Miss Graham?"

Helen watched as Robert got onto the elevator, then faced the nurse. "Fine. I'm just a bit tired."

"Lynn is awake if you want to go in."

Helen grabbed her purse. "Her legs? Has the feeling come back?"

The nurse smiled. "She can move a little now. It's a good start."

"Oh, thank God." She slipped her shoes on her swollen feet and rushed past the nurse. Lynn was lying on her back, moving one leg from side to side.

Helen rushed to her daughter's side and kissed her. "Are you very sore, honey?"

She groaned. "A bit. I could probably move my leg more if it wasn't so sore."

"The doctor said the soreness will go away a little every day. How does the rest of you feel?"

"Like I've been hit by a car."

Helen frowned.

"Sorry, Mom. Bad joke. When can I get out of here?"

Just as Lynn asked the question, the doctor walked in. "I can always tell when my patients are getting better by the questions they ask. So, you want to get out of here, young lady, huh?" he asked, as he pulled the blanket from her waist.

Helen moved aside so that the doctor could perform his examination.

"It's just like we said before – no broken bones and no other injuries. The pain will subside as time passes. When she goes home, Miss Graham, you'll have to make her take it easy for a while," he said more to Lynn than Helen. "You don't feel better one day and go dancing the next day, young lady. "He patted Helen's hand. "I'll look in on her later."

When the doctor left, Helen returned to her daughter's bedside.

"So, you'll be able to go home soon," Helen said feeling good for the first time.

"Yeah, and did you notice that the doctor was kind of cute, Mom?"

Helen laughed. "No, I didn't notice. Now, lie back and be still. I can tell that you're still in pain."

"I'm sorry to cause all this fuss, Mom. I know I must have scared you to death."

Helen fixed the pillows for Lynn. "No, honey. I only had a couple of heart attacks. But once I saw you, I felt much better." She kissed her daughter.

A knock on the door interrupted them. A young man, who looked to be about the same age as Lynn, entered holding red roses. His eyes looked from Lynn to Helen and Helen could tell he was speechless.

He looked at Helen again. "Hello, my name is Sidney James." Then, turning to Lynn, he held out the roses. "These are for you." He swallowed hard. "I'm the driver of the car that hit you. I prayed that you weren't hurt too badly. Well, actually I prayed that you weren't hurt at all, but I knew you were. I just didn't want it to be bad. This was the most horrible experience I've ever had in my life. Well, except when Billy Joe fell out the tree and landed on top of my Daddy's new truck. But, he wasn't hurt."

Helen and Lynn looked at each other, then back at the

young man. Helen took the roses from him and set them on the bedside table. She stared at Sidney as he continued to babble, with a dopey smile on his face and she finally excused herself from the room. Last night, she wanted to kill the person that did this to her daughter. But after seeing the poor, frightened kid, she felt sorry for him. At least he hadn't run away. Elaine told her that he had stayed until the paramedics came and now he was willing to face the music. Now, he's facing the music all by himself. Poor kid. He's probably a good kid at that, thought Helen.

Sidney sat in the chair next to Lynn's bed and smiled. He couldn't believe he had been able to do this. His father had told him to stand up to the situation like a man – he had told him to go see the girl and apologize.

Lynn smiled at the tall, thin young man. His blonde hair was combed back from his face. Lynn could tell that if she didn't smile, he would take off running.

"Thank you for coming, Sidney."

"I couldn't sleep at all last night. I had the worst night-mare." He trembled just at the thought. "I can't say how sorry I am. Do ya have any broken bones or anything?"

"No, it's not too bad. I guess you could say that I was lucky. At first, I couldn't move my legs…"

"Oh, God, you're not crippled, are ya? He jumped from the chair as if he was ready to run and hide.

"Oh, no. I can move them now. I'm just a bit sore. In fact, I will be going home soon."

He eased back into the chair and took a deep breath. "I just don't know what to say, except that I'm very sorry. If you need anything at all, just give me a holler. I'll leave my number."

"Thanks, Sidney." Lynn said noticing his easy smile. "You can come and visit me when I go home, if you'd like."

"Your parents won't mind?"

"It's just my mother and you've already met her. She doesn't bite." Lynn smiled as his face turned red with embarrassment.

"Gee, thanks, Lynn." He stood and stuffed both hands in his pockets. "Well, I guess I'd better go so that you can rest. Maybe I'll come back tomorrow."

"That would be nice."

He smiled, walked out the room and bumped right into Helen. "Oh, I'm so sorry!" he said blushing again.

"That's okay. Thank you for coming to visit my daughter."

"I was so scared. I don't even know how it happened. But, it's a good thing that man was there waving his arms and screaming. That's what made me put on the brakes. If it wasn't for that gentleman, I hate to think what would have happened. I guess he saved her life..."

"What gentleman?"

"You know, the one who rode in the ambulance with her. Well, I won't keep you any longer. Good-bye now."

Helen stood aside and watched him walk down the hall. Robert saved my daughter's life, she thought. She thought he had told her all the details, but obviously he had left something out. What was she going to say to him now? She'd already said, thank you, a dozen times. But she knew she had to do more. Lynn could be dead today, right this minute if it weren't for Robert. She knew in her heart that it was God who placed him there that very day, that very second. The older she got, the more she realized that life had so many twists and turns, and one never knew in what direction.

As she was about to go back into Lynn's room, she heard footsteps and she smiled as she saw Elaine and Dan. They made such a nice looking couple. Elaine was smiling and Dan put his arm around her shoulder as they walked together.

Elaine hugged Helen, then rushed into the room. She sat a pink stuffed animal on Lynn's lap. "How's our girl today?"

"She's all right," Helen said.

"I'll be just fine in a few days, Aunt Elaine."

"In a few weeks," Helen corrected.

"Well, she looks great to me. What do you think, Dan?"

"I think she'll beat all of us running in a few weeks," Dan answered.

Lynn laughed as she held the stuffed animal.

"I'm just so glad that you're all right, Lynn," Elaine said. "She's lucky, isn't she, Helen?"

Helen nodded and noticed that Lynn seemed to be getting sleepy. "You're tired, aren't you?"

"A little. And I think you should go and get some sleep yourself, Mom." Helen looked at her watch. It was already one o' clock. "Well, while you're taking a nap, I think I'll go and do the same. I'll be back after dinner. I'll pick you up a few magazines and a nice gown."

Lynn nodded and waved her hand. Helen kissed her and walked out with Elaine and Dan.

"Do you want us to take you to the hotel?" Elaine asked.

"No, I can use Lynn's car while she's in the hospital. She told me where the car is parked. Can you drop me off there?"

"Sure. Are you sure you don't want to stay with us?" Dan asked.

"Yes, I'm sure. I have to figure out something for Lynn when she leaves the hospital. I think she and I should stay together for a while."

"But, where will the two of you stay?" Elaine asked with concern.

"I don't know yet, but don't worry. Something will work out."

They dropped Helen off at Lynn's car and then she drove to the hotel, grateful to have a few hours to herself. She climbed into bed and fell asleep before her eyes were closed. When she woke up, she felt like a new person. After calling Lynn, she took a long shower, then slipped into jeans and a matching blouse. She ordered room service and listened to the news on television while she ate the bean soup and ham salad sandwich. She was off to the hospital in the next hour.

As she got off the elevator to go to Lynn's room, she ran into Robert. Her heart started beating faster.

He smiled. "I left the office early so I could see if you and Lynn were all right."

"That was very considerate of you." She didn't smile, just looked directly in his eyes.

He took her hand and led her to the couch they had sat on before. "Have you decided what you're going to do when Lynn gets out of here?"

"No, not yet. There's just so much to think about," she said shaking her head. She looked away from him. "I can't help but feel that I should have been here with her." When she turned back to look at him, tears were rolling down her face and he wiped them tenderly with his handkerchief.

"Even if you were here, Helen, you wouldn't have been able to stop a car from hitting her."

She nodded her head in agreement. "You're right. But when she's better, I'm going to go back to Atlanta and sell my place. I want to move back here as quickly as I can. My daughter and my sister need me."

"It's not how I imagined it, but I am glad that you're moving back here. What made you decide to do it?"

"There's nothing left for me in Atlanta."

"Well, what about Darlene? I'm sure she'll miss you."

Helen lowered her head. She couldn't say anything. It was still too soon to talk about Darlene. But she had to tell him. He didn't know. "Darlene is dead, Robert. She died a few weeks ago." Her voice was a whisper.

He squeezed her hand. "Oh, baby. I'm so sorry." He took her in his arms. "I wish I had known, Helen."

She gently pulled herself from his arms. "I needed you..." She turned her back to him and wiped her eyes.

"I know. I'm so sorry. I was so stupid and I have paid a high price for it."

"Yeah, sure," Helen said.

"Helen, I still want to marry you."

She put both of her hands up. "Please, Robert. I can't talk about this right now. I don't think I'll ever be able to...after that girl."

"Helen, I love you."

She looked into his eyes, eyes she thought she would never look into again. God help her. They still mesmerized her. She was still in love with him, too. Her legs almost weakened with the thought of loving him. Maybe that was why God had made sure Robert was there with Lynn.

"I really want you and Lynn to stay with me. I promise I won't bring up the subject of marriage again. I won't press you for anything."

She gave a long, deep sigh, feeling as though she was being pushed into a corner. She wanted to stay with him, but for all the wrong reasons. She wanted to be near him, see him off to work every morning. But, she couldn't think about herself – she had to think of Lynn and what was best for her. And, they did need a place to stay. She looked at him. "No strings attached?"

He gave her a wide smile. "No strings." He held out his hand. "Is it a deal?" he asked hopefully.

She laughed. "It's a deal."

They went into Lynn's room together to tell her the news and Lynn was pleased. She had been worried about where they would stay and she knew that had been bothering her mother as well. Now, Helen seemed relieved. Maybe this would be a new start for her mother and Robert.

"So, it's settled?" Robert asked as he touched Lynn's hand.

Lynn answered before her mother could. "Yes and I can't wait."

They stayed with her until Lynn was tired enough to go back to sleep. As they walked out of the hospital, Robert said,

"Why don't you follow me home so that I can show you around the house?"

Helen smiled and nodded. She followed him and was impressed with the house. He proudly walked her through the first floor.

"This is wonderful, Robert. Lynn will love the back yard," she said as she walked outside to the patio. "And the view. I bet it is even more beautiful at night."

"It is. You can see lights shining all over the city. Come on, let me show you the rest of the house."

He showed her his office and the room he had hoped would be her office, but he didn't mention that. He led her upstairs to the third bedroom that was still without furniture, in hopes that one day Helen would agree to marry him and furnish the rest of the house any way she wanted. She smiled as she walked from room to room.

"This is beautiful. I can see why you brought this house. You have good taste."

He was proud that she was pleased. They returned to the living room. "You can check out of the hotel tomorrow. I'll give you a key tonight."

She smiled at him and he felt his heart melt. "I appreciate everything you're doing for us."

He stood up. "Why don't we open a bottle of wine?"

"That would be nice." She followed him into the kitchen. "Do you cook a lot?" she asked as she looked around.

"Sometimes, but nothing fancy. Omelets, sandwiches."

She laughed. "You don't cook sandwiches, Robert."

"Oh, yes, you can. You can fry lunch meats and bacon and stuff like that for sandwiches. I can fry some good chicken, too."

"Well then, I'll just have to make a few good meals."

"I can't wait. Helen, I'm really glad that you're here. I mean it."

She looked serious. "Thank you, Robert. I'm glad I'm here, too." She really was happy that she had taken him up on his offer. Lynn would be comfortable here.

And as Robert watched her he thought of his drive home with Helen following him. He drove home with a smile on his face. It would be good to have Helen and Lynn so close to him, and to think that they would all be in the same house together. His day had gone well, including today in court. This case was the hardest in his career. A murder case, a gang shooting. It was hard to find the little bastards guilty, but he had. He worked day and night on this case, turned over every rock until he found the evidence needed to convince the jury that they were guilty. The shooting was retaliation for a shooting the night before. There were two brothers and one was shot by a rival gang member for a beating the week before. The next day, they went out together and shot the wrong person. A sixteen-year-old and a student who had planned to go to college. He was shot in the streets, left crawling on his hands and knees. The young boy couldn't even make it across the street before he collapsed. During the trial, the two brothers were always smiling, and the more they smiled, the tougher Robert got. He made his mind up, he was going to get the two brothers and he did.

The picture of the dead boy's mother, the two brothers smiling, was constantly in his mind, day and night. Robert was tough, straightforward with every question. He looked his victims straight in their eyes and shot their testimony straight to hell and everyone's that testified on their behalf. And when their mother got on the stand and lied about their whereabouts the morning of the shooting, he made sure that she left the stand crying. He was hard on her, when she finished her testimony, she was dishonored. He stood tall, his concentration fast and fierce, walked backward and forward, giving her time to sweat and wonder what he would ask her next. But, she broke on the stand. He won. That was his way of getting retribution for the murder of an innocent child. A child that could have had a wonderful life ahead of him.

Yes, this was a good day for Robert and he would do what ever it took to make Helen and her daughter comfortable in his house. He smiled. Who knows where this can lead to, he thought, turning into his driveway, knowing that Helen was right behind him.

Chapter 26

The next morning, Helen was awake by eight, though she could still feel the effects of the wine she'd shared with Robert last night. Her eyes wandered to the keys to Robert's house that she had dropped on the dresser when she returned to the hotel. Now as she sat in bed, she wondered if she had made the best decision. The thought of living in the same house with him was nerve wracking. She leaned her head against her knees that were propped up in front of her and sighed long and deep.

She called room service and ordered wheat toast and coffee. After eating, she took a shower, then made a list of all that she had to do. But first, she called Elaine and told her the plan to stay with Robert during Lynn's recovery. Elaine sounded a bit confused, but Helen reassured her, this would help Lynn. Maybe this would be recovery for her too. Maybe she would be able to go on with her life without Robert. Maybe.

Her second call was to Valerie. At the sound of Valerie's voice, Helen felt her eyes burn with tears and a lump form in her throat. The pain hadn't lessened since Darlene's death, but Helen knew it would with time. She and Valerie didn't talk long – each reminded the other too much of Darlene.

She packed the rest of her things and checked the room to make sure she wasn't leaving anything behind. Then, she left to run errands. She ran from Sav-On Drug Store to Lynn's room on campus. Helen packed, then stood in the middle of the room and checked the list she'd been given by Lynn. Now, she had to take everything to Robert's house and then go to the hospital. Lynn would be released in the morning. After leaving Lynn's room, Helen went to the supermarket. After all, she had promised Robert a home-cooked meal.

By five o'clock, she was at the hospital and she wasn't surprised to see Sidney James visiting Lynn. He was just about to leave and Helen smiled as he said his good-byes.

225

"So, how was your day?" she asked Lynn.

Lynn frowned as she moved her legs under the blanket. "I had three visitors today. Two from school and Sidney. He's very nice, Mom."

"I can see that."

"Did you get my things from the dorm today?"

"Everything you asked for. Are you feeling all right, Lynn?" Helen was concerned. Her daughter looked tired.

"I'm a bit sore, but that's it. Actually, I'm more worried about you. You haven't had a break. First Darlene's death, then this. I'm sorry to put you through all of this."

Helen touched her daughter's hand. "I'll be all right. I'm going to bed early tonight and by tomorrow, I'll be a new person. You won't recognize me when I come to pick you up. It'll be nice for us to spend some time together. And then, when you're feeling better, we can look at some houses."

"I would love that!" Lynn exclaimed.

Helen touched her daughter's hand. "I was hoping that once I moved out here, you would move in with me."

Lynn smiled, but didn't say anything. Her mother still thought of her as her little girl, but she had gotten used to being independent. Lynn's plans were to work as a writer for the L.A. Times and get a place of her own. But, she wouldn't tell her mother that right now.

"Anyway, how was dinner?" Helen asked.

Lynn made a funny face. "Meat loaf, mashed potatoes, peas and ice cream. The ice cream was the best of all."

"Did you eat all of it?"

"I tried to, but it wasn't very good, Mom."

Helen pulled a bag from her purse and Lynn's eyes got big as she read "Fat Burger" on the face of the bag. "How about a burger and fries?"

"I don't believe this," Lynn said as she opened the bag. She bit into the hamburger. "Delicious," she moaned. "This is the best hamburger I've ever tasted."

"I know how hospital food tastes and I knew that right about now, you would appreciate a good burger. In other words, my dear, I love you," Helen mused.

While Lynn ate her hamburger and fries, Helen flipped

through the magazines she'd purchased for her daughter. They talked for over an hour before Lynn finally fell asleep. Helen kissed her on the cheek and tiptoed out of the room.

She was driving down Slauson when she decided to turn on Victoria and onto West Boulevard. Her cousin, Mary, lived on this street. She drove until she spotted the brown, beat-up, Buick Mary had been driving at her mother's funeral.

She got out of the car and rang the doorbell three times before it was opened. Mary stood there, high as a kite. She was wearing a short, black satin nightgown. Her hair, without her wig, was braided in small braids all over her head. She stood at the door for a full minute before she recognized Helen.

"Aren't you going to ask me in, Mary?"

Wordlessly, she motioned for Helen to come in. She pushed the door closed with her butt and stood against it. Helen stood in the middle of the shabby living room. The carpet, couch and recliner were old and dirty. The walls looked gray and overflowing ashtrays were on every table. The smell of alcohol combined with tabacco made Helen choke.

Finally, Mary said, "Well, have a seat, Helen."

Helen sat on the edge of the couch and cleared her throat. "I was just passing by and thought I would stop and say hello. I haven't heard from you since the funeral, you know."

Mary sat in the recliner opposite Helen. "Yeah, I know. When did you get here?"

"Four days ago. Lynn was in a car accident."

Mary's mouth opened wide and her gown slid up her thighs. She lit a cigarette and poured herself a glass of Southern Comfort from the bottle that was sitting on the table.

Helen frowned without realizing it.

"You'll have to excuse this place, Helen, but I've been under the weather." She sat back in the chair. "So, how is Lynn? I hope she wasn't hurt too bad."

"She's doing better. She'll be leaving the hospital tomorrow."

Suddenly, Mary laughed out loud. "Remember when we were kids running around like wild fools and I got hit by a car?"

Helen crossed her legs and looked at Mary as she took

long swallows from her glass. "I was just thinking about that yesterday when I went to visit Lynn," said Helen. "I thought Daddy was going to kill us all, that day, the way we were running from one side of the street to the other."

Mary tilted her head back and closed her eyes. "Was that at y'all's house or my daddy's house?" she asked Helen.

"It was at our house, Mary. Don't you remember?"

Mary saw the expression on Helen's face and took another long swallow. She was embarrassed. She hated that Helen had caught her in this condition and she was ashamed. At least Helen was being a lady about it and not looking down her nose. She wiped the tears that were rolling down her cheek, falling onto her gown.

Helen saw the silent cry for help. "What's wrong, Mary?"

She shook her head. "I'm just a bit tired." She took another drink and it spilled down her chest. "Shit! How did I do that?" She wiped it with the back of her hands and looked up at Helen. "Where are you staying? I have a room if you wanna stay here."

Helen's eyes widened. "Oh, no. I have a place to stay. In fact, I should probably be going now. And since you're feeling a bit under the weather…" Helen got up.

Mary stood. "Don't go so soon, Helen. You're the only family that has come to see me in a long time. Nobody cares, Helen. My brother and sister don't care about me. Every one thinks they're better than me." Mary's voice was low and soft. She flopped back down on the couch. "Why do people always think they're better than others?"

"People are people, Mary. They always see the worst." Helen put her hand on her cousin's shoulder. Mary felt so thin; Helen could feel Mary's bones against her hand. "That's just the way life is, Mary. But, I will come back to see you soon."

Mary held her face in her hands and cried. "I know that I drink too much, but I can't stop, Helen. I have no reason to stop."

Helen sat on the arm of the chair and lifted Mary's chin. She looked her cousin in the eye. "You do have a reason to stop. Stop for your own good. Stop for Mary."

Mary was still crying. "No, that's not enough of a reason for me."

Helen wrapped her arms around her cousin. "You really do need to stop, Mary. I can help you, if you want."

As Mary continued to cry, Helen led her cousin to her bedroom. The room was musty, clothes were piled on the floor and an empty wine bottle lay next to the bed. She helped her into the bed, and covered her with the blanket. Helen wondered just how much her cousin had been drinking. She turned out the lights and walked from the room.

In the living room, Helen wondered where to start first. She found a trash bag and emptied the ashtrays and threw away the empty bottles that were throughout the house. She washed the dishes and cleaned up the kitchen and living room. Finally finished, she turned the lights out and walked out of the house. Once in her car, she picked up the paper off the seat. Lord, what's on this list of things to do next?

Chapter 27

The next morning, Helen checked Lynn from the hospital and took her to Robert's. Robert was home, waiting to welcome them. Robert watched as Lynn walked around on her crutches, checking out everything in the living room. She looked so much like her mother. At that moment, he wondered what it would be like to be her father. Wonderful, he thought, as she looked at him with round, smiling, innocent eyes.

"Welcome home, Lynn," he said.

"Thank you for having us, Robert. Your home is beautiful. May I take a look around?"

He helped her walk to the sliding glass door leading to the backyard. Helen was supporting her on the other side.

"I love your yard. Now, this is where I'll be spending all my time."

When Robert looked at her, he saw her mother's smile. Against her protests, he carried Lynn upstairs to her room.

"Thank you, but you won't have to do that every time I come up. I need to start exercising my legs anyway."

"I don't mind, Lynn," he said in a deep, soothing voice. "I'll leave you ladies alone for a while. Call if you need anything." He walked out, leaving Helen and Lynn looking after him.

Helen sat on the bed next to Lynn. "We'll have to share this bed. The other rooms are not furnished yet."

"I don't mind, Mom. This room is nice and big anyway." Lynn limped to the window. This gave her a backyard view where she could see the city. "Look, Mom. This is gorgeous. I wonder how far you can see from here?"

Helen walked over and stood beside her. "I stood here for a while last night. It is beautiful." She turned to her daughter. "Why don't you lie down before you get too tired? Remember what the doctor said. You're not supposed to be

230

standing too long." Helen closed the blinds and when she turned back to her daughter, she could see that she was tired. "What's wrong, honey?"

"Nothing. I'm just bored stiff. Maybe I'll be able to go back to my dorm next week."

"Don't be ridiculous, Lynn. You're thinking too far ahead." Helen sat next to her and put her arm around her shoulder.

"But, I can walk all right and the pain is not as bad as it was in the beginning."

"That's because you're following the doctor's orders. We'll see how you are next week and then we'll decide." Helen got up and helped her out of her clothes.

As Lynn laid on her back, looking up at her mother, she said, "Mom, there's something I've been wanting to tell you." Lynn fixed the pillows and sat up straighter. "My father was here."

Helen didn't say anything for a full minute. "You're father came to see you? When?"

"The day you arrived in San Francisco. I was going to tell you when you got home, but then I had the accident..."

"Well, he did come after all. What did you think of him?" Helen looked serious.

"I don't know yet. He seems all right, but I'm not sure if I like him yet. He says I look a lot like you, except for my eyes. He say's their his mother's eyes."

"They are."

"I think that maybe I could like him."

"I think you will. Just take it slowly – you have all the time in the world. He must really have wanted to see you to come all the way to Los Angeles."

Lynn smiled. "He did come a long way, but I think his company sent him and he decided to see me while he was here."

"Well, you just get some rest. Why don't you read some of these magazines I brought you?"

Helen left Lynn alone and went downstairs. Robert was sitting at the kitchen counter. When he saw her, his eyes lit up with pleasure.

"How is Lynn?"

"She'll be all right in no time."

"Does she have everything she needs?"

"Yes, thank you." She sat on a stool next to him.

"And what about you, Helen? Do you have everything you need?"

She looked into his eyes. He was outrageously hand-some. "Yes, thanks to you. Thanks for having us here."

"I just want to make you comfortable."

She touched his hand. "We are. I picked up everything we would need when I was out yesterday. It was a long day."

"What did you do?"

"Well for one thing, I went to see my cousin, Mary. Remember her?"

"Yes, I saw her at your mother's funeral. I met her before, but I can't remember where."

"Well, seeing her was not good. Robert, it was pitiful. She was so drunk, I had to put her to bed. And that house," Helen started, shaking her head in disgust. "She needs to move into a decent place. I don't know where she is going to end up."

"If my memory serves me correctly, she was drunk when I first met her. Is she trying to stop?"

Helen shook her head. "No, but I want to help her."

"Well, no one can help her until she wants it.

"I know," she agreed. "I just worry about her. But, you're right." She touched his hand. It was warm and strong. "Thanks Robert."

"For what?"

"For saving my daughter's life, for being there for her. The young man who hit her told me that he heard you yelling and that's when he put on the brakes. I hate to think of what would have happened…" It gave her chills to think about it.

Robert closed his eyes, remembering how horrifying the accident was. He squeezed her hand. "I only wish that I could have done more."

"Well, she's recovering. She's talking about going back to her dorm next week."

Robert looked disappointed. "Isn't that a little too soon?" he asked with concern.

"Well, she has no broken bones or serious injuries. And,

she can walk, a little. But, I think it's too soon, too. We'll see how she's feeling next week and what the doctor has to say."

"Does that mean you'll be leaving, too?"

"I don't want to impose on you. After all, this isn't something we planned. I can go back to the hotel if I stay longer."

"You don't have to leave – since you're here anyway. Why go back to a hotel?"

She smiled, but said nothing. What could she say? So much had happened between them – all the hurt and pain. Yet, being here with him felt so right. She didn't want to feel anything for him, except gratitude. But it was impossible. Every time he touched her hand, every time he sat close to her or looked at her, she felt her legs weaken. No, she couldn't stay much longer.

That night in his bedroom, Robert got up, wearing only his shorts, and stood at the window looking out at the city. The night was still and the warm breeze blew against his face. This view was meant to be shared with someone, someone you could hold in your arms. Someone you could whisper beautiful words to as the bright stars shined down.

Helen should be in his arms, but even though she was in his house, she was so far away. He couldn't touch her face, her lips, her body,and it was driving him out of his mind. But he couldn't give up. He had a few more days and he would make things right between them again. He shook his head, trying to clear it. He looked down and decided from the bulge he felt, this would be a long night.

"What's this?"

"Your breakfast," she said.

Robert looked her up and down. She was wearing jeans and a tight sweater. Her hair was pushed up in the back. She looked young and sexy to him. Seeing her like this, reminded him of the long night he'd had.

She pointed to the table. "Sit. I'll pour you coffee."

He smiled and hung the jacket he was holding on the chair next to him. "It's been a long time since anyone had my breakfast ready and served."

"Well, it was obvious that you don't cook breakfast for yourself. You had no food inside the refrigerator." She took two slices of toast from the toaster. They ate bacon, scrambled eggs and toast.

"A man could get used to this," he said, teasing her.

Their eyes met and she looked down at her plate. Why did he have to say such things, she thought? They ate the rest of the meal in a comfortable silence. When they finished, she cleared the table and she could see him watching her out of the corner of his eyes. Finally, he stood and put on his jacket. When she turned to him, their eyes held and they stood staring at each other for several moments. The silence was broken when Lynn entered the room.

Saved by the bell, thought Robert. He was about to kiss her and he knew he would have been pushing his luck. It was too soon. "Good morning, Lynn. I hope you slept comfortably last night," Robert said.

"Yes," she smiled at him. "Gee, it smells good in here."

"I have some bacon ready for you. I just have to scramble some eggs and put some bread in the toaster," Helen said as she glanced at Robert.

"Was it hard for you to walk down the stairs?" Robert asked.

"Not too hard. I just walked slowly and took one step at a time, instead of running and taking two at a time, the way I would if I wasn't sore."

"Ah, youth," Robert mused as he smiled at her. "Just take it easy and don't push too hard." Robert looked at his watch. "It's time I got out of here. You girls have a nice day."

Helen felt like she should walk him to the door, but she didn't. She smiled, said good-bye, and finished cooking Lynn's breakfast. "Elaine will be here soon," she told Lynn. "She wants to see you."

After Helen finished cooking, then cleaning up, she roamed through the house. She stood in the doorway to Robert's bedroom. She inhaled the smell of his cologne that lingered. She stood at his bed, so neatly made. He was a very neat man, to say the least. He had so many good qualities, she couldn't find anything wrong with him. Except for the fact that he had an affair. She groaned and walked down the stairs. She stood at the picture window in the living room. The woman across the street was working in her flower bed, wearing a large straw hat to block out the sun. This was a beautiful neighborhood, she thought. Baldwin Hills was where she always wanted to live, but now, Robert was here. And, she couldn't bear the thought of running into him with another woman. She folded her arms in front of her and stood for a few more minutes, when Elaine pulled up in her black Acura. Helen ran out to greet her.

"It's a beautiful day," Elaine said, hugging her sister.

"And, I'm glad you decided to come by. You'll be good company."

"You have Lynn."

Helen frowned. "Come on, let's go inside." She led Elaine into the house. "Lynn's already talking about being bored. She's been complaining all morning."

Elaine laughed. "All the young ones are like that, Helen. Besides, she has so much energy."

"Yeah, see what you have to look forward to," Helen said, pointing to Elaine's growing stomach. Helen led her to the kitchen where Lynn was sitting drinking orange juice and flipping through a magazine.

Elaine kissed her on the top of her head, then suddenly held her breath. "Oh dear. We'll have to go into the living room. The smell of food in the morning like this, makes me ill."

Helen took one look at her sister's face and guided her by the arm. "Come on. You'll be comfortable in here. I'll make a cup of tea for you." Helen left her on the couch and returned to the kitchen.

Elaine sat in the chair and laid her head back. "It's this morning sickness," she said. She placed her hand on her stomach.

"Is it really bad?" Lynn asked.

"Yes, it's awful. I hate it."

Helen returned with a tray with tea and toast and looked at her sister with concern. She looked a little better, not as flushed.

"Aunt Elaine, do you want a boy or girl?"

"It doesn't matter to me as long as my baby is healthy with ten fingers and toes. But, Dan wants a girl. His brother

235

has boys and his mother only had boys." Elaine turned to Helen. "When you were pregnant, what did you want?"

"I wanted a girl and that's what I got!"

Lynn laughed.

"Have you talked to Harriet lately?" Helen asked Elaine.

Elaine shook her head. "No. She calls less and less these days. I have a feeling that soon, she'll stop calling all together. And, whenever I call her, she's always too busy to talk."

Lynn stood. "I think I'll go into the backyard and get some sun. Anybody want to come?"

"No, thanks," the sisters answered. "Maybe we'll join you later," Helen said.

The two of them sipped their teas. Helen could tell that her sister was still curious about their living arrangements and she decided to tell her. "I guess I should tell you something about Robert and myself."

"You know, I've been wondering about the relationship between you two. Especially after the way you treated him in the hospital. That wasn't like you at all."

Helen told Elaine everything about her and Robert. "I was so in love with him and couldn't believe we had this second chance together. I think I've always been in love with him. But now, I've been so hurt and confused by my feelings."

"Sometimes, it's hard in the beginning of a relationship, Helen."

"I know, but we started off so strong. I trusted him with all my heart. Have you ever had so much trust in anyone in your life?"

"Not until Dan came along. You don't find someone like that often, Helen. Maybe you should reconsider your feelings about walking away from Robert. Your love for him will always be there, and I don't think he'll hurt you like this again." Elaine refilled her teacup, then continued. "I have to be honest, I knew about you and Robert."

Helen was surprised. "How?"

"I'm not the simpleton everyone seems to think I am. It was none of my business, so I didn't ask any questions. But, you could have told me," Elaine said, as if her feelings were hurt.

"I know and I'm sorry. I didn't say anything to you because of Harriet. In the beginning, I didn't feel comfortable about it myself."

"I understand how it could have happened between you and Robert. After all, you had him first. I think he never stopped loving you, just like you've never stopped loving him. You are in love with him, right?"

"I am, but I'm fighting my feelings like hell. I'm going to have to get out of this house real soon. It's hard being under the same roof with him."

"I'm sure it's hard on him too. If you ask me, he loves you. I can see it every time he looks at you. Even with the way you treated him at the hospital, his eyes lit up when you walked in the room." She held her sister's hand. "Just don't be blind, Helen and don't be a fool. If there was someone else in his life, surely she would be here and not you and Lynn."

Helen sighed. "I'm not sure of that. You see, she's dead, Elaine. If she weren't, maybe she would be here." Helen's voice revealed the pain she felt just at the thought of Robert being with another woman.

"Oh, goodness. What happened?'

"An old boyfriend shot her. But, I still wonder about her with Robert. Why was she so irresistible to him? Why wasn't I enough?"

Elaine sat back and rubbed her stomach. "I don't think that was it. He's a man, and he made a mistake. And, long distance relationships have a hard time working."

Helen nodded her head in agreement.

"He needs you here, just as you need him near you."

Helen paced the floor and threw her hands up in the air. "I just don't know anymore. I just damn don't know."

"You should give it a lot of thought if you love the man. Talk to him and see where his head is at."

"It's in his ass if you ask me."

"Now, Helen, don't talk like that."

She sat back down next to Elaine. "I wouldn't know what to say to him. I never even planned to see him again. Even when I planned to move back here, I knew there was a chance of running into him, but I had no plans of seeing him." Helen sighed. "Anyway, what do you think of me moving back here?"

"I'm happy about it. It's going to be wonderful having my sister so close. I want my baby to know my family, not just Dan's. I just wish Harriet wanted to be a part of our lives."

Helen got up and straightened the painting on the wall and then sat back down. "Harriet will be all right, Elaine. She doesn't need us."

"I guess you're right. It's just that we have each other and she has no one."

"It's her choice," Helen said. "Do you want more tea or toast? How's your stomach feeling?"

Elaine nodded. "I'm fine now. I'm feeling a little too relaxed. I can feel myself getting lazy." Elaine shifted on the couch. "I am so glad you're going to be moving here. I know you miss Darlene."

"I miss her everyday. We used to talk almost everyday and on the days that we didn't, it was all right because we knew the other was there. And, we could talk about anything." Tears began to form in her eyes. "God, I miss her."

Elaine shook her head, understanding what her sister felt. And, she could never tell Helen how she used to be jealous of her relationship with Darlene. They were so much like sisters and Elaine had wished for the same kind of relationship with Helen.

"It wasn't until Darlene died that I decided to move out here. I knew Lynn wanted to stay and now there's no reason for me to stay in Atlanta. Besides," she said smiling at Elaine. "You'll need me after the baby is born."

Elaine put her hand on her stomach and felt the baby move. There was such a sadness in her sister's eyes and she wished she could help her. "Any ideas for another book yet?" she asked changing the subject.

"No, not with all the interruptions going on in my life right now. I've got to sell my place and then get settled out here before I start a new book. My latest book will be on the market in a couple of months."

Elaine looked at her watch. "I think it's time for me to leave. I have a couple of things I have to pick up for the baby and then meet Dan for lunch."

Helen walked her out to her car and helped her get in.

"Now think about what I said. Give some serious thought to Robert. Make sure you're absolutely sure before you shut him out of your life completely."

Helen shut the door. "I'll think about what you said. I know that I'll have to make a decision eventually. I thought I had already made my decision. It's funny how things change. I feel now that I had taken one step forward and now two steps back."

"Well, this all happened for a reason, Helen."

Lynn walked outside and stood on the front steps and Elaine yelled out for her to stay there. "I'll see you in a day or two, Lynn. Maybe next week, you'll be well enough for us to have lunch together."

"I'd love to," Lynn yelled back.

"I'd better get going so that I can meet my husband on time. He's having lunch brought to his office since he can't get away."

"How romantic," Helen laughed.

"Maybe not, but that's where it all started with us." She drove off, waving.

It was such a beautiful day that Helen didn't want to stay in the house and they decided to have lunch at the Soup Plantation in the Marina. Helen had a salad and bran muffin, while Lynn filled her plate with everything in the buffet.

"Gee, how do you stay so slender? You have three different breads on your tray."

Lynn looked down as if she hadn't realized how much she'd taken.

"Oh, I don't know. Maybe I stay this way because I'm on the move too much to gain any weight."

"That, and the fact that you're still young."

"Mom, you're still slender."

Helen laughed. "But I have to work on it. I have to go to the market. Do you feel up to going with me or should I take you home first?"

"I'm fine, Mom. It's just good to get out for a while."

"Girl, you sound like you've been in for months."

"It feels like it," Lynn said as she bit into her muffin.

"I'm just not used to being stuck inside for so long. What do you need from the market?"

"I thought I would cook a nice dinner. Maybe I can get you to eat some real food while I'm here."

"Don't worry about that. Once you move out here, I'll always eat at your house." Lynn ate the last of her vanilla pudding.

Since it was the middle of the afternoon, the market was almost empty. Lynn stayed in the car while Helen shopped for collard greens, pot roast, sweet potatoes and carrots.

When Robert entered his house that evening the aroma from Helen's cooking led him straight to the kitchen. She was just putting a pan of cornbread muffins into the oven and had her back to him. He stopped, watching her, then glanced through the glass doors where Lynn was sitting beneath the lemon tree reading a book. He turned back to Helen. If things were different, he would take Helen upstairs, undress her and make wild, sweet love to her. If things were different, he thought.

Helen turned around, screamed and jumped as the pot holder in her hand, fell to the floor. "You scared the living daylights out of me." She nervously pushed her hair from her face.

Robert took two steps to pick up the pot holder and they both bent down at the same time. They stared at each other, then burst into laughter. They laughed until their eyes began to water.

He spoke first. "I'm sorry I frightened you, Helen. I was going to say something and then Lynn caught my eye," he lied. "It smells delicious in here. And, I'm starved," he said, inhaling the smell of the food.

"Then, you came to the right place." She took a few steps back, putting distance between them. They were standing too close. "The muffins will be out in ten minutes."

"Good. I'll say hello to Lynn and change into something more comfortable."

"Remember, ten minutes," she yelled behind him.

He stuck his head back into the kitchen. "Thanks, Helen. Thanks for being here."

240

She felt tears burn her eyes. PMS, she thought. Why else would I cry so easily? She set the table and had everything ready by the time Robert and Lynn walked into the dining room. He had changed into a pair of jeans that fit tight against his hard thighs, and a blue T-shirt.

They chatted easily through dinner.

"Mom is the best cook and you should taste her sweet potato pie. Melts in your mouth," Lynn said.

"Oh, I've tasted it," Robert replied, smiling at Helen.

Lynn smiled. She liked Robert. She liked the way he watched her mother when he thought no one was looking. She liked the way he made her feel comfortable and she felt like she'd known him much longer than she had. It was hard to imagine him married to her Aunt Harriet. They seemed so different and she wondered how they'd ever gotten together.

She looked from Robert to her mother. They seemed so comfortable, but somehow, they also seemed strained. She wondered how long it would be before the two of them got together – because she was sure they would end up together.

"Mom, since you cooked, I'll do the dishes."

"I'll give you a hand, honey," Helen said.

"No, I feel okay. I want to get back to doing things for myself since I'll be going back to my dorm in a few days."

Robert sat straight up in his chair. He and Helen exchanged glances.

"You don't think it's too soon?" Robert asked. "You and your mother are welcome to stay as long as it takes to get you better. There's no reason for you to rush."

"Thank you, Robert. But even when I leave, Mom doesn't have to. She may want to stay a little longer to make sure I'm all right. You know how mothers are."

"That's a good idea, don't you think, Helen?"

It was too much for her. Robert was trying to push her against a wall and she knew it. She wanted to slap that silly grin from his face. And, what was Lynn up to? "If I stay any longer, I can go to a hotel. But, I do appreciate your offer, Robert," Helen said as she rolled her eyes at Lynn.

Lynn smiled, but lowered her eyes. She could tell that Helen knew they had just double-teamed her. Robert looked from Helen to Lynn and had to hold back his laughter. He knew that he'd have to keep Lynn here longer, in order to keep Helen with him. Soon, Helen would realize that this was where she belonged and would agree to marry him. But getting to that point would take some time.

Helen didn't want to leave so soon, but what choice did she have? Lynn's health was the only reason she was here and she knew this little arrangement couldn't last forever. She looked into his handsome face. She didn't know what she was going to do, but this could easily become a habit.

Lynn cleared the table while Robert and Helen took their glasses of wine to the patio table in the backyard.

"It's so peaceful out here," Helen said.

"It is...I come out here and sit when I have something on my mind. It's quiet and I can think clearly."

"I guess everyone has their favorite spots. I have a large chair in my bedroom in front of the window. That's where I go when I need to think. I watch the stars and the city lights and I feel like I'm the only one who's awake in the entire city. But this place you have here – this is a dream."

"I love it. I just hope I won't have to live here much longer by myself."

She couldn't take her eyes off him when he said those words, but she didn't have an answer for him. Hell, she didn't have an answer for herself. It would be three, maybe four days before Lynn would be ready to leave. She felt a familiar ache in the pit of her stomach. Damn, she wanted him. She needed him, needed to be near him. She wanted to touch him and have him touch her body the way he touched her heart.

"Helen," he said her name softly.

"Yes?"

"I was just thinking. The day Lynn leaves, why don't we go out to a movie or something before you go? You haven't had any time to yourself since you got here."

She was disappointed. She thought he was going to ask her to marry him again, even though she didn't know how she would have responded. She hesitated for a few seconds before she answered. What harm would that do? She really did want to be alone with him. She looked at him and smiled. The idea was appealing to her. "I think that is a good idea, Robert. I'd love to go out with you."

Four days later, Lynn returned to her dorm and Helen made reservations to return to Atlanta. No matter what happened with her and Robert, she had to put her home up for sale.

Before he came home that night, Robert stopped at Conroy's on LaBrea to purchase a dozen red roses. He wanted everything to be right. By tomorrow, he wanted her to be madly in love with him. He had to make her understand that he loved her and Mona meant nothing. He wanted to marry her, only her. He came home an hour early and Helen was watching the dark clouds that had begun to form in the sky.

"Surprise!" he said as he entered the house.

She smiled and almost ran to the front door. "I am surprised," she said looking at him, her eyes dancing. She looked younger without makeup. She was barefoot and had on a short, blue terry cloth bathrobe. He handed her the flowers. She stood on her toes and kissed him on the cheek. They heard what sounded like rain and they both walked to the window. It thundered, and rain came down hard and fast as if the sky had opened up.

"Well," he said taking her hand and leading her to the couch. "We can stay in and build a fire in the den. We can eat in there and listen to some music. What do you think about that, Helen? Is it still a date?"

She smiled. "I say, it sounds great!" She looked toward the window. The rain was coming down even harder. "I can make some sandwiches if you're hungry."

"That sounds good. I'll change and meet you in the den."

She ran upstairs behind him and changed into jeans and a sweater. She returned to the kitchen and made the sandwiches and got a bottle of wine. By the time she took it all into the den, Robert had started the fire. He was wearing jeans and a white V-neck, T-shirt, that revealed the black hair curling on his chest. Helen sat the tray on the floor, where he had put two large pillows. There was no furniture in the room. This was another room he was waiting for Helen to furnish.

They sipped their wine and sat facing each other.

"You know what's missing?" Robert asked her.

She looked around the room. "No."

"Listen. What is it that you don't hear?" He paused.

"Music. Soft music. We were supposed to go out for dinner and dancing. Well, we have the sandwiches and now we only need the music." He jumped from the floor like a young, excited boy and ran from the room.

She stared after him and felt sadness in her heart. This was their final time together and she didn't know what to do about it. Why couldn't she just forgive him for the mistake and accept what he had to offer? Was it because she felt deep in her heart that she feared it might happen again? She tried to shake that from her mind. Tonight, all she wanted to do was enjoy being with him.

Robert knew that this was his last chance with Helen. This was his last chance to convince her that he wanted her. Tonight would determine the rest of his life. He returned to the room with a boom box. He plugged it into the wall and Barry White came out soft and clear.

"Is this better?" He looked at her with that familiar look of desire in his eyes that made her feel all warm inside. She was glad that she was already sitting down because she knew her legs wouldn't hold her up if she were standing.

He held out his hands to her, pulling her from the floor. He put one arm around her waist and she fell into step, following the music and his movement. He pulled her closer and she laid her head on his shoulder. She felt safe and she needed him. Helen wished the music would go on forever. Robert whispered her name and lifted her face. When they kissed, every sound disappeared, except for what she heard inside her chest. She moaned from deep inside her throat and locked her arms around his neck. His hands slid over her hips, bringing her closer, fitting her against his body as one. They didn't know how long they stood there because the song had changed. Her jeans, then his, fell to the floor, then another piece of clothing. They needed each other. It went on and on, over and over until they were too exhausted to do anything else but lie and hold each other. It wasn't until then that she heard the music and the rain again. Before she closed her eyes, she heard him whisper, "Helen, I love you."

They made love again before he left the next morning and when he returned home that evening, she was already on a plane headed back to Atlanta, Georgia.

Chapter 28

He walked in and called her name. No answer. He called again and again, but still no answer. Robert ran from room to room and finally looked inside the closet where she had kept her clothes. Empty. Maybe she had gone to see Lynn, but inside he knew that wasn't true.

He sat in the chair and ran his hands through his hair. He had wanted to phone her all day, but he was in court. He laid back and closed his tired eyes. Now what, he thought? But, he had no answers. He'd done everything to get her back. Maybe she just didn't love him anymore. Maybe it was too much water under the bridge for Helen to forgive or forget. Maybe he had hurt her too much. Maybe after all that had happened since the accident, and the fact that she could still walk out so easily was proof that she couldn't take him back. Maybe this was what he needed to realize it was just too late for them.

Maybe. Maybe. Maybe. Too many maybes in his life at this moment. He got up and walked past the phone when he noticed the white envelope.

Dear Robert:

Last night was the most beautiful night I've had since the last time we were together, and it is probable that I will never spend another time in my life with such beauty and closeness. I guess there is still too much that I remember and I haven't fully recovered. I've lost too much in my life these last few months to trust so easily and fall back into the same situation. Walking out today isn't easy, but it is better than suffering the consequences later. I will never forget you, Robert, and hope with all my heart that you will be happy.

Love you always, Helen.

He snapped and snarled as he lashed out with his foot and kicked the phone off the hook. And, she has the unmitigated gall to say she hopes I will be happy? Bull shit. He balled the letter in his hand and threw it on the floor. How could she? He picked up the phone, started to call her and threw it against the wall. "I won't call her again," he said aloud. "It's over. It's over. It's over," he continually repeated. "I should fly to Atlanta and tell her this to her face."

Instead, he called Joyce and made a date for dinner. She'd been trying to get him into bed for months – from the moment he'd met her at one of the attorney's birthday party. If I'm going to be dropped for sleeping with another woman, I'll sleep with a bunch of them. The time has come. Helen doesn't belong here anymore.

The minute Helen put her key in the door and turned the lock, she knew she'd made a mistake. She missed him already. She looked at her watch. He was probably home and had read her letter. She kicked off her shoes and leaned back on the couch. She'd been gone for twenty-five days and this was not a happy homecoming. She phoned Lynn to let her know that she had made it home safely.

"But, I don't understand why you changed your flight and left earlier, Mom."

"I had some important phone calls to make that I'd forgotten about. How are you feeling, honey?"

"Don't worry about me. I'm doing fine. Aunt Elaine called to ask if I needed anything but I told her that my room looks like a supermarket. But, I will be happy when you move out here, Mom."

"I'll be happy too, honey. I miss you already. But the sooner I get started, the sooner I'll be back. Now, I want you to take it easy and don't move too fast."

"Yes, Mom. I love you."

Helen hung up the phone in tears. When the phone rang, she jumped. It was her realtor. She had called him from Los Angeles. He was the same one who had sold her the town-house, so he was familiar with the area.

Finally, she took her suitcases upstairs and threw herself across the bed. She couldn't hold it in any longer and she

cried. There was no Darlene to talk to until she felt better.
There was no one there for her. She had to leave Atlanta and
start all over. "Dear God. I am so tired of the hurt and the pain
I feel from missing everyone I love," she whispered. She got
up and put on a pair of jogging shorts. After the realtor left,
she would go out and run. Run until she was too tired to think.
Too tired to think about the ache in her heart for Robert.

Chapter 29

"Miss Graham. I have an offer for your townhouse. I just got the offer today."

"I'm impressed. I didn't expect this so soon."

"You do want to sell?"

"Yes. As soon as possible," Helen said, as she stood and looked around the room as if it was the last time.

"When can I bring the offer over for you to review it?"

"Today. As soon as you can."

"Terrific. I'll see you in an hour."

Precisely an hour later, her doorbell rang. When she opened the door, he peered up at her through his thick-rimmed glasses that seemed to need cleaning. She was taller than he and could look down at his bald spot in the middle of his head. He entered the townhouse quickly, like he was in a hurry to move on to his next sale. Helen smiled and motioned for him to have a seat on the couch.

"Would you like a coke or glass of water?" she asked him.

"No thanks, I'm just fine." He set his briefcase on the coffee table and pulled out the purchase agreement.

She read the offer. "This looks good, Mr. Jones."

"No counter offer?"

"No, I accept this. It's three thousand dollars more than I said I would sell for." She signed it and gave it back to him.

"The young man will be very pleased." He looked at Helen and felt dampness spring to the top of his head. Any man still breathing with a brain in his head would appreciate those long shapely legs around his waist, and he was a breathing man, and had a brain.

"How long is the escrow?" Helen asked.

"Oh, I'm sorry, Miss Graham, what did you say?"

"How long is the escrow?"

"He wants to close as soon as possible. We're looking at thirty days."

"The sooner the better for me, Mr. Jones."

He stood, holding his briefcase. "What are you going to do now, Miss Graham?"

"I'm moving to Los Angeles. I have a daughter and two sisters there," she said happily.

"Yes, I remember your daughter. She was a pretty little girl, but she's almost grown now, isn't she?"

"She's in college," Helen said with pride. "I'll be renting an apartment until I found a house that I want."

He moaned. "Too bad you'll have to move twice. It's so much work."

"I know, but there's no easy way to do anything, Mr. Jones," she said sadly.

"I hope things work out for you, Miss Graham."

When she closed the door behind him, she thought about Robert. If she were moving in with him, she wouldn't even wait the thirty days for the escrow to close. Why can't I just forgive him? she asked herself.

That night, she tried to sleep, but tossed and turned from one side of the bed to the other. She got up, warmed a glass of milk and took it back to her bedroom. She sat in her favorite chair and looked out on the city. She sighed and felt a tear roll down her cheek. The last time she felt this way, Darlene had marched into her living room like a hard wind and talked her out of it. This time, she had no one. And when she got to Los Angeles, it wouldn't be much different. Lynn would finish school and live her own life. Elaine had a family of her own and Harriet didn't want to see any of them.

She closed her eyes and tried to think of Robert with another woman, but she kept hearing a little voice that said, "Maybe the other woman didn't mean anything to him like he said." Helen shook her head. Maybe he did tell her the truth. Maybe. Maybe. Shit. Helen tried to drink her milk, but couldn't swallow. Finally she put the glass down and forced herself to sleep.

The next morning, she didn't get out of bed until after nine. She was still tired from jet lag, but she had so much to do. After dressing in jeans and an oversized sweatshirt, she sat at the kitchen table, with her cup of coffee and wheat toast, and made a to-do list. As she ate, the phone rang. She didn't recognize the woman's voice at first.

"Oh, Miss Lettie. How are you? You have a cold? I'm sorry about that, but it's good to hear from you. I've been trying to keep myself busy since Darlene passed." Helen poured herself another cup of coffee and continued chatting. "I just got back from L.A. My daughter was hit by a car and I had to go and take care of her. Luckily, it wasn't too serious."

Miss Lettie invited Helen to come over.

"I don't want to bother you if you're feeling a bit under the weather. What? You have tea cakes? I'll be right over." As she hung up the phone, Helen felt much better. It would be good to see Miss Lettie. She was a lifelong friend of Darlene's mother and treated Helen like family too. She was 75 years old, with white hair that was always pinned up in a ball on top of her head. She was tall, heavy, and sat around watching talk shows and soap operas all day when she wasn't cooking or baking. She knew everyone's business, just by the sound of their voice, or the expression in their eyes and face. She said that was something being over 70 taught her. She'd look at her neighbor and say, 'Her husbands ain't lovable toward his wife', 'Miss Whatchamacillits had a good night. Chile, I can tell by the pep in her step. Now, you take Mr. Whatchamacillits in the green house across the street over there. He's whoring around on his wife. Come in all hours and time of the night. If he was a husband of mine, I would put his ass out in the streets, his entire ass in the middle of the streets. Clothes and all.' Helen and Darlene would laugh all the way home, but they loved visiting her, and Miss Lettie had a good head on her shoulders, she had wisdom and a big heart.

Helen was at Miss Lettie's door at one. She opened the door while wiping her hands on her pink apron.

"Hi, honey. I was just making a meatloaf cause Sonny Boy is coming over later today."

"Oh, no," Helen replied.

"I know he picks on you, but chile, he only do it cause he wants you for hisself."

Helen sighed. "Did I stop you from cooking dinner, Miss Lettie?"

"Now what if you did? I can mix a meatloaf and talk at the same time."

Helen laughed and followed Miss Lettie down the long, narrow hall that led to the kitchen. "It smells good in here, like it always does." Helen took a seat at the round table, covered with a red and white table cloth. The white nylon curtains in the kitchen window looked like they were freshly washed and ironed. Her large black and white stove had pots hanging on the rack on each side. She set a plate on the table in front of Helen with two cups of steaming tea.

"I started to make fresh donuts with the Beignet mix that Anna sent me from New Orleans. Sent all kinds of goodies to me last week." As she spoke, she changed the channel to Sally Jesse Raphael's show. "Now, that's my girl, there," she said as she looked at the TV screen. "She has all types of fools on her show. But, she's good. I don't miss her show. I could watch her and Oprah all day and never get tired."

Helen sipped her tea. "Oh, I love it when you put honey in it. Darlene used to fix my tea this way."

"Honey, I knew you would like it. Where do you think Darlene got it from?" She watched Helen closely. "What's bothering you, chile?"

Helen looked up from her cup and tears began to form in her eyes.

"Is it Lynn?" Miss Lettie asked as she sat at the table.

"No, she's fine. It's me, Miss Lettie." The tears were falling uncontrollably now.

Miss Lettie moved into the chair next to Helen and held out her arms. Helen laid her head on the older woman's shoulder. "It can't be that bad, baby."

"Yes, it is that bad," Helen whispered between sobs. "It's worse than bad, Miss Lettie. My life is falling apart and I don't know what to do about it. First, I lose Darlene, and now Robert." She told Miss Lettie the whole story.

"Now, let me get this right. Because of one screw up before your marriage, you walk out and make your life miserable and his too? One screw up and you run? Well,

I'm surprised at you, Helen. I thought you were stronger than that."

Helen sat up straight in her chair. "But, I'm being strong by not taking him back."

The older woman was standing again. She put both hands on her hips and leaned closer to Helen. "No, you're not being strong, you're being a fool. He is a man, that's all, and that woman put the silver tray out there for him, then served it. He probably would have turned her down if you were living in L.A. Think about it for a second, baby."

Helen was still wiping her eyes.

"You're a smart woman," Miss Lettie continued. Just think about it. Some men will accept it even when they don't really want it and it don't have to be good either. It don't mean he loves the woman. It don't have to mean anything to him. And you're mad over a dead woman?"

Helen nodded and Miss Lettie returned to her seat.

"Open your eyes, honey." She pointed a finger at Helen. "Look at what you're doing to yourself and to him. Listen to me, Helen."

"But, it hurts so much, Miss Lettie. It was so disappointing."

"Life is disappointing, Helen. Look around you. How many people in this world haven't been disappointed a time or two?"

Helen held her head down. "Everyone has been, I suppose."

"You're right about that, chile. Now, I can't make you go back to that man, but why sit here and be unhappy, crying your eyes out? It sounds like this man is a once in a lifetime man. You are trying to punish him, but you're hurting."

"I hadn't thought of it that way."

"Well, honey, ain't no woman gon sit around and wait for you to forgive and make up your mind. Chile, if I was younger, I'd give you a run for your money with him."

Helen laughed between tears. "I knew you would make me laugh, Miss Lettie."

They talked a bit more before Miss Lettie said, "Did you hear that Jimmy died? Not too long after Darlene."

"No, I didn't know that. Darlene wanted to go by and see him."

"Well, enough of this kind of talk. He was never nice to that chile anyway. Now, eat some tea cakes while they're still warm and let's see what damn fools Sally Jessie got on her show today. After she goes off, I'll turn it to my girl Oprah."

Chapter 30

"Robert, Miss Anita Taylor is here to see you, but she doesn't have an appointment."

Robert stood up and smiled. "She doesn't need one. It's okay, send her in." He was standing when Anita entered, closed the door and walked into outstretched arms. "Gee, it's good to see you, Anita. I've missed you."

She kissed him on the cheek and sat in the chair opposite his desk. Her eyes glanced around his office. "You have a real nice set up here, Robert." She rubbed her hand against the large oak desk. "Nothing like the cheap stuff in the City Attorney's office." She noticed the two large plants in the corner. "I'd love to work in a place that looks like this."

"I'll talk to them and get you in here. We can always use someone as good as you."

She knew he was serious. "Thanks, but I'm leaving Los Angeles."

For a moment, he thought she was joking, but then he knew she spoke the truth. "Leaving? But why, Anita? Where would you go?"

"Back to Mississippi. My mother is very ill so I have to go."

"I'm sorry to hear that." He looked at his watch. "Have you had lunch yet?"

"No, and I could surely use something."

They walked to the Red Lobster in the next block and Robert requested a table where they could talk without being disturbed.

"How's everyone at the office?" he asked.

"Everyone's all right. A little busy, but nothing has changed. I hate leaving, but I have to." She looked at Robert closely and noticed that his eyes were red as though he hadn't gotten enough sleep.

It was hard to believe that she was leaving. That job was her life, he thought as he listened to her. "When are you leaving?"

"In a week. My mother has cancer and somebody has to take care of her. My brothers and sisters are too involved with their own lives to take care of her."

"Has the doctor said how long she has?"

Anita got misty-eyed and he reached across the table and held her hand. "Not more than a year, if that long. Her twin sister is with her now, but I think one of her children should be there."

"I agree, but I'm going to miss you, Anita. We've been friends for a long time, you know."

"We'll still be friends. We'll keep in touch. You can even come out and visit me."

"You can count on that. You were always the closest thing I ever had to a sister. And, I love you for that," he said sincerely.

"I've always loved you too, Robert." And, he didn't know that she meant it in every sense of the word. She had always been in love with him.

"Is there anything I can do for you before you leave?"

"No, I've got everything under control. Today is my last day."

"Did you ever find a replacement for Mona's position"" he asked with a sad look in his eyes.

"Yes, she's in her middle forties, married with three children and is not looking for a man," Anita laughed.

"It was a terrible thing that happened to Mona."

"Yes, it was."

"But the way she messed up my life and I only touched her once..." he said, shaking his head.

"You haven't been able to convince Helen of that, have you?"

"No."

The waitress brought their lunch of steak and lobster.

"Maybe some day Helen will realize what she's missing and come around. Maybe it's still too soon for her," Anita said.

"I understand, but how much time does a person need if

she really loves someone? If the tables were reversed, I think I would have believed her, Anita."

"Think about it, Robert. There were pictures. It's not as easy as just believing, you know."

"I know."

As the restaurant got busier, they chatted and looked out the window. Anita looked into Robert's handsome face. Helen Graham, she thought to herself, wherever you are, you had better make up your mind fast before another Mona comes along.

After lunch, Anita and Robert said their good-byes at her car.

That night, Robert sat in his study, trying to concentrate on the book in front of him. Joyce had wanted to cook dinner for him, since he'd taken her out to dinner the last time they were together. But, he wasn't interested. She was attractive and he knew he could like her, if he'd give himself the chance. But he couldn't get Helen out of his mind. He hadn't even taken Joyce to bed, though that had been his intentions. But, he knew it wouldn't fix anything for him.

But, there was nothing he could do. He had promised himself that if he and Helen had ever gotten together, he would never let her go. He would not lose her again. But, he had. For one stupid mistake, that Helen couldn't forgive.

Well, there was nothing he could do. He had to go on with his life. She had told him that it was over and that was that.   Here it was Friday night and he was alone reading a book. He sighed. He wondered if he would ever get over her.

The doorbell rang. "Hell," he murmured. He wasn't expecting anyone and thought about not answering. When he opened the door, he was stopped in his tracks. He looked at her from head to toe. She was wearing a black dress that revealed her shapely figure and the neckline of the dress was so low, he could see the top of her breasts. Her hair was lying over her shoulders like silk. He was speechless, and she looked more beautiful and sexier than he had ever seen her before.

She ran her tongue over her bottom lip. "May I come in, Robert?" she whispered in a low voice.

He was too shocked to answer and he moved aside to let her pass. She stood close to him and he inhaled the soft fragrance of her perfume. They looked at each other for what seemed like hours before she fell into his arms. "Helen, are you here for good?"

She held him close. "Yes, Robert, if you'll marry me."

"Welcome home, baby." They embraced and he whispered over and over again his love for her and this time, she opened her heart and let him in. She didn't want to live without him.

It wasn't long before they were upstairs in bed. In the middle of the night, he sat up on one elbow and watched her sleeping peacefully. Her lips were slightly parted and her hair was wrapped around his finger. She was finally his. He touched her smooth thighs and she moaned deeply, wanting more of him. When she opened her eyes, she moaned again as she yielded to him completely. Nothing would come between them again.

The next morning, Helen phoned Elaine and told her that she and Robert were getting married and the two sisters cried their happiness over the phone.

"It's about time," Elaine said. "I'm so very happy for you."

Lynn was also excited for her mother and Robert. She was happy they'd be living in the same city again. The accident made her realize how much she needed and missed her mother.

Two weeks later, Robert and Helen were married and in forty days the escrow on her townhouse closed. She spent the next week moving into Robert's house and enjoying her new life. A few days later, while she was working in the upstairs bathroom, the phone rang.

"Miss Graham, this is Lorraine, the office manager at the 52nd Street school."

Helen's eyes widened. "Is my sister okay?" she asked and sat in the chair near her.

"Yes, and I'm sorry if I frightened you. We are having a baby shower here at the school. I wanted to invite you and ask if there was anyone else I should call?"

She released a deep sigh of relief and held her head back, still feeling her hands tremble.

"I know her due date is in two weeks," Lorraine continued. "And, we're pretty late, but we've been so busy with the new construction of the school."

"When is it?"

"Friday. I hope that's convenient for you. We would like to surprise her."

"Sure, just give me all the details and I'll be there." Helen smiled as she wrote down the information. "See you on Friday."

When Helen hung up, she left a message for Lynn. They had to go shopping and only had two days. At least it would be slightly easier to find a present, since Elaine had told her she was having a girl. My niece, Helen thought. That sounded so strange. Elaine's baby would be her first niece.

Helen continued trying to get the house in order. She furnished her study with the same furniture she had in her townhouse. Her bedroom suite went into the guest bedroom. She put the rest of her furniture in storage for Lynn. Helen and Robert were settling in to a wonderful married life and they both knew that this was the way their marriage would always be.

Helen and Lynn were already at Elaine's baby shower when Elaine walked into the classroom. There were balloons hanging from the ceiling and a small table in the corner with sandwiches, a cake and a bowl of punch. There were twenty teachers, and Helen had invited Elaine's neighbor. When everyone yelled, 'surprise,' Elaine jumped and looked around, taking in everything at once. She looked at Helen and Lynn and then the gifts stacked in the corner. Her eyes started to water and Lorraine held her arm and led her to the chair that was decorated for her. Helen and Lynn stood by her side.

"Are you really surprised, Aunt Elaine?" asked Lynn.

Helen gave her a tissue. "I knew you would need these. Pregnant women cry a lot."

As Elaine greeted her guests, Lorraine walked up to Helen. "It's a pleasure to meet you." Lorraine shook Helen's hand. She was a short blonde, with light blue eyes and didn't look older than twenty. "Is this your daughter?" Lorraine asked as she smiled at Lynn.

Lynn said hello and looked around at the decorations. "Did you do all the decorating, Lorraine?" Lynn asked.

"Most of it. I work in the office, so I had more time than the teachers."

"Okay, let's have cake and punch and Elaine can open the gifts."

The baby shower was over at five and all the guests helped Elaine carry the gifts to the car. She said good-bye to everyone. This was her last day at work and she wasn't exactly sure when she'd be back. Dan wanted her to stay home with the baby for at least a year before going back to work.

Two weeks later, at two in the morning, the phone rang. Robert switched on the lamp and Helen sat up straight in the bed. It was Dan, calling from the hospital. Helen and Robert jumped out of the bed, grabbing their clothes.

"No, Robert. Get back in bed. You have to be at the office in the morning."

He stood for a few seconds and hesitated. "Well, I am working hard on this closing for tomorrow."

"Then, you need your rest and clear head," she said, slipping into her jeans. "Besides, we were up pretty late," she smiled mischievously.

"Yeah. You wouldn't keep your hands off of me."

"I couldn't help myself," she said as she appraised his body. She motioned for him to get back in bed.

"No, I'll walk you to the car." He followed her into the garage and kissed her. "Drive carefully, Helen." Robert knew how fast she could drive.

Helen parked in the Kaiser parking lot and ran inside the hospital. When she got off the elevator, she saw Dan and his brother.

"Is she all right?" Helen asked.

"Yes, I came out so that the doctor could examine her," Dan said nervously.

Helen looked at Roger, Dan's brother. "Hi, Roger. It's good you're here with Dan. He looks frightened to death."

Roger looked in his brother's direction, laughed and patted him on the back. "I already have two boys, so when he called me, I could hear the fear in his voice. And, I knew he needed me with him. I understood how he felt," he said more to Dan than to Helen.

The doctor came out of the room and as he talked to Dan, his eyes kept shifting in Helen's direction. Dan introduced Helen to the doctor as his wife's sister.

"Can we go in to see her now?" Helen asked.

"Sure. It shouldn't be more than a couple of hours now, Mr. Smith."

Helen left the two brothers outside and walked into the small room. Elaine was lying on her back and her eyes were closed. She opened them when she heard Helen whisper her name. She took Helen's hand as Helen sat in the chair. Elaine's hair was in disarray and she looked as though she had been crying.

"Oh, Helen, I'm so glad to see you and I'll be glad when this is over."

"The doctor says it won't be long now. Just hang in there."

A momentary spasm of pain deepened the wrinkles in Elaine's forehead and she groaned. Helen pushed Elaine's hair from her face and held her hand tight.

"You're going to have a beautiful baby soon, honey. Just think, I'll be an aunt," she said with a wide smile that turned into a frown when she felt Elaine squeeze her hands as tears ran down her face. Elaine's pains were coming stronger and closer together. Dan walked into the room and Helen moved aside. Dan took Elaine's hand and instructed her to breathe the way the instructor taught her in class. He kissed her forehead and talked to her.

"I'm trying, but Dan, it hurts."

"I know, honey. But it won't be long now. Just hold on a while longer." Taking deep breaths, he breathed with her, holding her hands and rubbing her stomach. Helen looked into his face and saw beads of sweat across his forehead as he whispered softly into Elaine's ear. "There, baby. It'll be soon."

Helen walked out of the room to give them the time alone. Dan had sent his brother home, but Helen was determined to stay. She walked to the vending machine and bought a cup of coffee. Outside of the room, she could hear Elaine's scream and the bottom of her stomach felt as though it turned upside down. She sipped on the strong coffee. Another scream, and she put the coffee in the trash can. She paced up and down the hall with her hands covering her ears. Another scream and Helen said a prayer. A half-hour passed. She was halfway out of her mind when Dan walked out, smiling from ear to ear.

"It's a girl! An eight-pound beautiful girl, Helen." Dan and Helen hugged each other, then Helen pulled away.

"How does she look?"

"She has a head full of red hair," he laughed.

"Shit!" She laughed and ran to the phone booth to call Robert.

"Honey, it's me."

"I was hoping you'd call before I left."

It was soothing to hear her husband's strong voice. She looked at her watch; it was six. "Robert, she just had an eight-pound girl. Can you believe it?"

"Yes!" he laughed. "She was big enough. Congratulations. You're an aunt. How is she?"

"Dan says she's all right."

"Well, when you get home, make sure you get some rest. I'll try to be home earlier today."

She smiled as she hung up. She had called her husband. Husband, the word sounded good to her.

The new baby was named Danielle Renee Smith and Helen was delighted that Elaine had given the baby the same middle name as Lynn. Danielle was as beautiful as her mother predicted, with her father's red hair. Elaine cried when she held her daughter in her arms. She had never felt such happiness.

Helen finally left the hospital at eight-thirty. She went home and slept four hours. That evening, she returned to the hospital with Robert and Lynn. They chatted with Elaine, Dan, Roger and Roger's wife, Diane.

A few days later, Elaine checked out of the hospital and Helen was at their home getting everything ready for the baby. She had cooked dinner, and baked a chocolate cake, decorated with Danielle's name. Coming home was special for Elaine. She was coming home to a husband and a baby. A year ago, she hadn't known what would become of her life. And now, she had a family of her own.

Chapter 31

Lynn met her father in Westwood at a small restaurant where they could sit outside and eat. It was a warm, sunny, May day and she wore a short sleeve shirt and jeans. From the start, she sensed this meeting would be different from their first one. For one thing, he had let months past before he had contacted her and told her he was coming back to Los Angeles. It didn't seem like they were going to be able to develop a close relationship.

As they sat at the table, he seemed quite surprised about her being in the hospital. "I just don't understand why you didn't call to tell me what happened," he said, sounding insulted. "And I can't believe your mother didn't call me."

Lynn looked at him like he was stone crazy. After all these years, why should her mother call and tell him anything. Lynn wished that she had just told him she had to study, when he had called. She was only half-listening when he mentioned again that Helen should have contacted him.

"Dad, I was fine. Mom probably felt that there was no need to call you since you don't normally talk to each other."

He shook his head. What could he say? "Has she started a new book yet?"

"No. She just finished one a couple of months ago."

"Maybe I'll call her when I get home."

"You don't have to wait until you get home. Mom lives here now."

He looked at her as if he didn't know what to say. His eyes lit up. "You mean, she's here in Los Angeles? Why didn't you say something before?"

"Because I thought you came to see me, not her," she snapped, with displeasure reflecting on her face.

He could hear the irritation in her voice and decided to change his tactics. She was quick like her mother.

"Sweetheart, of course I came to see you. Why would you think differently." He reached across the table and touched her hand.

Lynn was annoyed. Why should she waste anymore time with him? She pushed her plate away and stood up.

He looked up at her. "Now come on, sweetheart, relax and finish your lunch. I saw a chocolate cake and thought we could have a slice for dessert."

Maybe she was being too hasty. She sat back down and he smiled at her.

"How's school?" he asked with very little interest.

"It's okay. I'll be glad when I'm finished. I have to go back to my room soon so that I can study before I go to work this afternoon."

He looked surprised. "You mean, you work, with all the money your mother has?"

"Of course. Mom says I don't have to, but I like earning my own money and it isn't interfering with my schooling..." She looked at him questioningly, not understanding his reaction. And then, it hit her. She didn't want to waste anymore time with him and decided to put all of his curiosity to rest. "Did you know my Mom got married?" She watched his mouth fly open. "Yes, she's married to a lawyer. He's very nice and she's very happy."

Lynn stood with a smirk on her face and waited until he completely digested the shock of what she had said. She picked up her purse. "Good-bye, Dad. And have a good life. Next time you're in L.A., don't bother to call." She walked away with tears in her eyes. "The old bastard," she hissed. Her feelings were hurt. She thought he wanted a relationship with her, but he was just using her to get to her mother and her money.

He didn't try to stop her and sat staring at his glass of water. He looked at Lynn's plate. She had barely touched her food. After twenty minutes, he walked out without picking up the tab. No need to pay for food that wasn't touched. He would patch things up with Lynn, but he would give her time to mellow out. The only problem was, if Lynn was anything like Helen, that could take a long time. He sighed. Guess I'll have to figure out another way to get my house out of foreclosure, he thought as he ran across the street.

Lynn rang her mother's bell twice before Helen answered the door. She walked in, past her mother. Then she stopped and hugged her.

"What a nice hello," Helen said as she looked into her daughter's face. She closed the door behind Lynn. "Come into my study while I sign off the computer."

"Were you writing?"

"Yes, but only notes and names of places that I'm going to write about. I've been so busy decorating, that I can't seem to remember all the ideas I have up here," she said pointing to her head.

Lynn followed her mother and stood silently staring at a picture of her mother and Darlene.

"Why the long face, honey? Didn't your lunch go well?"

"No. Mom, he never wanted to know me. It was always about you and your money."

"I don't have that much money, Lynn."

"You have more than he does, Mom. Enough to live comfortably for the rest of your life."

"He must be pretty bad off because money never excited him before. The only thing that excited him were parties and other women." Helen could see that Lynn was irritated and disappointed. "You know, Lynn, he made me believe that he wanted to get to know you. I'm telling you, if I ever see him again, he'll get an earful from me. He will hear about this," she said simmering with anger. She put her arms around her daughter. "I'm sorry that you had to go through this, honey. But, you don't need him."

"I know, Mom. You were always there for me like my mother and father."

"Well, enough talk about this. Let's make us some sandwiches, since my guess is you didn't eat much at lunch."

They went into the kitchen.

"Hey, do you have any peanut butter and jelly?"

Helen laughed. "You know I do," Helen said as she opened the refrigerator and handed Lynn the peach jelly. "The peanut butter is in the cabinet over there," she pointed.

They chatted through lunch and finally Lynn had to leave.

"Well, Mom. At least I know who my father really is. I feel much better now."

Helen smiled and hugged her daughter. "I'll see you tomorrow at Danielle's christening." Helen stood at the door and watched Lynn drive away.

"I think I have a plot for a new book. That is when I get time to write again. I've been writing down ideas for weeks, but just can't seem to put any of it into motion."

Robert smiled and Helen leaned back in the car enjoying the fresh air blowing against her face. She grinned mischievously, when Robert leaned over and put his hand on her knee. Finally, they reached the church.

"I see Lynn is already here," Robert said and parked right behind her. "There are quite a few people here."

Robert and Helen took seats behind Lynn. Helen looked around the church to see if Harriet had come. Of course, she had not. The church was small, but there were at least twenty people there. Helen recognized a few people from the baby shower.

The christening started with two women singing, "You've Been Good To Me" and it made Helen think of her mother and father. The pastor then asked everyone to stand for prayer and he recited a prayer for Danielle. Danielle just awakening from her nap and Helen smiled. Her niece was now five months old with curly red hair. She was wearing a white dress and shoes.

The pastor sprinkled a few drops of water on Danielle and said another prayer. Elaine cried and Dan wiped the tears from her eyes.

After the christening, everyone met at Dan and Elaine's house. There was a long table lined with a lace tablecloth, on the shaded patio, and food from one end to the other. Helen played with the baby while Elaine finished setting out the food. Elaine looked out at Danielle and Dan and she had to stop for a moment. This was her family. God, she thought, so much had happened in their lives in the last year and a half.

Lynn smiled as she looked at her mother and walked over with her new friend. "Mom, I'd like you to meet Cassandra," Lynn said making the introductions. "She is Aunt Elaine's neighbor."

Helen extended her hand. "I'm happy to meet you, Cassandra."

Lynn asked if she could hold Danielle. Helen left Danielle with Lynn and walked outside when she bumped into a tall man.

"I'm sorry, Miss."

She looked up and smiled, then, looked into his face carefully. "Ronald, Ronald Kenny?"

He looked down at her and threw his head back and laughed. "Oh, no, it's not you, Helen?" His eyes smiled as he remembered so many years ago in high school, when he stole a kiss from her in the parking lot.

"Oh, yes, it sure the hell is me."

He picked her up and kissed her on each cheek. When he put her down, he stepped back to take a good look at her. "You're prettier than you were the last time I saw you and that was twenty years ago."

"Yes, it has been a long time," she said laughing up at him. He was still handsome and she felt so good seeing him. From the corner of her eye, she could see Robert watching her, but she didn't know what he was thinking.

Robert kept his eyes on his wife. He didn't particularly like the way the man was looking at Helen. And, the man seemed to be alone. He wondered if he were one of Helen's old boyfriends. He watched the man touch Helen's arms and shoulders and he wanted to go over and remind Helen that she was married. Robert watched Helen walk away, refill her glass with champagne and return to the man. Robert also noticed that the man never took his eyes off of Helen. They seemed to have too much to talk about and Helen seemed to be enjoying his company. As the seconds ticked by, Robert was getting angrier. He wasn't used to feeling jealous and he didn't like the way he felt. Maybe he loved her too much. Could a man really love his wife too much? Or maybe it was because he had waited so long for her and now he felt threatened.

Robert couldn't take it any more and decided it was time to put an end to this madness. As he stood and started in their direction, a woman walked up to the man, hugged Helen and kissed the man on the mouth. Then, Helen and the woman embraced again just as Robert approached. Helen grabbed Robert by his arm.

"This is the wonderful man I was telling you about. This is my husband Robert. Robert, this is Ronald Kenny and his wife Janet. You had transferred to Dorsey High when the three of us were in high school together."

Robert and Ronald shook hands and suddenly, Robert didn't feel the resentment he'd felt only moments before. Helen stood close to her husband and looked into his eyes. Robert was suddenly reminded of that morning and how she had lain in his arms. He looked into her brown eyes and it hurt him deep inside. At that moment, just like other moments he had had with his wife, he felt something inside that was so familiar, so strong and so deep. Something he would remember for the rest of his life. Christ, I'm in love for the first time in my life. And, for the last time, he knew.

Chapter 32

"I was so sure that she would have lived at least nine or ten months, Robert. But the stroke took her right out of this world. It happened so fast, she couldn't even hang on until my brother arrived." Anita's eyes watered and Robert handed her the box of tissues from his desk. "But, it's best this way. I didn't want my mother to suffer. Have you ever seen anyone suffer through the pain of cancer, Robert?"

"No, but I've heard what it's like."

"It's harder on the loved ones," Anita said, with pain in her eyes. She sighed. "So, I'm back earlier than I had planned. I called personnel to let them know I'm back, but I need another month off. I have to find another apartment and get settled before I can return to work."

Robert looked at Anita with concern. She had lost weight and he could tell she was still grieving. But he wanted to change the subject to cheer her up. He looked at his watch.

"We still have some time. Helen's not expecting us until six and she will be glad to see you."

"Oh, how is she?"

"Her writing keeps her busy and she's decorating the house. She also has to learn her way around L.A. again."

Anita saw the light in his eyes as he spoke of his wife. "I'm so happy to see that you're happy again, Robert."

He leaned back in his chair and relaxed. "You know, Anita, it may sound strange, but being so happy and having my life complete is a strange feeling sometimes."

"Why?" she asked, slightly confused.

"For years, I only existed. I got up in the morning, went to work, took a holiday off, met new people, and smiled because I was supposed to. I was thankful for my life, my health, my strength and of course a good job. But now, I have

all of this *and* love. It's the most beautiful, gratifying feeling
that any human being can experience. It's strange, but beautiful."

Anita nodded in agreement. She'd had it once, but not
for a very long time. Robert was lucky, but so was Helen. "I
know, Robert. Listening to you makes me miss being in love,"
she said sadly. "I'll bet you don't take your love for granted,
do you?"

"You're damn right I don't. Now, let's go. Helen's probably waiting."

Helen looked at her dining room table once more. It was
perfect. She wanted the entire night to be just right for Robert's
guest. He'd told her about Anita before and she was saddened
when Anita had phoned to say that her mother had passed. At
least she was close to her mother, Helen thought.

She heard the car pull into the driveway and felt her heart
jump as it did everyday when Robert came home. She
wondered how long this feeling would last – she hoped it
would be forever. She quickly moved through the living room
and dining room to make sure she hadn't forgotten anything.
She was still standing in the dining room when Robert walked
in and called her name. She kissed her husband on his cheek
and she and Anita smiled at each other.

Helen held out her hand. "I feel as if I've known you
forever and I'm glad you could make it for dinner. Welcome to
our home."

Anita gave her a warm smile. "I feel like I've known you
forever too."

The two women took to each other immediately and they
talked, laughed, made plans to go shopping and have lunch
together.

Helen served roasted chicken, wild rice, mixed vegetables and hot rolls. After dinner, they went into the den and
had coffee and cake and talked some more. Anita had spent the
evening studying Helen. There was no doubt they would
become friends and since she couldn't have Robert, she was
glad Helen was in his life. Robert looked so at peace. Their
home was warm and friendly and Anita enjoyed herself.

"This was just what I needed," Anita said. "To be among
friends and relax. I've been staying with my cousin and her

two kids, so it was good to get out for a while," she said with relief.

Helen and Robert walked Anita to her car and watched her drive off. After cleaning up, they went to bed.

Helen woke up in the middle of the night and quietly got out of bed. She went into her study, turned on her computer and started to write. When she stopped, the sun was creeping through the blinds. The crystal clock on her desk told her it was six. Where did the time go? she wondered. She went back upstairs, brushed her teeth and climbed back into bed, into her husband's arms.

That morning as Helen was working in the backyard, she heard a car pulling into her driveway. Who was it, she wondered? She smiled. Maybe it was Robert pulling one of his tricks like he had last week. She had been in the kitchen that morning when she heard the front door open. She went into the livingroom and there was Robert, standing in the middle of the room, waiting for her. He grabbed her and kissed her hard.

"What are you doing here at this time of day?" she had asked him with a wide grin.

"I forgot something this morning," he had said with deviltry dancing in his eyes.

"What?"

He was still holding her. "A quickie, that's what."

She laughed, even though she knew he was serious. He kissed her again, moving one hand slowly up her thigh.

"I'm glad you're wearing this little robe. It makes it all easier."

They kissed all the way to the extra bedroom down the hall until they tumbled onto the bed. She helped him undress and he slowly made love to her.

When they finished, she whispered in his ear, "I thought this was supposed to be a quickie?"

"It was, but I changed my mind."

"I'm glad you did..."

Now, she walked into the house, waiting for Robert with anticipation. She loved these little surprises. What was keeping him so long, she wondered? She walked to the front door, opened it and to her surprise, Anita was standing there.

"I do apologize for not calling first, but I was so close by, I decided to drop in and say hello."

Helen opened the door wider for her to enter. "No apology needed. Come on in."

"Are you sure you don't mind, Helen? I can come back another time."

"Goodness no, Anita. Have a seat." Anita followed Helen into the den. "Really, I could use the company. Would you like a cup of tea?"

"No thanks, but I would like to take you to lunch or maybe we could just window shop. It was so nice of you to have me here for dinner last week, Helen."

"It was my pleasure." Helen could tell in Anita's eyes that something was wrong.

Anita cleared her throat. "I couldn't sleep last night. I think my mother's death is getting to me. I'm trying to cope with it, but it's so hard."

"Yeah, I know. I lost my mother and father." Helen suddenly realized that two years had already passed since her mother died. She was amazed the time had gone by so quickly. "I also lost my best friend. We were like sisters, much closer than some."

"I'm sorry, Helen. Robert did mention that to me. Look, I know a nice place we can go to lunch. Is that okay with you?"

Helen agreed and Anita took her to the Marina, to a small restaurant with a view of the pier. The skies were clear with birds flying across the ocean. It was a warm, clear day and the scene was peaceful.

"I guess I just needed the company. I'm glad you could come, Helen."

"Thank you for asking me."

"I fell asleep early last night, then had a dream that kept me up for the rest of the night. It was about my mother."

"I'm sorry about that Anita, but it may happen for a while and then it'll get easier. It still happens to me sometimes. So, you're staying with a cousin?" Helen asked trying to change the subject.

Anita nodded.

"Have you ever been married?" Helen asked.

"Yes, but it only lasted two years and that was eighteen years ago."

"And you never wanted to remarry?"

Anita looked hurt and Helen was sorry that she had asked. Helen put up one hand. "I'm sorry. Stupid me. That is none of my business. Here, I should be making you feel better and look what I've done."

Anita leaned across the table. "Oh, no, Helen. I don't mind talking about it. I think we should get to know each other." She patted Helen's hand. "And, yes. I did want to get married again, but I wasted so much time on one man. I spent five years with a man who kept promising to marry me. I did everything I could to prove my love to him. I brought him expensive gifts, gold rings, watches, four-hundred-dollar suits, everything and anything he wanted."

"Wow and you two never got together?"

"No. My mother hated the man. She told me that he was using me and that he was no good. She said I was only looking at his pretty face. My mother knew he would never marry me. Helen, that man broke my heart in two."

"Well, you're not the only one something like that has happened to. We've all had to learn. It's just that some men are worse than others."

"I know," Anita said. "But the worst thing was that eventually he did get married – to someone else who was ten years younger."

"Bastard," whispered Helen.

"They live in a little community called Phillips Ranch in Pomona and have children, I understand." Anita sighed. "So, I don't think of marriage anymore, Helen. That part of my life is over with. I've accepted my life the way it is." She smiled a peaceful smile. "But there is something that bothers me."

"What?"

"When I hear these young girls talking about what they buy their men, I want to tell them, they're wasting their time. It doesn't matter what you buy them or what you do for them. Honey, if they don't want you, they don't want you. That's just the way it is."

"Yeah, I heard that, girl," Helen said.

Anita reached across the table and touched Helen's hand. "I'm glad I've met a friend."

"I am too, Anita."

They chatted through lunch and finally Helen asked, "How much time do you have before you have to go back to work?"

"Three weeks. We've got to get together before I go back." Helen was quiet for a moment and Anita wondered if she had said something out of place. "Did I say something wrong?" Anita asked.

"No, it's not you. I wanted to ask you something. Did you know the woman who was shot – you know, the woman that Robert was working with?"

"Oh, Mona." Anita looked at Helen closely. "Uh-huh, she worked under me. Helen, all I have to say about that situation is that you never had anything to worry about. It was you that Robert wanted and you that he married. You know, men are blind to certain things. Robert thought Mona was bright and a hard-working angel. But, he didn't want her. I saw straight through her." Anita sighed. "Robert just made a stupid mistake without thinking."

When Helen just nodded, Anita continued, "He talked about you all the time and I tried to console him when you two were apart. And believe me, honey, he needed it. He was a mess." Anita smiled. "But now, put that all behind you."

"Okay, I just had to ask."

"Because you're a woman," Anita laughed. "I would have asked too." Anita motioned for the waitress to bring them the check. "I'd better get going. I have another apartment to look at in Culver City."

The new friends chatted easily as Anita drove Helen home, and when she parked in front of Helen's house they hugged.

"Honey, I needed this today. Thank you so much for your company. Today was a good day."

Helen returned her smile. "It was all my pleasure." She got out of the car and went inside the house. Today was a good day, indeed.

Chapter 33

"How is my little niece today?" Helen took the baby out of her playpen and kissed her rosy cheek. Danielle laughed and pulled at Helen's hair. "Elaine, she's getting prettier everyday."

Elaine's smile was a proud one. "You sound like her father. He tells me everyday how his daughter is prettier than she was the day before."

"And, what does her mother say?" Helen asked.

"The same," Elaine laughed.

Helen smiled at the thought of Dan. "His baby girl and his only child," Helen said as she played with the baby. She glanced at Elaine. "All right, sit down and tell me what's wrong."

"Now, why would you think that anything's wrong?"

"Honey, I can tell by the little wrinkles on your forehead."

Elaine took a deep breath. "I called Harriet yesterday and again today. She wouldn't even accept any of my calls. Her secretary said that she was too busy and would call me back. But of course, she hasn't. What did I do to her? Why is she so cold?"

Helen could see that Elaine was really hurt by this, but Helen knew that Elaine would have to accept Harriet's separation sooner or later. "Elaine, you've done all you can. You invited her to your wedding and the christening. Face it, she doesn't want to have anything to do with us and we can't force her."

"I know, but it still hurts. Anyway, I tried to call *you* all day yesterday. Where were you?"

"I went to lunch with Anita, Robert's friend. She had dinner with us the other night. We got to know each other yesterday – you know, a lot of girl talk. I'll bring her over to meet you one day."

Elaine smiled, but she didn't look happy. She didn't want to be jealous of Helen's new friend. "I thought we were going to see more of each other when you moved here."

Helen was surprised and turned to face her. "Honey, we are. She just dropped by. I didn't invite her." Helen felt as if she had to defend herself. "I really want the two of you to meet."

Elaine sat back on the couch. "Now, I'm being silly. I woke up this morning with a headache and it put me in a bad mood. My throat is getting sore too, but there's no reason to take it out on you."

"Well, I'll tell you what. Why don't you get a few things ready for Danielle and I'll take her off your hands for a while. You can take a nap and get some rest."

"I can't just put her off on you."

"Why not? I'm her aunt. Now get up and get some things together so Danielle and I can get going."

After Elaine put together a bag for Helen, she put the baby in the car seat and drove off. Helen turned on the radio and sang while the baby laughed and tried to clap her hands together. Just as they arrived at her house, Helen heard the phone ringing and ran inside to answer it. She smiled when she heard Lynn's voice.

"Guess who's here with me? Danielle, I'm baby-sitting for Elaine. She wasn't feeling well."

"That sounds like fun. I'm coming over."

Helen was in the backyard with the baby when Lynn drove into the driveway. When Helen opened the door for her, Lynn immediately took Danielle from her mother's arms.

"Are you hungry, sweetheart?"

"Yeah, what you got?"

"Corned beef and cabbage."

"That sounds good."

"Keep the baby company and I'll fix you a plate"

Lynn sat at the kitchen counter and played with Danielle. "I got a letter from Maria yesterday. She sounds happy. You know, it's a pity, Mom. They found out her father died, just a week after Maria got home. But now, she's happy and I hope her mother is too."

"I hope so," Helen responded.

"Maria says she doesn't have to work as hard since her sisters are helping out. They moved into a larger house down the street from her aunt."

Helen set the plates on the table. "Here, I'll take the baby so that you can eat." She placed the baby on her lap. "I'm happy for Maria. Will she be coming out to visit anytime soon?"

"No. She's saving her money so that she can move back next year. We're talking about finding an apartment in the same complex after I graduate."

"Maria is a good girl, and a smart one, too," Helen said, thinking of the hard times the child had had in her life. She suspected that it had been even harder than she'd told Lynn.

Helen smiled. "You'll be finished with school in a year. The time went by so fast."

They chatted and played with the baby for another hour before Lynn started gathering her things. "I have to do some studying."

"I am so glad we're living close now," Helen said and kissed her daughter. "Atlanta was just too far away." She picked up the baby who was crawling around on the floor. "It's time to take you home, little one. I'm sure your mommy is waiting for you now."

Lynn laughed out loud. "I'm surprised she hasn't called for her yet."

"Give her a little time. She will. That's why I want to get her home. Wait for me, while I gather her things."

They walked out the house together, then went their separate ways. When Helen got to Elaine's house, she had the door opened before Helen could even ring the doorbell.

"Well, you look refreshed," Helen said as she stepped inside. "I enjoyed your daughter."

"I really appreciate this, Helen. I feel so much better now. But, as bad as I felt, I missed my baby. Do you want a cup of tea?"

"No, I'd better be getting back home so I'll be there when Robert gets there." She patted Elaine on her arm. "Take care of yourself and call me tomorrow if you need me to come over and get the baby."

"I will. Thanks again."

Helen looked at her sister. "Harriet still hasn't called back?"

"No, but I really don't expect her to."

Helen patted Elaine on her shoulder. "I'll check in with you tomorrow."

As Helen got in her car and drove off, she wondered if Harriet was all right. It had been over a year since she'd seen her sister, but they had been separated for long periods of time before. Maybe she would try to find out about Harriet, through a cousin who attended the same church.

By the time Helen got home, she had time to prepare dinner and freshen up herself before Robert got home. As soon as he walked in the door, she could tell from his face that something dreadful had happened. He kissed her on the cheek and held her tight. She pulled away and looked into his eyes.

"What's wrong, sweetheart?'

He put his hand around her waist and led her to the den. They sat on the black leather couch. "You remember me telling you about my aunt?"

"Yes, you said you wanted me to meet her."

He sighed and held her hand, remaining silent for several moments. "Well, she died last night."

"Oh, honey, I'm so sorry."

He pulled Helen into his arms. "Well, she was eighty-five and she died in her sleep. At least she didn't suffer."

"That's good."

"We can leave tomorrow night. Is that all right with you?"

"Of course it is," Helen responded. "But what about work? Aren't you in the middle of a big case?"

"I gave it to Martin today. He can handle it for me for a few days."

"Let me get you some dinner now. We can turn in early and watch TV in bed."

After dinner, Robert made reservations while Helen cleaned up the kitchen.

"Our flight is ten tomorrow night and we'll arrive in Shreveport early in the morning. Her funeral will be the day after."

The next day, Helen packed. She stood in front of the closet and looked at five dresses before she decided which one

277

she wanted to wear to the funeral. She pulled out Robert's navy Hugo Boss suit, jeans and slacks. They would only be there from Wednesday to Friday. She called Lynn and Elaine to let them know that she and Robert would be leaving. They took a cab to the airport and when they arrived in Shreveport, they took another cab to the hotel. Robert called his cousin's house and she said she would pick them up.

"Have you ever been to Louisiana before?" he asked Helen as she unpacked.

"Only New Orleans, but that was about ten years ago. I'm sure a lot has changed since I was there."

The phone rang and the desk clerk said that someone was coming up to their room. A few minutes later, they heard a soft knock on the door and Robert opened it. A tall, slender, pretty lady wearing a pair of black jeans and a low-cut blouse that revealed her full breasts, smiled back at him.

"Hi, I'm Willa Mae. Remember me? Your cousin, Lester's sister?"

Robert returned her smile. "I wouldn't have recognized you if you hadn't told me. Come in, we're ready."

Willa Mae stopped when she saw Helen. "We?"

"Yes, my wife and I," Robert said, turning to Helen. He held Helen by her hand, clearly seeing the shock in Willa Mae's face. "Honey, this is my cousin, Willa Mae."

"Glad to meet you," Helen said.

"Glad to meet you, too. But no one knew you had a wife," she said turning back to Robert. "We all heard that you were divorced, Robert. "We didn't know you married again so soon."

As Willa Mae looked Helen up and down, Helen frowned. She would have to watch this one. They were cousins, but not first cousins. And, it didn't seem to matter to Willa Mae anyway.

"I'm surprised that you all didn't hear that I was remarried and happily remarried, I must say."

Helen didn't miss the look of disdain from Willa Mae.

"Well, come on. I think we should be getting along." Willa Mae walked in front of Robert, strutting every inch of her figure.

This is not a good thing, Helen thought to herself.

Helen thought they would never stop riding the rocky dirt roads before they got to the house.

"This is Auntie's same old house, Robert. But I live in the city. Lester lives out here in the country, but not as far back in these woods as Auntie."

Robert got out of the car and stood in front of the house, remembering the times he visited his aunt – the nights he spent, the days he spent playing in the yard.

His cousin Lester walked out the door and grabbed Robert's hand. "It's good to see you, man, mighty good," Lester said. "I was glad when you said that you could come."

"So was I," said Willa Mae. She looked at Helen and turned her back.

"Who is this beautiful lady, Robert?" Lester asked.

Robert grabbed Helen's hand. "This is Helen, my wife," he said with a proud smile.

Helen looked at Willa Mae and smiled. "Are you married, Willa Mae," Helen asked.

"No, I'm not," she snapped.

Helen kept her smile. "Well, when you do get married, I hope you're as lucky as I am." Helen knew that she had made Willa Mae angry and loved every minute of it.

They walked inside and Helen and Robert took seats on the couch. "What would you like to drink? We have some iced tea," Lester said.

"That'll be fine," Helen answered.

"Make that two," Robert added.

Lester sat in the chair opposite the couch while Willa Mae went to get the drinks.

"Auntie lived a good life, Robert. Sure, she had hard times, but we all did. But she had some stories to tell. When she was younger, she worked hard for just pennies a day. But the good thing was, when she got older she could relax and rock in her rocking chair all day." Lester leaned forward in his chair. "But, Robert, she was sure proud of you. She used to say, 'That boy didn't move to California and forget us old folks. He calls me every month and sends money too.'"

Robert wiped a tear from his eye as Willa Mae returned with the iced teas.

"Robert, do you remember when we were younger and you told me that we would get married when you came back home. That was the last thing you said to me before you got on the bus to California. You said, 'Willa Mae, I'm going to marry you, girl. Just you wait and see.'"

Robert and Helen looked at each other and laughed.

"You were just a kid. How do you remember that, Willa Mae?" Robert asked.

"Because I thought you meant it," she snapped.

"Yes, I'm sure I did mean it. But, I was only thirteen at the time. I think you were only six." He laughed again. "It was such a long time ago."

"It doesn't seem so long ago to me, Robert," Willa Mae said softly. She was truly humiliated now.

Helen turned to face Robert. "Why, you said the same thing to me over twenty years ago," she said with a smile. "So you see, Willa Mae, men just can't be trusted."

Everyone laughed, even Willa Mae.

"Hey, Willa Mae, why don't we put on some music?"

As Willa Mae went to the stereo, Lester got up and looked closely at Helen. "Damn, I know who you are now. My girlfriend has your latest book. You're a writer," Lester said.

Willa Mae turned to Helen and smiled. "A writer, huh? That's nice." Suddenly, Willa Mae's attitude changed and Helen was glad. She didn't want to play any more of these silly games

"I hope you guys are staying for dinner. Willa Mae is a fine cook," Lester said.

"Oh, no, Willa Mae, has enough to do," Helen said. "We can all go out to dinner before we leave."

The phone rang and Lester excused himself.

"That phone hasn't stopped ringing," Willa Mae said. "But I knew that once the word got out about Auntie, people would call. It happened so fast, just overnight. She wasn't even sick. I'm going to miss her. When my mama died, I depended on Auntie and Lester. She was more like a grandmother to me than an Aunt. She and Lester were close, too." She looked directly at Robert. "I'm glad you're here for Lester, Robert. We can't find Fred. He hasn't been home for almost three years."

"No one knows how to reach him?" Robert asked.

"No. Lester thinks he might be in jail. He was always doing something he had no business doing." Willa Mae sounded so sad, Helen felt sorry for her.

Lester returned to the room. "That was Julia. She said that she couldn't find Fred. That brother of mine. I'm telling you, he'll never change."

"He's probably far away from here by now, anyway," Willa Mae said. "Lester, you and me are the only two fools who stayed around here."

They all chuckled.

"What time is the service tomorrow?" Robert asked.

"Eleven. You can meet us here," Lester said sadly.

Robert got up and hugged him. "We're going back to the hotel and have dinner. We'll get the bed early so we can meet you guys in the morning."

Lester reached into his pockets and pulled out his keys. "I'll drop you guys off."

The ride back was short and Robert and Helen walked into the small restaurant in the hotel. Robert ordered white wine while they looked over the menu.

"I want some sort of seafood. You know, down here it's really good. And, frog legs – it's been years since I've had any." Robert looked at the sour expression on his wife's face and smiled.

"I'll just have the catfish and a salad. You can keep those frog legs to yourself," she said as she laughed and closed the menu.

They ate dinner quickly and returned to the room. Helen changed into her white lace gown that she had purchased at Victoria's Secret. She stood in front of the mirror and brushed her hair back. Robert walked up behind her and slipped one strap off her shoulder, not taking his eyes off her in the mirror. She leaned her body into his. He cupped her breast and she moaned with pleasure. She closed her eyes as he slid the other strap from her shoulder. Her gown fell to the floor, gathering around her feet. As his hands cuddled her breasts, a fire blazed in the pit of her stomach. His hands teased her. He led her to the bed and gently laid her on her back, planting light kisses over her breasts, neck and then her stomach. His tongue felt hot against her thighs and as he went lower, she heard a moan that she didn't recognize as her own. And, when she did the same to him, he held her down, slid deeply inside her and they became one.

Helen heard the water running in the shower and she turned over, smiling as she remembered the night before. She got out of bed and went to the window. The sun was shining and she could tell it was warm. As she heard the shower stop, she turned, looking for her robe. Robert came from the bathroom, still drying himself off. He stopped and looked at his wife. She took the towel from his hand and dried his back, kissing him between his shoulders.

"Good morning, honey," she whispered.

He turned around and kissed her. "Good morning, my love."

"I'm going to take a shower and then do my hair."

"Don't take too long. I'm calling room service so that we can have breakfast before we leave. What do you want?" He asked looking at the menu.

"French toast and bacon. And, some coffee."

"What happened to your wheat toast and coffee."

"After last night, I'm starved, thank you," she smiled. She kissed him on the cheek and ran into the bathroom. When she came out, she was wearing the nightgown she had intended to wear last night.

"You finished just in time," Robert said pointing to the food on the table.

She looked at her watch. It was just eight. Good, she thought. They wouldn't have to rush. Leisurely, they ate breakfast and then dressed.

"We can get a taxi in front of the hotel. I saw them lined up when we came back last night."

Helen looked at her husband, handsome in his double-breasted navy suit. "When are we going back home?"

"I made arrangements for tomorrow around noon."

"That's fine with me."

They held hands as they rode down in the elevator and into the lobby. A taxi took them back to Robert's Aunt's house and when Robert and Helen walked in, there were two other couples already there. Robert stopped and smiled recognizing his cousin Jake.

"Hey, man," Robert said as they shook hands and patted each other on their backs.

"It's been a long time, man," Jake said. "This is my wife Susie."

Susie stood and walked toward her husband. She was wearing a white suit that was too tight, but she was a nice-looking woman. She was at least fifteen years younger than her husband and she was taller than he. With a warm smile, she extended her hand to Robert.

"And, this is my wife, Helen."

Susie and Jake smiled at Helen. Willa Mae came into the room and stood against the wall like she was bored stiff. Helen believed it was just her nerves. She would probably take her aunt's death harder than anyone. Willa Mae walked outside and Helen excused herself to follow her.

Willa Mae was standing outside, dabbing her eyes with a tissue and she turned around when she heard Helen's voice. "Is there something I can get for you, Helen?"

"No, I just wanted to see if you were all right."

"Yeah, I'm all right," she snapped.

"There's no need to be unfriendly. It's not going to change anything, you know." Helen could hear Willa Mae's sigh. "Did you really think that after so many years, he would have remembered his promise and married you, Willa Mae?"

She turned around to face Helen. "He may have. I saw him over ten years ago, but he didn't see me. He was visiting Auntie and by the time I found out about it, he was heading for the airport. I jumped into my car to try to catch him, but I got there just as he was boarding the plane. I could see him, though. He was so tall and so handsome. I decided at that moment that I would marry him. But then, he married someone in California. I'd given up then. But, Lester told me Robert was coming to Auntie's funeral and that he was divorced. I figured I'd give it my best shot. Shit, he's married again. What a disappointment."

"Even if he wasn't married, it doesn't mean he would have married you. Nothing is that sure in life."

283

"I would have done anything to make him like me and take me away from here."

Helen walked closer to her. "You can leave this place on your own. Why wait for someone to marry you and take you away?" Willa Mae turned her back to Helen, but Helen walked around to face her. "Look, let's clear the air, so we can both forget about this ridiculous dream of yours. Robert is already married, happily married. Forget about him, let it go. We're leaving tomorrow and he may never come back, so you need to get over this and grow up."

Helen walked away, leaving Willa Mae standing alone, with her mouth still open. Helen walked back inside like nothing had happened.

"Have you seen Willa Mae?" Lester asked.

"She's outside," Helen said. "I think she wanted to get some air." Helen sat on the couch next to Susie.

"I read your last book, Helen. I thought it was great. Like real life, too."

"I'm glad you liked it."

"I always wanted to write or do something like that. Do more with my life. But there isn't much to do or write about around here. I don't work either," she whispered. "My husband is too jealous to let me leave the house every day. And, I don't have any children or much family either."

"So, what do you do all day?" Helen asked.

She leaned closer to Helen so that her husband couldn't hear what she was saying. "I do leave the house sometimes. I mean, I'll go crazy if I stayed in all the time. But when I'm home, I watch soap operas and talk shows. Sometimes, he'll let me go get my hair and nails done. And then, I do a little shopping." Susie pushed her long, black hair from her face with her nails that were too long. Helen noticed the fake diamond in each of Susie's fingernails, but then she wondered if they were fake? The long, dangling earrings that she wore, could have been diamonds too. Susie's entire outfit looked as if she were going to a nightclub rather than a funeral.

"Why do you put up with that?" Helen asked.

"Hell, it's no secret. Everyone knows that I married Jake for his money. He takes real good care of me. Treats me better than any other man I've been with. But, I'm good to him too and since we've been married, I've grown to love him."

Willa Mae and Lester returned to the room and Willa Mae looked as if she'd been crying.

"I think Willa Mae is getting nervous," Susie said. "She came around Auntie a lot and I don't know what she'll do without her. Except for Lester, she'll be pretty much by herself. She wants to get married, but no man will marry her because, chile, she has slept with every man in this town."

Willa Mae stood and came towards Susie and Helen. "Would you guys like something to eat? We have lots of food with what everyone brought over," Willa Mae said, looking at Helen.

Helen was surprised by Willa Mae's offer. "No thanks, we had breakfast at the hotel."

"And, I cooked breakfast for Jake and I before we left home."

As they all got ready to leave for the funeral, Helen took Robert's hand. Lester had decided on a graveside service. The Pastor gave a short sermon and a woman sang two songs. It was a short funeral.

They went back to Auntie's house and ate. After dinner, Willa Mae called a taxi for Robert and Helen. They said their good-byes and left for the hotel.

"So are you and Willa Mae all right now?" Robert asked Helen.

Helen laughed. "You devil. You knew what she was trying to do and you didn't say anything."

He hugged his wife. "I don't even remember saying anything like that to her. For her to remember it *and* believe it was just too much. She's quite a character."

"Shame on you, Robert. Telling women that you'll marry them and then forgetting all about it."

"I've never forgot the day I told you, darling."

She squeezed his hand and laid her head on his shoulder. "Well, Willa Mae and I did clear the air...so to speak."

They both laughed.

Chapter 34

"Hi, we're home."

Lynn laughed as she heard her mother's voice. "When did you guys get back?"

"About thirty minutes ago. You're the first person I called. How are you, honey?"

"Fine, Mom. Did you have a good trip?"

"Let's just say it was interesting."

"I had dinner with Aunt Elaine last night. Mom, Danielle is growing fast."

"Just like you," Helen said, as she laughed through the phone. "I still can't believe you are almost twenty years old already. That makes me old, Lynn."

Now Lynn really laughed. "Mom, nothing will ever make you old!"

"Thanks, honey. Well, I just called to let you know that we're home. By the way, Robert says hello."

"Tell him I said hello, too."

She hung up and called Elaine. "I'm back!"

"You were only gone for a few days and I missed you. Did you like it there?"

"It was all right to visit, but not for very long. There's not much to do except eat and get fat. I am glad to be home."

"Well, it's good to hear your voice. What do you have planned for the weekend?"

"Absolutely nothing. We need to rest. Why don't we get together on Monday?"

"That'll be great. See you then."

As Helen hung up the phone, Robert came into the room.

"I just finished unpacking," Robert said.

"You're just too good."

He kissed the tip of her nose. "Say that tonight."

Helen laughed and went into the kitchen.

"Do you want a glass of wine?" Robert asked.

"Yes, that would be nice."

While Robert got the wine, Helen fixed a tray of cheese and crackers. They went into the den and he turned on the television. The first thing they heard was a report about a gang shooting.

Helen shook her head in disgust. "You know, all this bad news makes me think of a song I used to like by Kathy Mattea, A Few Good Things Remain. The song starts off with the news about shootings and fires, but when she sees her lover, she tells him that there are a few good things that remain. Seeing him was one of them. Just like when I see you," Helen said as she sat on the couch next to Robert.

Robert pulled a video from a box on the table. "This is better than the news." Helen sat back and leaned into his arms.

"It's good to be home, isn't it?" Robert stated.

"Hell, yes. I want you to relax and enjoy this weekend. Just watch TV or do whatever you want. You were working pretty hard before we left."

"Are you going to spoil me, Helen?"

"That's the plan." She smiled and refilled his glass.

He put his arm around her and pulled her closer. "You know, if I stay in bed late, I want you right beside me," he said.

"I like that plan, too," she laughed. "You know, we still don't act like married people."

"How do we act?" Robert asked.

Like lovers."

"But darling, we are lovers," he said and kissed her hard on the mouth.

By ten that night, they were in bed, happy to be home and looking forward to a fabulous weekend together.

Monday morning, Helen was up with the sun. She'd gotten up in the middle of the night and wrote until it was time to fix breakfast for Robert. After he left, she cleaned the house and began to prepare lunch for her and Elaine. As she went upstairs to change, she heard her fax machine and went into her office to see what it was. It was the newsletter from Romance Writers of America and she noticed the date of the next meeting. She would try to make it. She went into her bedroom and the phone rang.

"Hi, Helen. I was just calling to see how you were doing."

"Hi Anita, good to hear from you. Are you all settled in now?"

"Trying to…"

"Listen, what are you doing for lunch? My sister is coming over and I really want the two of you to meet."

Anita agreed and they made plans. After dressing, Helen decided to call Miss Lettie. She hadn't spoken to the woman since she had moved to Los Angeles.

Miss Lettie was thrilled to hear from Helen. "I'm glad my talk did some good, baby. I knew you were a smart girl and would do the right thing. How is that man of yours?"

"He's fine, Miss Lettie. We are really doing good."

"I knew that you guys would do well. You just needed a push in the right direction."

Helen told Miss Lettie that she loved her and would stay in touch.

A half-hour before she was expecting anyone, Helen heard a car pull into the driveway. She opened the door for Anita. The two women embraced, then Helen offered her a cup of tea.

Anita followed Helen into the kitchen. "I came a little earlier so that I could talk to you about something."

Helen looked concerned. "Is there anything wrong, Anita?"

"No, not wrong," Anita said as she took the tea from Helen. "I think I met someone."

"Really?" Helen said as she led Anita into the den. "Tell me about him."

"Well, the other day, I went to the mailbox and he was standing there going through his mail or at least pretending to. He introduced himself and I told him my name."

Helen didn't miss the light in Anita's eyes. "So, he lives in your building?"

"Uh huh. He's single, forty-five, but seems to live a quiet life – at least from what I've seen. And, guess what? He invited me to a party that his sister gave last Friday night."

"Did you go?"

288

"Yes. I wasn't going to turn that down. It's been a long time since I've gone on a date. His sister took me aside and told me that he's a good man. She said he had told her about me."

"That's a good sign."

"Yes, but I don't know what to think about this. It's all happening so fast."

"That's the way it was with me and Robert. I kept trying to walk away, but it wasn't possible. Do you like this man, Anita?"

"Yes, girl. I think that I like him a lot. He's all I think about lately."

"In other words, he's all that," Helen laughed. "Why don't you give it a try and see what happens."

"I want to, but I'm afraid to let myself go and love again. I can't take another disappointment in my life. I'm too old for that."

"Look, girl. First of all, you are not too old and you still look good. Maybe this is the right man for you. You have to give it a shot."

"I guess all that I can do is take it day by day."

"And, enjoy it! Maybe one evening, we can all go out to dinner. I'm sure that big brother Robert will spot any imperfections in this guy."

Anita agreed that that was a good idea.

"Anyway, how is work? Are you happy to be back?" Helen asked.

"It's all right," Anita sighed. "You know, Helen, I think I've come to a point in my life where I'm just not satisfied with the same things anymore. I used to love my job, love the authority and the training I had to do with the other girls, but I don't enjoy it like I used to."

Helen put her cup down. "Can you apply for another position?"

"Yes, but what? I don't know what I want to do anymore. It's like there's something missing inside of me. I want to improve myself and I don't know how yet."

Helen listened to Anita chatting and a bell went off in her head. She'd been spinning her wheels trying to think of something different for her next book and now the idea came to her. She would write a book for women – on self-esteem and improving their lives. For women who were in the middle of their lives and couldn't decide where to go next.

"Helen?"

She looked as though she had drifted a million miles away. "I'm sorry, Anita. It's just that I have an idea. When Robert and I were out of town, I talked with two of his cousins that felt the same way you do. They couldn't articulate it, but both of them were at crossroads in their lives too. I couldn't think of anything to tell them, but you just brought something to the light."

Anita looked confused. "What did I say?"

"Well, it's what you're looking for. You know there are so many women like you. Some are divorced after twenty years, some have been working in the same job, some have raised their children and don't know what to do next, some just have a fucked-up life, or whatever. But, they all have something in common."

"What's that?"

"They're stuck with nowhere to go, nothing to do. But, they know there's got to be more than what they're getting out of life. They want to go forward, improve themselves. And after all they've been through, it's their turn. Do you see what I mean?"

"I'm beginning to," Anita said, nodding her head slowly.

"I knew there was some reason I had to see you today, Helen. You're good for the soul. Maybe it's time for me to do what I've wanted to do for a while. You know, I've been dreaming of opening a small bookstore, but there was always something holding me back. But now, maybe it's time I should try to do it for myself."

"Girlfriend, that's what I'm talking about."

"Will you have time to help me get things set up?"

"Damn right. Then, I'll write my book to encourage other women."

The doorbell rang and it was Elaine. Anita played and held Danielle while Helen prepared lunch. They told Elaine their plans and she loved the idea.

"I'm not going back to work for a while, so call me if

you need any help," Elaine said enthusiastically. "If I hang around you two for a while, I might be getting into something that I never dreamed of. I really love the book idea."

"The book will be a lift for all women, especially Black women."

"Yes, but this is a universal cause. All women have experienced this problem," Elaine said.

"You're absolutely right," Anita said. "And, I'm so happy to be part of this great idea."

Helen stood up. "Come on, let's talk about this over lunch."

Chapter 35

"I'm glad you could meet me for lunch today," Anita said as she led the way to the table. She picked a table by the window with a view of the pier full of boats. The sky was light blue, almost gray and the water was calm. It was eleven-thirty and the lunch crowd had not yet arrived.

Helen ordered her favorite fruit salad and Anita ordered tuna with lettuce and sliced tomatoes.

"So, today is your last day of work, and the first day of your new life. Now, how does that sound to you?" Helen smiled.

"Good, but it's kind of scary, you know. But, I am happy, Helen. Happier than I've been in a long time."

"And, you deserve every bit of it. We all do."

Anita let out a deep sigh. "I'm taking most of my savings to do this," she said, sounding a little scared.

Helen reached across the table and touched her hand. "It'll work out, Anita. And, I've thought of something else for you. Once I finish my book, I'm going to do some tapes that can be sold along with my book. We can do the tapes together and split the profit."

Anita smiled and the wrinkles on her forehead seemed to disappear. "You know, the one thing that is good is that Jerry is behind me all the way."

"Speaking of Jerry, how is it going with the two of you?" Helen asked.

"I'm happy, Helen. We sit for hours and talk and laugh. We really listen to each other. I remember Robert telling me the same thing about you and him. I was so envious because I never had that kind of relationship before. So, it feels good now."

"That's great, Anita. I'm happy for you." Helen pushed her face from her forehead.

"Are you okay, Helen?" she asked with concern.
"You look a bit tired."

"I'm fine. It's just that I didn't sleep well last night. One of my sinus headaches, that's all. I'll feel better once I get something in my stomach."

Anita frowned and for the first time noticed that Helen wasn't wearing makeup. Not that she needed any, she looked just fine. But Anita was concerned. "Well have some tea, now."

Helen sipped on her tea. "That feels good."

They chatted through lunch and Helen began to feel better.

"You know, Robert will be home early all next week. Why don't I fix dinner for you and Jerry? I'll call Elaine and Dan too."

"That sounds good," Anita smiled.

"I'll speak to Robert about it tonight, and we'll set a date." Helen laid her hands flat on the table. "Now, when can we start looking for a place for your bookstore."

"I thought you would never ask. I've been looking in the newspaper for some places. I don't want it to be too far from my apartment. I saw some places around Slauson and LaBrea. I thought we could go look the day after tomorrow. Will you have time?"

"Sure," Helen said. "Just call me and I'll meet you there. Have you thought of the name for the bookstore yet?"

"No, not really. I've mulled over a few in my mind, but they didn't sound right – not catchy enough."

"Maybe at dinner with the guys, we can bring it up and get a few ideas."

Anita nodded, but remained silent.

"I have an idea," Helen started. "Why don't you just name it, 'Anita's.'"

"I don't know. I thought of that, too." She looked at her watch. "I have to meet my brother at two-thirty."

"Okay. I think I'll go home and take a nap."

After paying for the lunch, the two women hugged and went their separate ways.

Helen went straight home and changed into shorts and a T-shirt. She lay across the bed but she couldn't sleep. Finally she got up and called her publisher to tell her about the idea for her new book. They talked for an hour before Helen hung up and went into her office. She turned on her computer and typed five lines, then deleted all five. She stared at the computer for almost ten minutes before she started typing again. This time, she typed fifteen pages before she stopped. She deleted the last six pages, then typed seven more before she heard movement behind her. She jumped, her heart beating fast against her chest. She turned around and it was Robert.

"Lord, what time is it?" she asked as she noticed he had already changed his clothes. He was wearing a pair of shorts and no shirt. She looked at her watch; it was already four-thirty. "Oh, dear. I haven't cooked." She kissed him on the cheek and started to go to the kitchen when he grabbed her arm and kissed her.

"What's your hurry?" he whispered in her ear.

"Aren't you hungry?"

He looked deep into her eyes and smiled. His smile pulled the deepest secrets from her heart. "No, and when I get hungry, I can make myself a sandwich. One for you too."

She put her arms around his neck and held him close. "You are just too sweet, and I'm so lucky," she said.

"Are you tired enough to take a break?" he asked seductively.

"Yes, quite tired," she said and laid her head against his chest.

He took her by the hand and led her to the couch in the den. She flopped down and noticed the beer he had in his hand. He sat down next to her and she laid her head on his shoulder.

"Tell me about your day," he said.

She told him about her meeting with Anita and her idea of having Anita and Jerry over for dinner. They agreed that they would do it within the next few days. After a few minutes, they went into the kitchen and made sandwiches for their dinner.

"I'm telling you, Robert. I don't know where the time went. I was just going to put a few ideas on paper and before I knew it, the day was gone." They were sitting side by side at the kitchen counter. "I should have cooked you a hot meal."

"Don't worry about it, baby. You were working and I understand." He tenderly pushed her hair from her face.

She looked into his eyes and she knew, she was the luckiest woman alive.

A few days later, Helen was preparing for the dinner party. As she took steaks and chicken from the freezer, she remembered that she needed to get a couple of bottles of wine from the cellar. Returning to the kitchen, she put the wine in the refrigerator, then made a checklist in her mind of all she had to do. She had purchased pies from Marie Callendar's and had taken out the hamburger meat for Lynn. She really hoped that the evening would go well.

Finally satisfied that everything was in place, she took a book and the phone outside to the patio and sat in one of the lawn chairs. She laid her head back, closed her eyes and fell asleep within minutes.

"Mom, Mom, Mom, wake up. It's Lynn. It's me, Mom. Wake up."

Helen was swinging her arms and crying out. Lynn continued shaking her mother and finally she opened her eyes. Helen was disoriented. She looked up at the tree, but it wasn't the big lemon tree in her parent's backyard. She was home. Oh, thank God, she was home.

Lynn got down on her knees and put her arms around her mother's shoulder. "What were you dreaming of? You frightened me to death, Mom."

"I'm sorry. That was a scary one. I was dreaming that my mother was beating me. It was strange because my mother never did that, at least not with a belt or her hand. She would beat me down with her mouth." Helen shook her head as if she was trying to wake up from a deep sleep. "I feel better now and I'm glad you're here."

Lynn stood and took her mother's hand pulling her from the chair. "Are you sure you're all right?"

"I'm just fine. Now enough. Let's go inside." She put her arm around her daughter's shoulder. "You know, I love that you only live twenty minutes away. I get to see you whenever I want."

"I love it, too," Lynn said, suddenly serious.

"What's wrong?" Helen asked as they went into the kitchen.

"I received a letter from my Dad a week ago, but I haven't answered. I see no reason to."

Helen remained silent. She understood how Lynn felt and was sure that Thomas understood too. Helen started seasoning the steaks and chicken.

"So, you don't have any opinion about what I should do about the letter?" Lynn asked.

"Nope. I told you before, this is up to you. But whatever you do, I will support you."

Lynn smiled. "Thanks, Mom." She watched her mother preparing the dinner. "Why didn't you guys just go out somewhere?"

"Well, I thought if I had dinner here, it would be easier for Elaine. You know, with Danielle."

"I'll see to Danielle," Lynn said. "She and I can eat in here together."

Helen smiled. "You're good with her, honey."

"I love being with her. She feels more like a niece than my cousin. I feel kind of responsible for her."

"That's because you're so much older than she." Helen put the food aside. "I'm going upstairs to change. Make yourself comfortable."

Helen went upstairs and changed into red pants and a matching sweater. She pinned her hair up and returned downstairs to finish the dinner. Lynn was lying outside on the patio. Helen was standing at the sink, when Robert sneaked up behind her and kissed her on the back of her neck.

"I didn't even hear you come in," Helen said.

"I was outside with Lynn and I guess you were upstairs. It smells good in here," he said.

"Thanks. Everything is ready. Everyone should be here in less than an hour. You know, Anita is going to be talking about her business tonight, but you haven't said much about it."

He pulled away and put his hands in his pockets. "I know, I guess I'm kind of jealous. I've gotten used to having you here when I come home. It's nice coming home to you,

296

Helen. That's why I bring work home rather than stay at the office."

She put her hands on her hips. "And, who said that I won't be home, Robert? Remember, it's Anita's store, not mine. I'll be helping her out, but she knows that I have other things to do. She knows I want to be home and she knows that I have a lot of writing to do. Don't worry. I want to be here when you come home at night."

He looked at her long and hard. "You really mean that, don't you?"

"Hell, yes. You are number one in my life."

He pulled her into his arms. "Baby, I sure do love you," he said as his lips grazed her ear.

"Love you too," she whispered. She held him tight and kissed him on his neck. "Now, go upstairs and get comfortable before our company gets here."

Helen was in the bathroom, checking her hair and makeup when she heard the doorbell ring.

"I'll get it," Lynn yelled.

Helen could hear Danielle's giggles, then she heard Robert's voice greeting Elaine and Dan. She went into the kitchen and got the tray of vegetables and blue cheese dip. She set the tray on the table and kissed Elaine and Dan. At that moment, the bell rang again.

"You guys have a seat and make yourselves comfortable," Helen said. "I'll get the door."

Anita was glowing. She wore a black jumpsuit with a thin, white collar and black low-heeled shoes. Her dark eyes were smiling as she looked at Jerry. And, Jerry was exactly like Anita had described him. He had a medium build, dark smooth skin and his hair was cut close. Helen thought they looked great together and she liked the way Jerry looked at Anita.

Anita introduced Jerry to Robert and Robert introduced everyone else. Robert put on soft music and they chatted until Helen told everyone to come into the dining room.

"Helen, these steaks are perfect," Jerry said as he looked around the table.

"Thanks, Jerry. I love to cook when there's someone around to eat my cooking. Before Robert and I were married, I hardly ever cooked. Now, I do almost everyday."

"And, I enjoy it," Robert said, looking at his wife who was sitting beside him.

Dan laughed. "I heard that, Robert.Elaine has spoiled me, too."

They all laughed and after blessing the food, they passed the platters around. As they talked through dinner, Robert kept his eye on Jerry. He wasn't sure if he liked the man, but he could see that Anita was taken with him. Well, he wouldn't judge him right now. It was a little too soon. He watched Anita smile when Jerry looked at her and he could tell she was happy.

"Robert, Robert," Helen was trying to get his attention.

"Oh, I'm sorry, baby." He touched her hand under the table to let her know that everything was fine.

"Anita tells me that you're a writer, Helen. She showed me your books when we went to look at some of the bookstores in the area. I'm not big on reading myself, but I've heard your name. How did it feel the first time you walked into a bookstore and saw your books?" Jerry asked.

"I felt as though I had conquered the world. I felt like I had made my mark on this earth. I love it." Helen looked around the table. Everyone was sitting up and looking at her.

"Now, let me tell you," Elaine said. "The first time I went inside a store and saw my sister's book, I almost screamed with excitement. I showed Helen's book to everyone I knew."

Anita cleared her throat. "So tell me Robert, what do you think of me owning a bookstore?"

"I think it's a good, sound business as long as it's in a busy location."

"I agree with Robert," Dan said. "When I'm out shopping or just kicking around, I'll walk into a bookstore to just look around. And, I usually end up buying something."

"Precisely," Robert said. "You have to be in a location that is open so everyone can see it."

Jerry looked at Anita and smiled. "I know the perfect spot."

"Where?" Helen asked with wide eyes.

"Centinela and LaTijera. It's a shopping center that's always busy. There's a grocery store and a Sav-On Drug, besides a lot of smaller stores. We can ride through there on the way home."

Robert nodded his head in agreement. "It's a prime location."

"I know where it is and I don't think you can lose," Dan said. "I've been through there myself. It's always very busy."

Helen and Elaine were excited and Anita beamed.

"Let's go there tomorrow, Helen."

"That's fine. Can you join us, Elaine?"

"I can't tomorrow, but I'm free all next week."

Robert was pleased with Jerry's suggestion. Maybe he would turn out to be the man for Anita after all, Robert thought. He was certainly friendly enough and seemed to want to help.

"I heard that you and Anita live in the same building, Jerry," Robert commented.

"Yes, I've lived there for seven years now. I saw Anita when she first moved in and decided I wanted to get to know her."

After dinner, they went into the living room. Helen served more wine and they talked about her tapes that would go along with her new book. Helen told them that she wanted Anita to make the first tape.

"But what will I say?" Anita asked.

"You'll talk about the way you felt before you retired from one job and starting something new. Tell how bored you were and what inspired you to take this step. Anita, you'll be telling people about courage. So many women just dream about doing things like this, but they are afraid. These tapes will inspire."

"That's very cleaver, Helen," Dan said.

Elaine nodded in agreement. She knew her sister was very smart.

They were all excited about Helen's ideas and tossed more thoughts and ideas out to discuss. After a while, Elaine went to look for Danielle, so that they could leave.

"Helen, can I help you clean-up?" Anita asked.

"Of course not. You guys are the guests."

"Then, we should be leaving too. Jerry has to be at work at 5:30 in the morning. I promised him that we would be home early."

Jerry and Robert shook hands. "It was nice man," Jerry said. "Next time, dinner will be on me."

"I'll hold you to that," Robert said as they all began walking to the door.

Jerry touched Helen's shoulder. "You sure are a hell of a cook."

"Thanks. It was finally good to meet you, Jerry."

Anita hugged Robert and Helen. Everyone looked in Elaine and Dan's direction when they walked out of the bedroom with a sleeping Danielle in her father's arms.

Robert and Helen walked outside with their guests and watched them drive off.

"Well, Jerry seems to be a nice guy, don't you think, Robert?"

"He's all right."

Helen grabbed his hand and they walked back inside. "He is nice, Robert."

"Okay, okay. He may turn out to be nice, but this was only our first meeting. We'll just have to see." He kissed her on the cheek. "The dinner was fabulous, baby."

"Thanks. Why don't you go up to bed while I clean up?"

"No, baby. I want to help."

"No, that's okay. You have to get up early. I'll be right up."

He took the stairs two at a time. Helen finished in the kitchen and then looked in on Lynn who had decided to spend the night. She was sound asleep. Helen went upstairs to her bedroom and fell asleep almost instantly. It had been a good day.

The next morning Helen was in the kitchen, when Lynn peeked in. "It smells good in here, Mom."

"Sit down. You want some coffee, tea or orange juice?"

"Orange juice."

Helen gave her a glass of juice, then placed a plate in front of her filled with pancakes, eggs and bacon.

Robert walked in and poured himself a cup of coffee. "How are my two favorite girls this morning?"

Helen kissed him on his cheek. He sat down and she put his plate in front of him. He looked up at her. "You're not eating?"

"No, I've been nibbling on bacon all morning." She had a slice of wheat toast and coffee.

"What do you have planned for today, Lynn?" Robert asked. She put her glass down. "I'll be at school most of the day."

"Ah, school days. I remember them."

"But, what you do now is so interesting," Lynn said.

"When I graduate, I want a job that keeps me on the go like you."

He looked at his watch. "Yeah, I'm always on the go. Like now, I can't even finish breakfast. I've got to get going," he said grabbing his jacket. "I've got a full day. I'll be lucky if I can even squeeze in lunch."

Helen walked him to the door and kissed him good-bye. When she returned to the kitchen, Lynn was putting her plate in the sink.

"I'm glad I spent the night, Mom. No one cooks breakfast like you do." She kissed Helen on the cheek. "I've got to go, too. You're the greatest, Mom."

Helen looked at the window and watched her daughter drive off. She cleaned the house and got ready for Anita to pick her up. Anita was right on time. They drove to the shopping center that Jerry had told them about last night.

"Let's get out and walk around to see if there are any empty spaces. Jerry said he thought he saw a couple last weekend."

They passed an empty storefront and Helen jotted down the number. They peeked through the window, trying to see inside.

"I think it's worth calling and coming back, don't you think?" Helen asked.

"Yeah. It looks like it is the right size, too."

They walked through the rest of the center and Helen wrote down the number to another empty space.

"This is getting exciting," Helen said.

"I know. I feel a thrill creeping up my back."

"That's the thrill of knowing something good is about to happen. And, believe me, Anita, it will."

As they started to walk away, Helen noticed that there was someone inside. She put her face against the glass. "Look, there's someone in there. Knock on the door, Anita."

A man opened the door and smiled. "What can I do for you ladies?"

"I'm looking for a small storefront to lease. Is the owner here or do you know where he can be reached?" Anita asked.

The man smiled and stood straight with his arms crossed in front of his chest. Helen noted his straight, white teeth and high cheekbones. His chin was square and he was nicely built, like he had played football when he was younger.

Finally, he spoke, "Miss, you're talking to the owner."

"Oh, I'm sorry. I didn't mean...I just thought...I just meant..."

"That's quite all right, Miss." He found this woman amusing.

"I'm really sorry..."

"Miss, would you like to see this place?"

"Yes, thank you."

Anita and Helen walked through the storefront. It was small, with a bathroom and a kitchen that could be used for storage.

"I think it's cute, don't you, Anita?"

Anita cocked her head to one side. "Yes, it's cute."

"You don't have to make up your mind on the first place you see. There is still the other one."

"I could really decorate this nicely." Anita stood in the middle of the store and turned around. I would use bright colors to lighten the place up. I need colors that will attract people, Helen."

The owner scratched his head and waited patiently as the two women walked from one corner to the other. They walked in back and took one last look.

"Do you know who owns the empty storefront across the parking lot?" she asked.

"Yes." He didn't say anything else.

"Well, who?" Anita asked impatiently.

"I do. Would you like to see that one, too?" He smiled.

Anita sighed heavily. "Yes, please."

"Follow me, ladies." He locked the door and walked to his car. "See you ladies over there." He drove off and Helen looked at Anita and laughed.

"Do you believe this shit? He didn't even offer us a ride," Helen laughed.

Anita was still standing with her mouth open. They

looked across the lot and he was leaning against his truck with his arms folded across his chest like he was getting impatient.

"You know, Anita, if this wasn't so important, we could just get in the car and drive off. But, you know, I like his style. He's just doing this because you made him feel like anyone would own this place but him." Helen started laughing again.

"Okay, so I deserve this. Come on, before he leaves us or changes his mind."

They walked to the other side of the shopping center.

"I was beginning to think that you ladies had changed your minds," he said with impatience in his voice.

"No, we were just admiring the parking lot," Helen said.

He looked as if he were at a loss for words, but smiled in spite of himself. "Well, come on. I hate to rush you, but I have things to do." He looked at Anita and smiled.

Anita looked him up and down the length of his body as she walked by him. She and Helen looked at each other and followed him inside the store.

"This is it," Helen exclaimed. "This is the place for your bookstore."

"Is that what you're going to do? Open a bookstore?"

"Yes and what's wrong with that?" Anita snapped.

"Why, nothing. I think it's a good idea. People will walk out of the supermarket and right into your bookstore. I'm surprised someone hasn't thought of this before."

"Sir..."

He held up his hands. "Miss, if we're going to do business together, then call me Raymond."

Anita and Helen walked through the store some more and Anita was very pleased. This would be her bookstore.

"Raymond, can we talk business?" Anita asked.

"Certainly can."

"Okay, you can call me Anita and this is Helen."

Anita and Raymond discussed the lease while Helen looked around visualizing the store. She stood in the door and looked at all of the other businesses in the center. This would be a good place.

"Would you ladies like a ride back to your car?" he asked Anita.

"No thanks. We want to walk through the shopping center some more."

He said good-bye and told Anita that he would get with her in a few days. Anita grinned all the way to the car.

"So, how do you feel?" Helen asked.

"Great, just great. Helen, I can't wait. I want to get started as soon as he says it's mine."

"And, I'll help you all the way. I'm so excited for you, Anita. Well, now that you've found yourself a bookstore, I have to go to the cleaners and the market and then I've got some writing to do."

"And, I've got some planning to do," Anita responded. "Let me drive you home so that we can both get started."

When they returned to Helen's home, the two women hugged and Helen watched Anita drive off. Helen got into her car and drove to the cleaners and the market. It was such a beautiful day, that she decided not to return home right away. She would drop by to see if Mary was doing better.

There was a strange car in the driveway and Helen sighed. At least, Mary was probably home. Helen rang the doorbell once and waited a few seconds before she rang it again. She heard footsteps and then, Mary opened the door. She smiled at Helen.

"Now, what brought you to this side of town, Helen?" Mary stepped aside. "Come on in, girl."

Helen noticed that she didn't smell alcohol on Mary's breath. "I was out and thought I would come by and see if you were doing all right, Mary."

They sat in the living room and Helen looked around. The house was clean. Everything was in place and there were no empty wine bottles or empty glasses. Helen heard footsteps. A tall woman walked in and stood in the door. She gave Helen a warm smile, then walked over to Mary and kissed her hard on the mouth. Helen sucked in her breath, then sighed quietly. What in the hell was going on here, she wondered? The woman stopped kissing Mary, but held onto her hand.

"Helen, this is Shirley."

The woman was almost six feet tall and she smiled at Helen.

"Shirley," Mary continued. "This is my cousin, Helen. The only family I have that looks in on me every now and then."

Shirley extended her hand. "Glad to meet you, Helen. I appreciate your coming by to see Mary. We met at our AA meeting a month ago and she has been doing real good, too," Shirley said with a proud smile.

Helen was lost for words.

Mary spoke up. "Shirley is good to me, Helen. I don't know what I would have done if it weren't for her. She's been the best friend any one could have."

Helen looked from one to the other. Shirley kissed Mary again and Helen wanted to turn her head, but she couldn't move.

"I guess I'd better be going so I won't be late for work, honey," Shirley said. She turned to Helen. "I hope I get to see you again, Helen."

"Wait here, Helen. I'm going to walk Shirley to her car."

They walked out and Helen peeked through the faded shade hanging at the window. She watched as they kissed in the middle of the street like man and wife. When Shirley got inside her blue Toyota, Helen walked back to the couch as if she hadn't seen anything at all.

Mary returned to the chair opposite Helen. "Sorry, you got such a surprise, Helen. But like I said, Shirley is good to me."

Helen was trying to find the words to ask her. "Do you love her, Mary, or is she just good to you?"

"I love her and she loves me."

"Well, I guess that's all that matters, isn't it?"

"Then you understand?"

"I wasn't born in the Stone Age, Mary. I may have acted that way at first, but I was shocked. But yes, I do understand that these things happen."

Mary wanted to laugh, but just smiled with understanding. "I met Shirley when I was at my worst. She found me sitting in an alley in the back of the AA meeting place. I was so drunk, I didn't know where I was. When I woke up the next day, I was sleeping on her couch. She told me that someone said that three men had me in the alley, Helen. I guess they were drunks, too. But, I don't remember any of it, thank God."

Helen felt chills traveling up her back. "Did you feel anything the next day?"

"Hell, yes. I wasn't wearing any panties and my ass was sore. I was tested for aids, but so far, I'm clean. That shook me up. I knew then that I had hit rock bottom. I cried on Shirley's shoulder the entire next day. That night, she took me to the AA meeting with her. I know it hasn't been long, but I haven't had a drink since then, Helen. Not only have I been clean since I met her, but I'm going for an interview tomorrow at the company where she works. And, our plans are that by next weekend, we can move in together so that I can get out of this dump!" She looked around as if she was disgusted, but then she turned back to Helen and smiled. "I know you might be surprised at this relationship, but she is the best thing that ever happened to me. All of the men in my life just used me or beat me. I don't want another man, Helen."

Helen nodded.

"Shirley understands what I need," Mary continued. "She makes me feel loved and wanted like I never felt before." Tears began rolling down Mary's cheeks.

"I understand Mary. The best thing is that you look good." Helen walked over and held her hand. "I'm going now, but this time, I can leave and know that you will be all right. I'm happy for you, Mary. Keep it up."

Mary hugged her. "Thank you for coming to see me, Helen." She walked Helen to the door. They hugged again before Helen left.

Helen was home for only a few minutes, when Robert came in. She met him at the door.

"You're early."

He kissed her on the forehead. "I finished and came straight home to you. Come upstairs with me while I change out of my suit."

Holding hands, they walked up the stairs together and he told her about his day.

"I spoke to Anita today," he said.

"Really? Did she tell you about the place we found?" Helen asked.

"Yeah, but you know, she kept talking about that Jerry. I'm not that fond of him, you know."

"Why not?" Helen asked. "You only met him once."

"I don't know what it is."

"Maybe you'll feel differently after you've known him for a while."

"Maybe. I think I've seen him someplace before, but I can't remember where."

"I hope it wasn't in court for murder," Helen said, hanging his pants on the hanger.

"That's not funny, Helen."

She laughed at the serious expression on his face. "Well, you know that your opinion is important to Anita. You're like a brother to her, so you should be careful what you say. I think Jerry's a nice guy – until he's proven different. Now, are you hungry?"

"Starved. I didn't have lunch today. Just crackers and peanut butter from the vending machine.

She kissed him on the cheek as she passed by him. "Oh, poor baby." He slapped her on her butt.

They had a quiet dinner and afterwards, went into the den to watch television.

"How long do you think it will take Anita to get the bookstore up and running?" Robert asked.

"I don't know. A couple of months. Why?"

"I thought once she opened up, you and I could get away. Do you realize we haven't taken any time off? We didn't even have a honeymoon. It's time, don't you think?"

She held his hand and sat closer to him. "Yes! Where will we go?"

"I don't know. We can make plans. Where do you want to go?"

"Let's go someplace romantic, Robert. Oh, I can't wait, honey," she said as she laid her head on her husband's shoulder. "You know I stopped by my cousin Mary's house today."

"How is she?"

"Sober, but she's living with another woman – her lover."

Robert sat up straight and Helen told him about her visit. He shook his head as Helen spoke.

"Well, if that works for her," Robert said still shaking his head in disbelief.

"It seems to be working just fine. Do you want a glass of wine?"

"No, I just want to sit here and hold my wife close to me. I still can't believe that we're together. This is all I've ever wanted." He ran his hand up her thighs. Her short blue dress had risen to reveal her upper thighs. He took Helen by the hand, lifted her from the couch and led her upstairs. "It's getting cold down here, don't you think, darling?"

"No, love. It's getting hot to me, but the bed is always better." They laughed as they went into the bedroom.

The next day, Helen met Anita back at the storefront.

"So, you decided on this one?" Helen asked. "I love it."

"Yes. Raymond told me to come and get the keys. I wrote him a check and now this place is mine." Anita turned in a circle. "I'm going to put my desk in the corner over there," she pointed.

Helen stood in the corner. "This will be good. You can see people as they come in and have a view of the outside, too."

They discussed how she would set up the store and what kind of displays she would use.

"You know, I've been reading a lot on starting a book-store. And Jerry's given me some ideas, too."

An hour later, the women left and went their separate ways.

Anita parked her car in the garage, but didn't see Jerry's car. She didn't want to tell Helen, but she hadn't seen Jerry since the night they all had dinner together. He had called her from work, but he didn't mention getting together. She felt like their relationship was changing and she didn't know why. She was sure that he wasn't working every night and that probably meant there was another woman.

But, she wasn't going to pressure him. She'd been hurt enough in her lifetime and things were going too well for her to drop everything and hurt over Jerry or any other man.

For the next few days, Anita focused on everything she had to do for the bookstore. She and Helen visited other book-stores, like Crown Bookstore, to get an idea of how the stores were set up. She had started contacting distributors and book clubs. She wanted to be completely ready for her opening day.

Anita was home one night, doing paperwork, when she

heard a light knock on her door. She opened it without hesitation. Jerry was standing in the hallway, with his hands stuffed in his pockets.

"Hi, baby. I was waiting until I thought you were home."

She stepped aside, so he could come in. He turned to her and gave her a long kiss.

"Damn, I've missed you," he said as he held her.

She smiled, but he noticed her smile was different. She seemed cooler, as if she didn't miss him at all.

He told her about his busy week at work and she listened, but asked no questions. She didn't want to hear any lies. As they sat on the couch, Anita noticed that he kept checking his watch. He had only been there for a half-hour, when he said he had to replace someone on the night shift. He told her that tomorrow would be their night together.

Anita agreed. "Until tomorrow..." she said as he walked out the door. She sat back on the couch and smiled to herself. Did he really think she was stupid enough to believe him?

The next night was Wednesday and Jerry brought Chinese food and wine. They made love and he was up at five in the morning. Over the next week, he called her everyday, making excuses until Wednesday, when he came by again. The same thing happened the following week and Anita realized he was only going to see her on Wednesdays. Didn't he realize she would notice the pattern?

The next Wednesday, when he called for his Wednesday night screwing, he asked if she would be available at seven.

"Sorry, but I'm busy tonight, Jerry. I'll be busy next Wednesday too." She heard him sigh. "And, Jerry?"

"What, Anita?"

"Kiss my ass." She hung up and laughed. All of a sudden, she felt a relief that she hadn't felt in weeks. It was over with Jerry.

Anita didn't mention anything to Helen about her experience with Jerry. She didn't want to talk about it and Helen, being a good friend, didn't ask.

She was at home a few days later, when the phone rang. At first, she didn't recognize the deep, sexy voice. It was Raymond.

"Hello, Anita. I have a shelf that I think you might be interested in. If you like, I can get these shelves for your store."

She made an appointment to see him the next day. The next morning, she took extra time dressing. Damn, she felt good about herself these days. She applied her make-up and combed her hair back, which made her look younger. Her short haircut lay silky against the back of the neck. She wore a navy wool dress and pumps.

She met Raymond as planned. He stepped inside the store and she was standing with her back to him. He hadn't noticed before that she had great legs. She turned to face him and he took in every inch of her from head to toe. She was a small woman, but he liked that. He liked the way she carried herself. Stern and businesslike, but pleasant.

She smiled. "I really appreciate your help with my store, Raymond."

"Well, I try to please my clients. If there is something I can do, I do it. We're all just trying to make it."

She watched as he went to his truck to get the shelf. It was a beautiful, cherrywood. He laid it against the wall and watched the pleased expression in her eyes.

"I can get more where this comes from, if you like it."

"I love this!" she said smiling.

"See how lucky you were to lease a place from me? I take care of my people, especially the pretty ones," he said playfully.

She looked into his eyes and felt the heat rise in her face. She wondered if she was really pretty to him and she felt herself smiling widely. Anita cleared her throat. "This is perfect and you can get me all I need?"

"This is so good, Raymond." Anita stood in the middle of the floor, looking at the shelf from every angle. Anita saw from the corner of her eye that Raymond was watching her. Must be the dress, she thought. "You know, Raymond, things are really falling into place for me."

"Some things are just meant to be, Anita. You seem to be a businesswoman, and I believe you would do good at whatever you decide to do."

"Thanks," she said.

"I guess I had better go. I have to stop by a couple of my

310

other places. I can have the shelves here for you on Thursday. Is that all right?"

They made plans to meet on Thursday and after he left, Anita remained at the store waiting for her desk to be delivered. She called Helen.

"If you feel like coming over, we can try one of the restaurants here for lunch. We can try the Loves BBQ. We can just walk over there."

Helen told her that she would be there in an hour. When Helen drove up, Anita was standing in the door with her arms folded.

"Gee, you look great today," Helen said. "I love that dress. And look a there, the girl got legs."

Anita laughed and they walked inside.

"I love your desk and it's perfect here," Helen said as she ran her hand over the top of the chair. "And look at this shelf, it's beautiful. Did you buy this at the same place you got your desk and chair?"

"No, actually Raymond gave it to me. He's bringing the other shelves over on Thursday," she said in a matter-of-fact manner.

Helen smiled. "Raymond, huh? Now why am I not surprised?"

"What do you mean?"

"I saw the way he looked at you the first day we met him. And, I'm sure he got an eyeful of you today," Helen said as she looked Anita up and down. "You look good, girl."

"I just wanted to wear a dress for a change. I woke up feeling good today."

"Well, I think Raymond is a nice man. He gave you a good deal on your lease and now he's helping you."

"He is helping. It's better than what Jerry is doing." Anita walked into the back room to get her purse.

As they walked from the store to the restaurant, Anita told Helen what had happened with Jerry. "He thought I was a fool, Helen. Why do men think we are too stupid to see when they are trying to use us?"

"I'll tell you why. The ones that are single have had weak women in the past. They are used to telling them anything and they get away with it. So, they think they can treat every woman the same." Helen shook her head. "Which goes to show you how much damn sense is in their heads. Now, was he really fool enough to think that you didn't know he was screwing around with someone else?"

Anita just shrugged.

"You don't seem too disappointed, Anita."

"I'm not. I guess I saw it coming and I have great things going on in my life now. I need a man who is sure of himself, who has confidence, who is strong and who will support me totally in what I'm doing. Jerry wasn't that man."

But Raymond might be, Helen thought to herself.

Anita didn't mention Jerry's name again as the two friends enjoyed their lunch.

The next couple of weeks were busy for Helen and Anita. Helen worked on her book day and night and Anita worked on the store. Elaine and Lynn helped Anita set up everything and people constantly came into the store inquiring about it's opening.

Helen finished her book at 6:30 one rainy Saturday morning. Robert hadn't noticed that she hadn't been to bed all night, but when she told him she had completed it, he was delighted. He pulled her from the chair and led her upstairs.

"You go take a hot shower," Robert said. "I'll cook breakfast and then after you eat, I want you to go to bed." She started to say something, but he held up his hands stopping her. "Don't argue, Helen. I want you to get some sleep. You've been working so hard on this these past few weeks."

She laid her head against his chest and nodded in agreement. He turned her in the direction of the bathroom and gave her a gentle push. After breakfast, Helen slept, getting the best four hours of sleep she'd had in weeks. When she awakened, she heard voices downstairs. She washed her face and brushed her teeth before changing into a jogging suit. When she went downstairs, Anita and Robert were sitting in the den.

"You know, Robert, I can't believe this has really happened. Everything is all set up. I can't even sleep, I'm so excited."

Helen walked in and kissed Robert on the cheek. She touched Anita's hand as she sat down.

"Robert tells me that he made you get some sleep," Anita said. "You needed it, Helen."

"I know and I feel a hundred percent better. But, I did finish the book this morning. So now, I'm all yours."

"I think I'll leave you two ladies alone for a while. I have some work to do in my study." He kissed Anita on the cheek. She was holding a glass of Pepsi in her hand. "Can I get you anything, Helen?" he asked.

"No, love. I'm all right."

Robert smiled at them as he left the room.

"You know, we've got a lot to do next week, Helen."

They made a list of everything and discussed the timetable. They wanted the store to open in two weeks.

"I guess we've covered everything," Helen said, as she quickly went over the list and read it back to Anita.

"Oh, what about decorating the store the night before I open?" Anita asked.

Helen smiled. "Perfect. What colors will you use?"

"The same – orange and yellow."

Helen nodded in agreement. "That will look good because it's the same color as everything else in the store. I'll ask Lynn if she will do the decorating for you. She's good at that."

"Thanks, and Raymond said to count him in for anything we need. He's been such a good friend, Helen. He checks on me everyday."

"Good, we'll need his help, too."

"So, what are you and Robert doing tonight?"

"Nothing. He has some work, but I'm not going to do anything else. You and I have been going non-stop for three weeks now," Helen sighed. "But you're almost there, girl."

Anita touched Helen's hand. "With your help and encouragement, Helen."

"Well, this is an experience for both of us. And, I can't

wait for you to do the tape for my book. My agent thinks this is a great idea."

Anita smiled and stood, placing her glass on the table. "Well, I think I'm going to stop by the store on my way home. I want a thick steak for dinner. I've been living on sandwiches for I don't know how long. I'm tired of them."

Helen walked her to the door and watched as she drove away.

For the next two weeks, they all worked day and night to prepare the store for the opening. Helen noticed that Raymond was always there, right by Anita's side. Helen wondered if her friend even noticed that Raymond was quite taken with her. Helen doubted it. Anita had been so busy and so excited, she couldn't see anything except for the store.

The night before the opening, Helen, Lynn and Elaine were with Anita until midnight. Lynn decorated the store with orange and yellow balloons. Elaine checked every book on the shelf to make sure that they were all placed in alphabetical order and Helen was working on inputting the inventory into the computer. At midnight, the women stood at the door, smiling with pride.

The store opened at 10:00 the next morning. Robert and Helen were the first customers and of course, Raymond was already there. Anita and Raymond were becoming closer by the day and Robert seemed to really like him.

When Elaine, Dan and Lynn arrived, Anita stood in the middle of the floor and spoke. "I want to thank all of you for your help and support. I couldn't have done this without my friends." She looked at Raymond and felt her face get hot. He had been there with her every step of the way. She had never had that kind of support or that kind of relationship before, and she knew she was blessed. But the best part was she had the feeling that the real blessings were still to come.

Harriet was home that afternoon reading her Bible, when she felt the pain in her stomach. She hadn't gone to work in three days, due to the flu and upset stomach. She was beginning to have chills again and took another aspirin for her aching body. She got up to turn off the stove. Her chicken soup should be well cooked by now. She would just stay warm, read her Bible and take it easy for the rest of the weekend. They could do without her at church tomorrow. Besides, she had been working too hard for one person. She had lost ten pounds in two months, which pleased her, because her blood pressure was too high and she was twenty pounds overweight. Maybe this was a good time for her to put her life into some sort of order. She was lonely and had no family or friends to be with on days like this one. I always feel sorry for myself when I'm sick, she thought, as she sat at the table sipping on her soup. Sure, she had family in the church, but she had no blood family. Was there anything that she could have done differently in her life? Maybe she should have stayed in touch with Elaine, but what did they have in common? She missed her mother so much, her dear, sweet mother, who took care of her, when no one else cared.

When Harriet got out of bed on Monday, she felt better. She went to work and caught up on all the work that had piled up on her desk while she was out. She made plans for the Bible class on Wednesday night and went to the cemetery to put flowers on her mother's grave.

By the time she got home that night, she was smiling. As soon as she entered her door, the phone rang. And she stiffened when she answered it. It was Elaine. She told Elaine she couldn't talk very long, because she was just about to leave.

"How is Helen and her daughter," Harriet asked. "I forgot her daughter's name." But before Elaine could answer, Harriet remembered. "Oh, yes, Lynn. Now I remember. And how is your child, Elaine?" It was strange to her that after all this time, she and Elaine were talking on the phone.

The conversation didn't last very long. When Harriet hung up, she baked cookies for the Bible study she was having at her house that evening with some of the ladies from her church. She looked forward to this time. She knew the Bible from front to back and enjoyed discussing it with others like her. She frowned as she felt another pain in her stomach and she took a tablespoon of Mylanta. She had been living on that recently, but minutes later she felt better. She heard a knock on the door – it was Sister Watson and Sister Jones.

"You ladies come in and have a seat. I have oatmeal

cookies and hot coffee." Harriet felt better now that her friends were here. "Oh, Sister Talbert will be here shortly and then we can begin."

The ladies sat on the couch chattering and Harriet came out with the refreshments. When Sister Talbert arrived, Harriet stood in the middle of the living room with her Bible in her hand. She smiled. "Are you ladies ready to get started?" she said with a wide smile and a light in her eyes. Yeah, she felt better, she thought as her class began. This was where she belonged.

Helen was working on a new book, when the phone rang. It was Anita.

"Girl, I was up until two last night. Robert walked into my study and led me to bed." Helen took the cordless phone and went down to the kitchen.

"I was up late too, doing some paper work for the store," Anita said.

"And, how is it going?"

"Busy, I hired a young girl to help me out."

"Good. I told you you'd need someone soon."

"Helen, what are you doing today?"

Helen looked at the clock on the wall as she poured herself a cup of tea. "I was just going to stay in and write while I'm on a roll."

"Good for you," Anita said. "I'll pop in on you tomorrow on my way to the store."

"Good, you know where to find me," Helen laughed and hung up the phone. She went back into the study and sipped her tea. She was so happy. Life was so different now. She thought of the years she lived in Atlanta and the good times she and Darlene had together.

The phone rang again, and she picked it up. It was Elaine.

"I just wanted to tell you that I spoke to Harriet yesterday," Elaine said.

"Really? How is she?" Helen asked.

"She seems fine. She even asked about you and Lynn."

"That's surprising. I'm so surprised that you finally caught her."

"Well, we didn't talk long. She said she had a Bible meeting at her house."

"But at least she did talk to you. That is something, Elaine."

"Well, I'm not going to get my hopes up. You know how she can be."

"I know, but knowing that she is fine, makes me feel good. She sounds all right?"

"She sounds like herself, so I guess she's all right."

"Well, who knows. Maybe one day she'll come around and want to see us."

When they hung up the phone, Helen went back to her computer. It was time to do more work.

Robert had been home for a while, but he couldn't concentrate. Every time he looked up, Helen would pass his office. He shook his head, trying to clear it and keep his mind on his work, but whenever he tried, she would pass again in her short, blue satin robe. She walked by again.

"Damn." He wouldn't accomplish anything tonight until she went to bed. He left his study and walked into the den where she was watching TV. Her robe was short enough to show her perfect thighs. She looked up and smiled mischievously, as if she had willed him into the room with her and she was waiting patiently until he got there. He sat next to her on the couch. He took her face in both of his hands and kissed her.

"What was that for?"

"Just because you're you." He sat back and she laid her head on his shoulder. "I have to go to San Francisco next month for a day. If you go with me, I'll stretch it into two days. We'll stay at the Carlton."

"Will you be working all day?"

"Most of the first day, but then I'm yours all night and the next day."

"I can't wait," she said, kissing him on his neck.

"We can go on the Golden Gate Bridge Cruise. It goes under the bridge by way of Sausalito, past Angel Island and then around Alcatraz. I think you'll like that. I went the last time I was there which was about four years ago."

"I think I'll love it. The last time I went to San Francisco, I didn't get to do anything fun."

"That was when you had to rush here for Lynn's accident,"

Robert said, remembering. He felt her tremble slightly and he held her close. "This trip will be different, I promise."

"I know, love and I can hardly wait."

"Good," he said as his hands went up and down her thighs, feeling her tremble to his every touch. "This is why I couldn't work in my study," he whispered in her ear. "And I'm going to punish you for that."

"Punish me, baby," she said and they both laughed all the way to their bedroom.

Chapter 36

Harriet walked into the house at precisely 8:00 PM. She drove on the freeway for two hours before she decided to come home after a long, tiring day. She stood in front of the fireplace, trying to decide if she should make a fire or light the heater. No, she thought. It really wasn't cold enough. Besides, she wasn't in the mood for building a fire. She doubted if she would feel the heat anyway. Her house was just a cold house.

As she stood there, she found herself gazing at an old family photo on the mantel. It showed her mother, father and two sisters. They were all smiling. God, we were all so close, then. She hadn't looked at or touched the picture for a long time. "Family album," she murmured as she fingered the edge of the gold picture frame. But now, she had no family. There was no one there for her anymore. She only had the church as her family and she had the Lord. He was her family, the family she could rely on and that loved her unconditionally.

"Lord, I've tried. You know that I've tried to consider my sisters as my family..." But, the feeling or meaning of sister, just wasn't in her heart any longer. She thought of the conversation she had with Elaine just a few weeks ago. It was short, polite, but she didn't have anything to say. She couldn't talk about church; her sisters were sinners and didn't go to church.

She set the picture back on the mantel, touching her finger to her father's face. Suddenly, she jerked her finger back quickly. "Uh-huh, looks like you took residence with the devil himself, old man. You took my family with your evil words. You took them all away from me," she whispered. She remembered all the things he had said that day. In just minutes, he had taken everything. Because of him, Helen and Elaine had each other, but she had no one.

She walked into the kitchen and made herself a black cup of coffee. When she returned to the living room, she stopped again in front of the fireplace and picked up another picture of just her and her sisters. She sat on the couch and held the picture in her lap. They were sisters, then, and they loved each other. They had something in common, until she became the outsider.

Her cousin, Melvia, always told her about what was going on with Helen and Elaine. She knew about Helen and Robert and Melvia told her all about Danielle and how beautiful she was. They all had wonderful lives. It was like her sisters had gotten a second chance after their mother's death. But there were no chances for her.

The doctor had just told her that she had cancer of the stomach and it was too late to operate. Now, everything was just in the hands of the Lord. She wasn't afraid. She would pray and if the Lord was ready for her, then she was ready, too. She sat in the same spot for hours, looking at the clock on the wall. It was midnight, but time didn't matter to her any longer. She wasn't sleepy. She wasn't anything – not sad, not afraid. Just tired. Never did she imagine that what she'd been feeling these past few weeks was cancer eating the insides of her body, killing her as the days passed. She closed her eyes and thought of her mother.

"Maybe you handled it all wrong, Mama," she whispered. "Maybe you should have made us a loving family, instead of dividing us and making a battleground in our home."

She would make out a will and leave everything to the church. She thought of Danielle and Lynn. They were her nieces, but they were strangers to her. Harriet decided to leave the gold bracelet that had belonged to her mother to Lynn and the necklace to Danielle. It was only right to leave it to them. The jewelry did belong to their grandmother. At least, she wouldn't be leaving it to complete strangers.

She laid her head back. So much had happened in her life. After she had found out about her father, she thought she would never be happy. But then, she'd met Robert and she thought she would be happy forever. She remembered the first night they were together, so long ago.

It was 1973 and Harriet's only friend, Doris, had made plans with her to go to the annual dance in the Jefferson High School gymnasium. They were wearing matching red and white outfits and the gym was overflowing with students. The first boy Harriet danced with was sweaty and leaned his head against her face the entire time they danced. She was glad when the music stopped and she patted her hair in place. He walked her back to the corner and went to the next girl.

"He's cute," Doris whispered.

"No, he's not. You think every boy is cute, don't you?" Harriet snapped at her.

Doris stiffened and rolled her eyes. Harriet was different than anyone she knew. She never had anything nice to say, Doris thought.

Harriet had been excited about the dance, but now that she was here, she was not having a good time. Her spirit had been dampened by the argument between her parents the day before. It was always the same argument. Her mother saw the effects it was having on Harriet and her heart bled for her daughter. Helen was strong – she could take care of herself and would take care of Elaine. But, Harriet had no one, only her. Odessa knew she would have to do anything she could to make Harriet feel better and she tried to pay more attention to her than anyone else in the house. She gave Harriet all the love and attention she could, after all, all of this was her fault.

Now as she sat at the table, she was bored and wanted to go home.

"Hi, Harriet, is Helen here with you?"

She turned to the sound of his voice. Damn, everyone always asks about Helen. "No, Robert. I came here with Doris. You know her, don't you?"

Yes, everyone knew her, thought Robert. He looked at Harriet just sitting there with her hands folded in her lap.

Harriet looked up at Robert and was struck by a great idea. "Actually, Robert, Helen went out tonight. I just remembered that she said she was going out with Thomas. They're seeing a lot of each other you know," Harriet said as sweetly as she could.

Robert was angry. He called Helen twice, that day and

she had never returned his calls. Now, he knew why. He remembered how he had caught Helen slow dancing with Thomas last week. What did she see in that cocky idiot anyway? Thomas would surely break her heart and then move on to the next woman, but he guessed she would have to see that for herself, because no one could tell Helen what to do. Robert loved her and knew that she loved him too; she just had a difficult time expressing her feelings. But, it looked like she had moved on.

"Oh, I'm so sorry, Robert. Did I say something I shouldn't have? I thought you knew. After all, everyone else does."

"I guess," Robert said.

"I'm sorry, Robert. I don't know what she sees in him," Harriet said with a spark in her eye.

Robert wondered if she were really sorry. Everyone knew that there was no love lost between the sisters. He looked at Harriet's shiny black hair. She was friendly tonight and talking much more than usual. Funny, he hadn't noticed before, how pretty she was. She was dressed sexily and he smiled at her. He decided that he didn't want to be alone and he asked Harriet to dance.

They danced close together for the rest of the night. Doris had left with her friend, Harvey, so Robert offered Harriet a ride and she anxiously accepted his offer. Neither of them were ready to go home and Robert was enjoying her company. He parked his car around the corner from her house and they talked hours before he attempted to kiss her. She welcomed the feeling of being wanted by a boy as popular and good looking as Robert. And it felt good, because he almost belonged to her sister. He kissed her over and over again. Each time, the kiss lasted longer until they were making love in the back seat of the car.

Harriet was now in love and she had never been so happy. Robert was gentle and loving and now he was hers.

Helen had stayed home the next day and called Robert twice on the phone. But he wasn't there. She had already told Thomas, to leave her alone. The only person she wanted to be with was Robert. But as she waited all day, Robert did not return any of her calls.

"Men, they're all alike," Helen murmured.

Helen was in the living room watching television, when Harriet came in.

"You look pretty, Harriet. Going someplace special?" Helen asked. Helen noticed that Harriet was smiling. There was something different about her. She had been smiling all day and talking about old times.

"I got a date."

"Must be someone special, huh?"

Harriet's smile got wider. "Do you really think I look pretty, Helen?" she asked, standing in front of the long mirror hanging on the closet door.

"Sure do."

The doorbell rang and Helen jumped off the couch. "Don't go anywhere until I get back. I'm going to comb my hair. I want to see your lucky date for myself," Helen said as she ran into the bathroom.

"I'm sure you do, Helen," she said under her breath. Harriet opened the door and threw her arms around Robert's neck. She kissed him on the mouth just as Helen came out of the bathroom. Helen stood frozen, her eyes wide and full of pain.

Robert felt her presence and stopped. His eyes met Helen's and held, then he watched as she ran into her bedroom.

Harriet looked behind her when she heard movement. "I wonder just how long she was standing there?" she asked Robert, innocently. "She wasn't there when you came to the door."

They walked out and Robert closed the door quietly behind him. He felt sick.

Helen sat on the edge of her bed. She realized then, that Harriet really did hate her. As tears ran down her face, she knew that she loved Robert, but now she may have lost him forever.

The next day, she confronted Harriet. But Harriet laughed at her.

"You can't have everyone you want, Helen. Just like I can't help it if Robert wants me and not you."

Helen took a step closer to her sister, her dark brown eyes full of hostility. She was so close that Harriet could feel her warm breath as she spoke. "You're an evil bitch, Harriet. You always have been. And now, you'd better stay out of my way."

Helen went back to Thomas. When she got pregnant, she and Thomas married and moved to Atlanta. It was after Helen left, that Robert asked Harriet to marry him. She accepted – that was the fastest way to get from under her father's roof.

Harriet opened her eyes. She knew that even after they married, Robert always loved Helen. How many times over the years had he called her Helen? Many. She looked at the clock on the wall. Time just didn't matter – especially since she had such little left.

She went into her bedroom and crawled into bed, closing her eyes wishing sleep would come quickly. She was so tired, but she had a lot to do. Tomorrow, she would make out her will and begin to prepare for the end. She was going to die with dignity and no one would know about it until it was over. She turned over and fell asleep.

It was in the middle of February and it was rainy and cold. It had been that way for two weeks. Helen was cooking stew, when she stopped at the kitchen window and noticed how green the grass had become. She looked at her watch to see if it was time for her husband to come home. She dropped potatoes into the pot and put the cornbread in the oven.

All of this rain concerned her. She had already checked to make sure that Lynn was in her room at her dorm. Now, if Robert would get home, both her loved ones would be safely inside.

The moment she thought of 'loved ones', Harriet came to her mind. They hadn't talked in so long. Helen picked up the phone, then hung it back up. Her sister had made it clear that she didn't want anything to do with them. Helen had to respect her wishes, but she just didn't understand why Harriet had been on her mind so much lately.

When she heard the front door open, she ran to greet her husband. He was taking off his coat when she walked in.

"It's raining like hell out there," he said.

She took his coat and he kissed her on the cheek. Robert ran upstairs and she went into the kitchen to take the cornbread from the oven, before she joined him in the bedroom.

"Was the traffic terrible?"

"Yes, but I kept telling myself that I was going home to my wife," he said, smiling.

"Did that help?"

"It got me home faster, I think."

He was standing in his underwear. She looked at his wide shoulders and his long strong legs. She walked up behind him and wrapped her arms around his waist. He pulled her in front of him and led her to the bed.

He kissed her neck and whispered, "Good thing I made an honest woman out of you." He kissed her on the mouth.

Helen had never been so happy. He undressed her and they made love. Afterwards, they laid in a comfortable silence, listening to the rain hitting against the window.

She propped herself up on her elbow. "I hope that it will always be this way between us," she said looking into his face.

He opened his eyes and held her tight. "It will be, as long as you behave yourself." He kissed the tip of her nose.

She cocked her head to one side. "As long as I behave?"

"Just don't say no when I pull you into bed and start tearing your clothes off and make wild, crazy love to that beautiful brown body of yours."

She laughed. "I could never say no. Maybe I'll say more, but never no."

"That's a good thing."

They laughed. He rolled over on top of her. She welcomed him by opening her arms and holding him close. She would never let him go.

The next day, the rain stopped and Helen decided to go to Macy's for the white sale. She parked her car on the second level of the Beverly Center shopping mall and went into Macy's. She was wearing black jeans, knee boots and a short, black leather jacket. She saw a man watching her and she smiled.

"Sorry, fellow," she thought. "I have the man I want."

She walked through the store, looking first at linens and then moving over to the Junior's department for Lynn. She hoped to find a suit or a dress Lynn might like for graduation.

"Helen?"

Helen turned around and saw her cousin Melvia who she

hadn't seen since Danielle's christening. Helen held her packages under her arm so that they could embrace.

"It's good to see you, Helen."

"You too, girl. I thought I would get out of the house to get some fresh air, since it finally stopped raining."

"Girl, that is exactly what I had in mind," Melvia responded. "I called in sick today. I just needed a day to relax. But I ended up coming out here and spending money I don't even have. How's your daughter, Helen?"

"She's doing really well, and your children, Melvia?"

"My girl is doing all right, but that boy of mine is in jail again. This time for selling dope. I knew when he came into this world that he was going to be just like that good for nothing daddy of his. I knew it the day he gave me so much trouble at birth."

Helen shook her head in sympathy.

"You know, Helen. I was going to call you anyway, but now I'm glad we ran into each other," Melvia paused and said nothing for a few seconds. "Did you know that Harriet and I go to the same church?"

"Yes. You told me that last time we were together," Helen sighed.

"It's too bad you sisters never cleared up your differences."

"Look, Melvia. Let's get one thing straight. Elaine and I don't have any problems with Harriet. We can't make her see us if she doesn't want to."

"I know, Helen. But this is just not the time for such foolishness."

Helen was getting impatient. "We are not the ones who are being foolish."

"Well, I think it's foolish, because Harriet is dying of cancer. I haven't seen her for weeks, but Pastor Jones announced last Sunday that we should pray for Harriet because she is in her last days. He says it could be anytime now, Helen."

Helen had to lean against the clothes rack to keep her balance. Her eyes had darkened and she looked as if she were going to faint. Helen's mouth dropped open as she tried to digest the news. "My sister is dying? This can't be true," she whispered.

"Like I said, I was going to call you. I didn't know if you guys had been told or not."

"How dare she keep something so serious from Elaine and I?" Tears began to roll down Helen's face. She was still leaning against the rack like she couldn't stand on her own. Her heart ached for her sister. She was alone. Helen thought back to when she had almost called her yesterday. Now she knew why her sister had been on her mind lately. "Is she home, Melvia?"

"No, she's back in the hospital. Pastor Jones thinks this will be her last hospital stay. Her time is near."

"I had better go and see Elaine. She needs to know," Helen said, her voice shaking. "And, I've got to call Robert. No, I'll tell him when he gets home." Helen didn't know what to do first.

Melvia felt sorry for Helen. "Are you going to be all right, Helen?"

"Yes, thank you. I have to go now." Without saying good-bye, Helen rushed through the mall to her car and drove as fast as she could to Elaine's building.

When Elaine opened her door, she knew immediately that something was wrong. Helen led Elaine to the couch. "I just had a talk with Melvia. We ran into each other at the mall." Helen paused. "Melvia says that Harriet is very ill. She has cancer and she's in the hospital."

Elaine wrung her hands. "Oh, my God. What are we going to do now, Helen?"

"We go to her, of course. She's our sister. We try to give her all the comfort and understanding she needs."

"You sound as if she is going to die."

"She is, Elaine. She's dying."

"But what if she tells us to get out when we get there? What if she doesn't want us there?" Elaine asked.

"She won't tell us that. She's saved by God and will want to go knowing that she made peace in her life, and that is all we can give her right now, Elaine."

"Okay, Helen. Let me just get my purse."

"Wait, Elaine. What about the baby?"

"Oh, Lynn's here. She's in the back with her," Elaine

said. "Lynn," she yelled out. "Your mother's here."

"Hi, Mom," Lynn said as she came out of the back room with Danielle at her side. "What are you doing here?"

Helen repeated her conversation with Melvia and told Lynn to watch Danielle while she and Elaine went to the hospital. She asked Lynn to call Robert at his office and tell him.

"We'll be at Daniel Freeman Hospital. I know Robert will want to see her right away."

They drove to the hospital in silence and walk briskly into Daniel Freeman, afraid of what awaited them. They reached the nurse's station and talked to one of the nurses about their sister's condition. She told them that Harriet was in pain and that all they could do was try to make her comfortable.

The nurse gave them a curious glance. "We had no idea she had family," the nurse said.

As Helen and Elaine walked into the room, Helen's stomach did a somersault. She held Elaine's hand tight to keep her from crying out.

Harriet was small. She had lost a lot of weight and now looked fragile. Her coloring had darkened, but her beautiful black hair was braided. She looked so different and Helen had to hold her breath to keep from choking on her tears.

Helen bent down so that Harriet could hear her speak. "Harriet, honey," she whispered. "Honey, it's Helen and Elaine. We came to see you. We want you to know that we are here for you," she said softly and held Harriet's hand in hers.

She opened her eyes slowly and smiled at them. "I know it's you, Helen." They had to bend closer to hear her. Harriet looked at Elaine. "Melvia says your baby has red hair, Elaine."

"Yes, her father has red hair," Elaine said, trying to control the trembling in her voice.

"Melvia says she's a beauty. Just like Lynn." Harriet looked at Helen.

"Danielle is such a joy. When you go home, Harriet, I want to bring her by to see you."

Harriet closed her eyes and didn't say anything for a few seconds. "I won't be going home, at least not on this earth. When I do go, it will be with the Lord," she said as she breathed heavily.

Helen rubbed her hand. "Don't say that, Harriet," Helen said. "People get better everyday. You are a church-going woman and you know what the Lord can do."

"Yes, but this is His will, not ours."

Helen pulled two chairs by the bed so they could sit close.

"I've missed you, Harriet," Elaine said.

Harriet tried to raise her hand, but it fell back on the bed.

"Don't be silly, Elaine. You have a husband and baby now. How do you have time to miss me?"

"Harriet, can I get you anything?" asked Helen. "Would you like me to read the Bible to you? There's one on the table here."

"No, Helen. I'll just fall asleep while you're reading. Pastor Jones comes by and reads to me sometimes." She talked slowly. "How's Robert?"

"He's doing well. Just busy with his new cases."

Harriet tried to nod. "He was always busy, but that was when he was happiest." She closed her eyes again and the nurse walked in, motioning to Helen and Elaine to come into the hall.

They tiptoed out of the room.

"It's time to leave her for a while. She's very tired and was in such agony last night. She didn't get much sleep at all."

An agonizing sound came from Harriet's room and one of the nurses ran inside.

"Oh, my God, what is it? What's wrong?" Helen and Elaine held onto each other. The sound continued to come into the hallway. The nurse finally walked out of the room as if she was tired.

"It's best if you come back later. She's sleeping now and will for a while."

"How often does she have that pain?" Helen asked as if she could feel the excruciating pain herself.

"Often, whenever the medication wears off." The nurse looked at them with sympathy in her eyes. "It won't be very long."

Helen and Elaine were still holding each other and Helen could feel Elaine trembling.

"Why don't you come back in an hour or so," the nurse said before she walked away.

As they walked outside, the air felt fresh and free from the pain and worry the two sisters carried inside their hearts.

"I wonder if she has already made funeral arrangements," Elaine said as they got into the car.

"Now, Elaine. You know Harriet never leaves any loose ends. I'm sure she took care of everything months ago, when she first found out she was sick. She's always been one to take care of business. Even when she was a child," Helen said. "She was always after me for doing things at the last minute."

"I don't remember that," Elaine said.

"You were too young."

They pulled up in front of Elaine's building and walked inside hand in hand. Danielle came running into her mother" arms.

"Mom, did you see Robert?" Lynn asked.

"No, did you contact him?"

"Yes, he came here and then was headed to the hospital."

"How was he?"

"Very upset. But he was really concerned about you and Aunt Elaine."

Helen nodded. "You know, I better go home so that we can go back to the hospital." Helen hugged Elaine and then kissed Lynn and left to go home.

"Harriet, Harriet?"

She heard his voice and opened her eyes slowly. It took her a moment to recognize him. "Robert, is that you?"

"Yes, it's me." He put her thin, long fingers in his hand and held them firmly. Christ, she looked so weak and sick. She didn't look anything like the woman he married twenty years ago.

"What are you doing here?" Her voice was almost a whisper.

He was taken aback by her question. "I'm here to see you. Why didn't you call me and tell me you were sick? I would have come sooner. Helen and Elaine would've come, too."

"You should know me better than that, Robert. I would never call for anyone's pity."

"It's not pity, baby. It's love and caring. You have people who care about you. Not only me, Helen and Elaine. But, you have two beautiful nieces."

She closed her eyes feeling tired and weak. She knew the time was nearing. Her body was slowly leaving her, floating into another world, as if she was disappearing slowly from the face of this earth. Finally, she opened her eyes. "To tell you the truth, I wish that I could have known Helen's daughter. That is the one regret I have, Robert."

"Lynn is a terrific kid."

"Funny, how we realize things when it's too late," she whispered. "But, if you tell Helen what I said, I'll deny it." She tried to smile, but held his hand tighter and moaned deeply as the pain burned through her body. She closed her eyes once again.

"Harriet," his voice quavered. "I wish I could take the pain for you."

When she opened her eyes, she saw tears running down his face. "I wasn't very nice to you when we were married, Robert. I'm sorry about that."

"Harriet, don't talk about that now. Just hold on to my hand and relax."

"No, I have to say this. There were so many things that were unsaid and I should have said them long before now. I'm sorry about what I did to you and Helen. I hope Helen know what a good man you are."

"I think she does," he tried to smile.

"She'd better or I'll haunt her." She closed her eyes and thought of the first time they were together. They had danced to all of James Brown's slow songs that night. She squeezed Robert's hand again. "Robert one other thing. Don't let Helen feel guilty about my death. Make Helen and Elaine understand that this was all my choice. Can you do that for me, Robert?"

"Yes, I promise."

A nurse came into the room and checked Harriet. "She's asleep now, sir. But you can sit with her for a while if you like." The nurse walked out the room.

An hour later when Harriet opened her eyes, Helen and Elaine were sitting beside her bed.

"I thought Mama and Daddy were here. I could have sworn I heard his voice. It was deep, wasn't it, Helen?"

"Yes, honey. It was very deep."

331

"I dreamed that we were all wearing white dresses that Mama made for us."

Helen moved closer to the bed and held Harriet's hands. Her heart was heavy, but she was trying to hold on for Harriet's sake "You were probably dreaming about the Easter dresses that Mama made us."

"I remember that, too," Elaine said in a whisper.

Harriet's breath seemed to shorten and was becoming more labored. She turned her head slightly and saw the tears running down Helen's cheeks.

Harriet whispered, "I won't tell them, Mama. Oh, Mama, please stay with me."

Her words shocked Helen and Elaine, but then, Helen made a decision to help her sister this one final time. Helen spoke the words in a low, soothing voice. "Mama's here, Harriet. Mama's here to love and take care of you." Helen leaned over and kissed Harriet's cheek that was wet with tears. "I love you, Harriet," Helen said. She felt Harriet's hand fall open, but she held onto it. She knew Harriet was gone. She brought Harriet's hand to her face and cried. "Oh, God, Harriet, why didn't you call us sooner?"

Elaine ran into Robert's arms. "She's gone, Robert."

He hugged her quietly and led her down the hall, sitting with her on the small bench. He left her there, for a moment. He had to make sure his wife was fine. When he walked inside the room, Helen was still silently holding her sister's hand. Robert took Harriet's hand from her and laid it by her side. The doctor and nurse walked in and asked them to wait outside. He led Helen to where Elaine was sitting.

"She's gone now, baby," Robert said as he held her tightly. "She won't feel any more pain. She can have some peace now."

"I know," Helen cried. How could this happen? In one day, she finds out that her sister is sick and then she loses her. But, Helen thanked the Lord that they had at least this time with Harriet.

As Elaine cried softly, Helen knelt in front of her. "Shush, honey, it's over." She held her sister. "Let me drive you home, now."

Elaine nodded and stood, the tears still falling.

"I'll call Pastor Jones when I get home. I'll get his number from Melvia. I know she made arrangements, but I want to make sure that everything is in order."

Robert walked them to Helen's car and kissed his wife. "I'll see you when you get home, baby."

By the time Helen got home and called Pastor Jones, he had already gotten the news. "Her funeral will be Friday morning at 11:00. She was the one that chose the time."

For the first time that day, Helen smiled. It was just like Harriet to do something like that.

"She said that she hated going to funerals in the middle of the day. So, she wanted hers in the morning so that people could get it over with and go on with their lives. She also asked to be buried next to your mother."

"That makes sense," Helen said.

That night, as she lay in Robert's arm, they talked until midnight, both unable to sleep. They acknowledged how lucky they were to have each other and promised that they would always be this close, never have any secrets, and never go to bed angry. They made that promise and then fell asleep.

At midnight, Dan walked into the living room and found his wife standing at the large window. He stood behind her and placed his hands on her shoulders. "I know you're hurting, Elaine, but you have to try to get some sleep."

"Dan, it hurts so much."

"I know, but this was her time and she's no longer in pain. I had an aunt who died from cancer, so I know what it's like to watch someone suffer." He led her to the couch.

"I just keep wondering if Helen and I could have done more. The two of us were so happy, while our sister was across town dying."

"Elaine, you tried to stay in touch with Harriet, isn't that true?"

"Yes," she answered.

"And, when you did speak to her, did she tell you that she was sick?"

"No. She sounded all right on the phone. I couldn't tell."

"Exactly. That's just the way she wanted it. Harriet lived

her life the way she wanted to. You can't blame yourself or
Helen for that."

Elaine nodded.

"You invited her to our wedding and Danielle's christening. She has a twenty-year-old niece that she knows nothing
about. She wouldn't take your calls or let you come visit.
There was nothing else you could have done," Dan said as he
held her hand. "And, in the end, I believe she knew that you
loved her, Elaine."

"Do you really think so?" Elaine's voice was hopeful.

He nodded. "Of course."

Elaine laid her head on her husband's shoulder. "What
would I do without you, Dan?"

He took her by the hand. "It's time for bed, dear. I have
a store to open in the morning, but I can't sleep unless my wife
is in bed beside me." Dan turned out the light and they went
into Danielle's room to check on her. They put the covers that
she had kicked off, back over her, then walked hand in hand
into their bedroom. It had been a long day.

Helen stood at the bedroom window, watching the stars
shine down on Los Angeles. She thought of the last time she
and Darlene had sat at her kitchen table and had one of their
monthly dinners. They had always been so close. She always
thought of Darlene when she needed someone to talk to.
Darlene understood her – the way she thought, the way she felt.
Darlene knew that Helen wanted a relationship with Harriet.

God, I should have tried harder, Harriet. I'm so sorry,
Lord, I'm so sorry. Helen thought of yesterday, when she had
picked up the phone to call Harriet. She squeezed her eyes
closed and tried to force the thought from her mind.

She wouldn't think of times like that. She would remember
when they all played jacks together. Or, when they slept in the
same bed laughing and talking. She didn't hear her husband
get out of bed. He held her shoulders and turned her around to
face him. Tears were rolling down her face. He led her to the
bed and they sat, holding each other.

"I had a talk with Harriet before you and Elaine arrived,"
Robert started. "She asked me to do something for you, Helen."

Helen wiped her eyes. "What?" she asked cautiously.

"She told me not to let you feel guilty. She said that you tried, Helen, and that there was nothing you could do."

"Maybe I didn't try hard enough, Robert."

"Harriet didn't feel that way. She wanted to go in peace and it was important to her that you and Elaine not feel guilty about her or her illness. I know in my heart that she was happy and relieved because in the end, you and Elaine were there with her."

Helen laid her head against her husband's chest and cried. She cried for her mother and father, Darlene and Harriet. She cried until she fell asleep.

Chapter 37

Helen looked up at the sky, and pulled her long, black coat tighter against her body. The weather was colder than it had been the day of her mother's funeral. Harriet's last request was to have a graveside ceremony to be completed in less than an hour. Harriet's family met the sisters and brothers from the church including a man named Charles who cried throughout the entire ceremony. Why was he taking her sister's death so hard? she wondered.

"Sister Harriet was a good woman. She worked in the church, she taught Sunday school, did all the church accounting, and taught Bible classes. Yes, Sister Harriet lived for the Lord. But now, He has called her. She has gone to a better place where she will no longer feel any pain. Let us bow our heads and pray," the pastor said, holding his Bible with both hands.

After the service was over, they all met at Pastor Jones' house on Morningside Park. People gathered in the large den where there were long tables with fried chicken, potato salad, red beans, rice and cold drinks and coffee. Pastor Jones and Harriet's family were in the dining room.

"You all may not know this. Harriet left everything to the church. But then, two days before she died, she changed her will." Pastor Jones looked at Helen and wet his bottom lip with his tongue. "And, I wasn't disappointed at all."

Helen and Elaine exchanged glances.

"Harriet left $15,000 to each of her nieces. The money is to be given to her niece, Lynn, upon her graduation from college and the same goes for Danielle. Of course, this is contingent on them graduating." The pastor was reading from the will he held in his hand. Pastor Jones then pulled out a small, black suede box that Helen recognized as their mother's.

"This gold necklace and bracelet were also left to her nieces." He handed the box to Helen.

She opened it and stared inside for seconds before she pulled the necklace out and handed it to Elaine. "It was Mama's," she whispered. "I wondered what happened to it."

"Harriet said that it was only right for her nieces to have them. She said that she wished she had gotten to know them better." He handed the will that he had been reading to Helen. "As you can see, it was dated when she was in sound mind."

Helen saw tears rolling down Lynn's cheeks and she put her arm around her shoulder. Elaine was choking back her tears and she held Dan's hand tight for support. Helen fought her own tears. Harriet didn't like crying, weak women and she would stay strong. Today was Harriet's day.

The pastor hugged each of them, then they all walked out of the dining room and talked with some of the people they recognized.

Mary walked up to Helen and pulled her aside. Helen noticed the smart navy suit and pumps Mary was wearing. "How do I look, girl? Shirley brought this suit for me for the funeral."

Helen walked around her and looked at her from head to toe. She smiled. "Honey, you looked like you just stepped off the cover of a magazine."

"Oh, hell, Helen, I don't look that good.

Helen squeezed her hand. "You look good, Mary, damn good to me."

"I'll tell you who looks damn good."

"Who, girl?" Helen asked.

"Look over there in his gray suit."

Helen burst out laughing. "Don't even go that way. He's my husband, and I know he looks good. So, just look the other way, honey."

They both laughed and Mary said her good-byes, then left.

A few minutes later, the entire family decided to leave and Helen, Lynn and Elaine walked out in front of the men. They stopped when they got outside.

"It's still beautiful," Elaine said and closed the box. She looked up at her husband. "Let's go home to our daughter,

Dan. It's been a long day." Elaine and Dan said good-bye and drove off.

Helen and Robert kissed Lynn, then held hands as they watched her drive away. Finally, they went to their car and Robert pushed her hair from her face.

"Have you brought a new dress for Anita and Raymond's wedding?"

"No, not yet. I still have a week, but I did-see one that I liked."

He smiled at her.

"I'm so glad that we'll be on our way to San Francisco in a couple of weeks. We can use it now."

Robert started the car. "Let's go home, Helen," he said and kissed her on the forehead. "We've had enough for one day, don't you think?"

"Hell yes, and it's over," she said, thinking of Harriet. She still couldn't believe her sister was gone. Robert turned the car in the direction of their home.

Order Form

Milligan Books
1425 West Manchester, Suite B,
Los Angeles, California 90047
(323) 750-3592

Mail Check or Money Order to:
Milligan Books

Name _____ Date _____

Address _____

City_____ State _____ Zip Code_____

Day telephone _____

Evening telephone_____

Book title _____

Number of books ordered ___ Total cost .... $_____

Sales Taxes (CA Add 8.25%) .... $_____

Shipping & Handling $3.00 per book .... $_____

Total Amount Due..$_____

· Check   · Money Order   Other Cards _____

· Visa   · Master Card   Expiration Date _____

Credit Card No. _____

Driver's License No. _____

Signature _____   Date _____